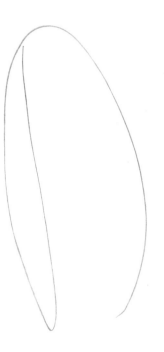

CHARLEY'S
WEB

ALSO BY JOY FIELDING

Heartstopper
Mad River Road
Puppet
Lost
Whispers and Lies
Grand Avenue
The First Time
Missing Pieces
Don't Cry Now
Tell Me No Secrets
See Jane Run
Good Intentions
The Deep End
Life Penalty
The Other Woman
Kiss Mommy Goodbye
Trance
The Transformation
The Best of Friends

CHARLEY'S
WEB

A NOVEL

JOY
FIELDING

ATRIA BOOKS

NEW YORK   LONDON   TORONTO   SYDNEY

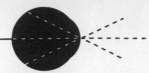

**This Large Print Book carries the
Seal of Approval of N.A.V.H.**

ATRIA BOOKS

A Division of Simon & Schuster, Inc.
1230 Avenue of the Americas
New York, NY 10020

This Atria Books large-print hardcover edition April 2008

ATRIA BOOKS and colophon are trademarks of Simon & Schuster, Inc.

For information about special discounts for bulk purchases, please contact Simon & Schuster Special Sales at 1-800-456-6798 or business@simonandschuster.com.

Designed by Jaime Putorti

Manufactured in the United States of America

10 9 8 7 6 5 4 3 2 1

ISBN-13: 978-1-4165-8694-4
ISBN-10:   1-4165-8694-6

For Annie,
I adore you

CHARLEY'S WEB

1

FROM: Irate Reader
TO: Charley@Charley'sWeb.com
SUBJECT: YOU ARE THE WORST COLUMNIST EVER!!!
DATE: Mon. 22 Jan. 2007, 07:59:47–0500

Hey, Charley: Just a brief note to let you know that aside from being THE WORST COLUMNIST WHO EVER LIVED!!! you are quite possibly THE MOST SELF-ABSORBED WOMAN ON THE PLANET!!! It's obvious from your photograph—the long, wavy, blond hair, the knowing glance from large, downcast eyes, the subtle smirk on those no doubt Restylane-enhanced lips—that you think the sun rises and sets on your lovely shoulders. Your insipid columns about shopping for the perfect stilettos, searching for just the right shade of blush, and coping with the demands of a new personal trainer have only solidified my assessment. But what on earth would make you think there is anyone who is even moderately interested in learning about your latest foray into the world of the sublimely shallow—a Brazilian wax?!!! Before your graphic and unnecessarily lurid description regarding the denuding of your nether region in Sunday's paper—(WEBB SITE, Sunday, January 21)—I actually had no idea there even **was** such a thing, let alone that any grown woman—I know from a previous column that you celebrated your thirtieth birthday last March—would willingly consent to such a barbaric procedure. I wonder how your poor father reacted when he read about his Harvard-educated daughter infantilizing her body in such a demeaning way. I wonder how your mother manages to hold her head up in front of her friends with the constant public airing of such private—dare I say, pubic?—matters. (At least they have two other daughters to keep their spirits buoyed!!! Kudos to Anne, incidentally, for the stunning success of her latest novel, **Remember Love**—number 9 on the **New York Times** bestseller list, and climbing!!! And to Emily, who made such a lovely impression when she subbed for Diane Sawyer on **Good Morning America** last month!!!) Those are truly daughters to make any parent proud.

And speaking of daughters, what must your eight-year-old think when she sees you parading around the house in the nude, as I'm sure you do, judging from how much you obviously enjoy exposing your-self in print!!! Not to mention the teasing your five-year-old son will be subjected to in his kindergarten class from other children whose parents were no doubt similarly appalled by Sunday's column! Last week's article about sex toys was bad enough!!

Can you not look beyond the tip of your pert little nose—courtesy of the best plastic surgery money can buy, no doubt—and consider the effect of such indis-creet blathering on both these young innocents?! (Al-though what can one expect from a woman who prides herself on never having married either of her children's fathers?!!!)

I've had it up to here with your inane yapping about **all things Charley**. (Thank you for not using your given name of Charlotte. At least you spared us the desecration of that most wonderful of chil-dren's books!) After three years of reading—and shaking my head in dismay!!!—at your dimwitted musings, I have finally reached the end of my rope. I would rather hang myself by my own still intact pubic hairs than read one more word of your puer-ile prose, and I can no longer justify supporting any newspaper that chooses to publish it. I am there-fore canceling my subscription to the **Palm Beach Post** as of today.

I'm sure I speak for many disgusted and disgrun-tled readers when I say, WHY CAN'T YOU JUST SHUT UP AND GO AWAY?!!!!

Charley Webb sat staring at the angry letter on her computer screen, not sure whether to laugh or cry. It wasn't just that the letter was so nasty that had her feeling so unsettled—she'd received many that were worse over the years, including several this very morning. Nor was it the almost hysterical tone of today's letter. Again, she was used to reader outrage. And it wasn't the wildly overused punctuation either. Writers of angry e-mails tended to view their every sentence as important and therefore worthy of capital letters, italics, and multiple exclamation points. It wasn't even the personal nature of the attack. Any woman who devoted a thousand words to her recent Brazilian wax had to expect attacks of a personal nature. Some—including a few of her colleagues—might even say she invited them, that she prided herself on being provocative. She got what she deserved, they might say.

They might even be right.

Charley shrugged. She was used to controversy and criticism. She was used to being called incompetent and lightweight, as well as a host of other more unflattering epithets. She'd grown used to having her motives questioned, her integrity impugned, and her looks dissected and disparaged. She was also used to being told it was those same looks that had gotten her a byline in the first place. Or that one of her more famous sisters must have pulled some strings. Or that her father, a highly esteemed professor of English literature at Yale, had used his influence to get her the job.

She was used to being called a bad daughter, a worse mother, a terrible role model. Such slurs usually rolled off her "lovely shoulders." So what was it about this particular e-mail that had her trapped between laughter and tears? What about it made her feel so damn vulnerable?

Maybe she was still smarting from the fallout from last week's column. Her neighbor, Lynn Moore, who lived several doors away from Charley on a once-decrepit, now verging-on-fashionable, small street in downtown West Palm, had invited her to a so-called Passion Party, just before Christmas. It turned out to be a variation of the old neighborhood Tupperware party, except that instead of a variety of heavy-duty plastic containers on display, there were vibrators and dildos. Charley had had a wonderful time handling all the assorted **objets**, and listening to the hyperbolic sales pitch of Passion's perky representative—"And this seemingly innocuous string of beads, well, ladies, let me tell you, it's nothing short of miraculous. Talk about multiple orgasms! This is truly the Christmas gift that keeps on giving all year round!"—then performed a neat evisceration of the evening in her column the following month.

"How could you do this?" Lynn had confronted Charley in person the day the column ran. She was standing on the single step outside the front door of Charley's tiny, two-bedroom bungalow. Charley's column was scrunched into a tight ball in her clenched fist, her fingers curled around Charley's paper throat. "I thought we were friends."

"We **are** friends," Charley had protested, although, in truth, they were more acquaintances than actual friends. Charley didn't have any actual friends.

"Then how could you do this?"

"I don't understand. What have I done?"

"You don't understand?" Lynn had repeated incredulously. "You don't know what you've done? You humiliated me, that's what you did. You made me look like a sex-crazed fool. My husband is furious. My mother-in-law's in tears. My daughter is beside herself with embarrassment. The phone's been ringing off the hook all morning."

"But I didn't say it was you."

"You didn't have to. **My hostess**," Lynn recited from memory, "**a fortyish brunette sporting tight capri pants, two-inch crystal-studded nails, and three-inch heels, lives in a charming white clapboard house filled with fresh-cut flowers from her magnificent garden. A large American flag waves proudly from the tiny, manicured front lawn**. Gee, I wonder who that could be."

"It could be anybody. I think you're being overly sensitive."

"Oh, really? I'm being overly sensitive? I invite you to a party, introduce you to my friends, pour you not one, but **several** glasses of champagne . . ."

"For God's sake, Lynn. What did you expect?" Charley interrupted, annoyed at having to defend herself. "I'm a reporter. You know that. This sort of story is right up my alley. Of course I'm going to write about it. You knew that when you invited me over."

"I didn't invite you over as a reporter."

"It's what I do," Charley reminded her. "It's who I am."

"My mistake," Lynn said simply. "I thought you were more."

There was a moment of awkward silence as Charley struggled to keep Lynn's words from sinking in too deep. "Sorry I disappointed you."

Lynn brushed off Charley's apology with a wave of her two-inch nails. "But not sorry you wrote the column. Right?" She began backing down the front walk.

"Lynn . . ."

"Oh, shut up."

WHY CAN'T YOU JUST SHUT UP AND GO AWAY?!!!!

Charley stared at her computer screen. Was it possible Lynn Moore was her Irate Reader?

Wary eyes skipped across the words Irate
Reader had written, searching for echoes of
Lynn's subtle southern drawl, finding none. The
truth was that Irate Reader could be anyone. In
her thirty years on this planet, three at this
desk, Charley Webb had managed to ruffle an
awful lot of feathers. There were plenty of
people who wished she would just shut up and
go away. "I thought you were more," she repeated under her breath. How many others had
made the same mistake?

FROM: Charley Webb
TO: Irate Reader
SUBJECT: A reasoned response
DATE: Mon. 22 Jan. 2007 10:17:24–0800

Dear Irate:

Wow!!!! That was some letter!!!! (As you can see,
I, too, have an exclamation mark on my computer!!!!!) Thanks for writing. It's always interesting
to find out how readers are responding to my columns, even when they aren't always positive. Call
me crazy, but I sensed you haven't been too thrilled
with my columns of late. I'm truly sorry about that,
but what is it they say? You can't please everybody
all the time? Well, I learned a long time ago that it's
pointless to try. Reading is such a subjective en-
deavor, and one person's heaven is another person's

hell. Clearly, as far as you're concerned, I'm Satan incarnate!!!!!

Now, while I rigorously defend your right to be wrong, I feel I must address some of your more egregious utterances. (I'll see your **indiscreet blathering** and raise you one **egregious utterance!!!**) First, I do not now, nor have I ever, used Restylane to enhance my lips. My lips are the lips I was born with, and while they're perfectly adequate as far as lips go, I've never considered them to be particularly noteworthy, or I probably would have written a column about them by now. Also, I broke my nose when I was seven, running into a brick wall to get away from my younger brother, who was chasing me with a garter snake he'd found in our backyard. The result has been a lifelong fear of reptiles and a nose that veers slightly—some might say charmingly—to the left. I've never felt the slightest need to have it fixed, although now that you've declared it "pert," I may have to reconsider.

I'm surprised you'd never heard of a Brazilian wax before you read about it in my column, because I can assure you they've been around for a long time. But once you realized what I was writing about, and that such a topic was an affront to your obviously delicate sensibilities—a lot of that going around these days—why on earth did you continue reading?!!! (Finally, I got to use the ?!!! It's fun!!!!)

As for what my father thinks about his Harvard-educated daughter **infantilizing** (good word!) herself in this way, I suspect he doesn't know—cocooned as he is in his ivory tower at Yale—and if he does, he doesn't care, since we haven't spoken in years. (Regular readers of WEBB SITE should know this!!!) As for my mother, she doesn't have to worry about holding her head up in front of her friends, since, like me, she doesn't have any. (Possible fodder for an upcoming Mother's Day column that you will, unfortunately, miss.) My children, on the other hand, have lots of friends, all of them happily oblivious to the **inane yapping** of their mother, and since—surprise!—I actually **don't** make a habit of parading around the house in the nude, they haven't had to pass any unnecessary artistic judgments on the **denuding of my nether region**. Wow—that's quite a mouthful, even in writing!!! As for my never having married either of my children's fathers—nor lived with them, I might add—well, at least I haven't subjected them to the unpleasantness of divorce, unlike both my more successful sisters, who have four-and-a-half divorces between them—Emily, three, and Anne, one divorce, one recent separation. (Incidentally, I'll pass on your congratulations to both of them for their recent, much-deserved triumphs.)

As for my column, you should realize that I am doing exactly the job I was hired to do. When I came to work at the **Palm Beach Post** three years ago, the editor-in-chief, Michael Duff, told me he was interested in attracting a younger readership, and that he was especially interested in what people my age were thinking and doing. In short, unlike you, he was deeply interested in **all things Charley.** What he **wasn't** interested in was objective journalism. On the contrary, he wanted me to be totally subjective—to be honest and forthcoming and, hopefully, controversial as well.

It would seem from all the e-mail I've received this morning that I've succeeded. I'm sorry you consider my prose puerile and that you're canceling your subscription to our wonderful paper, but that is certainly your prerogative. I will continue to do my job, commenting on today's social scene, reporting on the morals and habits of America's youth, and tackling important issues such as wife-abuse and the proliferation of porn, alongside my continuing forays into **the world of the sublimely shallow**. Sorry you won't be along for the ride. Sincerely, Charlotte Webb.

(Sorry. Couldn't resist.)

Charley's fingers hovered over the SEND button for several seconds before moving to the DELETE button and pressing it instead. She watched the words instantly vanish from her screen as all around her, the busy sounds of Monday morning began encroaching: phones ringing, keyboards clicking, rain pounding against the floor-to-ceiling, third-floor windows of the airy, four-storey building. She heard her colleagues

talking outside her tiny cubicle, inquiring pleasantly about one another's weekend. She listened
to their friendly banter, full of laughter and
harmless gossip, and wondered briefly why no
one had stopped by her desk to ask about **her**
weekend or congratulate her on her latest
column. But no one ever did.

It would have been easy to dismiss their attitude as stemming from professional jealousy—
she knew most of them considered her columns,
and, by extension, **her**, to be silly and inconse-
quential, and resented her high profile—but the
truth was that her colleagues' ever-increasing
coldness was largely her own fault. Charley had
purposefully shunned their overtures when she
first came to work at the **Palm Beach Post**,
thinking it was better, **safer**, to keep relationships on a strictly professional level. (Just as
she'd never believed it was a good idea to get too
chummy with the neighbors. And boy, had she
been right about that.) It wasn't that she was
unfriendly exactly, just a little aloof. It hadn't
taken her colleagues very long to get the message. Nobody liked rejection, especially writers,
who were already too used to being rejected.
Soon the casual invitations to dinner stopped,
along with the offers to tag along for a drink
after work. Even a polite "Hi. How's it going?"
had stopped coming her way.

Until this morning, she thought with a shudder, recalling the obscene leer that senior editor Mitchell Johnson had given her when she'd walked by his glassed-in office. Never subtle to begin with, Mitch had stared directly at the crotch of her Rock & Republic jeans and asked, "How's it growing? **Going.** I meant **going**, not **growing**," he corrected, as if his slip had been unintentional.

He thinks he knows me, Charley thought now, leaning back in her brown leather chair and staring past the dividing wall that separated her tiny space from the dozens of other such cubicles occupying the editorial department's large center core. The big room was divided into three main areas, although the divisions were more imaginary than concrete. The largest section was comprised of journalists who covered current events and filed daily reports; a second section was reserved for weekly and special-interest columnists such as herself; a third area was for fact-checkers and secretarial staff. People worked at their computers for hours on end, barking into headphones, or balancing old-fashioned black receivers between their shoulders and ears. There were stories to uncover and follow, deadlines to be met, angles to be determined, statements to be corroborated. Someone was always rushing in or out, asking for advice, opinions, or help.

No one ever asked Charley for anything.

They think they know me, Charley thought. They think because I write about Passion parties and Brazilian waxes, that I'm a shallow twit, and they know everything about me.

They know nothing.

WHY CAN'T YOU JUST SHUT UP AND GO AWAY?!!!!

FROM: Charley Webb
TO: Irate Reader
SUBJECT: A reasoned response
DATE: Mon. 22 Jan. 2007 10:37:06–0800

Dear Irate: You're mean. Sincerely, Charley Webb.

This time Charley did press the SEND button, then waited while her computer confirmed the note had indeed been forwarded. "Probably shouldn't have done that," she muttered seconds later. It was never a good idea to deliberately antagonize a reader. There were lots of powder kegs out there just waiting for an excuse to explode. Should have just ignored her, Charley thought, as her phone began ringing. She reached over, picked it up. "Charley Webb," she announced instead of hello.

"You're a worthless slut," the male voice snarled. "Someone should gut you like a fish."

"Mother, is that you?" Charley asked, then bit down on her tongue. Why hadn't she checked her caller ID? And what had she just decided about not deliberately trying to antagonize anyone? She should have just hung up, she admonished herself as the phone went dead in her hand. Immediately the phone rang again. Again she picked it up without checking. "Mother?" she asked, unable to resist.

"How'd you know?" her mother replied.

Charley chuckled as she pictured the puzzled expression on her mother's long, angular face. Elizabeth Webb was fifty-five years old, with shoulder-length blue-black hair that underlined the almost otherworldly whiteness of her skin. She stood six feet one in her bare feet, and dressed in long, flowing skirts that minimized the length of her legs and low-cut blouses that maximized the size of her bosom. She was beautiful by anyone's definition, as beautiful now as she'd been when she was Charley's age and already the mother of four young children. But Charley had few memories of this time, and fewer photographs, her mother having disappeared from her life when she was barely eight years old.

Elizabeth Webb had reappeared suddenly two years ago, eager to renew contact with the offspring she'd abandoned some twenty years earlier. Charley's sisters had chosen to remain loyal to their father and refused to forgive the woman who'd run off to Australia with, not another man, which might have been forgivable, but another woman, which most assuredly was not. Only Charley had been sufficiently curious—spiteful, her father would undoubtedly insist—to agree to see her again. Her brother, of course, continued to shun contact with either of his parents.

"I just wanted you to know that I thoroughly enjoyed your column yesterday," her mother was saying in the quasi-Australian lilt that clung to the periphery of each word. "I've always been very curious about that sort of thing."

Charley nodded. Like mother, like daughter, she couldn't help but think. "Thank you."

"I called you several times yesterday, but you were out."

"You didn't leave a message."

"You know I hate those things," her mother said.

Charley smiled. Having only recently settled in Palm Beach after two decades of living in the outback, her mother was terrified of all things remotely technical, and she owned neither a computer nor a cell phone. Voice mail continued to be a source of both wonder and frustration, while the Internet was simply beyond her comprehension. "I drove into Miami to see Bram," Charley told her.

Silence. Then, "How **is** your brother?"

"I don't know. He wasn't at his apartment. I waited for hours."

"Did he know you were coming?"

"He knew."

Another silence, this one longer than the first. Then, "You think he's . . . ?" Her mother's voice trailed off.

". . . Drinking and doing drugs?"

"Do you?"

"Maybe. I don't know."

"I worry so much about him."

"A little late for that, don't you think?" The words were out of Charley's mouth before she could stop them. "Sorry," she apologized immediately.

"That's all right," her mother conceded. "I guess I deserved that."

"I didn't mean to be cruel."

"Of course you did," her mother said without rancor. "It's what makes you such a good writer. And your sister such a mediocre one," she couldn't help but add.

"Mother . . ."

"Sorry, dear. I didn't mean to be cruel," she said, borrowing Charley's words.

"Of course you did." Charley smiled, felt her mother do the same. "Look, I better go."

"I thought maybe I could come over later, see the children . . ."

"Sounds fine." Absently, Charley clicked open another e-mail.

FROM: A person of taste
TO: Charley@Charley'sWeb.com
SUBJECT: Perverts
DATE: Mon. 22 Jan. 2007 10:40:05–0400

Dear Charley,

While I'm normally the kind of person who believes in LIVE AND LET LIVE, your most recent column has forced me to reconsider. Your previous column on sex toys was bad enough, but this latest one is an affront to good Christians everywhere. What a vile and disgusting pervert you are. You deserve to BURN IN HELL. So **DIE, BITCH, DIE**, and take your bastard children with you!

P.S.: I'd keep a very close eye on them if I were you. You'd be horrified at what some people are capable of.

Charley felt her breath freeze in her lungs. "Mother, I have to go." She hung up the phone and jumped to her feet, upending her chair as she raced from her cubicle.

2

O kay, Charley, try to calm down."

"How can I calm down? Some lunatic's threatening my children."

"I understand. Just take a few deep breaths, and tell me again. . . ."

Charley took two big gulps of air as Michael Duff got up from behind his massive oak desk and walked to the door of the large, glass-walled office that occupied the southwest corner of the floor.

A small group of reporters had already gathered outside the office to see what all the commotion was about. "Problems?" someone asked.

"Everything's fine," Michael told them.

"Everything's **Charley**," she heard a woman mutter dismissively as Michael closed the door.

"Okay, so tell me exactly what the e-mail said," he instructed, signaling for Charley to sit down.

Charley ignored the two green leather chairs in front of Michael's desk, choosing to pace the sand-colored carpet instead. Outside the rain pelted against the windows, the sound competing with the din of traffic from nearby I-95. "It said I should burn in hell, and I should 'die, bitch, die,' and take my bastard children with me."

"Okay, so obviously not your biggest fan . . ."

"And then it said that I should watch them carefully, that you never knew what people were capable of."

Michael's brow wrinkled with concern as he perched on the side of his desk. His brown eyes narrowed. "Did it say anything else?"

"No, that was it. That was enough."

Michael rubbed his strong jaw with his large hand, pushed back some gray hair that had fallen across his wide forehead, then crossed muscular arms over his expansive chest. Charley watched each move, noting that everything about the older man was oversized, something she might normally have found comforting, but which this morning only served to underline her growing sense of helplessness. Listening to the effortless boom of his voice, seeing the casual authority inherent in even his smallest gesture, she felt reduced and insubstantial. Looking at him, she understood, for the first time, what people meant when they said someone "assumed control." **Assumed**, she thought. Not took. Not seized. A man like Michael Duff never had to fight for control, as she always seemed to be doing. It was his—naturally. Something he took for granted, something he just **assumed**.

"I shouldn't have come barging in here like that," Charley apologized, replaying in her mind the dramatic way she'd burst into the room without so much as a knock on the door. She glanced toward the reporters sitting at their desks beyond the glass wall. She knew that even though they were no longer looking in her direction, they were still watching her. Judging her.

"You're understandably upset."

"It's not that I've never gotten nasty e-mails before. Or even death threats." High-profile reporters routinely received such unpleasantries, and most were as meaningless as the proposals of marriage that also came their way. Along with the abuse also came letters of congratulations on a job well done and more than a few declarations of love. Some readers submitted suggestions for future columns, others forwarded nude pictures of themselves, and a surprising number were looking for someone to pen their life stories. Charley had received two such requests in recent weeks. She'd turned them down as gently as she could—other commitments, I'm not the right person for the job, you should try writing it yourself—but then, some people couldn't help but take such rejection personally. "It's just that this is the first time anyone's threatened my children," she said, her eyes filling with tears. "You think I'm overreacting, don't you?"

"Not at all. We take threats like this very seriously. Please tell me you saved the letter."

"Of course."

"Good. I'll report what's happened to the police, forward them a copy of the e-mail, and see if they can trace it."

"Whoever wrote it probably used an Internet café."

"I wouldn't be too sure about that," Michael said. "Most of these nut cases aren't very bright. Wouldn't surprise me at all if the creep used his home computer."

"**His?** You think it's a guy?"

"Sounds like masculine posturing to me."

"So, what do I do now?"

"Not much you **can** do, except be extra careful," Michael said, with a shrug. "Don't open your door to strangers; try not to antagonize anybody; keep a close eye on your kids; let the police handle it. I don't think he'll bother you again. Guys like this are basically cowards. He shot his wad when he sent that e-mail."

Charley smiled, feeling safer already. "Yesterday's column seems to have upset a lot of people."

"Just means you're doing a good job."

"Thanks."

"Try not to worry," Michael said as she opened the door to his office and stepped outside.

"Everything all right?" one of the secretaries inquired as Charley walked past her desk.

"Everything's fine," she answered without stopping or looking back, afraid if she did either, she'd burst into tears.

"The hairless wonder," someone whispered, loud enough to be heard.

"Must itch like hell."

Muted laughter followed Charley back to her cubicle. What I wouldn't give for a door to slam, she thought as she stepped inside and stooped to right her fallen chair. The threatening e-mail had disappeared from her computer screen and been replaced by her screen saver: a year-old photograph of her children. Charley stared at their beautiful faces, silently counting up the changes the past twelve months had brought—Franny's toothless smile was shyer in the picture than it was now that her two front teeth had finally grown in, and her brown hair was shorter and lighter than it had since become, although she had the same sparkle in her luminous green eyes. One freckled arm was draped across her younger brother's shoulders in what looked like affection but was probably just an attempt to keep him still. James, at four, was a little butterball of nervous energy, even when he wasn't moving. And while his cheeks had thinned and his body was now taller by several inches, he'd lost none of that energy. He might look like a little cherub with his mop of white-blond hair and navy-blue eyes, she thought, her fingers reaching out to stroke the dimple in his chin, but he was a regular little imp. She adored him. Glancing between him and his sister, Charley couldn't believe she'd managed to produce anything so absolutely perfect. Sometimes her body actually ached with the love she felt for her children. Why had no one prepared her? Why had no one ever told her it was possible to love this much?

Possibly because there'd been no one to tell her.

Charley sank down in her chair as she reached into the top drawer of her desk. She retrieved a copy of her sister Anne's latest novel, **Remember Love**, sent to her two weeks ago, and which she'd yet to read. If the cover hadn't been enough to turn her off—a picture of a young bride, her tear-filled eyes only partly obscured by her wedding veil—the dedication would have. **To my wonderful father, Robert Webb.** What was that all about? Whose father had **she** had? Charley thought of the cold and bitter man in whose house she'd grown up, a house full of angry silences and the echo of stern rebukes. Had her father ever had a kind word to say? To anyone?

Charley flipped to the title page. **To Charlotte**, her sister had scribbled in an elaborate series of loops and swirls she'd no doubt worked weeks to perfect. **With best wishes, Anne.** As if they were no more than strangers. Which perhaps was exactly what they were.

She turned to the first chapter, read the opening sentence: **The first time Tiffany Lang saw Blake Castle, she knew her life had changed forever.**

"Oh, dear."

It wasn't just that he was the handsomest man she'd ever seen, although that was undeniably true. It wasn't the blueness of his eyes or even the way they seemed to look right through her, as if he were staring straight into her soul, as if he could read all her most secret thoughts. Nor was it the insolent way he occupied the center of the room, his slim hips tilted slightly forward, his thumbs hooked provocatively into the pockets of his tight jeans, the pout on his full lips issuing a silent invitation, daring her to come closer. Approach at your own risk, he said without speaking.

"Dear God."

"Whatcha reading?" came a voice from behind her.

Charley quickly closed the book. "Something I can do for you, Mitch?" she asked without turning around.

"Understand you had a death threat."

Charley swiveled around in her chair. Mitch Johnson was a middle-aged man with a beer belly and a receding hairline who, for reasons Charley had never been able to fathom, thought he was irresistible to women. He stood leaning against the wall of her cubicle, in a studied pose Charley assumed he considered sexy, wearing a frown on his round face and trying to look serious.

"Should have come to me with that," he admonished. "I'm the senior editor. Your direct superior," he reminded her, subtlety never having been one of his strong suits. "Shouldn't go running to Michael every time you have a little problem."

"I didn't consider it a little problem."

"Still should have come to me first," Mitch said, in the annoying way he had of dropping pronouns from the start of his sentences.

"I'm sorry. I wasn't really thinking."

"Think next time," he said.

"I'm hoping there won't **be** a next time."

"Might try writing something a little less provocative for next week's column, in that case," he said, his gaze drifting toward her crotch. Charley folded her hands across the book in her lap in order to block his view. "Not that I personally didn't enjoy yesterday's little exposé, as it were. Been trying to convince my wife to go Brazilian." He winked. "Guess she's not as adventurous as you."

Charley turned back to her computer. "I'll forward a copy of that e-mail to your computer," she told him, punching in the appropriate keys.

"You do that. And next time . . ."

"You'll be the first to know."

"Good. Always liked being the first."

Charley could feel him wink even with her back to him. What was it with some guys? she wondered. Had they never heard of a little thing called sexual harassment? Did they not think it applied to them? Although she doubted she'd find many sympathizers on this floor. Didn't she invite this kind of sex-based banter with the columns she wrote? she could hear her fellow columnists ask. Don't expect any sympathy from us.

Don't worry, she thought, flipping over the book in her lap. I long ago stopped expecting anything from anyone.

Charley found herself staring at the glamorous photograph of her sister on the back cover of the book. Anne was sitting on a pink velvet sofa, surrounded by decorative white lace pillows, her long auburn hair piled loosely on top of her head, a few photogenic ringlets falling around her heart-shaped face. There was no denying her beauty, despite the layers of heavy makeup she wore. But no amount of mascara or smoky shadow could disguise the sadness in her eyes. Charley had read in the tabloids about Anne's recent separation from bad-boy husband number two. Rumor had it he was asking for alimony and threatening to sue for custody of their young daughters if he didn't get it. If Charley remembered correctly, Darcy was two and Tess only eight months. What a mess, she thought, reaching for the phone. She retrieved her sister's number from her mental files and dialed New York before she could change her mind.

"Webb residence," the housekeeper announced crisply, answering on the first ring.

"Can I speak to Anne, please? It's her sister."

"Miss Anne," the housekeeper called out. "It's Emily."

"No, it's . . ."

"Em, how are you?" her sister said, coming on the line.

"It's not Emily," Charley corrected.

"Charlotte?"

"Charley," she corrected again.

There was a long pause.

"Anne? Are you still there?"

"I'm here."

"I thought for a minute we'd been disconnected."

"I'm just surprised to hear from you, that's all. Is everything all right?"

"Everything's fine."

"Our mother?"

"She's fine. Our father?"

"Fine."

"Good."

Another pause, even longer than the first.

"So, how are the kids?" Charley asked.

"Well. And yours?"

"They're great."

"I take it you've heard about A.J. and me splitting up."

"I'm really sorry."

"Trust me, I'm well rid of the miserable s.o.b. The turd cheats on me with two of my best friends and still has the nerve to ask for alimony. Can you beat that?"

Charley wasn't sure what surprised her more: that her soon-to-be-ex-brother-in-law had slept with two of her sister's best friends or that Anne had so many.

"How's Emily?" Charley asked.

"Em's wonderful. You saw her on **Good Morning America**, I take it."

"Actually, no. I missed it. Nobody told me . . ."

"She was terrific. Apparently the network is considering a permanent spot for her."

"That would be great."

"Yes, it would. How's Bram?"

"Okay. Have you heard from him lately?"

"Are you kidding? He phones even less than you do. Why? Is something wrong?"

"No."

"What's going on, Charley? Why are you calling?"

Why **had** she called?

"Has anyone contacted you from **People**?" Anne asked.

"What people?"

"**People** magazine. My publicist has been trying to convince them to do a piece on me. She was thinking of using the whole Brontë thing."

"What?"

"Emily thinks it's a great idea. They haven't called?"

"No. Not yet. Look, the reason I called . . . I just wanted to thank you for your book. It was very nice of you to send me a copy."

"Oh, yeah. That was my publicist's idea, too. She thought you might write something about it in your column. I told her you probably wouldn't even read it. Have you?"

"Not yet, but I intend to start it this weekend."

"Sure."

"I hear it's really good," Charley ventured.

"Everyone says it's my best."

"Number nine."

"Actually, number six as of next week."

"That's wonderful."

"Everyone's very pleased."

"They should be."

"I'm booked solid for speaking engagements for the next two months."

"Really? Any chance you'll be down this way?"

"Maybe. I'm not sure of my exact schedule."

"Well, call me as soon as you know anything."

"Why?"

The question was piercing in its simplicity. "I thought maybe we could all get together," Charley improvised, trying to remember the last time she'd seen either of her sisters in person.

Another pause, this one the longest yet.

"Maybe. Look, I better go. Thanks for calling."

"Thanks for the book."

"Enjoy," Anne said before hanging up.

"Enjoy," Charley repeated, replacing the receiver and closing her eyes, trying to pinpoint the moment her family had begun its slow and steady disintegration. Her father would undoubtedly put the blame on her mother, insisting her desertion had damaged the family unit beyond repair. Her mother would no doubt issue a counterclaim, insist it was Robert

Webb's coldness that had driven her into the arms of someone else. That that someone was a woman had only added fuel to her father's angry flame.

It shouldn't have been that way.

On the surface, Robert and Elizabeth Webb had been the ideal couple, good-looking and educated, young and in love. Even their names were a perfect match, especially for an esteemed professor of English literature. Robert and Elizabeth, just like Robert Browning and his wife, Elizabeth Barrett Browning, the famous romantic poets. How wonderfully appropriate, they'd joked. Except that Robert Webb had turned out to be anything but romantic, and it hadn't taken Elizabeth long to discover that while she'd fallen in love with a Robert, she'd married a Bob.

They'd had four children in eight years. Charlotte arrived first—**Charlotte's Web** having been her mother's favorite children's book, and the play on words was just too delicious for an English scholar to resist—followed two years later by Emily, and then Anne two years after that. "Our very own Brontë sisters," her mother had told anyone who'd listen. And then came the boy her father had been hoping for all along. They'd actually considered naming him Branwell, after the Brontë sisters' only brother, but since, unlike his famous siblings, Branwell was an abject failure at everything he tried, they'd settled on Bram, after Bram Stoker, author of **Dracula**, the bloodsucking count. The name change hadn't helped. Just as the Webb sisters had followed the example of their more illustrious namesakes, Bram did his part as well, following in Branwell's footsteps by never amounting to much. "It's destiny," he liked to say, citing Branwell's addiction to both drugs and alcohol as the inspiration for his own.

Once again, Charley reached for the phone. She should call Bram, she was thinking, although speaking to her younger brother was always an exercise in frustration, and she was already feeling frustrated enough. Especially after his no-show over the weekend, when she'd driven all the way down to Miami in holiday traffic—in south Florida, the holiday extended from December through March—only to find his apartment empty and her brother nowhere around.

There was a time when this might have concerned her, but no longer. It had happened too often. "See you at eight o'clock," he'd say, only to turn up at midnight. "I'll be there Friday at six for dinner," he'd confirm, arriving the following Monday at noon. Charley had known about the drugs for years. She'd hoped their mother's reappearance in their lives might help turn things around. But after almost two years, Bram still refused to have anything to do with her. If anything, he was worse now than he'd been before.

"Knock, knock," said a woman from behind Charley's desk.

Charley swiveled her chair around to see Monica Turnbull, early twenties, jet black, closely cropped hair, a silver loop pinching her right nostril, blood-red nails clutching a plain white envelope.

"You've got mail," Monica chirped. "And I don't mean that virtual crap. I mean a real, actual letter," she continued, dropping it into Charley's outstretched palm.

Charley stared at the girlish scrawl on the front of the white envelope, then had to glance twice at the return address. "Pembroke Correctional? Isn't that a prison?"

"Looks like you have a fan."

"Just what I need." The phone rang. "Thanks," Charley said as Monica wiggled her fingers good-bye. "Charley Webb," she said, picking up the receiver.

"This is Glen McLaren. I have your brother."

"What?"

"You know where to find me."

The line went dead in her hands.

3

W here's my brother?" Charley said, bursting through the heavy front door of Prime, the chichi nightclub that was Palm Beach's current place to be and be seen. Prime boasted a clientele of mostly young, mostly rich, mostly beautiful—or those whose money qualified them as beautiful—people. They came to mingle, toss their layered blond hair around photogenically, show off buff bodies swathed in the latest designer fashions, and hook up—with old friends, future lovers, and discreet dealers. Charley had referred to the place as Prime Meat in a recent, none-too-flattering column that had done absolutely nothing to slow the club's ever-burgeoning popularity.

The first time Charley had visited Prime was in the early morning hours of a late October weekend. Like most people her age, she'd initially found the combination of mirrors and mahogany, loud music and dim lights, expensive perfume and sweating, well-toned bodies, to be amazingly seductive. In the five minutes it had taken to navigate her way through the meticulously underdressed crowd to the impressively overstocked bar that occupied the entire left side of the room, she'd been approached by a trio of handsome men, a woman with fake, balloon-sized breasts, and a chorus of seemingly disembodied voices offering to sell her everything from Ecstasy to heroin. "You name it, I've got it," someone had whispered tantalizingly in Charley's ear as a young socialite swayed past her on unsteady heels, white powder still clinging to the underside of her nostrils. Noise and laughter had followed Charley to the bar, stray hands carelessly groped her buttocks as she walked, the continuous beat of the music blocking out conscious thought. Charley had realized how easy it would be simply to give herself over to the meaninglessness of it all, to dance, to drift, to deny . . . everything.

I think not. Therefore I am not.

It had been so appealing.

But now, in the unflattering light of a rainy morning, the room retained little of its after-hours glamour or decadence. It was lifeless, like an overexposed photograph. Just another big, empty space with a deserted wooden dance floor.

About twenty tables, each seating four, were crowded together in the far right corner of the room for patrons who actually wanted to eat, while a series of high-tops, seating two, were scattered throughout the room, guarded over by towering bronze sculptures of blank-faced nude women, their elbows bent, palms facing forward, fingers pointing toward the twenty-foot-high ceiling, in gestures of abject surrender.

"Where's my brother?" Charley said again, her eyes returning to the bar where Glen McLaren sat perched on a tan leather stool, the morning paper, open to the sports pages, stretched out along the brown marble counter-top.

McLaren was dressed all in black. He was maybe thirty-five, tall and slim and not quite as good-looking as Charley remembered from their previous encounter. In daylight, his features were coarser, his nose broader, his brown eyes sleepier, although she could still feel them undressing her as she approached. "Miss Webb," he acknowl-edged. "How nice to see you again."

"Where's my brother?"

"He's okay."

"I didn't ask you **how** he was. I asked **where** he was."

"Would you like a drink?" Glen asked, as if she hadn't spoken. "Some orange juice perhaps or . . ."

"I don't want anything to drink."

". . . a cup of coffee?"

"I don't want coffee. Look. You called me. You said you had my brother."

"And **you** said a lot of very unflattering things about me and my club in your column last month. Or so I understand." He grinned. "Personally, I never read your column."

"Then you shouldn't be too upset."

"Unfortunately, a lot of other people, including our esteemed mayor and the chief of police, don't have my discerning taste. I've been getting a lot of unwanted attention these past several weeks."

"I'm sorry about that."

"Are you?"

"Not really. What's any of this got to do with my brother?"

"Nothing. I'm just making conversation."

"I'm not interested in conversation, Mr. McLaren."

"Glen," he corrected.

"I'm not interested in conversation, Mr. McLaren," Charley repeated, transferring her oversize beige leather handbag from one shoulder to the other. "I'm interested in finding my brother. Do you have him or don't you?"

"I do." McLaren smiled sheepishly. "God, the last time I said that it cost me a fortune." He lowered his chin and raised his eyes flirtatiously. "What—not even a little grin? I'm trying to be charming here."

"Why?" Charley glanced around the room, saw no one but a waiter wiping down the tables on the far side of the dance floor.

"Why am I trying to charm you? Oh, I don't know. Because you're beautiful? Because you're a reporter? Because I'm trying to get into your good graces? Or maybe because I'm just trying to get into your pants."

Charley's impatient sigh filled the room. "I'm not into revenge fucking, Mr. McLaren."

Glen shrugged, his eyes drifting back to the sports pages of the morning paper. If he was shocked by her coarse language, he gave no indication. "Interesting, since you seem to have no trouble at all fucking people over."

He's quick, Charley thought. She'd give him that. "I guess that'll teach you not to talk to reporters."

"Except that, if you recall, I had no idea you were a reporter the last time we spoke. I didn't have a clue there was such a thing as WEBB SITE. Clever title for a column, incidentally."

"Thank you."

"I was simply under the impression I was talking to a beautiful young woman, one I was trying very hard to impress."

"One you promptly stopped trying to impress the minute you realized she wasn't going to sleep with you."

"I'm a man, Charley. I'm only interested in so much talk."

"Then why are we talking now?"

Glen smiled again—something he did with alarming regularity, Charley thought—causing the skin around his sleepy brown eyes to crinkle. "I'm just having fun, playing with you a little," he admitted.

"I don't like being played with."

"Is that what your little literary temper tantrum was really all about? You felt you were being played and it hurt your feelings?"

"This isn't about hurt feelings," Charley said, trying not to enjoy the phrase "little literary temper tantrum." "And it's certainly not why I left work this morning to drive all the way over here in the pouring rain."

"Aw, it's not **that** far," Glen pointed out.

"Where's my brother?"

Glen nodded toward the rear of the club. "In my office."

Immediately Charley darted in that direction.

"Turn left," Glen said, following after her.

Charley quickly reached the back of the club and pushed open the hand-carved mahogany door to Glen's office, her purse slapping at her side. The blinds were partially closed and the wood-paneled room was mostly in darkness, but even so, she could make out the figure of a man sprawled on his back across a red velvet sofa, right leg on the floor, left arm tossed dramatically over his head, light brown hair lying limp across his forehead. "My God. What have you done to him?"

Glen flipped on the light. "Take it easy. He's just sleeping."

"Sleeping?" Charley dropped her purse to the floor and rushed to her brother's side. She knelt down, laying her head against his chest, listening for the sound of his breathing.

"Passed out, actually."

"Passed out? What did you give him?"

"Well, I tried to give him a cup of coffee, but he's stubborn. Like you. Said he didn't want any."

"Bram?" Charley said, shaking his shoulder gently. And then not so gently. "Bram, wake up." She looked from her brother back to McLaren. "I don't understand. What's he doing here?"

"Oh, so now you want to talk?" Glen sank into the second, smaller sofa positioned at a right angle to the one on which Bram had apparently spent the night.

"How do you even know my brother?"

"I don't," Glen admitted. "First time I laid eyes on him was last night when I asked him to leave."

"What are you talking about?"

"According to my bartender, your brother arrived around ten o'clock last night, had a couple of drinks, hit on a few young ladies, then became quite belligerent when they turned him down. He started mouthing off, being generally obnoxious, telling everyone within shouting distance he was really here to score some dope, and where were all the dealers he'd read about in his sister's column?"

"Which was how you knew he was my brother," Charley stated with a roll of her eyes.

"That, plus I checked his wallet for ID after he passed out."

"Which was when exactly?"

"Around one o'clock."

"How'd he get that bruise on his face?" Charley ran a wary finger along her brother's pale cheek. She felt him flinch, although his eyes remained closed. "Did you hit him?"

"I had no choice."

"What do you mean, you had no choice?"

"He was drunk, and probably stoned as well. I told him I was gonna call a cab to take him home, but he refused, said he was perfectly capable of making it back to Miami on his own. Well, I couldn't let him do that. So I followed him to the parking lot, told him he was in no condition to drive, and he said to try and stop him." Glen shrugged. "Like I said, I had no choice."

"You were being a good samaritan?"

"I just didn't want him driving drunk and maybe killing somebody. The last thing I need right now is a lawsuit."

Charley saw a flash of lightning from behind the half-closed metallic blinds, followed seconds later by a crack of thunder. "So you brought him in here?"

"Would you have preferred it if I'd left him outside?"

"I hope you're not expecting me to thank you," Charley said.

"Perish the thought. I just thought you might like to know where he was."

"Are you always so dramatic?" Charley asked, mimicking his voice on the phone. **"I have your brother. You know where to find me."**

Glen laughed. "Just having some fun. You already think I'm a gangster. Figured I might as well act like one."

"I believe the term I used was 'hoodlum wannabe.' Not quite in the same league as 'gangster,' " Charley corrected.

"Ouch." Glen clutched his chest, as if he'd been mortally wounded.

"**Are** you a gangster?" Charley asked seconds later, curious in spite of herself.

"Off the record? Promise I'm not going to read about this conversation in next week's paper?"

"I thought you never read my columns."

Glen smiled. "I'm not a gangster." He looked toward her sleeping brother. "He do this kind of thing often?"

"That's really none of your business."

"No, but it's my sofa. You could at least try to make nice until he wakes up."

"Sorry. I've never been very good at making nice."

"Why doesn't that surprise me?"

"Because you're a man of great intelligence and perception. How's that for making nice?"

"A little heavy-handed."

"Take it or leave it."

"Oh, I'll take it. Does this mean you'll reconsider sleeping with me?"

"Not a chance."

Another bolt of lightning. Another crash of thunder.

"Storm's getting closer," Glen observed.

"Great," Charley said sarcastically. "I always loved driving I-95 in the pouring rain."

"I don't think you're going anywhere for at least a little while."

Charley looked from the window to her brother, now snoring contentedly beside her. "Great," she said again.

"How about reconsidering that cup of coffee?"

"Why are you being so nice to me?"

"You have a problem with people being nice to you?"

Charley lifted her hands into the air, in a gesture of surrender remarkably similar to that of the faceless bronze statues in the other room. "Sure, let's have coffee," she said. "Why not?"

"Why not indeed?" Glen echoed, going to the door. "How do you take it?"

"Black."

"Thought you'd say that. Back in a flash," he said, as another bolt of lightning shot through the sky. It was immediately followed by a spectacular crack of thunder.

"You're missing quite a display," Charley said to her sleeping brother, as she pushed herself to her feet and walked to the window. She opened the blinds with a flick of her fingers and stared at the ferocious downpour. The rain in Florida was like nowhere else in the world, she was thinking, watching huge drops, like angry fists, pound against the panes of glass. It came at you relentlessly, obliterating almost everything in its path, blinding you. If she'd been driving, she'd have been forced to pull over and wait it out.

Could that be any more uncomfortable than waiting it out in the office of the man she'd disparaged in print as a "hoodlum wannabe," while her brother slept off a drunken stupor on that same man's red velvet couch? "Why do you do these things to me?" she asked him, as another bolt of lightning lit up the sky, illuminating her dented, silver Camry in the parking lot next to Bram's ancient, impeccably maintained, dark green MG. "You always loved that car more than anything else on earth," she muttered as another clap of thunder rattled the palm trees and shook the premises. "God, Bram. What's the matter with you? Why do you keep screwing up?" She returned to the sofa, sank down beside him. "Bram, wake up. Come on. Enough of this crap. Time to grow up and go home. Come on, Bram," she said again. "Enough is enough."

Bram said nothing, although his long, dark lashes fluttered provocatively, as if he might be persuaded, with a few well-chosen words, to open his eyes.

"Bram," Charley said, impatiently poking at his arm. "Bram, can you hear me?"

Still nothing.

"You can't keep doing this, Bram," Charley lectured. "You can't keep fucking up and expecting people to rescue you. It's getting old. And you're not getting any younger," she added, although at twenty-four, he was hardly a candidate for a retirement community. "It's time to get a life." She sighed. Her brother had pretty much given up on life a long time ago. "Our mother called this morning," she continued, recalling that of the four children, her brother had seemed to adapt to their mother's desertion the best.

Maybe because he was only two at the time she'd left, and too young to realize what exactly was happening. He'd cried for his mommy for several days, then blithely crawled into the arms of the woman their father had hired to take her place. A needy child, he'd basically stayed there until the woman quit two years later in a salary dispute with their father. She, too, had left without saying good-bye. After that, there'd been a succession of housekeepers, as plentiful and as faceless as the bronze statues beyond Glen's office door. No one ever stayed very long. Their father's unyielding coldness saw to that. "She's worried about you," Charley told her brother now, thinking of her own children, and wondering, as she always did when she thought too long about her mother, how the woman could have walked out and left them the way she did.

"I wanted to take you with me," her mother had tried to explain when she'd reentered Charley's life two years earlier. "But I knew your father would never let me take you out of the country. And I had to leave. If I'd stayed in that house any longer, I would have died."

"So you left us to die instead," Charley told her, refusing to let her off the hook so easily.

"Oh, but look at you," came her mother's instant response. "You've done so well. All my girls have done so amazingly well."

"And Bram? What about him?"

To that question, Elizabeth Webb had no answer.

"Bram," Charley said now. "Bram, wake up. It's time to go home."

She smelled the coffee even before she turned around to see Glen standing there. "Making any progress?" he asked from the doorway, his arm extended toward her.

She shook her head. "That smells wonderful," she acknowledged, taking the mug from his outstretched hand as the steam climbed toward her nose.

"You got lucky. Paul just made a fresh pot."

Charley took a long, slow sip. "It's very good. Thank you."

"You're welcome." He resumed his seat on the other sofa.

"You're not having any?"

"I'm not much of a coffee drinker."

"Really? Why is that?"

"I find it interferes with all the cocaine in my system," he said with a straight face, and for an instant, Charley wasn't sure whether or not he was serious. "That was a joke," he qualified quickly. "Although, obviously not a very funny one. Especially under the circumstances." He looked toward her brother.

"You think he's doing coke?"

"I think he's going to have one hell of a head-ache when he wakes up," Glen said, without answering the question. "What's his problem anyway?"

Charley took another sip of coffee as another flash of lightning streaked across the sky. "You really think I'm going to discuss my brother's problems with you?"

"Problems?" Glen repeated, stressing the final **s**.

"Figure of speech."

"Or a slip of the tongue."

"My brother's a bit of a lost soul," Charley admitted, another clap of thunder serving to underline her words.

"How long has he been wandering?"

Charley almost smiled. It appeared the "hoodlum wannabe" had a bit of a poet's soul. "I'd really rather not talk about it," she said, although the truth was she was suddenly desperate to talk about it. **He's been screwed up as long as I can remember,** she wanted to shout. **He's been drinking since he was fourteen, and doing drugs at least that long. As a teenager, he was kicked out of every private school in Connecticut. Then he flunked out of Brown in his first year, and headed south to join me in Florida, where he enrolled in night school at the University of Miami, and where he's been languishing ever since, taking one aimless course after another, rarely even bothering to write the final**

exams. He lives in a furnished apartment in a nasty part of town, works as little as possible, and only then when he needs to supplement the small inheritance our paternal grandmother left us, and which our beloved father, as trustee of her estate, elected to dole out in meager monthly increments. "Probably one of the few smart decisions he ever made," she muttered out loud.

"Sorry?" Glen asked.

"Smart decision, to have coffee," Charley amended, wondering if she was fooling him. If she was fooling anyone.

"Anytime." The phone rang. Glen pushed himself off the sofa and walked to his desk in three easy strides. "McLaren here," he said into the receiver. "Well, how are **you**?" he asked, his voice dropping, becoming instantly soft and seductive. He held one hand over the mouthpiece, whispered to Charley, "I'll just be a minute."

"Would you like me to leave?"

He shook his head. "Not necessary." He sat down behind his desk and swiveled around in his high-backed, black leather chair to face the window. "Of course I'm glad you called. No, you're not interrupting a thing."

Charley frowned. Outside the storm was growing a little less fierce. She could now actually make out the tops of a row of giant palm trees bending in the wind. "Wake up, Bram," she whispered between clenched teeth. She returned to the sofa, trying not to eavesdrop on Glen's conversation.

"No, I have no plans for tonight after work," she heard him say.

A nice clap of thunder would be good right about now, she thought, hearing him laugh, and wondering if there was anything she could do to blot out the sound of his voice. She reached across the floor for her purse, thinking she could call Emily in New York, since Emily was the only sibling she hadn't seen or spoken to today. And certainly Emily would be as delighted as Anne to hear from her.

"Of course I'd love to see your new apartment," Glen was practically purring.

"Oh, for God's sake," Charley said out loud, forcing a smile onto her lips as Glen's head poked around the side of his chair to see what was the matter. "Just looking for something," she whispered, pulling a white envelope out of her purse. "Found it," she exclaimed, although the truth was she barely remembered stuffing the letter into her purse before fleeing her office.

You've got mail, she heard Monica say.

Charley turned the envelope over in her hand,

studied the return address. **Pembroke Correc-tional.**

Looks like you have a fan.

Blocking out the sound of Glen's suggestive banter, Charley tore open the letter, pulled out the lined white paper filled with girlish script, and started reading.

4

January 17, 2007

Dear Charley,

Hi. I hope you don't mind my writing to you. I know how busy you must be, and that you probably get tons of mail, although maybe not too many from prisons. Gee, I still can't believe I'm really here, even though it's been over a year now. I was really afraid of coming to this place—have you seen all those scary movies about life in women's prisons?—but I have to admit, it hasn't been all that bad. After all the death threats I received from supposedly law-abiding citizens on the outside, it's actually been something of a relief, to tell you the truth, and so far, nobody's tried to rape me with a broom handle or anything awful like that. It's been fairly quiet, to be honest, and I'm happy to say, relatively clean, since I'm a bit of a neat freak.

The other prisoners have all turned out to be pretty nice—most of the women are here on drug-related issues—although for a long time, nobody would speak to me. But I've tried to be on my best behavior and put my best foot forward, always being pleasant and helpful, and now almost everyone has more or less come around. One woman, in here because she stabbed her best friend with a pair of scissors over an argument about which TV show to watch—even told me she thinks I have a pretty smile. I think she might have a crush on me, although I've done nothing to encourage her in that regard. There are still a few women, mothers of small children mostly, who won't have anything to do with me, but I'm working on them, and I feel their resistance beginning to wane.

This might sound strange, and I hope you won't take it the wrong way, but you've always been kind of a role model for me. I want you to know how very much I admire you. Before I was sent to prison, I used to read your column every week. My favorite columns were the ones you wrote about the time an ex-boyfriend talked you into going bungee jumping—I could really relate, having been talked into a few ill-advised outings myself—and about the problems you had deciding what to wear when your daughter's father got married and you didn't want to upstage the bride. I thought that was so funny. But touching, too, the way you took everyone's feelings into account.

I even wrote several letters to your website, and you were kind enough to respond. You probably don't remember. And there's no reason you should. I wrote them about three years ago, just after you started doing your column. This was way before anything bad happened, and I didn't sign my real name, so you wouldn't have had any reason to connect me to that monster you wrote about later. The Beastly Baby-Sitter, you called me. I felt really awful about that—still do—since I hate that you have such negative feelings about me. I want you to like me. Your opinion is very important to me.

Anyway, the first time I wrote you, it

was about my older sister, Pamela, who's always been a real pain in the you-know-where. I'd borrowed an old blouse of hers—I swear I didn't know it was her favorite—and my boyfriend accidentally spilled some red wine on it. This boyfriend's name was Gary. (You may remember him—he testified against me in court.) When we tried to get the stain out with water, we only made it worse. (I didn't realize the blouse was silk, and that it had to be dry-cleaned.) Anyway, Pam has this really bad temper—so does my whole family—and I was afraid to tell her I'd ruined her blouse, so, coward that I am, I threw it in the garbage. But then I felt so guilty, 'cause she was crying and tearing up the house looking for it. So, I wrote to you, asking for your advice. You told me that you weren't an advice columnist, but in your opinion, I should tell her the truth and offer to reimburse her for the blouse. I thought that was very good advice, and I often wish I'd taken it. But I just couldn't. I was too afraid of her temper. (Plus I didn't have the money.)

The second time I wrote you I was having problems with Gary. I told you he was very controlling, and trying to get me to do things I was real uncomfortable about doing, but that I was afraid of losing him if I didn't go along. Again, you made it very clear you weren't an advice columnist, but that, in your opinion, I shouldn't do anything that made me uncomfortable, and that I should worry less about losing him and more about losing myself. Those words touched me very deeply, even if I didn't heed them.

Please don't think there was anything wrong with your advice just because I wasn't strong or wise enough to take it. You were absolutely right. I did end up losing myself. That's how I found myself in this awful mess.

I want you to know I never planned for any of this to happen. I never intended to hurt anyone. I still can't believe I played any part in the horrible things they say I did. It doesn't seem possible that I could have been involved in any way. I'm really a very good person at heart. I hope you believe me. I even hope one day we might be friends.

Which brings me to the reason for this letter.

In the past year, I've had a lot of time to think. About all sorts of things. Not just the terrible things that landed me here, although obviously they're very important, but about how a person with my background and upbringing— my parents have been together for almost thirty-four years, and are regular churchgoers, plus I have an older brother and sister who've never been in any trouble with the police. Not to mention, I've always been very considerate of others. I wouldn't even step on an ant. I swear, if I saw one inside the house, I'd pick it up in a tissue and carry it gently outside. So, how could I possibly be guilty of doing such horrible things to actual human beings? It doesn't make sense.

Of course, at first everyone thought that Gary was to blame, that he was the true mastermind behind what happened. That was so not true. Gary couldn't mastermind his way out of a paper bag, as my mother used to say. And though I hate to admit it, she was right. (Don't tell her I said so.) Besides, even though Gary was technically my boyfriend at the time of the murders, I'd already moved on. Some people still think he had something to do with what went down. They can't believe a girl could commit the heinous crimes I've been accused of all on her own.

Maybe they're right.

Am I whetting your interest?

I'm facing a lot of issues these days, and I'm starting to question everything. Trouble is, I don't always know the right questions to ask. Which is, hopefully, where you come in. Even though I don't get to read your columns as frequently as I used to, and they're usually old by the time I get to see them, I still enjoy them, and think you're a wonderful writer. You have a way of getting to the truth, and expressing it clearly and without pretension. You're sensitive and caring, but you don't take crap from anyone. You stand up for what you believe, and you aren't afraid to take an unpopular stance. Even when you were writing all those unflattering things about me, I still admired you. That's an amazing talent for someone to have.

And I have an amazing story to tell.

Which is what I'm getting at.

I think it's time to tell my story—all of it—and I think you're the only person who can do it justice. Actually, it'd be more of a collaboration, since it would involve you and me spending a lot of

time together. I don't think that would
be all that unpleasant for you. I'm really
not the way the media—yourself included—portrayed me. I'm not the beast
you wrote about. Despite those awful
tapes they played at my trial, I'm not a
monster.

People think they know me.

They don't.

Actually, I think we have a lot in
common. (Please don't be angry with
me for saying that.)

But look at the facts: We're both attractive young women. (Okay, you're
beautiful!) Yes, I'm only twenty-two, but
that's not that much younger than you
are. And we both have brothers and sisters, although you're the oldest, and I'm
the baby of the family. We're both blond
and bosomy. And I think we have similar taste in men. We both seem to fall
for good-looking older guys who aren't
always the best choices for us. We like
our men to be strong and take charge,
but then we chafe at the restrictions
they try to put on us. Is that why you
never got married?

Personally, I've always wanted to get
married. I dream of a fairy tale wedding
with all the trimmings. Before all this

happened, I used to practice writing my vows and designing my dress. I had sketches all over the house. I pictured a long white dress, strapless, but not low-cut. I always think it's tacky when brides expose too much cleavage, and I wanted something very classy, very Vera Wang-ish. She's always been my inspiration, although I'll never be able to afford her. It's a moot point now anyway, since Pembroke Correctional doesn't allow prison weddings. Not that there's a whole lot of opportunity to meet suitable men in here. (They keep the men and women segregated, although occasionally we manage to find ways of getting together. Hint: there's way more than reading going on behind the bookshelves of the prison library.) Lots more about that if you agree to do the book.

Please, PLEASE, PLEASE consider my offer. I really think we'd make a great team. I promise to be very forthcoming and answer all your questions as honestly as I can. I won't hold anything back. I'll tell you all about my childhood, my parents, my brother and sister, my boyfriends, my sexual experiences. (Like you, I started very young. Unlike you, it wasn't my choice.) In short, I'll tell you every sordid detail, including facts never before made public about the unfortunate deaths of little Tammy Barnet and Noah and Sara Starkey.

I recognize that as the mother of two small children yourself, you are no doubt repulsed by the very idea of getting to know me better. You probably think you already know more about me than you ever wanted to know. Believe me when I tell you, you're wrong.

So, take all the time you need to arrive at a decision. And rest assured that you are the only candidate I'm considering for the job. Naturally, I'm hoping to hear from you sooner rather than later. I fully understand that you're a very busy woman, and that there are all sorts of demands on your time. You have a family to look after and a column to put out every week. But isn't it true that every journalist dreams about writing a book?

You're already well known in Palm Beach, but a story like mine could make you famous across the country. You deserve that, just as I deserve to have the true story of what really happened to those three sweet children made public.

Naturally, I'm not expecting anything in the way of financial remuneration. Aside from the law that says criminals can't profit from their misdeeds, money doesn't concern me. Whatever you can negotiate with a publisher would be entirely yours to keep.

Mine is a story that needs to be told. I think you have the courage to tell it.

Anxiously waiting on your reply,

Jill Rohmer

P.S.: If you decide to accept my offer, or if you have any questions at all, please feel free to contact my lawyer, Alex Prescott. He has an office in Palm Beach Gardens, and I've already alerted him to the possibility you might call. Please do. I promise it will be worth your while.

Whatever you decide, I remain your steadfast fan.

Jill

"Holy shit," Charley said, dropping the letter to her lap, watching her fingers tremble.

"Bad news?" Glen asked from behind his desk.

Charley noted the phone was no longer attached to his ear. "What?"

"You're white as a ghost. Everything all right?"

"I'm not sure."

Glen came around the front of his desk. "Anything I can help you with?"

Charley shook her head, her eyes returning to the letter in her hand. "You remember Jill Rohmer?" she heard herself ask. "She butchered three little kids a couple of years back. Every media outlet had a reporter covering her trial. I even wrote about her in my column."

Glen's eyes narrowed, furrowing his brow. "Right. I remember. She was the nanny or something. I remember my ex was freaking out about it."

"You have kids?"

"A son, Eliot. He'll be six on Saturday." He reached into his pocket, pulled out a small photograph of a dark-haired boy with an infectious grin, showed it to Charley. "He lives with his mother and her new husband in North Carolina. I don't get to see him very much."

"I'm sorry."

"Yeah. Me, too. But they're bringing him down for the weekend. We're all taking him to Lion Country Safari for his birthday."

"Sounds cozy."

"Interesting choice of words," he said, not bothering to disguise the strain in his voice as he returned the picture to his pocket. "What about you? Any kids?"

"Two. A boy and a girl."

"But no husband." Glen looked pointedly at the empty ring finger of her left hand.

"No husband."

"In that case, how would the three of you like to join us at Lion Country Safari on Saturday? That way I can show you what a fine, upstanding citizen I really am."

Charley laughed.

"I'm serious," Glen said. "You'd actually be doing me a favor. It won't be quite so 'cozy' that way."

"Thanks, but . . ."

"Think about it. Offer's good till Saturday. So, why are we talking about this Jill Rohmer?" he asked in the same breath.

Charley held up the letter. "Apparently, unlike you, she's a fan."

"Mind if I have a look?"

Charley handed Glen Jill's letter, watching him as he read, and trying to gauge his reaction.

"So, did she whet your interest?" he asked when he was through.

"Oh, it's whetted all right."

"Does that mean you're gonna do it?"

"Do what?"

"Contact her? Write her life story?"

Charley made a dismissive sound with her lips that was half sneer, half whistle. "Why would I want to do that?"

"Because she's pushing all the right buttons.

Appealing to both your ego and your curiosity. Waving the chance for an exclusive in front of your face, along with the opportunity to be famous. Not to mention the possibility of uncovering the real truth and righting 'a grave miscarriage of justice.' "

"Please. There's been no miscarriage of justice. The woman's a psychopath. There's no doubt at all she killed those kids. Don't you remember the awful tape recordings the police found in her bedroom of her victims' dying screams?"

"I suppose someone could have planted them there."

"Which doesn't explain what **her** voice was doing on the tapes. She also had access and opportunity, plus her fingerprints were found at the scene, and her DNA was all over the victims."

"What—no videotapes?"

Charley shrugged. There'd been rumors of videotapes, but despite extensive police searches, they had never been recovered. "What are you suggesting? That you think I should actually consider going to see her?"

"Absolutely not."

"Good. Something we agree on."

"But you will."

"What?"

"You heard me."

Charley snatched the letter from his hand and

returned it to her purse, all the while shaking her head. Smug bastard, she was thinking. "You think you know me, don't you?"

People think they know me.

They don't.

"Well enough to know she's got you hooked."

"Is that so?"

Actually, I think we have a lot in common.

"Who's got who hooked?" Bram said from beside her, opening his eyes and lifting himself up on his elbows. If he was surprised to find himself in a strange room with his sister and the man who'd knocked him unconscious, his expression offered no sign of it. If anything, he looked rested and serene. "Did I hear you say something about Jill Rohmer?"

"Well, it's about time you woke up," Charley chastised, fighting the urge to shake him by the shoulders. Even with a large bruise sitting on his cheekbone, Bram was by far the best-looking of the four Webb children, with pale porcelain skin, large, luminous gray-blue eyes, and lashes so long and thick they looked as if they'd been pasted on.

"You know I used to go out with her sister," he said matter-of-factly, long slender fingers smoothing the front of his blue silk shirt.

Charley felt any patience she had left quickly abandoning her. "What are you talking about?"

"I went out with her sister—what was her name? Pamela?"

"What are you talking about?" Charley said again, louder this time.

"I went out with . . ."

"When, for God's sake?"

"I don't know. A few years ago. Right after I came to Florida. We took a few classes together."

"Why didn't you ever tell me this?"

"Why would I? It was just a couple of dates. It didn't mean anything."

"You never said a word about knowing Jill Rohmer all through her trial."

"I **didn't** know her. I knew her sister. Why are we talking about Jill Rohmer anyway?"

Glen walked to his office door. "I think your brother could use a cup of coffee."

"No, that's all right," Charley protested.

"I would **love** a cup of coffee," Bram said at the same time.

"Be right back." Glen closed the door behind him as he left the room.

"What's the matter with you?" Charley hissed at her brother.

"Whoa. Hold on there. What's **your** problem?" Bram grabbed the sides of his head, as if to keep it from falling off.

"What's **my** problem? **You're** my problem,"

Charley raged, trying to keep her voice down. "You're so damn irresponsible."

"Just because I got a little drunk . . ."

"You didn't just get a little drunk. You got a lot drunk. And God only knows what else. And you would have driven home in that condition if Glen hadn't stopped you."

Bram's hand moved gingerly to his cheek. "Yes, I vaguely remember something about that."

"Do you vaguely remember we were supposed to get together yesterday?"

"Do you have to talk so loud?"

"Do you think I enjoy driving all the way to Miami for nothing? Do you think I like being phoned at work by some guy I've insulted in print, telling me he's got my brother? What made you pick this place, for God's sake?"

"I read about it in your column. It sounded interesting."

It was Charley's turn to grab her head. "Okay, that's it. The rain's letting up. We're going home." She grabbed her brother's arm, dragged him to his feet. He loomed over her like a tall tree.

"My coffee," he protested, as Charley pushed him out of the office toward the front door. "I'll follow you in my car," he said as they reached the parking lot.

"You sure you're okay to drive?"

"I'm fine," Bram insisted. "I'll be right behind you."

"Promise?"

Bram nodded his silent consent as he folded his body inside the tiny MG.

But when Charley turned right on South County Road and looked into her rearview mirror only seconds later, he'd already disappeared.

5

O kay, that's it. I'm not doing this anymore,"
Charley exclaimed, tossing her cell phone
back into her purse as she turned off Old Dixie
Highway, and made her way through the twisting warren of streets behind the Palm Beach
Convention Center, heading for home. It was
almost three o'clock in the afternoon. She had
returned to the office after attempting many
times to contact her brother to no avail. She'd
even resorted to subterfuge, calling from a variety of different phones in an effort to get
around his caller ID, but still he wasn't answering either his home phone or his cell. She'd left
at least half a dozen messages. ("Bram, where
the hell are you? Stop being such an idiot.")
Not surprisingly, he hadn't answered any of
them. Clearly he didn't want to speak to her.
And after a few hours of aimless research for
her next column, she decided to call it a day.

"You want to get drunk and get yourself beaten up, end up in jail, or worse, that's your problem. Not mine," she said now, nodding at her reflection in the rearview mirror, as if to underline her newfound resolve. "I will not be the one riding to your rescue anymore. I will not show up at the morgue to identify your bruised, broken body. Let Anne do it," she said, reminded of her sister in her pillow-filled New York apartment, as she drove past tiny New York Street. "Maybe she can fit it in between speaking engagements. And maybe, just **maybe**," Charley continued, turning onto New Jersey Street and pulling into her driveway, "her publicist can even convince **People** magazine to send a photographer down with her. How's that for an angle?" she said, turning off the engine and climbing out of the car. "Beats the hell out of the whole Brontë thing," she said, recalling her sister's words. "Damn it, anyway. What's wrong with everybody?"

"Everything okay?" a voice asked, and Charley spun toward the sound. The house next door was undergoing extensive renovations, and a worker in a yellow hard hat was regarding her quizzically from the driveway next to hers, his hands resting on slender hips, sweat staining the front of his white T-shirt, a blue-and-gray-checkered shirt belted around his waist. "We tried to keep the dust and everything away from your property as much as we could," the young man explained. "If there's a problem . . ."

"Everything's fine," Charley said. Except for my brother, my mother, my sisters, and the fact I'm getting threatening hate mail, she thought of adding. Oh, and did I mention that I got a letter from a convicted child killer who wants me to write her life story? "Just fine," she muttered, feeling the worker's eyes on her backside as she walked up the narrow concrete path to her front door.

"At least it's stopped raining," the man said.

Was he trying to prolong the conversation? Charley wondered, glancing toward the still-gray sky, then back at the worker, who was approximately her age and quite cute under that yellow hard hat. She turned away before she could do something stupid, such as inviting him inside her house for a drink. The last time she'd impulsively invited a man into her home, he'd ended up staying for three weeks and fathering her son. "When do you think you'll be done?" she asked as she unlocked her front door.

"Oh, we'll be another month at least."

"See you around then."

"Count on it."

Charley smiled, deciding she liked his arrogance almost as much as the cut of his triceps.

"What's going on out here?" another voice suddenly interrupted.

Charley felt her shoulders slump. I should have gone inside while I had the chance, she was thinking. The last thing she wanted was to get into an altercation with yet another pissed-off neighbor. "Just asking how things are going with the renovation," Charley said, seeing the scowl on Gabe Lopez's face even before she turned around.

"Everything's right on schedule." Black eyes glared at her from beneath a bushy black uni-brow. "No thanks to you."

"Okay, well . . ." Charley said, pushing open her front door, ". . . good luck." She stepped inside and closed the door behind her. "Asshole," she muttered. "No wonder your wife left you." She kicked off her black slip-ons, stepped from the cold tile of the tiny front foyer onto the living room's warm hardwood floor. "Which wasn't my fault, incidentally," she yelled back in the general direction of the front door.

"Do you always have to talk so loud?" her brother asked from the sofa.

Charley gasped, stumbling back against a bamboo table that sat against one ivory-colored wall, almost upsetting a glass vase of red-and-yellow silk tulips. "My God! You scared me half to death. What are you doing here?"

"You said to follow you home," he reminded her, pushing his skinny arms above his head and stretching his reed-thin body to its full length, so that it seemed even longer than its six feet, two inches. At the same time, he brought his feet up to rest on the glass coffee table in front of him.

"Which you didn't."

"Only 'cause I knew a shortcut. Figured I could get here quicker. Which I did. Been waiting for you all day. Where've you been?"

"I went back to the office."

"Too bad. I was hoping you went grocery shopping. Do you know you're out of coffee?"

Charley shook her head in exasperation. "I don't believe you."

"It's true. You can check for yourself."

"I'm not talking about the coffee, you moron."

"Hey, hey. Let's not get nasty."

"Where's your car?"

"End of the block. In front of that house with the huge American flag. Isn't that the place you wrote about, where they have all those orgies?"

"It was a Passion Party," Charley corrected.

"Isn't that the same thing?"

"Oh, God." Were they really having this conversation? "I've been calling you all day. Don't you ever check your messages?"

"Battery's dead on my cell phone. Keep forgetting to plug the stupid thing in."

"You have an answer for everything, don't you?"

"And you have a question."

Charley looked helplessly around the room. What was the point in arguing? She'd never been able to win an argument with her brother. And besides, he was here, wasn't he? Which was what she'd wanted. (Be careful what you wish for, she thought.) And everything seemed to be in its proper place. The furniture was where it always was: two oversize rattan chairs sat facing the small beige sofa in the middle of the natural sisal rug; a floor-to-ceiling bookshelf completely occupied the north wall, so stuffed with hardcover books that some had recently formed their own shelf on the floor; photographs of her children covered the mantel behind the sofa, as well as the table by the front bay window. Nothing seemed to be missing. "How'd you get in here anyway?"

"Used my key."

"Where'd you get a key?"

"You gave me one."

"The hell I did," Charley protested.

"You did," Bram insisted. "That time I baby-sat . . ."

"(A) You've never baby-sat," Charley interrupted, "and (B) I never gave you a key."

"Okay, so maybe I found a spare one lying around last time I was here for dinner," he acknowledged with a sheepish grin.

"You took my spare key? I spent days looking for that."

"Should have asked me."

"Why would I ask you?"

"'Cause I had it." He smiled.

"You're enjoying this, aren't you?"

His smile widened. "I am, yeah."

Charley fought the urge to throw the nearby vase of silk tulips at his head. "Give me back my key."

"Aw, come on, sis."

"Sis? Since when have you ever called me sis? Don't give me this 'sis' shit."

"You know you have a bit of a lisp?" Bram asked provocatively. "I think it comes from yelling. Do you yell at your kids as much as you yell at me?"

"I never yell at my kids."

"No? You were sure yelling when you walked through that door. What was that about anyway?"

"What?" Charley shook her head, trying to clear it. Her brother had always been a master of keeping her off-balance.

"As I recall, the word **asshole** might have passed your lips."

"Oh, that. My stupid neighbor." Charley flopped into one of the rattan chairs and lifted her feet to the coffee table, so that her bare toes were almost touching the tip of her brother's black boots. "He's renovating, in case you didn't notice the mess next door. And his nose got all out of joint when the neighbors objected to some of the changes he wanted to make . . ."

"His neighbors being you?"

"I was one of them. He wanted to build this giant two-storey addition that would have totally blocked out all the sun from my backyard . . ."

"I seem to remember reading something in the paper about insensitive residents flouting long-standing bylaws and ruining lovely old neighborhoods." Bram folded his hands behind his head, pretended to be thinking. "Where could I have read that, I wonder?"

"Okay, so maybe I mentioned something about it in my column, but the whole street was upset. It wasn't just me. Besides, what's done is done. Get over it already. You want something cold to drink?" Charley jumped to her feet, headed for the white-and-brown kitchen at the back of the house.

"A gin and tonic?" Bram suggested hopefully.

"Fat chance of that. How about some orange juice?"

"How 'bout a beer?"

"How 'bout some orange juice?" Charley repeated.

"I think I'll have some orange juice," Bram said.

"Good choice." Charley poured them each a drink and returned to the living room.

"Why would he blame you for his wife leaving him?" Bram asked.

It took Charley a second to realize they were still talking about Gabe Lopez. "Trust me. I had nothing to do with that."

"Nothing?"

"I don't think I ever said more than two words to the woman in my entire life."

"By any chance, were those two words 'dump him'?"

"Very funny. You missed your calling. You know that?"

Bram took a long sip of his juice, made a face. "Something's missing, that's for sure. This could use a little vodka."

Charley sighed. "What are you doing, Bram? What's the matter with you?"

"Aw, come on, Charley. Don't start."

"You're way too smart to waste your life this way."

"I'm only twenty-four," he reminded her. "And I'm not that smart."

"You told me you were going into rehab. You said you were joining AA. You promised."

"And I will."

"When?"

"Whenever."

"Bram. . . ."

"Come on, Charley. You think I like waking up on some strange guy's sofa? Which, come to think of it, must be how you feel a lot of the time."

Charley rolled her eyes. "That was so not funny."

"I'm gonna clean up my act."

"Try starting with your mouth."

"Ouch. I think I touched a nerve."

"I'm not a slut, Bram." Charley walked to the front window, watching the young man in the yellow hard hat climb up a ladder to the roof of her neighbor's house. "Just because I had two children by two different men doesn't mean I'm easy."

Although what can one expect from a woman who prides herself on never having married either of her children's fathers?

"I'm sorry. I didn't mean to imply . . ."

"Of course you did."

Of course you did, her mother's voice echoed.

"Hey, I'm just yanking your chain," her brother said, taking another sip of his juice. "Just trying to get the focus off me."

Charley watched a small yellow school bus pull around the corner and come to a stop in front of her house. "Kids are here." She took a deep breath and walked to the front door, pulling it open. "Try not to say anything too stupid in their presence."

"Yes, Dad," she heard Bram mutter.

She felt a sharp stab of guilt, remembering the way her father had always spoken to his son. Bram was right, she'd realized. She sounded exactly like their father. "I'm so sorry, Bram. I didn't mean . . ."

"Mommy!" James shouted, jumping off the bus, all dimples and hair and moving parts. Even while standing at the curb waiting for his sister, he was in constant motion, right hand lifting in the air to wave hello, left hand tugging at the top of his khaki pants, his weight shifting from his left foot to his right in order to kick at a small piece of rubble, as his eyes darted from one end of the street to the other.

"Hi, sweetie pie," Charley called back, waiting as Franny made her way from the back of the bus to the front. Franny always liked to make sure the bus had come to a complete stop before getting up from her seat. Only then would she begin the trek from her seat near the back, latching onto the tops of the other seats on her way to the front.

She'd always been a cautious child, Charley realized, choosing careful deliberation over snap decisions, even as a toddler. Charley recalled the many times she'd stood beside her daughter at the playground while Franny tried to decide which swing to select. Her brother would have already taken a dozen plunges, face-first, down the giant slide, and still Franny would be standing beside the sandbox. It was the same at mealtime. James would be finished and squirming in his chair, having virtually inhaled his dinner in two quick breaths, while Franny would be taking her first tentative bites. Quiet, contemplative—the complete opposite of Charley—she never spoke unless she had something to say.

"She's a very thoughtful child," her grade-two teacher had pronounced at the start of the school year. "You can actually see the wheels turning."

She must get it from her father's side of the family, Charley thought now, picturing the broodingly handsome man who was Franny's father, as Franny grabbed her brother's hand, looked both ways, then led him across the street. As soon as they reached the curb, James broke free of his sister's grasp and raced up the front walk to Charley.

"We painted a picture today in school. I painted an alligator and a snake."

"You did?"

"Where's my picture?" James asked, as if she should know. He spun around. "Oh, no. I lost it."

"I have it," his sister said calmly, coming up behind him. "You dropped it on the bus floor." She offered it to Charley.

"Look," James exclaimed triumphantly, pointing to a shapeless blob of fluorescent green and a narrow streak of purple. "There's the alligator, and there's the snake. Can we tape it to the fridge?" Already he was racing through the front door.

"And how was your day, sweetheart?" Charley asked her daughter, who stood before her patiently, waiting her turn.

"It was good. How about you?"

"It was good," Charley echoed, deciding she wanted to be just like her daughter when she grew up.

"Hey, Franny," James called excitedly from inside. "Guess who's here."

"It's your uncle Bram," Bram announced, approaching the front door, James tucked under one arm.

Franny's face lit up, as it always did when Bram was there. "Hi, Uncle Bram. I like your shirt."

"You do?"

"Blue's my favorite color."

"Really? Mine, too."

"Mine, too," James squealed.

"You like purple," Franny reminded him.

"I **like** purple," James quickly concurred. "But blue's my favorite."

Franny smiled and said nothing. She knows when to keep quiet, Charley thought with growing admiration. She's made her point. There's no need to say more. "Anybody feel like some milk and cookies?" she asked.

"Me!" shouted James, now hanging upside down from Bram's arms.

"What kind of cookies?" asked Franny.

"I have an idea," Bram said. "Why don't we order Chinese food for supper? My treat."

"Yay!" James exclaimed.

"Can we, Mommy?" Franny asked.

"Absolutely," Charley said. "Maybe we could see if . . ."

"Don't even think about it," Bram interrupted.

. . . Grandma would like to join us, Charley finished silently.

"Don't think about what?" Franny asked.

"Absolutely nothing." Bram scooped Franny into his other arm and took off with both kids for the kitchen.

When did I end up with three children? Charley wondered, picking up the picture of the alligator and the snake that fell from James's hand, and following after them.

Later, after Bram had gone home and the children were in bed, Charley sat on top of the white comforter on her bed, rereading the letter from Jill Rohmer.

Dear Charley, Hi. I hope you don't mind my writing to you . . .

"Well, now that you mention it, I can't say I'm exactly thrilled."

This might sound strange, and I hope you won't take it the wrong way, but you've always been a kind of role model for me. . . .

"And look how wonderfully that turned out."

I'm really a very good person at heart. . . . I even hope one day we might be friends. . . .

"God forbid."

Mine is a story that needs to be told. I think you have the courage to tell it.

Did she? Charley wondered. Did she have the courage, the desire, the **stomach** to revisit the horrifying events that had held all of Florida in its terrible clutches for months? Even now, a year after the trial, and almost two years since the murders themselves, the details were never far from her mind.

Little Tammy Barnet was five years old when she disappeared one sunny afternoon from her fenced-in backyard. Four days later, her body was discovered in a shallow grave beside the intracoastal waterway. She'd been tortured and sexually abused before being asphyxiated with a plastic bag.

Five months later, Noah and Sara Starkey, six-year-old fraternal twins, vanished while playing catch on their front lawn. Their mother had left them for two minutes to answer the phone. When she returned, the children were gone. They were discovered the following week, the plastic bags still wrapped around their heads, their naked little

bodies bearing the grisly scars of dozens of cigarette burns and bite marks. Both had been vio-
lated sexually with sharp objects.

The killings sent shock waves throughout all
of Florida. Not only were the police most certainly dealing with a serial killer but someone so
deranged as to torture and kill innocent children. Not to mention, someone cunning enough
to snatch those children right from under their
parents' watchful eyes. Someone the children
obviously trusted, since no screams were heard.
Someone who was probably known to both families.

On the surface, the Barnets and the Starkeys
seemed to have little in common. The Barnets
were young and fairly well-to-do; the Starkeys
were older and just getting by. Ellis Barnet was
an investment banker; Clive Starkey was a
welder. Joan Barnet was a schoolteacher; Rita
Starkey was a stay-at-home mom. They moved
in completely different circles. Within weeks,
however, the police had discovered the common
link. Her name was Jill Rohmer.

The Barnets had hired Jill to baby-sit Tammy
every Saturday night when they had their "date
night." Jill was always punctual, and happy to
stay as late as needed. She'd play dolls with
Tammy and read to her for hours before putting
her to bed. According to interviews with her parents, Tammy adored her.

As did Noah and Sara Starkey, for whom she baby-sat every Friday, and then Saturdays as well, when those Saturdays suddenly freed up. Knowing the Starkeys were going through some tough times financially, Jill often refused to take their money. "The kids are fabulous," she'd say. "I should be paying you."

The police obtained a warrant to search the house Jill shared with her parents and older siblings. Under her bed, they found Tammy Barnet's bloody underwear, along with the tape recordings of all the children's dying screams. Jill's voice could be heard plainly. And her DNA was a match to the saliva found on the bodies. An open-and-shut case.

Rumors abounded about an accomplice, and both her brother and boyfriend were early suspects, but there was never enough evidence to make an arrest. Jill refused to implicate them, and declined to take the stand in her own defense. Her lawyer, Alex Prescott, tried hard to make a case for reasonable doubt, but ultimately there was none. Jill Rohmer was convicted and sentenced to die.

And now, it seems, she wanted to talk after all.

If you decide to accept my offer, or if you have any questions at all, please feel free to contact my lawyer, Alex Prescott. He has an office in Palm Beach Gardens, and I've al-

ready alerted him to the possibility you might call.

Charley pushed herself off her bed and padded down the hall to the larger bedroom at the far end of the hall where her children slept. She peeked inside, saw Franny asleep in her bed on one side of the room, James half in, half out of his bed on the other. Watching her children sleep, she wondered how a seemingly normal young woman could have committed such heinous acts. And what could she possibly have to say that could mitigate her behavior? Was it possible someone else was responsible? Someone who was still out there?

Charley walked to the kitchen, made herself a cup of herbal tea, then reached for the phone and called information. "Palm Beach Gardens, Florida," she instructed the recording. "Alex Prescott, attorney-at-law."

6

She called the lawyer's office first thing the following morning, seeking an immediate appointment.

"Mr. Prescott is in court until eleven o'clock," his secretary informed her in crisp tones that declared **I am an immaculately coiffed icy blonde, whose well-manicured nails match my perfectly glossed lips.**

Charley stared down at her brown blouse, its front stained by a wayward line of white toothpaste that must have dripped from her electric toothbrush while she was brushing her teeth. ("And you give me a hard time for not being able to manage a cell phone," she could almost hear her mother tease.) "I don't believe this," Charley muttered, balancing the phone between her shoulder and her ear as she began unbuttoning her blouse.

"Perhaps something later in the week, say Thursday . . ."

"No. It has to be sooner." Charley pulled her blouse off her shoulders and threw it on the floor. "He doesn't have anything available today at all?"

"I'm afraid not. He's in court till eleven, then he has a lunch meeting at twelve, another meeting at two . . ."

"Okay, fine. Never mind then." Charley clicked off her cell phone, then tossed it on her unmade bed. Obviously this was a sign her collaboration with Jill Rohmer wasn't meant to be. She walked to her closet and stared at her impressive collection of designer jeans and her less-than-impressive collection of everything else. "Who needs anything else?" she asked the empty house, the school bus having picked up Franny and James half an hour ago. Ultimately she settled on a rhinestone-studded, beige T-shirt, the bottom half of which was emblazoned with a skull and crossbones. Since she wouldn't be visiting Alex Prescott this morning, there was no need for more formal attire. "It just wasn't meant to be," she said again, this time out loud.

She was surprised, and somewhat dismayed, to realize how disappointed she was, especially since she'd more or less decided that she wanted nothing to do with Jill Rohmer or her sordid story. This, after a sleepless night spent tossing around in bed, weighing her options, figuring out how best to organize her schedule, and even drafting an outline in her head. I can't do it, she'd told herself repeatedly throughout the night, all the while composing a list of questions to ask Alex Prescott, and a further list of conditions that had to be met with regard to any possible collaboration. You'd just be asking for trouble, she'd cautioned herself minutes before dawn, trying to imagine her first meeting with Jill Rohmer, how she'd react when she saw her, what she'd say. By the time her alarm clock went off at 7 A.M., she'd gone so far as to visualize the book itself, her name in embossed silver letters below the title, or better still, above it. (A photograph of Jill Rohmer would undoubtedly fill the front cover, but her own far more glamorous picture would occupy the back. Maybe she'd even borrow her sister's white lace pillows.) "No, I can't do it," she'd said aloud, as she stepped into the shower and began washing her hair. Still, by the time her hair was dry, she'd settled on the simple opening line for the preface: **Yesterday I got a letter from a killer.**

Oh, well, she could always use that line to begin an upcoming column, she decided. She retrieved her cell phone from the bed and slipped it inside the back pocket of her jeans, then threw the bed's plain white comforter across the plain white sheets, so that at least it looked as if it had been made. One day I'll get my life in order, she was thinking as she scooped her purse off the uncarpeted hardwood floor and headed down the hall. I'll get nice sheets, I'll buy a rug, I'll wear some grown-up clothes.

Except what constituted grown-up clothes these days? Charley wondered. It seemed everybody wore the same things. There was no longer any dress code, no distinction between the generations. Three-year-olds wore the same styles as thirty-year-olds. Even seventy-year-olds dressed like thirty-year-olds. And thirty-year-olds dressed like teenagers. No wonder everybody was so confused.

"Times have certainly changed," her mother commented recently while shopping for a birthday gift for Franny. "When I was young, I wouldn't have dreamed of raiding my mother's closet for something to wear."

"I wouldn't know," Charley told her. "Your closet was empty."

The conversation had come to an abrupt end.

Had this blurring of the generations, this reluctance to let go of one's youth, the outright refusal to get old, contributed in some way to the increased sexualization of the young? Could current trends in fashion, reflective as they were of society's attitudes toward larger issues, be at least partly responsible for what had happened to little Tammy Barnet or Noah and Sara Starkey?

"Don't be ridiculous," Charley muttered,

pausing for a minute in the kitchen to jot down these ideas. (She kept pads of paper in every room in the house for whenever inspiration struck.) Even half-baked, the ideas were provocative enough to make for an interesting column at some future date. And it looked as if Charley's future was going to be a little more free than she'd imagined last night.

"It just wasn't meant to be," she repeated once more as she opened her front door, shielding her eyes from the bright sun that had replaced yesterday's gloom. When she looked up, she saw Gabe Lopez in her driveway, leaning against her car. The pinched expression on his face told her he wasn't waiting to wish her a good morning. What had she done now? "Something I can do for you, Mr. Lopez?" she asked, approaching cautiously.

"You can stop harassing my workers," he told her, his dark sunglasses preventing her from seeing his eyes. "I'm not running a dating service."

Charley felt every muscle in her body tense. "Okay. I guess that's good to know." She gritted her teeth to keep the word **asshole** from escaping. "Now if you'll excuse me, I have to get to work."

"I suggest you prowl for boyfriends in the personal columns," Gabe Lopez continued, as if not convinced he'd made his point.

"And I suggest you get the hell out of my way."

Gabe Lopez stepped back just enough to allow Charley room to open her car door. "Jackass," she muttered, her fingers trembling as she pushed her key into the ignition. Backing out of her driveway and onto the street, she saw the worker in the yellow hard hat watching her from the roof. When she turned the corner, she glanced back. The worker was still there, still watching.

"Mr. Prescott is in court this morning," his secretary told Charley at just past eleven o'clock, "and I'm afraid he's fully booked this afternoon."

Charley was somewhat gratified to note that although the forty-something-year-old woman was indeed an icy blonde, her hair was cut at an unflattering angle that accentuated her square jaw and did nothing at all for her overly tanned complexion. Her manicured nails, however, were a perfect match for the deep coral of her lips. "I was hoping I might catch him between appointments. Is he expected back before lunch?"

The secretary checked her watch. "It's possible. But he'll be in and out. Why don't I make you an appointment for later in the week?"

"If it's all right with you, I'd rather wait."

"I think you'll just be wasting your time."

"I'll take my chances." Charley perched on

the end of one of four dark green chairs that sat against the pale green wall.

The secretary shrugged and turned her attention to her computer, trying to look busy.

How did we ever manage without computers? Charley wondered absently, picking up a recent copy of **Time** from the stack of magazines on the small table beside her and thumbing listlessly through it. I certainly couldn't function without mine, she thought, trying to think of anybody who could.

Her mother, she thought.

Elizabeth worked at a small gift store on Worth Avenue three afternoons a week, selling "traveling jewelry," which was the Palm Beach way of saying "fakes," but that was more for something to occupy her time than because she actually needed to work. Her former "life partner," the woman with whom she'd escaped to the Australian outback, had died three years ago of cancer, leaving Elizabeth Webb her entire— and surprisingly considerable—estate. Elizabeth had immediately packed her bags and headed back to the States, with the highly unrealistic idea of dividing her time equally among her four previously discarded children and their offspring. Had she really expected them to tumble gratefully into her arms?

Charley shook her head in an effort to shake her mother from her thoughts, and focused all her attention on an article about a recent study on bone density that—surprise!—completely contradicted all previous studies. It seemed that the simple pill that had been touted as the miracle cure for osteoporosis might not be such a godsend after all. In fact, it might be more of a curse, responsible for a little something called necrosis of the jawbone. Even stopping the drug was pointless. Once the damn thing was in your system, it stayed there. Rather like mothers, Charley thought, catching a whiff of Elizabeth Webb's favorite perfume as she returned the magazine to the table. "I think my mother wears the same perfume you do," she told the secretary.

"Chanel Number Five," the secretary said without looking over. "It's been around forever."

Charley reached for the latest copy of **Vogue**, thinking it was very considerate of Alex Prescott to keep his magazines so up-to-date. She flipped it open, immediately zeroing in on a beautiful white lace blouse by Oscar de la Renta. "Only six thousand dollars," she noted wryly.

"I'm sorry. Did you say something?" the secretary asked.

"There's a blouse here for six thousand dollars."

"Amazing."

"And this purse," she sputtered seconds later, "this purse is seventy-five thousand. **Seventy-**

five thousand dollars! Who pays seventy-five thousand dollars for a purse?"

"As my mother used to say, the rich are different from you and me," the secretary said.

"F. Scott Fitzgerald," Charley said.

"What?"

" 'The very rich are different from you and me.' F. Scott Fitzgerald said it in **The Great Gatsby**."

"He did? Well, he must have borrowed it from my mother."

Charley chuckled. It always comes back to mothers, she was thinking, as the door to Alex Prescott's office opened and a handsome blur in a dark blue suit burst across the room.

"Shit, what a morning," he exclaimed, striding past his secretary's desk and into his inner office without so much as a glance in Charley's direction. Seconds later, the secretary's intercom buzzed and a disembodied voice asked, "Did I see somebody sitting out there?"

The secretary smiled indulgently. "She was hoping you might be able to fit her in."

"Not a chance. I'm up to my eyeballs. Have her make an appointment."

"Mr. Prescott, wait." Charley jumped to her feet, the magazine falling to the floor. "My name is Charley Webb. I was hoping to talk to you about . . ."

The door to Alex Prescott's inner office opened instantly. "**The** Charley Webb?" A smile played with his lips. "Well, then, how can I refuse? Hold my calls," he instructed his secretary as Charley picked up the magazine and tossed it on a chair on her way into his office. "Oh, and phone Cliff Marcus. Tell him I'll be a few minutes late for lunch. Please have a seat," he instructed Charley as he closed the door behind her. Settling into the chair behind his desk seconds later, he pushed his light brown hair away from his forehead, and stared at her with piercing blue eyes.

"Are you always this . . . busy?" Charley asked. She noticed his desk was immaculately clean and void of any family photographs.

"You meant 'manic,' didn't you?"

Charley smiled. "Actually, you remind me a bit of my son."

"Receding hairline, long nose, slight paunch?"

This time Charley laughed. "I didn't notice a paunch."

"Good. My trainer will be pleased. What can I do for you, Charley Webb?"

Charley took a breath for both of them. "It's about one of your clients."

"Jill Rohmer," he acknowledged.

"She wrote to me."

"She wants you to write her story."

"Yes."

"I don't think you should do it," he told her.

"What?"

"I don't think you should do it."

Charley didn't bother masking her surprise. "May I ask why?"

"Please don't take this the wrong way. . . ."

"But?"

"But I just don't think you're the right person to tell Jill's story."

"May I ask why?" Charley said again.

"Look, I'm a big fan," he began. "I read your column religiously every week. I find you provocative and entertaining, but . . ."

". . . shallow and lightweight," Charley finished for him.

"Well, I wouldn't have put it quite so harshly."

"But that's what you would have meant," Charley said, trying not to bristle at the all-too-familiar assessment.

"I'm not saying you don't write well. You do. It's just that Jill Rohmer is a very complicated young woman."

"And I'm too simple to grasp all that complexity," Charley stated.

"I didn't say that."

"You didn't have to."

"Have you ever written a book before, Miss Webb?"

"I've been writing my column for three years."

"Not exactly the same thing. Look, I can understand what would appeal to you about this project."

"You can?"

"Of course. It's dark. It's fascinating. It's sexy, in a sick, perverted way. . . ."

"You think sick and perverted appeals to me?" Charley folded her arms across the skull and crossbones on the front of her T-shirt.

"It's high-profile," he continued, ignoring her interruption. "It'll get you tons of publicity, maybe even make you a star."

"Only if I do a good job."

"Why would you even **want** this job?"

"I'm not sure I do."

"Then what are you doing here?"

"I had a few questions."

"Fire away."

Charley took another deep breath. Alex Prescott was exhausting, she thought, watching as he loosened his blue patterned tie and leaned back in his chair. He couldn't be much older than she was, she was thinking as she tried to formulate her first question. "In terms of this book, what do you think Jill has in mind?"

Alex Prescott paused, looked toward the window of his small, nondescript office. There wasn't even a painting on the wall, Charley realized. "I imagine she wants her side of the story to come out," he said.

"You think she has a side?"

"I think she has many sides."

"All of them guilty," Charley said.

"See. Now, that's just the kind of thing I'm talking about."

"What kind of thing?"

"Why you're not the right person to tell her story."

"Because I think she's guilty?"

"Because you won't give her a fair hearing."

"She's already had a fair trial."

"Jill's never been treated fairly in her entire life."

"You're trying to tell me she's innocent?" Charley heard the incredulousness in her voice.

"I'm saying there's a lot you don't know, a lot the jury didn't hear."

Charley squirmed in her chair, trying to contain her growing interest. "How did you get involved in this case, Mr. Prescott?"

"I believe in our court system," he answered, evading the question ever-so-slightly. "Even accused child-murderers are entitled to the best possible defense."

"How did Jill find you?" Charley pressed, trying to get him back on track.

"I'm not sure I understand the question."

"Well, Jill Rohmer has no money, you don't

work for the public defender's office, and you weren't appointed by the court. I checked the records first thing this morning."

"I'm impressed."

"So, what brought the two of you together?"

A slight pause, then, "The fact is I offered my services."

"You offered your services?" Charley repeated.

"Free of charge."

"Even though this type of case is a little out of your bailiwick?"

"I'd tried a number of murder cases before this one."

"But never anything as 'complicated,'" she said, using his word. "Or as high-profile."

"True enough."

"So why would you volunteer to take it on?"

He shrugged. "I guess because I thought it would make an interesting case."

"Or maybe because you thought it might get you a lot of publicity. Maybe even make you a star," she stated, again borrowing his words.

He smiled. "That might have had something to do with it."

"The details of this case didn't repulse you?"

"On the contrary, they repulsed me very much."

"Did you think Jill was guilty when you first met her?"

"I have to confess I did, yes."

"But you took the case anyway. The fact you thought she was guilty didn't stop you from giving her the best possible defense under the law."

"If anything, it made me even more determined to do a good job."

"Okay," Charley said. "To recap: You volunteered your services, you took the case despite the fact you had no real experience with crimes of this magnitude, and the fact it was high-profile and might make you famous admittedly crossed your mind. So, no disrespect intended, but what the hell gives you the right to sit in judgment of me? What gives you the right to question my motives and tell me I'm not qualified to write this book? Whether or not I think Jill Rohmer is guilty is beside the point. The point is that I'm the one she wants. Your client is sitting on death row, Mr. Prescott. What makes you think I could do any worse a job telling her story than you did?"

She released a deep breath. He did the same.

"That was some closing argument," he said with obvious admiration.

"Thank you."

"Anybody ever tell you you would make an excellent attorney?"

"My father wanted me to be a lawyer."

"But you never listened to your father, did you?"

Again Charley squirmed in her seat. "The only thing I'd enjoy about being a lawyer would be staring down some lowlife and saying, 'Tell it to the judge.' "

Alex laughed. "Doesn't happen very often."

"If I were to do this book," Charley said, returning to the original subject, "I'd have to have total access to Jill Rohmer's files."

"What's mine is yours."

"I'll also need the transcripts of the trial."

"You'll have them by the end of the day."

"I'll need to talk to her family and friends."

"I'll see what I can do."

"And, of course, I'll require access to Jill on a regular basis."

"We'll have to work that out with the prison officials."

"I insist on total freedom and absolute control. Jill has to understand she might not like the end result."

"You'll have to talk to Jill about that."

"When can you arrange a meeting?"

"How does Saturday afternoon work for you?"

Charley knew both Franny and James would

be spending the weekend with their respective fathers, but her mother had mentioned treating Charley to a day at a spa, six uninterrupted hours of mother-daughter bonding. Charley smiled across the desk at Alex. "It works fine," she said.

7

WEBB SITE

During a recent visit to a lawyer's office, I had time to glance through a number of magazines. Luckily for me, they were all recent editions, so I didn't have to waste time wondering why the movie world was just mourning the loss of Marlon Brando when I was pretty sure he'd died a few years ago.

Several items quickly caught my eye. One was a disturbing article about a popular drug for osteoporosis and a heretofore unknown side effect of this widely prescribed pill, a little thing called "necrosis of the jawbone," which has been occurring in an alarming number of women who've just had oral surgery. The dentist I subsequently contacted tells me it's every bit as awful as it sounds. "The jawbone literally disintegrates," Dr. Samuel Keller informed me. "Any woman on this drug who needs to have something as simple as a tooth extraction will be faced with a terrible dilemma."

That's not the only terrible dilemma women are facing these days.

"Okay," Charley said, rereading the opening paragraphs she'd written for this Sunday's column. "So far, so good."

Another dilemma is the price of tea in China. Or more to the point, the price of a purse on Worth Avenue. More precisely, the price of a cherry-red crocodile bag that, size wise, isn't even all that big by today's exaggerated standards, but that sells for the whopping figure of **seventy-five thousand dollars**.

Yes, you read that right.

Seventy-five thousand dollars.

For a purse.

The mind boggles. Who in their right mind would even consider spending that kind of money for a handbag?

"Is it lined in gold?" I queried the reed-thin saleswoman with the sleek, dark hair who greeted me at the door of the beautifully appointed Bottega Veneta store in the shopping heart of Palm Beach.

The saleswoman smiled the tight smile of someone who's had perhaps one too many nips and tucks, and said patiently, "It's handmade."

Oh, I see. That explains everything. "Can I see it?"

"We don't keep it in the store," the saleswoman said, as if this fact should be self-evident. "You'd have to special-order it."

"Isn't it against the law to make purses out of crocodiles?" I ventured further, receiving only a look of disdain in reply.

Who'd even want something made from the skin of a reptile? Charley wondered, literally shuddering at the thought.

I spent the next half hour checking out the other, somewhat less outrageously priced items that sat at respectful distances from one another on the long row of shelves on either side of the small store. Sprinkled among the gorgeous, latticed leather bags that are Bottega's trademark, were an array of stunning sling-back sandals, flats, and high-heeled shoes, all equally fabulous, and all mind-numbingly expensive, although even a seven-hundred-dollar pair of pumps starts to sound reasonable when it's sitting next to a seven-thousand-dollar bag. And what's seven thousand dollars compared to seventy-five thousand anyway? Why, it's a bargain, I thought, deciding I had to get out of there before it was too late.

Continuing down Worth Avenue, I visited a number of other shops. I found a long silk skirt for fifteen thousand dollars at Giorgio Armani, a simple cotton dress for eight thousand at Chanel, and a two-million-dollar yellow diamond pendant at Van Cleef and Arpel. In Neiman Marcus, I came across the six-thousand-dollar blouse from Oscar de la Renta I'd admired in the latest issue of **Vogue**. Hanging on a rack! In the middle of a bunch of other similarly priced items. As if this were normal. "Would you like to try that on?" a salesgirl asked matter-of-factly.

"Maybe another time," I answered, fleeing the premises, and heading for the ocean at the east end of the street in an effort to clear my head. "Who's buying these things?" I heard myself ask out loud, my voice carried out to sea by a gentle gust of ocean breeze. As I slipped off my sandals ($16.99 at Payless) to walk along the cool sand. . . .

"No, I don't like that. A little too **Remember Love**-ish for my taste," Charley muttered under her breath, deleting the last two lines from her computer, and pausing to reconsider what she wanted to say next.

Who's buying these things? I wondered, surreptitiously scrutinizing each woman I passed. Could that hideous handbag on the arm of the frump in the navy sweatsuit really be worth almost as much as my house? Did those oversize sunglasses hiding the pimples on the faces of the teenage girls giggling in front of Tiffany's really cost more than my monthly car payments? Was nobody else as

shocked as I was by the prices design-
ers were asking—and people were
paying—for their wares?

"Uh-oh. Maybe starting to sound a touch dis-
ingenuous," Charley said under her breath.

Don't get me wrong. I'm not naive
when it comes to what it costs to look
fashionable these days. I, myself, have
been known to shell out exorbitant
bucks for a pair of jeans just because
they have a little embroidered crown
on the rear pocket. But six thousand
dollars for a blouse? Seventy-five
thousand dollars for a purse? Is everybody nuts?
    And, in the end, where does such ex-
travagance get us?

Where does it get us indeed? Charley wondered,
not quite sure what point she was trying to
make.

Does it buy us better sex, better
health, a longer life?
    As we march our poor feet down the
street in our too-high stilettos, our
shoulders cramping under the weight
of those oversize crocodile bags, our

bones are already crumbling and threatening to disintegrate. Despite our best efforts at denial and the continuing advances of modern science, we are getting older. Necrosis of the jawbone is only one ill-conceived miracle pill away.

"Charley?" Michael Duff interrupted.

Charley swiveled around in her seat.

The editor-in-chief filled the entrance to her cubicle. "A police officer is here to talk to you."

"The police?"

"About that e-mail," he explained. "She's in my office."

"Oh." Charley pressed SAVE on her computer and stored the article she was writing for Sunday's column before getting up and following Michael to his office. The truth was she'd almost forgotten about Monday's e-mail. It seemed so long ago. "Do they know who sent it?" she asked, speaking to the back of Michael's green-and-white golf shirt.

"I think she just wants to talk to you," he said, opening the door to his office and stepping aside to let Charley enter first.

A uniformed officer promptly jumped to her feet. "Jennifer Ramirez," she said, introducing herself and extending her hand. Despite her slim build and shy smile, the officer's handshake was strong and firm. Her dark hair was pulled into a bun at the nape of her neck, and her brown eyes were the color of warm chocolate sauce.

"Charley Webb," Charley said.

Michael Duff took his seat behind his desk, then motioned for the two women to sit down. "You sure you wouldn't like a cup of coffee?" he asked the police officer.

"No, thank you. I've already had my quota this morning."

"Charley?" he asked.

She shook her head. "Do you know who sent me that e-mail?"

"I'm afraid not," Officer Ramirez said, pulling out her notebook from the pocket of her navy shirt. "Have you had any more?"

"Well, I get lots of e-mail every day."

"Ones that threaten your life?"

"Not usually, thank goodness. I always give copies of those to Michael." She nodded in his direction.

"We keep all threatening letters on file," he volunteered.

"We might need to see those later."

"Certainly."

"But this particular letter was the first one that threatened your children?" Officer Ramirez asked, although it was more statement than question.

"It said I should 'die, bitch, die,' and take my

bastard children with me. It also said I should keep a very close eye on them, that I'd be surprised by the horrifying things people were capable of," Charley recited, seeing the e-mail in her mind's eye as clearly as it had appeared on her computer screen earlier in the week.

"Which you interpreted as a threat?"

"You don't?"

"It's certainly not a very nice letter," Officer Ramirez said.

"But you don't think whoever wrote it is dangerous?"

"I think they're angry."

"Angry enough to harm my children?"

"Hopefully it's just some jerk who gets his rocks off writing nasty letters."

"That's what Michael said," Charley told her. "I probably just overreacted."

"Better safe than sorry."

"You haven't been able to trace the computer?"

"Unfortunately, no. So you haven't received any more threatening letters in the last several days, is that correct?"

"Not since Monday."

"Well, that's good. Pardon my ignorance, Miss Webb, but what sort of thing is it you write?"

Charley tried not to let her face register dismay that the officer was unacquainted with

her work. "I write a weekly column about various issues of the day. Whatever happens to be
on my mind," she qualified.

"I take it that what's on your mind is sometimes upsetting to other people," Officer Ramirez
stated.

Michael Duff laughed. "Charley has been
known to stir things up a bit."

"Sounds fascinating. I guess I'll have to start
reading your column. Tell me, Miss Webb, and
again, pardon my ignorance, but have you ever
targeted anyone in particular in these columns,
someone who might want to get back at you for
something you've written?"

"I'm sure there's a long list."

"I'd like to see it."

"Oh," Charley said, as the faces of Lynn
Moore, Gabe Lopez, and Glen McLaren flashed
quickly before her eyes. And those were only the
more recent examples. "Shouldn't you wait to
see if I get any more letters before you start
questioning anyone? Wouldn't want to antagonize them any more than I already have." She
tried to laugh, failed.

"Of course. This is all very preliminary," Jennifer Ramirez told her. "But I would like to have
that list. Just in case."

"In case of what?" Charley asked. "In case
something happens to me? Is that what you
mean?"

"Is there anyone else, someone from your personal life perhaps, that you think could have sent that e-mail? An ex-husband, perhaps? A co-worker you've pissed off?"

Charley shook her head. She was on reasonably good terms with both her children's fathers, although less so with Franny's stepmother. And while she wasn't exactly buddy-buddy with the other reporters on staff, she doubted any of them disliked her enough to threaten her or her children. "There's no one."

"It's probably just a disgruntled reader," Michael interjected.

"Probably." Officer Ramirez rose to her feet. "I wouldn't worry too much if I were you, Miss Webb. The odds are this was a one-time thing. Get me that list as soon as you can, and of course, if you receive any more 'interesting' letters, please contact me immediately." She handed a copy of her card to both Charley and Michael. "It was a pleasure meeting you. I can show myself out."

"You okay?" Michael asked Charley after the policewoman was gone.

"Fine." Maybe she should have told the officer about the "interesting" letter she'd received from Jill Rohmer, she was thinking. Now that's a name that would have gotten her attention, made her sit up and take notice. Except what would have been the point? Jill couldn't have sent that e-mail. Charley doubted that murderers were given access to computers while in prison. Wasn't that why Jill had contacted her by hand? No, mentioning Jill Rohmer would have served only to distract the officer. Jill would have highjacked the investigation before it even got off the ground.

Still, how ironic was it that Charley was considering meeting with a convicted child killer at a time when her own children had come under threat?

She almost laughed. Who was she fooling? She wasn't considering anything. She'd already made up her mind. Although in thinking back on her meeting with Alex Prescott, she wasn't sure quite how he'd managed to talk her into agreeing to see Jill. She smiled, again wondering who was fooling whom. The truth was that Alex Prescott hadn't talked her into anything. He'd been opposed to her telling Jill's story. The truth was she was the one who'd persuaded him.

"What's the matter?" Michael was asking.

"What?"

"What's on your mind?"

"Nothing. What do you mean?"

"You were a million miles away."

More like seventy-five, Charley thought, calculating the distance to the prison in Pembroke Pines. "Actually, I'm thinking of writing a book."

"Thinking or planning?" Michael asked, cutting right to the chase.

Charley smiled. "Planning."

"Does that mean you're also planning to ask for some time off?"

"No," Charley said quickly. "Unless, of course, you disapprove of the subject."

"The subject being?"

"Jill Rohmer." Charley immediately filled Michael in on the details of Jill's letter and her visit to Alex's office. "You think it's a bad idea?"

"On the contrary—normally I'd say it's an excellent idea."

"Normally?"

"Well, you've just received an e-mail threatening your children. Do you really think this is the best time to go one-on-one with a convicted child killer?"

Charley gave the question a moment's thought. Maybe it was precisely the threat to her children that was contributing to her willingness—indeed, her eagerness—to meet with Jill Rohmer. Maybe she had a need to understand the kind of mind that could do such horrible things.

Or maybe I just want to be famous, she admitted silently.

"Of course, if you do decide to proceed, I get first serial rights," Michael added, turning his attention to the papers on his desk. His way of signaling the meeting was over.

"Consider it done." Charley rose from her seat and left his office.

Her phone was ringing when she reached her cubicle. "Hello," Charley said, answering it just before her voice mail could click in.

"Charley?"

"Steve?"

"How are you?" he asked, as Charley pictured her son's father standing proudly beside a swimming pool he'd just helped install, shirt off, a glass of lemonade in his hand, courtesy of the wanton woman from the house next door.

That was how she'd met him, after all, she thought with a smile. After several weeks spent watching his gorgeous, half-naked body dig and plaster and tile a neighbor's new pool, she'd poked her head over her backyard fence and asked him if he'd like a glass of something cold. "What've you got?" he'd asked, following her inside her house.

Nine months later, James was born, the spitting image of his father, and while Steve had never been a permanent fixture in either of their lives, he made every effort to see his son several times a month. He was two years younger than Charley and still content to drift from job to job, yard to yard, lemonade to lemonade.

"I'm fine. You?" Charley wondered if something was wrong. It wasn't like Steve to call her at work.

"Great. Except listen, I have a slight problem with this weekend."

"What do you mean, a slight problem?"

"I can't make it."

"What do you mean, you can't make it?"

"Is that a problem?"

"Yes, it's a problem. I've made plans."

"I'm really sorry, Charley. You know I wouldn't do this unless it was really important."

"More important than your son?" Charley asked, then immediately wished she hadn't. It wasn't like her to lay a guilt trip on either of her exes. The truth was that neither of them had asked for parenthood, and the bigger truth was that she was more than happy to be a single mother. She'd never wanted either man to be a staple in her life, and had never asked them for anything, including child support. Still, Franny's father, Ray, had always insisted on being an active participant in his daughter's life, giving Charley money every month without fail, and even Steve contributed a little something from time to time. Both men had proved to be far more responsible than she'd had any right or reason to expect.

"Come on, Charley. Don't be like that."

"I'm sorry. New job?"

"New girl," he said, and Charley could actually feel the smile in his voice. "She wants me to meet her parents. They live in Sarasota."

"Sounds serious."

"Well, who knows?"

Charley felt a slight pang in her chest. She knew, even if he didn't. She also knew that women had a way of complicating things. Certainly everything had gotten a lot more complicated after Ray had married Elise, she thought.

"Maybe James can go with Franny," Steve suggested. "He's done that before, hasn't he?"

Steve was right. On at least two occasions, Franny had asked that her brother be included on weekend visits with her father, and Ray had generously agreed. So maybe he could be prevailed upon once again. "Don't worry about it. I'll think of something."

"Tell James I'll make it up to him real soon."

"I'll tell him."

"Thanks, Charley. You're the best."

"Yes, I am," she agreed. "Have a nice weekend."

"You, too."

So much for driving out to Pembroke Pines, she thought, hanging up the phone. She couldn't very well interview a child killer with her own child sitting on her lap. Still, the thought of having to postpone her interview. . . . She picked the phone back up, dialed Ray at home.

It was answered after five rings. "Hello?" a woman shouted over the sound of a baby crying.

Charley pictured the always frazzled woman

with the dark curly hair, bouncing her crying infant over her shoulder. "Elise, hi. It's Charley."

"Ray's not here."

Franny's father ran a small consulting business out of his home. Charley was never exactly sure what it was Ray consulted on, and truthfully, she didn't care. They'd met just after she moved to Florida. At the time he was working for a store that sold computers, and she was in the market for a laptop. She'd come home with both a new computer and the man who'd sold it to her. "Will he be back soon?"

"I doubt it. He just left. Is there something I can help you with?"

Charley took a deep breath, then plunged right in. "I was wondering if it would be possible for James to tag along with his sister this weekend," she began.

"You must be kidding."

"I know it's an imposition. . . ."

"You think?"

"It's just that James's father had to cancel, and I have to go out of town on business . . ."

"And that's somehow my problem?" Elise asked, as her baby continued to scream.

"No. Of course it's not your problem. Look, maybe I should wait and speak to Ray."

"Why? You think he'll be easier to manipulate?"

Charley said nothing. What could she say . . . yes?

"Look, it was bad enough before we had a baby of our own," Elise reminded Charley unnecessarily. Things had already been tense between the two women before Elise had given birth to Daniel. Now they were even worse. "I'm afraid you're gonna have to find a new patsy," Elise said before hanging up.

Charley quickly ran through her mental list of people she could call in a crisis. To her dismay, it was considerably shorter than the list Officer Ramirez had asked her to draw up, consisting only of her mother, who she knew had booked a weekend cruise to the Bahamas after Charley canceled their trip to the spa, and her brother, who'd basically canceled out of everything, period. There was no one else, she realized, reaching for the phone to call Alex Prescott and tell him she wouldn't be able to keep Saturday's appointment, when it rang. "Charley Webb," she said, unable to disguise the dejection in her voice.

"Something wrong?" the caller inquired.

Charley recognized Glen McClaren's voice instantly. "Just not my day."

"Anything I can do to help?"

The question stopped Charley cold. Could she do it? she wondered, inching forward in her chair. Then, immediately: what was the matter with her? She barely knew the man, for God's sake, and what she **did** know was unsavory, to say the least. A nightclub owner, a ladies' man, a "gangster wannabe." Hadn't she all but accused him of having mob connections? Still, her instincts told her he was a good man at heart, and it wasn't as if he'd be alone with her son. His own son would be there, along with the boy's mother and stepfather. And James loved Lion Country Safari. Still, what did it say about her—about any of them—that she trusted a relative stranger more than her own flesh and blood?

"Charley? You still there?"

"Listen, Glen," she began. "Is that offer still open?"

8

S ee that?" Alex Prescott asked.

Charley gazed out the front window of Alex's decade-old, mustard-colored Malibu convertible toward the flat, dull white structures in the distance. The bleak, armylike barracks stood in stark contrast to the rows of beautiful old pine trees that lined the approaching road. "That's Pembroke Correctional?"

"That's it."

"It looks awful."

"It looks even worse close up."

Charley tucked the hair that was blowing into her eyes and mouth behind her ears and adjusted her sunglasses, although there was no real need. The sun had stopped shining at just before noon, roughly the same time that Glen had pulled up in his silver Mercedes. Beside him sat his son. In the backseat sat his former wife and her current husband.

"You must be Eliot," Charley said to the round-faced, dark-haired boy clinging to his father's leg as the two of them walked into Charley's living room. "Happy birthday."

"What do you say?" Glen asked his son.

"Where's James?" Eliot shouted in reply, burying his face in his father's black pants.

"I'm on the toilet," James shouted back.

Charley laughed. "That's my boy."

"Nice house," Glen remarked.

"And you're all very nice for doing this. I owe you big time."

"Yes, you do."

Which was when James had come racing into the living room, almost crashing into Glen as he struggled to zip up the fly of his khaki shorts.

"Whoa, tiger," Glen had exclaimed.

"I'm not a tiger." James threw his arms into the air in exasperation. "I'm a boy, silly."

"Yes, you certainly are."

"Glen. . . . Eliot . . . this is my son, James," Charley said, trying to keep him still long enough to make the necessary introductions. "Where's the present for Eliot?"

James smacked his forehead with his open palm. "I forgot it."

"Then go get it."

"That really isn't necessary," Glen protested, as James ran from the room.

"Of course it is. Isn't it, Eliot?" Charley asked.

Eliot smiled, nodding his head emphatically.

"It's a book," James announced upon his return, dropping the brightly wrapped gift into Eliot's waiting hands. "Come on, Eliot. Let's go!"

"As you can see, he's very shy with strangers."

"Anything else I should know?" Glen asked as the two boys ran for the front door.

"Just don't let him out of your sight for a minute."

"I'll guard him with my life."

"You have to watch him constantly."

"I won't take my eyes off him."

"Make sure he doesn't get out of the car when he sees the lions."

"I'll sit on him if I have to."

"I should be home by six."

"See you then."

Seconds after the extended family took off in Glen's Mercedes, Alex had rounded the corner in his old Malibu convertible.

"You ready?" he'd called out, not bothering to get out of his car.

That had pretty much been the extent of their conversation until now. For almost the entire hour-and-a-half drive from West Palm Beach to the Pembroke Correctional Institution in Pembroke Pines, which was located south of Fort Lauderdale and due east of Hollywood, Alex had

been listening, via headphones, to a tape recording of legal precedents, in preparation for a case
he was working on. "I hope you don't mind. This
thing goes to trial on Monday, and I don't want
to leave anything to chance," he'd explained un-
apologetically as she'd climbed into the front
seat, which left Charley almost ninety minutes
to look at the scenery and silently berate herself
for having enlisted a virtual stranger and his
family to look after her son.

Charley glanced over in Alex's direction,
pushing all such troubling thoughts from her
mind, and hoping for a reassuring smile, but he
was staring out the front window, lost in his
tapes, and seemingly oblivious to the fact she
was beside him.

She smoothed her short, brown peasant skirt
across her thighs and absently checked the front
of her green T-shirt for errant toothpaste stains,
but everything seemed to be in order. It felt
strange to be sitting so close to a man who
clearly had no interest in her, she thought,
unable to remember the last time that had happened. She'd long since grown accustomed to
men falling all over themselves in an effort to
impress her. That Alex Prescott was so impervi-
ous to her delicate features, blond hair, and bare
legs was unsettling.

Was he married? She didn't see a ring, but

that didn't mean anything. He could be living with someone. Or otherwise involved. Or gay.

At first she'd been grateful for not having to make small talk. It had been nice to simply lean back in the tan leather seat, close her eyes, and let the breeze blow through her hair. But as the trip progressed and the wind picked up, the silence had become almost oppressive. She'd thought of turning on the radio, but hadn't wanted to interfere with Alex's concentration. She'd put him out enough already. It was Alex, after all, who'd made the necessary phone calls to prison officials, Alex who'd acted as the liaison between Charley and Jill Rohmer, Alex who'd volunteered to drive her to Pembroke Pines. She doubted this was simple altruism on his part. Clearly he wanted to keep tabs on the proceedings, make sure his client's interests were protected. If Charley ever found herself in need of a criminal attorney, she'd decided just seconds before he removed his headphones and pointed down the road toward the prison, he was the one she'd call.

"Sorry about that," he apologized, tossing the headphones into the backseat. "It's a tricky case."

"Can you talk about it?"

"Well, without going into the particulars, it involves the disgruntled heirs to a rather sizable fortune. We have brother against sister, sister against auntie, everybody against mother."

"Sounds familiar."

He smiled knowingly. "I guess every family has its issues."

"It's probably not even about the money," Charley said.

"Trust me," Alex demurred. "It's about the money."

Charley laughed as they turned down the road that led directly to the prison, taking note of the sudden lack of trees, the dry ground and dying grass, the twisted coils of barbed wire atop the high fences surrounding the premises. She pushed her sunglasses to the top of her head as they drew closer, able now to make out the bars on the windows, and register the high-powered rifles of the guards in their guard-houses, as well as the guns in the holsters of the officers on patrol. "They don't look very friendly."

"What do you know about our prison system?" Alex asked.

"Not much." Charley had been meaning to do some research, but between making sure her column was ready for Sunday's paper, getting Franny ready for her weekend with Ray, and worrying about James, she'd run out of both time and energy. Besides, she still hadn't decided if she was going to write this book. Nothing had been negotiated or agreed to. Everything depended on this afternoon's meeting.

"Well, according to Florida's Department of Law Enforcement, which has been compiling crime statistics since 1930," Alex began, unprompted, "the latest available figures show that over the past decade, the incidence of crime in this state has actually dropped by more than eighteen percent, and prison admissions have dropped nearly fifteen percent."

"Really? So how come I keep reading our jails are so overcrowded?"

"Well, first," Alex said, statistics spilling from his mouth as effortlessly as water from a glass, "under a 1995 law, inmates can't be paroled until they've served at least eighty-five percent of their sentences. And second, Florida law allows their correctional facilities to operate at one hundred fifty percent of capacity."

"What?"

"It's not as bad as it sounds. Most prisons have auxiliary facilities, so there are a lot of inmates in vocational camps and work release programs, or in hospitals and drug treatment facilities."

"How many people are in jail in Florida?" she asked.

"My guess is around seventy-five thousand."

The price of a purse at Bottega Veneta, Charley thought.

"Five thousand of those are women," Alex continued.

"What's the ratio at Pembroke Correctional?"

"The maximum inmate capacity is five hundred forty. The number of actual inmates is over seven hundred."

"I meant the ratio of men to women."

"They're all women."

"They're all women?" Charley repeated.

"You sound surprised."

"I'm sure Jill said. . . . Just a second." Charley pulled Jill's letter out of her purse, flipped through the pages. "Yes. Here it is. **Pembroke Correctional doesn't allow prison weddings. Not that there's a whole lot of opportunity to meet suitable men in here. They keep the men and women segregated, although occasionally we manage to find ways of getting together. Hint: there's way more than reading going on behind the bookshelves of the prison library. Lots more about that if you agree to do the book.**"

Alex laughed. "Well, there you go."

"Where exactly am I going?" Charley asked impatiently.

"Obviously she was trying to entice you."

"I don't like being lied to."

"Well, **technically**, it's not a lie. You could argue that since Pembroke Correctional is a women's prison, it is, by definition, segregated. And there **are** men on the premises—prison officials, staff, guards, workers. I'm sure they occasionally find ways of getting together with the prisoners."

"Maybe." Charley stuffed the letter back into her purse, unconvinced. "I just don't like to feel I'm being manipulated," she continued. "For this project to work, I have to be able to trust Jill. She has to be **completely** honest with me, not just **technically**."

"I understand. Look. It's not too late to turn back." Alex stopped the car about fifty yards short of the main gate. "If you're having second thoughts about doing this project, I can take you home right now."

"I haven't agreed to anything yet," Charley reminded him.

"Of course."

"This is just a preliminary meeting."

"Jill realizes that."

"The first time I catch her in a lie, I'm out of there."

"Perfectly understandable."

"Okay," Charley said, thinking he was right, that they should just turn the car around, head for home. She probably wasn't the right person for this job. She didn't have enough experience, with either books or psychopaths. But what the hell? They were already here. What sense did it make to have come all this way only to turn around at the last second? She might as well go inside, meet Jill Rohmer. She reached into her purse and pulled out her photo ID to show the guard. "Might as well get this show on the road."

Alex parked the car in the large, outdoor parking lot at the rear of the prison.

"Maybe you should put the top up," Charley advised. "In case it rains."

"It's not going to rain," he told her confidently, leaving the top down and walking quickly past her. "Coming?" he called back.

Charley picked up her pace, although it was hard to keep up in the platform sandals she was wearing. Why hadn't she just worn jeans and sneakers? she wondered. Whom had she been trying to impress by wearing an actual skirt and heels? Jill Rohmer? Or Jill's lawyer? And why should she give any thought to impressing either?

The fact was that Jill was already impressed. It was also a fact that her lawyer clearly wasn't, and probably never would be. He tolerates me, she thought, struggling to match his brisk stride as they rounded the corner of the building and headed toward the front entrance. He thinks I'm a lightweight.

Was he right? Charley wondered, reminded of

her father's scathing assessment of her talent. "Puerile and facile," he'd opined dismissively of the columns she'd sent him just after she'd started work at the **Palm Beach Post**.

"You didn't like them," she'd stated unnecessarily, grateful for the miles of telephone wire between them, so he couldn't see the tears filling her eyes.

"You know I have a low tolerance for drivel," came the final coup de grâce.

What had she expected? she wondered now, following Alex through the heavy glass revolving doors into the prison's main foyer. What could you expect from a man for whom criticism came as naturally as breathing, who was as ungenerous as he was ill-tempered, as sharp-tongued as he was unforgiving? Once her father had discovered that Charley was in contact with her mother, he'd cut her from his life altogether, refusing to so much as speak to her again.

"Miss Webb," Alex Prescott was saying now.

"What? Sorry. Did you say something?"

"I said, you might as well keep your ID handy. You'll have to show it a few more times."

"Oh. Okay. And please, you don't have to keep calling me Miss Webb."

"It's kind of hard to think of you as a 'Charley,'" he said, the only hint he'd realized she was female. Then, "Metal detector coming up."

Charley gave her purse to the female guard,

who rifled through it, then held out a large, callused hand for Charley's ID. The guard was a big woman, with massive shoulders, long fingers, and an incongruous patch of girlish freckles splashed across her nose and cheeks. Dark brown eyes shifted back and forth between Charley and the picture on her driver's license. "Empty your pockets," she said, nodding toward the conveyor belt.

"Charming," Charley muttered after they'd passed through the metal detector. Alex took her elbow and guided her down the hallway. She was surprised at the instant comfort his touch provided. She hadn't realized how unnerved she was at being here, how vulnerable she felt, how exposed. As if she were guilty of something, and was only moments away from being found out and handcuffed. They turned a corner and proceeded down another corridor.

"Another ID check coming up," he advised.

Charley opened her mouth to take a deep breath as they approached the next checkpoint, but the surrounding air tasted thick and pungent. "Eau de Disinfectant," she said, hoping for a smile, but Alex was already several steps ahead of her, and not listening.

It wasn't that the long hallways were particularly ugly, so much as they were aggressively institutional. Pale green and bare, the corridors were like a maze that wound ever inward, circling closer and closer to the abyss at its core, farther and farther from freedom. I wouldn't last a week in here, Charley was thinking as gates clanged shut somewhere behind her, and once again, wary eyes waited to peruse her driver's license.

"Well, well, well," the female guard stated, a wry smile playing with her wide mouth. She was a virtual twin of the first guard, except for the humanizing freckles. "So you're Charley Webb. I get quite a kick out of your columns."

Charley smiled, feeling strangely grateful. "Thank you."

"Yeah. They're certainly good for a laugh. And, of course, your sister's books are very popular here at Pembroke Correctional."

Charley's smile froze. "Of course."

"Nice to meet you, Miss Webb," she said. "Turn right at the first corridor, then left."

Again, Alex guided Charley down the long hall. This time, however, he didn't take her elbow. "So, your sister writes books," he said, as they reached a set of double doors, and yet another guard, this one male. He got up from his chair as they drew near.

"Take an immediate right," he said, after inspecting their IDs. "Room 118."

Room 118 was exactly as Charley had pictured it would be. Small, sparsely furnished with a cheap Formica table that was bolted to the concrete floor, and three uncomfortable folding chairs. The bare walls were the same green as the corridors, and recessed fluorescent lighting shone harshly down from the low ceiling. There were no windows, and only minimal air-conditioning.

"It'll take about five minutes for them to bring her down," Alex explained.

"Where are they bringing her from?"

"There's a separate section for the women on death row."

"Are there many of them?"

"A handful."

"Do they share a cell?"

"Actually, they're among the few Florida inmates who get their own cells. One of the perks about being sentenced to death."

"Almost makes it worthwhile," Charley noted sarcastically.

"Of course, that's only until the governor signs the death warrant. Then the prisoner is transferred to a 'death watch' cell, closer to the execution site."

"Which is where?"

"Starke. Near Raiford, the men's prison. North of Gainesville," he added, in case she didn't know.

"I know where Raiford is," she said, although in truth, she didn't. "So, when is Jill scheduled to be executed?"

Alex shrugged. "Probably in another twelve years."

"Twelve years?"

"That's the average length of time people get to spend on death row."

Charley debated jotting down this information, then decided against it. She didn't want to appear too eager. Nothing, she reminded herself again, had been decided. "Because of the appeal process?"

"Appeals, new trials, new hearings, court reviews, clemency pleadings—they all take time."

"And meanwhile, these women get to sit in their own, individual, air-conditioned cells."

"Death row isn't air-conditioned," Alex said flatly, a hint of irritation in his voice.

"Aw," said Charley, not bothering to disguise her own lack of sympathy.

"You don't think they suffer enough?" he asked.

"They eat, they sleep, they get an average of twelve more years than they gave their victims. It doesn't sound that bad to me."

"They also spend almost all their time in their cells, and have to be accounted for at least once every hour. Anytime they leave their cells, they're in handcuffs, except in the exercise yard and the shower, which they're allowed every other day."

Charley scoffed. "Jill made it sound as if she'd made a lot of friends."

"That was probably before they transferred her out of the general prison population. I think you'll be surprised, Charley. Jill Rohmer is a very easy girl to like."

Charley wasn't sure which unsettled her more—the idea that a convicted child murderer might be easy to like, or the way "Charley" had rolled seductively off the tip of Alex's tongue. "Yes, I understand her victims thought the world of her," she said, in an effort to keep that troubling thought at bay.

"I'm just asking you to keep an open mind."

With that, the door to the interview room opened and Jill Rohmer stepped inside.

9

In person, Jill was smaller than Charley had anticipated. Maybe five feet, two inches tall, with dark blond hair pulled into a high ponytail, dark brown eyes shyly downcast, small, bow-shaped lips, and a pleasant, heart-shaped face. Undeniably pretty, in a generic kind of way. Nothing too big or too small, no unsightly blemishes or irregular angles, no one feature that overshadowed the others, nothing that particularly stood out. Except maybe the garish orange T-shirt she wore, identifying her as a resident of death row.

To Charley's great surprise, the first word that came to mind when Jill walked through the door was **cute**. **Betty** as opposed to **Veronica**. Definitely nonthreatening. Even a little ordinary. Certainly there was nothing about her appearance to suggest the monster lurking within. Indeed, with her small bones and delicate

frame, Jill Rohmer looked more like an innocent victim than a cold-blooded killer. If Charley had seen her on the street and been asked
to guess her age, she would have said "sixteen."
Barely.

"Hi," Jill said softly.

Even her voice was childlike, Charley thought.
No wonder it had been so easy for her to gain
people's trust.

"Jill Rohmer, this is Charley Webb," Alex
began, introducing them in the manner that
Charley had earlier introduced Glen McLaren to
her son. "Charley Webb . . . Jill Rohmer."

"It's really nice to finally meet you in person,"
Jill said, extending her hand.

"Hello," Charley responded, pretending not
to notice.

The hand retreated. "I've been a fan of yours
for years. It was really nice of you to drive all the
way out here."

"Your lawyer did the driving."

"Thanks, Alex," Jill whispered, staring at the
floor. "I know how busy you are."

"Why don't we sit down?" Alex promptly
pulled out a chair and settled into it.

Charley sat down in the chair beside him,
watching as Jill sank into the lone chair across the
table and primly folded her hands in her lap.

"You're even prettier than your picture in the
paper," Jill told her.

"So are you," Charley responded grudgingly. It pained her that she could actually consider someone who had cruelly murdered three young children attractive.

Jill's face lit up instantly, her right hand moving to her ponytail, twisting it nervously between her fingers. "Thank you. They don't let us wear any makeup in here. We can't even color our hair."

"Your hair's fine."

"I think it would look better lighter. Like yours."

"I don't know," Charley said, amazed to be chatting about anything so mundane. "This color suits you."

"Yeah? Well, okay. That's good then. Is yours natural? It looks natural."

"It's had a little help," Charley admitted.

"Really? You'd never know."

"Thank you."

"Ladies," Alex interrupted. "Fascinating though this discussion truly is, I think we have more important matters to talk about."

Jill looked immediately chastised. She bowed her head toward her lap, her cheeks blushing a girlish pink. "Sorry," she said.

"You don't have to be sorry," Alex said quickly. "It's just that we only have a short period of time, and I don't think you want to waste it."

"Sorry," Jill said again.

"What exactly is it you want from me?" Charley asked, deciding to plunge right in.

Jill lifted her eyes, stared directly at Charley. "Like I said in my letter. I want you to write a book about me."

"And why would I want to do that?"

"Because you're a great writer," Jill answered immediately. "And great writers are always on the lookout for a great subject. Aren't they?"

"And that great subject would be you?"

"All I know is I have a story to tell."

"You'll have to be more specific."

"I don't understand."

"Murderers in and of themselves aren't necessarily interesting," Charley said flatly.

"You're saying I'm a murderer?"

"You're saying you aren't?"

"I'm saying there's a lot you don't know," Jill said.

"I know you were tried and found guilty."

"That's because the jury never heard the whole story."

"Why didn't you tell them?"

Jill fidgeted in her seat, looked toward the ceiling. "I couldn't."

"Why not?"

"I just couldn't."

"Why not?" Charley repeated. "Were you protecting someone?"

"No."

"Are you afraid of anyone?"

A slight flicker of hesitation in Jill's eyes. Then, "Not anymore."

"You're saying someone else was involved?"

Jill slowly turned her head from side to side, as if checking for eavesdroppers. "Maybe," she whispered, so quietly Charley found herself leaning forward in her seat, and even then she wasn't sure she'd heard Jill correctly.

"Maybe? Does that mean yes?"

Jill nodded slowly.

"So why tell me and not the D.A.?"

"The D.A. isn't interested. He's already got his conviction."

"And you're prepared to tell me who this person is?"

Again Jill nodded. "I'll tell you everything. I want people to know the truth."

"Which is?"

"That I'm not the monster they think I am."

"What kind of monster are you?" Charley asked pointedly.

Jill's eyes filled with tears.

Charley looked away, fighting the urge to apologize. She hadn't expected tears. Nor had she expected to feel anything but disdain for the convicted killer of three innocent children. "Why me?" Charley asked.

"Because I admire you. Because I like you. Because I think I can trust you."

"Ah, but can I trust you?"

"Yes. Yes, of course, you can trust me."

"You've already lied to me twice," Charley said.

"What? No!"

Charley pulled Jill's letter out of her purse, began reading. " '**The other prisoners have all turned out to be pretty nice—most of the women are here on drug-related issues—although for a long time, nobody would speak to me. But I've tried to be on my best behavior . . . always being pleasant and helpful, and now almost everyone has more or less come around. One woman . . . even told me she thinks I have a pretty smile. I think she might have a crush on me. . . .There are still a few women . . . who won't have anything to do with me, but I'm working on them, and I feel their resistance beginning to wane.'**" Charley lowered the letter to the table. "You want to explain that?"

Jill looked confused, glanced pleadingly at her lawyer.

"I told Miss Webb that prisoners on death row have their own cells, and rarely, if ever, socialize," he said.

"Yeah, but there are five of us, and our cells are side by side," Jill said quickly. "We talk to each other all the time."

"I didn't realize they sentenced women to death for drug-related issues. Even in Florida." Charley's voice dripped sarcasm.

"Well, no, of course they don't. I was referring to the women I met when I first got here. Before I was sentenced. When I was still part of the general prison population."

"That wasn't the impression you gave."

"I was just trying to give you an overall picture."

"So you lied."

"No. It wasn't a lie. I just took a little 'poetic license.' Is that the right term?"

"Is this also an example of 'poetic license?' **'They keep the men and women segregated, although occasionally we manage to find ways of getting together. Hint: there's way more than reading going on behind the bookshelves of the prison library.'** Did you think I wouldn't find out that Pembroke Correctional is for women only?"

"There are men here," Jill said defensively. "Maybe not prisoners, but . . ."

"Prison officials, guards, workers," Charley rhymed off. "I know."

"I was afraid to be more specific in my letter because . . . well, you never know who might open it and read it."

"And you're all busy having sex in the prison library you don't have access to, since you're only allowed out of your cells to shower and exercise."

The faint blush of pink reappeared in Jill's ashen cheeks. "I had access to the library before I was transferred to death row. I saw things you wouldn't believe."

"Why would I believe anything you tell me?"

"You're mad at me," Jill said, her voice cracking. "I've disappointed you."

"I don't care enough about you to be disappointed," Charley said, knowing she was being cruel and deriving a certain satisfaction from it, although less than she expected.

"You're right," Jill said, tears beginning to spill down her cheeks. "I don't deserve your interest or your time. I'm just a stupid girl who let herself get bullied into doing a bunch of horrible things. I deserve whatever happens to me."

"Who bullied you?" Charley asked, the question out of her mouth before she had time to stop it.

Jill shook her head. "I can't talk about that now."

"When then?"

"Not till you've heard my whole story."

"Which Miss Webb has made very clear she isn't interested in listening to," Alex said, already half out of his chair.

"Hold on a minute," Charley said. "I didn't say I wasn't interested."

"Are you?" Jill asked hopefully. "Are you interested?"

Charley had to concede that she was. "But that doesn't mean I'm on board," she added quickly.

"What can I do to convince you?"

"I'm not sure."

"You received my files and the transcripts of the trial?" Alex interjected.

"Yes. Thank you for sending them over so promptly."

"Have you read them?"

"I glanced through them."

"So you haven't actually read them," he stated.

"No. I haven't actually read them."

"So 'glancing through them' could be considered as a bit of 'poetic license?'" he asked, arching one eyebrow.

Charley found herself smiling. "I've been very busy, and your files are very . . ."

"Thorough?"

"Tedious," Charley corrected.

Jill laughed out loud. The laugh was big and boisterous, and her whole face was engaged. "She got you there, Alex."

"Yes, she certainly did."

"That's how I know you're the perfect person for this job," Jill told Charley.

"How's that?"

"You're not afraid of anyone," Jill explained. "You'll stand up to anybody, even Alex." She laughed again. "And you won't let me get away with anything either. You'll ask the tough questions, the **right** questions. You'll be able to draw me out, get at the whole truth. And you'll call me on any inconsistencies, like you did with my letter."

Charley was flattered in spite of her desire not to be. **She's pushing all the right buttons**, she heard Glen say. **Appealing to both your ego and your curiosity.** She cleared her throat. "There can't **be** any more inconsistencies."

"There won't be. I promise."

"What will you do if I say no?" Charley asked.

"What do you mean?"

"Where will you go? Who will you contact next?"

"No one," Jill insisted. "I told you that in my letter. You're my first and only choice."

"You're saying you're prepared to take the story of what really happened to those children to your grave?"

Jill sank back in her chair. "I hadn't thought about that. I guess I just assumed you wouldn't say no."

"Charley's sister is a writer," Alex said, as Charley's back stiffened. "Did you know that?"

"Of course I did. Her sister's Anne Webb. She's very famous."

"I'm afraid I'm unfamiliar with her work," Alex said.

"He'd never heard of you either," Jill told Charley, dismissing her lawyer with a wave of her delicate hand. "Anne writes romance novels," she explained, as if the two women were personally acquainted. "Not very good ones," she added. "If you don't mind my saying."

"You don't like them?" Charley asked.

"Not too much. They're kind of silly. If you don't mind my saying," she said again.

Charley was almost embarrassed to realize she didn't mind a bit. "Can't please everyone," she said.

"It's just that she writes the same book every time out. You know. The names are different, but it's essentially the same story. Boy meets girl. Boy loses girl. Boy gets girl in the end. Everybody lives happily ever after."

"I guess that's romance for you," Alex observed.

"Yeah?" Jill asked. "That's never been my experience."

"Nor mine," Charley agreed.

"See. I told you we have a lot in common."

"I don't think I'd go that far," Charley said icily.

"I didn't mean. . . . Please don't be insulted. . . . I'm really sorry. . . ."

"Stop apologizing," Jill's lawyer told her
sharply. "You didn't say anything wrong."

"I didn't mean to imply. . . ."

"She knows that," Alex said more gently.
"Don't you, Miss Webb?"

"Charley has another sister, Emily," Jill offered. "She's a television reporter. And a brother,
too. I don't think you've ever said what he does,
have you?" she asked Charley.

That's because he doesn't do anything, Charley thought. "He hasn't quite found his niche
yet," was what she said out loud. "Actually, he
used to date your sister. Did you know that?"

"What?" said Jill.

"What?" echoed Alex.

"Amazing, isn't it? Apparently they met at
night school a few years back and went out a
couple of times. I take it the two of you never
met."

"I don't think so. Pamela never brought her
boyfriends home. Not that she had a lot of boyfriends. Wow. Some coincidence, huh?"

"I'm not sure I believe in coincidence," Charley stated.

"Really?" Jill asked, her eyes growing wide
with wonder. "You mean you think it's like fate
or something?"

"I definitely don't believe in fate."

"Really? What do you believe in?"

"We're not here to talk about me," Charley said testily.

"I believe everything happens for a reason," Jill told her. "Even coincidences. If that makes any sense." She giggled. "So, I think this is a sign. Like we were meant to be."

Charley hid the impulse to shudder. "Are you religious?" she asked.

"Well, I was raised a Baptist, and my parents used to drag us to church every Sunday. But it was just so boring. I kind of got turned off. And Ethan, well, he just hated it. As soon as he was big enough to stand up to our father, he quit church altogether. Then I stopped. Only Pamela still goes." She chuckled. "I remember when we were little, Pammy used to talk about becoming a nun. That would make our father so mad. One time he hit her so hard against the side of her face that she lost partial hearing in one ear. 'We're not Catholic. We're Baptists, goddamn it!' he shouted," Jill said, then chuckled again.

"You find that funny?" Charley asked.

"Well, not the part where he hit her, of course. I don't find that part funny. Just the image I have of him in my head, standing there screaming, 'We're Baptists, goddamn it!' That's kind of funny."

"So you believe in God," Charley said.

"Don't you?"

"I'm not sure."

"Oh, you **have** to believe in God," Jill insisted.

"Do I? Why?"

"Because without God, nothing makes sense."

"And with Him, it does?"

Jill's face went blank.

"What sense does it make that three innocent children are dead by your hands?"

"I loved those children," Jill said.

"You had a funny way of showing it."

"I never wanted to hurt them."

"You tortured them," Charley reminded her. "You recorded their dying screams."

Jill began shaking her head back and forth in denial. "No . . ."

"Little children crying for their mommies . . ."

Jill brought her hands to her ears, as if to block out the sounds of those cries. "Please stop. Don't do this."

"Is that what they said? Did they beg you to stop?"

"No, please don't."

"Okay," Alex interrupted. "That's enough, Charley."

"Were there videotapes?"

"What?" Jill asked, her face awash in tears.

"There were rumors of videotapes."

"Strictly rumors," Alex said. "The police searched for months and didn't find anything."

"That doesn't mean they don't exist."

"They exist," Jill confirmed after a pause.

The room fell silent.

Charley found herself holding her breath. **There really are videotapes?** she wanted to shout. Instead she whispered, "Where are they?"

"I don't know."

"You must remember where you put them."

"I never put them anywhere. I never had them."

"But someone does?" Charley looked over at Alex, who stared back at her, looking every bit as stunned as she was.

"First time I'm hearing about this," he admitted, rubbing his forehead with his hand.

"You see, I told you she was the right person for the job," Jill said, a note of triumph pushing through her tears.

"You understand that if I ever so much as think you're being less than honest with me, if I ever catch you in the tiniest white lie, if I suspect you're playing games, all bets are off," Charley informed her, as she had informed Alex Prescott earlier.

"I understand."

"If I secure a book contract, you get absolutely no remuneration whatsoever. Not one dime."

"I don't want anything."

"If you don't like what I write, it's too damn bad."

"I know that won't happen."

"If it does . . ."

"Then it's too damn bad," Jill agreed.

"You'll sign a statement to that effect?"

"Absolutely." Jill looked to her lawyer. "Alex?"

"I'll draw up the papers first thing Monday morning," he concurred.

"Does this mean we have a deal?" Jill asked hopefully.

Charley swallowed the lump in her throat. What the hell was she getting herself into? "We have a deal."

10

You were right," Charley said, settling into the front seat of Alex's old convertible. Sometime during the hour they'd spent inside the prison walls, the clouds had dispersed, and the sky had turned a glorious shade of blue. "It didn't rain."

"Of course it didn't," Alex acknowledged with a smile.

Charley wondered if he was one of those men who were always right or just one of those who always thought they were. She reached inside her purse for her sunglasses as he snapped his seat belt into place and started the car. "You really didn't know about the videotapes?" she asked.

"I knew about the rumors." He backed the car out of its narrow space and turned toward the gatehouse.

"She never told you they actually existed?"

"Obviously there are a number of things about my client I don't know."

"Still think she's innocent?" Charley asked.

"I never said she was innocent. I said she was complicated."

"Complicated or just crafty?"

Alex gave Charley's question a moment's thought. "I guess you'll have to figure that one out for yourself."

"Any idea where the tapes are?"

"None whatsoever."

"You're sure she didn't give them to you for safekeeping?"

"Lawyers aren't allowed to hide evidence, Charley," he said, a hint of annoyance bracketing his words, as a guard waved them through the gate.

"What if you didn't know what was on the tapes?"

"Then I'd be an idiot," he said plainly, "which, trust me, I'm not."

"So you believe her when she says there was another person involved," Charley stated, although it was, in fact, a question.

"I've always believed that. Yes."

"Do you know who that person is?"

"No. She won't tell me."

"Do you have any ideas?"

"A couple."

"Care to share?"

"Well, her brother's a rather nasty piece of work."

"I thought he had an alibi."

"He claimed to be holed up with his girlfriend during the time Tammy Barnet was missing—the girlfriend backs him up, of course—and his father vouched for his whereabouts when the Starkey kids were killed."

"But you don't believe him?"

"The father's even worse than the brother. It wouldn't surprise me at all to learn that both of them were somehow involved."

"What about Jill's boyfriend?"

"Gary? Not likely. He was out of town when Tammy was killed, and he claims he was no longer romantically involved with Jill at the time of the Starkey murders."

"You feel like stopping somewhere for a cup of coffee?" Charley wasn't sure where that suggestion had come from. Her adrenaline was still pumping from her meeting with Jill, so the last thing her system needed was caffeine. Besides that, she was eager to get back to Palm Beach before Glen returned with James. Still, she felt the need for a time-out, a few extra minutes to absorb all that had happened. Everything was moving so quickly. She just wanted a brief respite to slow it all down.

"Can't," Alex said. "I really have to get back." He offered no further explanation.

"Family obligations?"

"In a manner of speaking."

"What manner?"

He smiled. "That case I was telling you about earlier. The one pitting brother against sister, sister against aunt. . . ."

". . . everybody against mother," Charley concluded. "Your wife doesn't mind you working so hard on a Saturday?" God, could she be any more obvious? she wondered, rolling her eyes behind her dark glasses. Why didn't she just ask him if he was married? Did she even care?

"I'm not married," he said.

"Divorced?"

"Nope."

"Not interested?"

"Is this a proposal?" He glanced over at her for the first time since they'd returned to the car.

Charley laughed. "Sorry. I didn't mean to pry."

"Of course you did. You're a reporter, aren't you?"

"Just trying to make conversation."

"Just trying to get information, you mean," he corrected.

"Is it classified?"

His turn to laugh. "Hardly." But he offered nothing further.

They drove in silence until they reached the entrance to the turnpike.

"So, what did you think of her?" he asked, taking a ticket from the tollbooth attendant and tucking it inside his shirt pocket.

"She's less imposing than I thought she'd be."

"Yeah, she's just a little bit of a thing."

"Still quite formidable."

"In what way?"

"I don't know. There's just something about her, something that lets you know she's the one calling the shots."

Alex looked surprised. "Interesting observation."

"You don't agree?"

"I'll have to think about it." He paused. "So, when do you want to see her again?"

Charley tried envisioning the weeks ahead, but the car was picking up speed, and the wind in her face made it hard to concentrate. She had to raise her voice in order to be heard. "Well, give me some time to read through the transcripts and your files, do a little research on my own, maybe contact a few publishers, write up a proposal. . . ."

"Next Saturday work for you?"

She pushed her hair behind her ears, held it there with both hands. "Uh . . . weekends aren't normally the best time for me. My kids . . ."

"That's right. I forgot you have children."

"You obviously don't," Charley said, although again, it was really a question.

"No. Never really saw myself with kids."

"You don't like them?"

"On the contrary. I think they're great." He shrugged. "Oh, well. You never know."

"You never do," she agreed.

They drove for several seconds in silence.

"So when **would** be a good time for you to see Jill again?" he asked.

Charley turned the pages of her appointment calendar over in her mind. "How's a week from Wednesday?"

"I'll see what I can arrange."

"Maybe we could set up a block of time every week, plus the occasional Saturday."

"Sounds like a good idea."

"Hopefully for longer than an hour. Maybe two, or even three?"

"Three is highly doubtful, but again, I'll see what I can do."

"Does Jill have access to a phone?"

"She has limited phone privileges."

"Well, she can call my office whenever she wants. Or my cell. And of course, she can always write letters. Maybe she could start with her childhood. Tell her not to leave anything out. I'll decide what's relevant and what isn't."

"I'll tell her."

"Okay." Charley sank back in her seat, suddenly exhausted. "Okay."

"You all right?"

"Just a little tired."

"Any plans for tonight?"

"No, nothing." Was he asking her out? If so, how should she respond? It probably wasn't a good idea to mix business with pleasure, she decided in that instant. Now she'd have to backtrack, make up some excuse he was too smart not to see through.

"Well, that's good," he said. "You can take a hot bath, order in Chinese, and just veg out in front of the TV."

So much for that, Charley thought, feeling a stab of disappointment. What was the matter with her? Why wasn't she feeling anything but relief? It wasn't as if she found the man particularly scintillating or attractive. Not that he wasn't either of those things. He just wasn't her type. He was too neat looking, too preppy. She'd always liked her men on the slightly scruffy side. Besides, hadn't she just decided it would be a bad idea to mix business and pleasure? What would happen if after a few dates, she tired of him? That was her pattern, after all. How would dumping him affect her working relationship with Jill? Would Alex be able to convince his client to drop Charley from the project altogether?

She sighed. The only reason she was even vaguely interested in Alex Prescott, she recognized, was because he hadn't shown the vaguest interest in her. And we always want what we can't have, she thought, shutting her eyes, her hair whipping at her closed lids.

In the next instant, she was sitting on the floor of her parents' bedroom, watching her mother throw a bunch of loosely folded blouses into a suitcase. "What are you doing, Mommy?"

"Mommy has to go away for a little while, darling."

"Where?"

"To a place called Australia."

"Where's that?"

"It's far away."

"Can I go with you?"

"No, sweetheart. I'm afraid you can't."

"Is that why you're crying?"

"Yes, sweetheart. That's why I'm crying. Because I'm going to miss you so much."

"Then why can't I go with you?"

"Because I need you to stay home and look after your brother and sisters for me."

"How long will you be gone?"

"I'm not sure."

"I don't want you to go."

"I know, sweetheart. But I have to."

"Is it important?"

"Yes, it is."

"More important than me?"

"Nothing's more important than you are," her mother said, crying even harder.

"Then why are you going?"

"Because I have no choice."

"Why?"

"Maybe one day I'll be able to explain it to you."

"Explain it to me now."

"I can't."

"Why not?"

"Because it's very complicated."

"What's 'complicated'?"

"For goodness sakes Charlotte. For once, can you not ask so many questions?"

"Charley," a voice said, sliding into her reverie, like an intruder at an open window.

Charley bolted up, her seat belt stiffening instantly, locking her in place.

Alex was staring at her. "You were having a nightmare," he explained gently.

It took Charley several seconds to reacquaint herself with her surroundings. They were still on the turnpike, the high volume of cars having slowed traffic down to a crawl. "What time is it? How long was I asleep?"

He checked his watch. "It's after four. You were out maybe forty minutes."

"I can't believe I did that. I never fall asleep in the afternoon."

"Must be all the fresh air blowing in your face."

"Did you get any work done while I was unconscious?" She noted the headphones wrapped around his neck.

"I tried. Couldn't concentrate."

"Sorry for not being better company."

"Do you have a lot of nightmares?" he asked.

"Not too many anymore."

"But you used to?"

"When I was a kid."

"What was this one about?"

"I don't remember," Charley lied, thinking it was easier that way.

"I never remember my dreams either," Alex said. "Bits and pieces maybe. Sometimes I wake up in the middle of the night in a cold sweat, thinking some guy's been chasing me with a knife . . ."

"I think I know that guy," Charley said.

"Big man in a black coat, face kind of fuzzy and indistinct?"

"That's the one."

"Yeah, well, you can have him."

"Thanks."

Alex smiled. "So, tell me about your kids."

"What can I say? They're perfect."

He laughed. "Of course. I wouldn't have expected otherwise. What are their names?"

"Franny and James. He's five. She's eight."

"Franny and James," he repeated. "Nice names."

"My sisters don't agree. They were expecting Franny and Zooey."

"Excuse me?"

"Franny and Zooey," she repeated, louder this time. "It's a book by J. D. Salinger. 'An inferior book by an inferior writer,' my father would say."

Alex looked appropriately confused.

"It's sort of a tradition in our family to give our children literary names. My sisters and I were named after the Brontë sisters," she confided, wondering why she was confiding anything in him at all, and deciding against regaling him with the additional anecdote regarding **Charlotte's Web**. "Both Anne and Emily continued in the literary mode. Anne named her kids Darcy and Tess."

"From **Pride and Prejudice** and **Tess of the D'Urbervilles**," Alex stated.

"I'm impressed," Charley said, and she was. Most of the lawyers she knew read only law journals and the occasional spy novel.

"And Emily?"

"Catherine, of course!"

"Of course. What else from the namesake of the author of **Wuthering Heights**?"

"You're very quick," Charley observed.

"Some might say glib."

"That's all right. I like glib."

Alex smiled, returned his full attention to the highway. "Almost there," he said, nodding toward the upcoming exit at Okeechobee.

Ten minutes later, he pulled the car to a stop in front of her house. "Thanks. I really appreciate everything you've done." She unsnapped her seat belt, pushed open the car door.

"It was my pleasure."

"Did you want to come in for a drink?" she asked, then bit down on her lower lip. What was the matter with her? Did she really want to prolong the afternoon? Hadn't they pretty much exhausted their supply of small talk?

"I really can't," he said. "But I'll call you after I've made some arrangements. Probably toward the end of the week."

"Sounds good." Charley got out of the car.

"Call me if you have any questions."

"I will. Thanks again." She waved as Alex drove off down the street, but he wasn't looking. Charley's fingers floated aimlessly in the air for several seconds before she realized someone was watching her. "Lynn, hi," she called toward her neighbor, who was glaring at her from behind the large American flag that occupied much of her front lawn.

But Lynn refused to acknowledge her, pivoting around on her exaggerated heels and hurrying up the path to her house. Seconds later, the sound of her front door slamming reverberated down the street.

* * *

Charley had just enough time to shower and change into her favorite jeans before Glen brought James home from their afternoon at Lion Country Safari.

"We had the best time," James shouted, tearing through the house toward the bathroom.

"Well, great," Charley called after him. "How about you?" she asked Glen, who was hovering at the front door, looking as rudely appealing as ever. She gave silent thanks that her instincts about him had proved correct.

"We had the best time," he reiterated.

"I can't tell you how much I appreciate . . ."

"You don't have to. How'd it go with Jill Rohmer?"

"Looks like I'll be writing that book," she said.

"Sure that's what you want?"

"I'm sure," she told him, realizing she was.

"Well then, good for you. Congratulations."

"Thank you. Now I just have to find a publisher."

"I can't imagine that'll be a problem."

"Hopefully not," she agreed, realizing she didn't want him to go. "Feel like a drink? I'm sure you could use one."

"No. I better not."

"Hot date?"

"Hot nightclub," he said. "And a hot date," he admitted in the next breath.

Charley tried to mask her disappointment with a quick smile. Two men had turned her down in one afternoon. That had to be a first. "I don't think you ever told me why you called the other day," she ventured. Surely it had been to ask her out.

"Just wanted to check that your brother was okay."

"Oh." God, she really **was** losing her touch. "James," she called toward the bathroom, louder than she'd intended. "Come say good-bye to Glen."

"I'm on the toilet," James called back.

"I think this is where I came in," Glen said, laughing. "Bye, James. See you again soon."

"Bye, Glen."

"I owe you," Charley reminded him.

He was halfway down the front walkway when he turned back toward Charley. "Don't worry," he said. "I fully intend to collect."

11

The next letter from Jill arrived at Charley's office the following Friday.

Dear Charley,

I can't begin to tell you how thrilled I was to meet you on Saturday. It was like my favorite fantasy coming true. You were everything I expected and more. Not only are you more beautiful in person than your picture in the paper—you really should think about having a new one taken, that one doesn't begin to do you justice—but you're every bit as smart and savvy as I knew you'd be. You didn't let me get away with a thing, and that's exactly what I need—what this book needs— to make sure the whole story gets told.

By the way, I hope that Alex isn't giving

you too hard a time. I know he's not especially keen on you for this project—he told me during our last phone conversation that he still thinks we should recruit someone with more experience and "intellectual clout," as he put it—I had to remind him you went to Harvard!— but please don't let his negativity get you down, or give you second thoughts about doing this book. It isn't that he doesn't like you. He does. It's just his way of looking out for me. I'm convinced in time he'll come to appreciate your talent as much as I do. So, let's prove him wrong, and write the best damn book we can. I can't stress enough how much I'm looking forward to our collaboration.

So, Mr. Prescott still doesn't think I'm up for the job, Charley thought, irritated at herself for being irritated with Alex's assessment of her limited "intellectual clout." "Pompous ass," she muttered.

Anyway, he told me he's trying to set up a meeting for next Wednesday, and while I'm disappointed that we have to wait so long to see each other again, I'm glad to know that things are moving in the right direction. I'm es-

pecially grateful for your kind offer to phone you whenever I want, either at your office or on your cell. Trust me, I won't take advantage of your generosity and goodwill, and will only call you if I think of something really important, or am afraid of trusting it to the mail. I don't want you to get tired of me, and I won't make a pest of myself, I promise.

In the meantime, I think your idea of writing letters is a good one. We can save a lot of time that way, and it might help you in preparing your questions. Not that I'm trying to tell you how to organize your time. I'm not. I'd never dream of telling a writer of your caliber what to do. I'm just so excited that we'll be working together, so please forgive me if sometimes I appear too enthusiastic.

Another side benefit of my writing these letters is that it gives me something to do. I spend so much time alone in my cell, and even though prisoners on death row are allowed a radio and a small black-and-white TV in our cells— did you know that?—sometimes you just want to have someone to talk to. (And I don't mean the other inmates.)

Admittedly, writing letters is a bit one-sided, but still I can pretend you're here with me, and I can imagine you looking at me, and really listening to what I'm saying, and hopefully trying to understand. Even if we achieve nothing else, I'd settle for that.

Alex said you thought I should start with my childhood. I think that's an excellent idea. We're all products of our childhood, after all. Everything we become as adults springs from who we were as children, how we were treated, who and what shaped our ideas and values. We are who we were—just taller. Do you agree?

Charley lowered the letter to her lap. " 'Everything we become as adults,' " she repeated out loud, " 'springs from who we were as children.' I guess I can agree with that." She took a deep breath, released it as if she were exhaling smoke from a cigarette. **We are who we were**, she reread silently. **Just taller.** "I bet you think you're terribly clever, don't you?"

"Well, yes. Now that you mention it," Mitch Johnson said from behind her.

Charley spun around in her seat. "Knocking would be nice," she said to her round-faced, round-bellied superior.

"A door would be nice, too, but what the hell, we make do with what we have." He moved closer to her chair. Charley caught a faint whiff of body odor as he approached. "More threatening mail?"

Charley turned Jill's letter facedown across her knees. "No. There's been nothing all week."

"Well, that's a relief."

"Yes, it is." She waited for him to either say something else or leave. "Is there anything I can do for you, Mitch?"

"Michael tells me you're writing a book about Jill Rohmer."

"Yes, that's right."

"It would have been nice to hear about it first-hand."

"It's still in the very early stages," Charley demurred. She was in no mood to have to deal with Mitch's bruised ego. "I don't even have a contract yet."

"A little out of your comfort zone, isn't it?"

"I guess I'll find out."

"I could help you . . . get comfortable. Dinner? Tomorrow night?"

Was he joking? Charley wondered. "I can't," she said. "But please tell your wife I appreciate the kind offer."

"Polly and the kids are out of town for the weekend. I was thinking we could try this new place that specializes in **Brazilian** food."

Charley shook her head. "This is really inappropriate, Mitch."

"Aw, come on, Charley. Lighten up. You didn't think I was serious, did you? Where's your sense of humor?"

"I don't have one, Mitch. Anything else?"

"This Sunday's column," he said after a pause. "Not your best."

"What's wrong with it?"

"Way too serious."

"Drunk driving is a serious subject," Charley said.

His eyebrows rose in unison. "Suppose you leave the serious subjects for the serious journalists."

The phone rang just as Charley was contemplating throwing it at his head. Mitch Johnson smiled and backed out of the cubicle. "Charley Webb," she growled into the receiver.

"Miss Webb, this is Ella Fiorio, Alex Prescott's secretary."

Charley pictured the deeply tanned woman with the unflattering haircut. She took a deep breath, tried to banish Mitch Johnson from her mind. "Yes. How are you?"

"Fine, thank you. Mr. Prescott asked me to give you a call regarding Jill Rohmer."

Charley wondered briefly why Alex wasn't calling her himself.

"He said to tell you he was able to schedule a

two-hour meeting for you and Miss Rohmer for next Wednesday, starting at one o'clock. I trust that works for you."

Charley quickly did the calculations. A two-hour meeting with at least ninety minutes of travel time on either side meant that, to all intents and purposes, she'd be tied up between eleven and five. Which meant she'd have to find someone to look after Franny and James when they got home from school. She thought of Glen and shook her head at her former audacity. She couldn't very well call on him again. She hadn't even heard from him all week. That hot date must have proved quite scorching.

"Miss Webb?" the secretary asked.

"Yes, that works fine."

"Good. I'll inform Mr. Prescott." She hung up before Charley had a chance to ask whether or not Alex would be present during the interview, or if she could expect to hear from him between now and then.

Another desirable man with no desire to talk to her, she thought. Unlike the Mitch Johnsons of the world. She returned her attention to the letter in her lap.

Okay, so where to start?
I guess we could start with the first
thing I remember, which, believe it or

not, is me standing in my crib, shriek-
ing my lungs out. I couldn't have been
more than two years old, and my
father insists it's impossible for
anyone to remember anything when
they're that young, but I swear I remember standing in that crib, holding
on to the bars and screaming because
my brother, Ethan, had taken my
stuffed bear and was sitting on the
floor, pulling the bear's arms so hard
they tore right off. And all the stuffing
came pouring out all over the carpet,
just like blood.

Ethan swears that never happened,
but I know it did because my sister,
Pammy, told me she remembers it, too.
She's three years older than I am, so she
would have been about five at the time.
And Pam has what they call a photo-
graphic memory. She just has to see
something once, and her mind records
it. Like a camera.

"Or a videotape recorder," Charley whispered.

I still can't get over the coincidence
with regard to my sister and your
brother. The next time I see her, I'll

have to ask her about him. (What's his name again? I remember from one of your columns that it was something like Brad, only different, more un-usual.) Not that Pam ever comes to visit me. You'll probably get to see her before I do. If you do, please tell her I miss her, and that I hope she can find it in her heart to forgive me for all the pain I've caused her. Tell her it was never my intention to hurt her, and that I'm truly sorry if she's suffered because of my weaknesses.

Sisters are funny, aren't they? Since you have two of them, I'm sure you understand what I mean. They're your own flesh and blood, cut from the same cloth, and you'd think we'd be more alike. Certainly Pammy and I share some of the same physical char-acteristics. We're both petite and blond, and we both have brown eyes, although mine are darker. Hers are bigger, and flecked with bits of gold. Fairy dust, our mother used to say, and I was so jealous because I didn't have any fairy dust in mine. Once I tried to fool everybody by going into this dirty old shed we had in our backyard and rifling around, trying to get dust in my eyes. Turned out I got it everywhere but **there. I was just covered in it. My mother thought it was really funny, but my father didn't laugh at all. He made me wear that filthy dress to a neighbor's birthday party that afternoon. I was so embarrassed and didn't want to go, but he said if I didn't, he'd cut the head off my pet turtle to teach me a lesson. So, of course I went to the party. I took the turtle with me—her name was Tilly—hiding her in the pocket of my dress. But she must have crawled out, because when I checked my pocket later, she was gone, and I never saw her again. Pammy said the neighbor's cat probably got her. My father said it served me right. My mother said it was God's will.**

Anyway, back to what I was saying about sisters. It just amazes me how different people can be, people who've come from the same two parents, and were raised in the same household, with the same set of values, etc., etc. To give you an example: Pam was always the good girl. She never got into any trouble, always did her homework, always got straight A's, unlike me, who was always in hot water about something. She had

lots of friends, although she was never as popular with boys as I was. She was an idealist, I guess you'd say. She used to talk about joining the Peace Corps, and going to Africa and helping the poor people dying of AIDS and stuff. My father said if she was so intent on helping poor people, she could stay at home and help him with my mother, who got diagnosed with MS about ten years back. And that's pretty much what Pam ended up doing. Even though she graduated high school at the top of her class, she never went to college. She took a few night classes a couple of years ago, but that was pretty much the extent of it. Then after I got in trouble, she became pretty much a recluse. She just stays in that house, looking after my mother, and cooking for my father and brother. Ethan's over thirty, but he still lives at home. Can you believe it? He was married for a little while, but his wife kicked him out after he kicked out two of her teeth.

Anyway, I seem to be getting ahead of myself, and the point I'm trying to make is that despite the fact we're sisters, Pammy and me couldn't be more different. (Should that be Pammy and I?) I was always the hellion, the one getting into trouble. It wasn't that I wanted to be bad. I didn't. I tried really hard to be good. Like at church. It was tough to sit there every Sunday listening to that preacher tell us we were going to hell for every little thing. I started to believe that even being in hell had to be better than being in church. I mean, he was really boring, and so I'd start to fidget, and next thing you know, my father would reach over and smack me on the back of my head. Soon I was getting mouthy and rebellious, falling behind in school. Until I met Wayne Howland, and he turned my life around, showed me a better way.

But again, I'm moving a little quickly here. You wanted to know about my childhood, and I keep jumping around. I guess that's just the way my mind works, why I was always getting into trouble.

So, what else do I remember about my childhood? Well, I remember my mother.

"I remember Mama," Charley said, leaning back in her chair and stretching out her arms and legs. She put down the letter and reached for the phone. "Mom, hi," she said when her mother answered after the first ring. "How are you?"

"Fine, darling. I'm so glad you phoned."

"I'm sorry I haven't returned your calls. I've been really busy."

"Of course, dear."

"How was your cruise?"

"It was fabulous. I had the most marvelous time. There was gambling. I won fifty dollars."

"Fifty whole dollars?"

"Well, you know me, darling. The minute I win, I quit."

"Actually, I didn't know that about you."

"I guess I'm not much of a gambler."

Charley was about to disagree. What would you call a woman who abandons not only her family but her entire way of life, to reinvent herself halfway around the globe, if not a gambler?

"And I met this very lovely gentleman," her mother continued, a strange note of girlish excitement creeping into her voice.

"You met a man?"

"A widower from Newark. His name is Phil Whitmore, which I think is a terribly handsome name, don't you? He's a retired investment banker, who's looking to buy a condo on the ocean. Which would be very nice, because I love the ocean."

"Mom?" Charley interrupted.

"Yes, dear?"

"You're gay," Charley reminded her mother.

"I think the word is **bisexual**, darling," Elizabeth Webb protested. "Something Phil found quite intriguing actually."

"I don't think I'm ready to have this conversation," Charley said.

Her mother laughed. "Oh, darling. You're such a sweet thing."

"Look, I'm actually calling to ask you a favor," Charley broached.

"Name it."

"I need to be in the Fort Lauderdale area on Wednesday afternoon."

"You want me to look after the children?"

Charley could hear the hopefulness in her mother's voice. "If you wouldn't mind."

"Mind? I'd be thrilled to death."

"It might turn into a weekly thing. At least for a little while."

"All the better."

"I should be home by five o'clock."

"Take all the time you need, darling."

"Maybe we could all have dinner together when I get home."

"I'll make something special," her mother said.

"You don't have to do that."

"Please let me."

Charley smiled. "Sure," she agreed. "Make whatever you like."

"You used to love my roast chicken. I made it with orange juice."

"I don't remember," Charley lied. The truth was that the aroma of her mother's roast chicken was already circling her head, so strong she could almost taste it.

"Well, I guess there's nothing really very special about roast chicken."

"Actually, it sounds wonderful. Please, if you wouldn't mind . . ."

"Of course I wouldn't mind. Thank you, darling."

"Don't be silly. I'm the one who should be thanking you."

"Nonsense. Well, I guess I'll see you on Wednesday," her mother said.

"If you could come around eleven o'clock?"

"I'll be there. I love you, sweetheart."

"See you Wednesday," Charley said, hanging up the phone, and closing her eyes to the tears she felt forming. I remember Mama, she thought again, remembering those awful days after her mother had left for Australia, the empty weeks that grew into months, the lonely months that faded into years, without so much as a phone call or a letter.

Of course it turned out Elizabeth Webb **had** called, and called often enough for Charley's father to get a new, unlisted number. And she'd written every day, although each of those letters had been returned, unopened. She'd even come back to Connecticut on one occasion to consult with a lawyer about being allowed to visit her children, but Robert Webb had refused his consent, and ultimately the courts had backed him up. Not that Charley or her siblings had known about any of this at the time. All they knew was that their mother had deserted them.

My mother was the peacemaker in our family, Charley read now, returning her attention to Jill's letter.

She was always trying to calm things down, keep us from killing one another. It couldn't have been easy, and I've always suspected it's one of the things that eventually made her sick.

Do you believe that? Do you believe our mental state can affect our physical well-being? I think it can. I remember I always used to get terrible stomach-aches whenever I got nervous or upset. Like before a big test or exam. And after little Tammy Barnet died, I was so sick I could hardly get out of bed.

Anyway, ours wasn't the easiest house to grow up in. My father had an awful

temper. He was constantly flying off the handle about something. Mom used to say he was a perfectionist, and that he was harder on himself than he was on anybody else, but I never bought that. As far as I could see, we were the ones who suffered, and he got off scot-free. (What does that mean—scot-free?) And I think that's a pretty lame excuse anyway. I mean, if you want to be a perfectionist, be one. Leave everybody else alone. Think what a great world this would be if we just followed the philosophy of live and let live.

I guess that sounds pretty ironic, coming from someone like me. But it's what I believe. In spite of everything.

My mother believed in trying to keep everybody happy. Whenever I think about her, and I think about her a lot, I picture her in her orange-and-brown-flowered apron, leaning over the stove, stirring a large pot of homemade soup. My mom's not very tall, even shorter than I am, and she only weighs about ninety pounds. At least she did. Since she's been in her wheelchair, I think she weighs even less. But I bet her hair's still the same style, curly and reddish brown, tied into a bun at the back of her head, the bun covered by a brown net, like the kind you see on food handlers at the supermarket. I remember getting my fingers trapped inside it when I was a little girl, and the netting caught on one of my nails and ripped, and my dad got angry and cut off all my nails with big scissors, right down to the quick, so that my fingers bled.

My mother didn't like it when my dad got physical with any of us. She tried to stop him, but he didn't listen. Sometimes her pleading only made things worse. Sometimes he'd hit her, too. One time, she overcooked the pork chops, and he got really angry and pushed her face into the mashed potatoes. When I started crying, he threw my plate down, then made me eat the food off the floor, like a dog.

We had a dog once. His name was Sam. My father and brother used to torture him something awful. They'd chain him up in the backyard and put his food dish just out of his reach. And the poor dog would scratch at the ground and try to get at that dish, but he couldn't. And he'd whine, sometimes for days, and Ethan would go out and kick him. It was really sad. My mother used to feed him scraps whenever she could, but my father caught her one day and beat her pretty bad. Then he shot the dog in front of us. We never had any pets after that.

"Dear God," Charley whispered, almost afraid to keep reading.

I'm probably making it sound much worse than it was. My mother always said I had a tendency to exaggerate. And I wouldn't want you to think there weren't good times, too. We had lots of those. Like the time my father took us all to Disney World. It was Pammy's tenth birthday, and he decided, just spur of the moment, to take us all there to celebrate. We took the car. I don't know if I mentioned that we're from a little town outside Fort Lauderdale—just past the airport—called Dania. Are you familiar with it? It's really small, and getting smaller all the time. It used to be quite a center for antiques, but it's becoming something of a ghost town. The main street is one creepy old store after another. People used to come from all over Florida to shop there. But things have pretty much dried up in recent years, probably because of the Internet and eBay, and a lot of the stores have closed. Too bad. Now there's nothing.

But, back to Disney World. We had the best time. We stayed at some motel with purple drapes and red walls. It was in Kissimee, which I used to pronounce Kiss-a-me, instead of Kiss-<u>ee</u>-me. Anyway, we couldn't afford to stay right in Disney World, but that was okay. We loved our tacky little motel, and we had two rooms, one room for my parents, the other for Ethan, Pam, and me. Our room had two double beds. One bed was supposed to be for Ethan, the other one for Pam and me. Except that in the middle of the night, Ethan carried me over to his bed and crawled in beside Pam. Then I saw him climb on top of her. Soon I heard her crying and telling him to stop. I thought he was tickling her, and I didn't want him to come over and tickle me, 'cause he tickled pretty hard, so I pretended to be asleep. The next day there was blood on the sheets, and I heard Ethan tell Pam that if she said anything, it would be worse the next time. I didn't know how you could get blood from tickling, and I guess I didn't want to know. At any rate, I learned soon enough. So we went off to Disney World, and I have to confess I had the best time. I forgot all about Pammy and the bloody sheets. We went on all the rides, and this time when I screamed, my father hugged me and called me his little cupcake. And that was really nice. I liked being his little cupcake.

There were other good times, too. Good times, bad times. Same as with every family, I guess. But I'm getting kind of tired, and my wrist is cramping, so I think I'll sign off for now. I'll write you another letter tomorrow, and look forward to seeing you on Wednesday. Two whole hours. Wow!

Anyway, I'm sure I've given you lots to think about, and I know you'll have plenty of questions. Try not to be too judgmental. Nobody's all good or all bad, and I've forgiven my family their imperfections. What is it they say in the Bible? "Forgive us our trespasses, as we forgive those who trespass against us"?

So, bye for now. Can't wait to see you.

Much love,
Jill.

P.S.: Any bites from publishers? Let me know the minute you get a nibble.

Charley folded up the letter and tucked it inside her purse. Then she got up from her chair, exited her cubicle, walked into the women's washroom at the end of a long hall, locked herself into the nearest stall, and burst into tears.

12

The worker in the yellow hard hat was watching from her neighbor's roof when Charley pulled her car into her driveway. She smiled up at him as she got out of the car, and he smiled back. "How's it going?" he called out.

"Okay," Charley called back. "What about you?"

"It's going. Looking forward to the weekend."

"Well, have a good one." Charley cast a wary eye around the premises. The last thing she was in the mood for was another set-to with Gabe Lopez. She was still smarting from her encounter with Mitch Johnson.

How dare he use her column to get back at her for turning down his advances, she thought as she unlocked her front door. The truth was that her upcoming column was one of her strongest in months. Maybe not as sexy as some of her more recent efforts, but her semi-serious suggestion that one way to stop people from driving drunk would be to drag them from their cars and shoot them on the spot was bound to be both controversial and provocative. It might even get her brother to sit up and take notice, maybe even persuade him to return some of her calls. Where was he anyway? She hadn't heard from him all week.

Yet another man who seemed to be avoiding her, she realized as she closed the door behind her and headed for her bedroom, feeling vaguely queasy.

Do you believe our mental state can affect our physical well-being?

I don't know what I believe anymore, Charley thought, entering her bedroom and exchanging the white T-shirt she was wearing for another one exactly like it. I believe that children have the right to grow up in a household where their pets aren't slaughtered before their eyes, where they aren't forced to eat off the floor, where they aren't beaten and sexually abused.

Was Jill telling her the truth? And even if everything she said or hinted at was gospel, could that excuse her behavior? Was the fact that Jill Rohmer had been hideously abused as a child any justification for her inhuman treatment of other children later on?

We're products of our childhood, after all.

Everything we become as adults springs from who we were as children, how we were treated, who and what shaped our ideas and values. We are who we were.

"Just taller," Charley said aloud.

Except how did that explain the thousands of children who were abused every year, and still grew up to be caring and responsible adults? Conversely, how did it account for the offspring of loving and attentive parents, who went on to kill without conscience or remorse? What made one sister dream of joining the Peace Corps, while the other conjured up murderous fantasies regarding the slaughter of innocents?

We may be shaped by our childhood, Charley decided as she headed for the kitchen, but there **was** such a thing as choice. We are what we **do**. "It's not just a matter of height." She opened the fridge and took out a ginger ale, drinking it straight from the can. Look at her own family, she was thinking. Then, no. Don't.

But it was too late. Her siblings were already lining up beside her: Emily with her neat blond bob and mellifluous TV reporter's voice; Anne with her soft auburn hair piled loosely atop her head; Bram with his elastic limbs and long lashes. We're all so different, Charley thought, trying to push them out of her sight line. And yet, not so different really. The sisters were ambitious and successful, all in related fields. Each had children from multiple failed relationships. They all nursed invisible wounds.

It was the way they dealt with those wounds that made them different.

And Bram?

He was more sensitive than his sisters, to be sure, more prone to self-destructive acts, more likely to give up without a fight.

Just . . . more.

And less.

We're products of our childhood, after all.

Was that why she was so determined to make sure her own children had the best childhood possible, why she was always there to greet them when they came home from school, why she'd never been away from them for more than two days? Was it also why she recoiled at the very idea of marriage, why she'd never had a relationship with a man that lasted more than two months, why she'd never allowed herself the luxury of falling in love?

"Or maybe I just haven't met the right person," Charley said, finishing the last of her ginger ale and checking her watch. The kids would be home any minute now, she knew, opening her front door and sitting down on the step to wait. She loved these few minutes of anticipation, moments spent picturing her children's faces, and the automatic way those faces lit up when they saw her. She wondered if her mother had ever felt the same thing. But whenever Charley tried to imagine her mother waiting for her by the front door, she saw only a blank space. Charley's strongest childhood memory of her mother was her absence.

And then suddenly, twenty years after she'd gone away, she was back. Charley still remembered that initial phone call word for word.

"Charlotte?" the woman had asked tentatively.

Charley had known instantly it was her mother. She'd been imagining this moment, preparing for it all her life. **Where are you? Where have you been? Do you think you can just come waltzing back into my life after all these years?** And yet when it had finally come, she was struck dumb. No words would form. No sounds were possible. She could barely breathe.

"Charlotte, darling, is that you? Please don't hang up," she'd added, as Charley was contemplating doing just that. "It's your mother, darling. You know that, don't you? Please say something, sweetheart. I know I don't deserve it, but please say something."

Where are you? Where have you been? Do you think you can just come waltzing back into my life after all these years?

"How did you find me?" Charley had finally managed to sputter.

"I hired a private detective. He said I should have just used the Internet, I could have found you myself. But I don't understand how that damn thing works, and, oh God, I'm just so glad to hear your voice. Are you well, darling? Can we meet? I'm here in Palm Beach. I can come over right now."

"Do you think you can just come waltzing back into my life after all these years?" Charley had demanded, finally mustering up the strength to push the words from her mouth.

"I know you're angry," her mother said. "I know I don't deserve your forgiveness. I'm not expecting it. I'm just hoping for a chance to explain. Please, Charley."

Charley's throat constricted and her eyes filled with tears. "Why did you call me that?"

"Well, I've read all your columns, dear. From your very first one a year ago. The detective found them for me. He had them printed out. So interesting and well written. I'm awfully proud."

"You liked them?" Charley heard herself ask.

"I **loved** them. And the name of the column, WEBB SITE, and your e-mail address, Charley'sWeb.com, so clever, darling, even if I don't understand a thing about computers. The detective suggested I contact you via e-mail, rather than risk contacting you directly—he even offered to do it for me when he saw how terri-

fied I was by the whole idea—but really, I just
wanted to hear your voice. Please, can we
meet?"

**No, we can't meet. You left us. You're no
longer a part of my life. I hate you.**

"All right."

"Oh, darling, thank you. When? I can come
right now."

"Do you know the fountain in the middle of
City Place?"

"No, but I'm sure I can find it."

"I'll meet you there in one hour." Charley
hung up before she could change her mind.

Her mother was already waiting when she arrived, even though Charley was twenty minutes
early. Both women recognized each other immediately, despite the passage of the years. Elizabeth Webb was every bit as imposing as
Charley remembered, her hair as black, her legs
as long. And although lines now creased her
pale white skin, and her dark eyes were clouded
over with tears, she was as beautiful as ever.
Charley had made a point of not putting on
any makeup or dressing up. She was wearing
the same jeans and navy T-shirt she'd been
wearing all day.

"God, you're beautiful," her mother had said.

The soothing sound of her mother's voice
was suddenly overpowered by the harsh sounds
of hammers from her neighbor's roof. Charley

looked up, saw the cute worker in the yellow
hard hat balanced on one knee next to another
worker, not so cute, also in a yellow hard hat,
the hammers in both their hands moving rhyth-
mically up and down, although what exactly
they were pounding was a mystery. The ham-
mering had been going on for weeks now. The
entire neighborhood had undergone extensive
renovations in recent years. What had once
been an uninteresting collection of small, run-
down streets in a largely neglected part of town,
populated primarily by the poor and the disaf-
fected, had been given a new lease on life with
the arrival on its doorstep of the spectacular
outdoor mall known as City Place, the magnificent Kravis Center for the Performing Arts, and
lastly, the cavernous Palm Beach Convention
Center. Each had brought more business, more
tourists, and more money into the area, and
with it more and more construction. No longer
simply a route one had to drive through—as
quickly as possible, with the car windows closed
and the doors locked—in order to get to Palm
Beach proper, this strip of Okeechobee between
Congress and Dixie had now become a prime
destination itself.

As a result, the surrounding area had become
increasingly gentrified. Expensive new condo-
miniums had sprung up, and existing homes had
been purchased, gutted, and replaced. Charley

had moved into her tiny bungalow just after Franny's birth, renting for the first few years, and then using the money her grandmother had left her as a down payment to buy it, her father having grudgingly given his consent. She'd been there when Lynn and Wally Moore moved in at the corner; she'd witnessed Gabe Lopez carry his then-bride across the threshold; she'd objected to the city council when the Rivers family next door started excavating their backyard pool. She'd watched as, step by step, old shingled roofs were replaced by new Spanish tiles, second-floor bedrooms were added, and kitchens were overhauled. Someone was always doing something. No sooner did one set of tools stop working, then another set started up. Only Charley's house looked pretty much as it had the day she'd moved in.

The school bus rounded the corner, and Charley jumped to her feet. Seconds later, Franny was leading her younger brother across the street, James proudly holding his latest work of art high above his head. "It's some deer drinking water from a pond in the middle of a forest," he said of the three oddly shaped brown blobs, a blue circle, and a bunch of straight green lines. "You see?" he asked. "See the deer? See?"

"Fantastic," Charley said, thinking it was. She turned toward her daughter. "How about you, sweetie? Anything to show me?"

"We don't have art on Friday," Franny said, with the voice of someone who has said the same thing many times before.

"That's right. I forgot."

"I'm thirsty," James announced.

"Did you remember to buy apple juice?" Franny asked. Her tone indicated she suspected this was yet something else her mother had forgotten.

Shit, Charley thought. "I'm sorry. I'll go out later and get some."

A black Chevrolet rounded the corner and pulled into the driveway of the house next door. Doreen Rivers, an attractive brunette in her late forties, pushed herself out of the car and started unloading groceries from her trunk.

"Here. Let me help you with that," Charley offered, walking over and taking a heavy bag of groceries from the surprised woman's hands.

"Do you want to see my picture?" James asked loudly, running to their side. "It's a bunch of deer drinking water from a pond in the middle of a forest."

"That's very good," Doreen Rivers said, her eyes widening as Charley grabbed a second bag from the trunk and carried both bags up the front walkway.

Why was she looking at her that way? Charley wondered, feeling the other woman's eyes boring into her back. True, the two women had barely spoken since Charley had voiced her objections to their backyard pool. But she wasn't **that** unfriendly. Was she?

"Did you buy apple juice?" James asked. "Our mom forgot."

"Well, no, I didn't," Doreen Rivers said. "But I think I may have some in the fridge, if you'd like some."

"Can we, Mom? Can we?"

"Well, I . . ."

"Of course you can." Doreen Rivers unlocked her front door and ushered a hesitant Charley and her eager children inside the cool interior. "The kitchen's at the back," she indicated.

"Your house is lovely," Charley said, noting the dark hardwood floors and the sleek minimalist furniture.

"I think the layout's the same as yours," Doreen said as they deposited the bags of groceries on the counter of the modern, black-and-stainless-steel kitchen. "Except we added a third bedroom, and of course . . . the pool."

"My dad builds pools," James said proudly, shifting his weight from one foot to the other as Doreen poured him and his sister a glass of apple juice.

"Yes. I believe he built **our** pool." She glanced warily at Charley. "Can I get you a glass of something cold?"

"No, thanks. We really shouldn't be bothering you."

"It's no bother. Actually, I think this is the longest conversation we've ever had."

"My mother doesn't believe in getting too friendly with the neighbors," Franny explained as Charley closed her eyes and prayed for a hurricane to strike.

"Yes, I suspected as much."

"Where are your children?" James asked in a voice that could cut glass.

"I only have one son. His name is Todd, and he's away at school."

"Finish your drink, James," Charley instructed.

"I want to see my dad's pool," James said. "Can I?"

"James. . . ."

"Of course you can." Doreen Rivers opened the sliding glass door to the back patio, beyond which a small, kidney-shaped pool took up most of the yard. "In fact, why don't you go home and get into your bathing suits, and then come back for a swim."

"Can we, Mom? Can we?" James asked, already pulling on her arm.

"I don't think so."

"Please!" James pleaded. Even Franny was looking at her longingly.

"Well, if you're sure it wouldn't be too much of an imposition."

"I wouldn't have asked if I considered it an imposition."

"Well, thank you. I guess it would be okay."

"Don't worry. You don't have to talk to me," Doreen said with a sly smile, although her words were all but drowned out by James's whoops of glee.

Later, after the children had had their swim and their supper, and were both tucked into their beds, Charley was surprised to hear a knock at the door.

"Who is it?" Charley asked, thinking it was probably Doreen Rivers. Come to borrow a cup of sugar, or bring her a piece of homemade coffee cake, or whatever else it was that neighbors did when they were being neighborly, exactly what Charley had studiously avoided doing all these years, because she hadn't wanted to risk . . . this. Contact, friendship, dependency. Whatever this was. Good fences make good neighbors, according to the poet, Robert Frost. Had all it taken been an impulsive offer to help carry a few groceries into the house to tear down the imaginary barrier she'd spent years constructing?

I think this is the longest conversation we've ever had.

Oh, well. Not to worry, she decided, thinking

of Lynn Moore and Gabe Lopez. Sooner or later, she'd find a way to alienate her again. Charley sighed and threw open the front door.

A handsome young man with curly brown hair and dimples in his ruddy cheeks stood smiling at her from the other side of the threshold. It took Charley a minute to realize who he was. She almost didn't recognize him without his yellow hard hat.

"I thought I'd take a chance you might be home," he said, pulling a bottle of red wine from behind his back. "Care to join me?"

Charley glanced behind her, half-expecting to see James and Franny standing there, observing them. But James and Franny were sound asleep, and it was Friday night, and she hadn't had a real date in months, she was thinking, not to mention, she hadn't had sex in even longer than that, and . . . what was the matter with her? "I don't think so, thank you," she told him.

"You're sure about that?" he asked, trying not to sound too surprised. A look of bemused disbelief played with his handsome features, telling her he'd used this ploy before, and wasn't used to being turned down.

What would it hurt? she asked herself. A few glasses of wine with a good-looking stranger, some sweet lies whispered into her ear, a few more whispered into his. Some soft, deep kisses, a few expert caresses, leading perhaps to a few hours of uncomplicated, impassioned lovemaking.

Where? On the sofa? In her bed?

Where her children could walk in and find them.

What would she say? How could she explain?

No, this man isn't your new daddy. I barely know him. No, he isn't staying.

Uncomplicated? she repeated silently. Since when had anything in her life ever been uncomplicated?

She remembered the first time Franny had attended a classmate's birthday party. "Where does Erin's daddy live?" she'd inquired when Charley arrived to take her home.

"He lives with Erin and her mommy," Charley told her.

The look of confusion on Franny's face had been replaced by wonder. "You mean mommies and daddies can live together?" she'd asked.

Charley stared at the muscular young man smiling seductively at her from her front step. He was even sexier without his yellow hard hat, she was thinking, feeling her resolve weaken and her body sway toward him. "I'm sure," she said, and quietly closed the door.

13

'Scot-free' is an expression that stems from a municipal tax going back to medieval times," Charley said as Jill Rohmer was ushered into the small interview room at Pembroke Correctional. "According to the Internet, it has absolutely no connection with Scotsmen, frugal or otherwise," she continued, trying to still the erratic beating of her heart as the guard removed Jill's handcuffs, left the room, and shut the door behind her.

Jill, dressed in her regulation orange T-shirt and baggy pants, pulled out a chair and sat down across from Charley, folding one small hand inside the other on the table between them, and staring at Charley with eyes the color of rich sable. "Tell me more."

"**Scot** is actually a Scandinavian word meaning 'payment,' " Charley continued, pleased to oblige because it gave her time to get her thoughts in order. Although she'd spent the last five days doing research and preparing questions, the sight of the ponytailed young woman in her death row uniform had temporarily rendered her mind a blank slate. All that remained was the information she'd been able to dredge up regarding the term **scot-free**, and which she now tossed out like handfuls of confetti. "The whole term was actually **scot and lot, scot** meaning 'tax' and **lot** meaning the **amount** of tax you had to pay. Apparently only those who paid their 'scot and lot' were allowed to vote."

"I'm not allowed to vote anymore," Jill interjected. Then, quickly, "Sorry. I didn't mean to interrupt. Go on."

"It's not really that interesting. I was just showing off."

"No," Jill protested. "It's **very** interesting. Please, go on."

Charley wondered briefly if Jill was toying with her. Or maybe she also needed a little time to relax, a few minutes to ease her way into the difficult hours ahead. "People were taxed proportionate to their own income," Charley continued, obligingly, "and that tax went to relief for the poor. Someone who evaded paying their share was said to get off 'scot-free.' And that's where the expression comes from," she concluded with an emphatic nod of her head.

Enough of this nonsense, the nod said. Time to get this show on the road. She pulled a tiny tape recorder out of her purse and set it on the table, along with her notebook and several black felt-tip pens.

"Wow. I didn't realize you'd be using a tape recorder."

"I thought you liked tape recorders," Charley said, biting down on her tongue as the color drained from Jill's heart-shaped face. What was the matter with her? Did she want to alienate the young woman before they even began? You catch more flies with honey than with vinegar, she was reminded, wondering where **that** expression came from. "Sorry. That was uncalled-for."

"You don't have to apologize," Jill said, although her skin remained ashen. "I know what you think of me."

"I thought it would be a good idea to tape record our sessions for a number of reasons," Charley offered. "First, because even though I'll be taking notes, there's no way I'll be able to write fast enough to get everything you say, no matter how slowly you speak. And I don't want you to have to even think about that. I want you to speak freely and as fast as you want, just like we were having a normal conversation." As normal as it can be, considering we're sitting in a locked room on death row, she thought, but didn't say. "And secondly, this way there'll be no confusion later on about what was said. We can avoid future arguments about you being misquoted, or my not understanding what you really meant. We'll have something concrete and absolute to refer back to. Also, it's a useful tool for me, something I can use to create context, or if I need to remember the exact tone in which something was said."

"It's a way of protecting yourself."

"It protects both of us."

"Okay," Jill said. "I'm fine with it."

"Okay," Charley agreed. "I should just test it to make sure it's working." She turned on the recorder.

Jill leaned forward, angling her shoulders toward the recording device and speaking directly to it. "Name, rank, and serial number?" she asked, then tittered nervously.

Charley pressed the PLAYBACK button. **Name, rank, and serial number?** echoed throughout the room, accompanied by waves of girlish giggles. "Seems to be working fine." She pressed the STOP button. "And you don't have to speak directly into it. It's small but it's powerful. It'll pick up whatever we say, so you can even get up and walk around, if you want."

"Wow. That's a lot better than the tape recorder I had."

Charley felt her breath catch in her chest. Could she have heard Jill correctly? "So, are you ready to start?" she asked when she was able to find her voice.

"Can I ask you a few questions first?"

"Of course."

"Did you speak to any publishers?"

"I spoke to a couple," Charley told her, "as well as to a few literary agents. They seem quite interested."

"Really?" Jill looked immensely pleased. "What'd they say?"

"They asked me to submit a written proposal, which I've already started work on. I hope I'll be able to get something to them by the end of next week."

"Pretty exciting, huh?"

"I guess."

"What does Alex think?"

"I haven't spoken to him."

"Really?" Jill looked disappointed. "Me neither. I guess he's pretty busy."

"Apparently."

"What do you think of him?" Jill asked.

Charley shrugged. "Seems like a nice enough person."

"He's a great lawyer."

"Yes, I read the trial transcripts. He did as good a job defending you as anyone could have, considering."

"Considering what?"

"The overwhelming evidence against you."

Jill's lips formed a pout of disgust, which quickly transformed itself into a bright smile. "Do you think he's cute?"

"What?"

"Alex. Do you think he's cute?"

"I hadn't really noticed," Charley lied.

"Well, I think he's cute. I mean, he's a little conservative and he'll probably be bald in a few years, but . . ."

"Jill . . ." Charley interrupted.

"I'm sorry," Jill said immediately, as if she was used to apologizing, even before she knew what she'd done wrong.

"We're not girlfriends here," Charley reminded her. "I'm not here so we can have a nice little chat about boys."

"I know. I'm sorry."

"It's just that we only have a few hours, and I don't want to waste any of it."

"I understand."

"We have a lot of ground to cover."

"Sorry. We can start now. I'm really sorry."

"You don't have to be sorry."

"Right. I'm sorry."

Charley sighed, pressed the START button on the recorder. "Why don't we begin with the letter you wrote me last week?"

"Was it okay? Was it what you had in mind?"

"It was very informative, yes."

"Good. I decided to wait to write more until I knew if you liked it."

"It's not a question of my liking it or not. . . ."

"No, of course not. I didn't mean that. I meant . . . I'm sorry."

"I know what you meant."

Jill breathed a deep sigh of relief. "Good."

"In your letter, you alluded to the fact you'd been sexually abused," Charley said, deciding it made more sense to plunge right in, rather than simply go over what Jill had written.

"I didn't say I was sexually abused," Jill protested vehemently. "I said Pam was abused."

Charley pulled the letter out of her purse, found the correct paragraph. " 'I didn't know how you could get blood from tickling, and I guess I didn't want to know,' " she read. " 'At any rate, I'd learn soon enough.' What does that mean exactly?"

"I don't know."

"What do you mean, you don't know?" Charley pressed. " **'At any rate, I'd learn soon enough.' "**

"I don't want to talk about that now." Jill folded her arms across her chest and looked toward the far wall.

"Why not?"

"Because it's too soon."

"Too soon for what?"

"To get into this kind of stuff. I feel like I don't know you well enough."

"You're saying you don't trust me?"

"I trust you," Jill insisted. "It's just that it's kind of like having sex on a first date, you know, before you're really ready. I need you to take me to dinner, maybe buy me a few drinks first." She rolled her eyes and stuck out her tongue, like a playful child.

"You want to be wooed?" Charley asked incredulously, wondering, not for the first time, what the hell she was doing here.

"I'm saying I'd appreciate a little sensitivity, that's all," Jill answered, the playful child gone, replaced by the stern adult.

Charley nodded. "I didn't mean to be insensitive."

"It's just that it was kind of a painful time in my life."

"I'm sure it was."

"I don't like talking about it."

"What would you like to talk about?" Charley asked, backtracking. Maybe the direct approach wasn't the best one to be taking after all. Maybe it was simply better to let Jill take control, to follow her down whatever path she chose to lead them.

"I don't know. How about Wayne?"

"That would be Wayne Howland?" Charley said, referring to her notes, although there was no need.

"Yeah. I feel like talking about him."

"Okay. Tell me about Wayne."

"He was my first real boyfriend."

"How old were you?"

"Fourteen. I remember because I'd just started getting my period. How old were you when you first got your period?"

Charley thought of telling Jill it was none of her business, reminding her again that they weren't girlfriends, here to share a pleasant trip down the memory lane of personal hygiene. She was here to write a book. A bestseller, if possible. Something of substance and weight that would shoot up the charts and silence her critics once and for all.

But maybe a girlfriend was exactly what was needed to get the job done. If it took a few shared confidences to get Jill to open up and reveal all her terrible secrets, so be it. Charley thought back. "I was twelve," she said.

"Yeah? Did you get a lot of cramps?"

"I don't remember." Charley's first period was memorable only because there was no one around to help her deal with it. Her mother was somewhere in Australia, her father was locked in his study, her sisters were younger and even more naive than she was, she didn't have any friends in whom she could confide, and their latest housekeeper referred to her own periods ominously as "the curse." What little Charley knew about such matters came from health classes and textbooks. It was terribly cold and clinical, when all she really wanted was for someone to put their arms around her and tell her everything was going to be all right, that the world of grown-ups she was now entering wasn't such a scary and terrible place to be. A little sensitivity would have been appreciated, she thought now, borrowing Jill's words.

"You have this funny look on your face," Jill said. "What are you thinking about?"

Charley shook her head. "I was just remembering the first time I used Tampax," she sidestepped. "I didn't realize you had to remove the cardboard."

"Ouch," Jill said, and they both laughed.

"This was in the days before they made plastic applicators. Anyway, you were talking about Wayne," Charley said, directing Jill back to the topic at hand.

"I thought he was so cool," Jill said. "He wasn't very tall. Probably shorter than you. How tall are you anyway?"

"Five-eight."

"That's all? You look taller."

"Five-eight," Charley repeated.

"Wayne would have been about five-six, which is pretty short for a guy, but I didn't mind.

I mean, I'm not very big either, in case you hadn't noticed." She made a sound that was more nervous twitter than laugh. "And it was kind of nice to have a guy who wasn't looming over me all the time."

"Like Ethan?"

"Yeah. Like Ethan." She sighed.

Charley jotted the sigh down in her notebook. "How old was Wayne?"

"Eighteen."

"An older man."

"I always liked 'em older."

"Them?"

"My men," Jill said with a big smile.

From big sigh to big smile, Charley jotted down. "So what was Wayne like?"

"He was real nice. He was the preacher's son, if you can believe that. Just like that old song, what was it? 'The only man who could ever reach me . . .' " she sang. "That was him. The son of our preacher. I think he thought he could save me or something."

"Save you from what?"

"From what was going on in my life."

"Which was?"

"He knew my father was beating up on us."

"Did he know about Ethan?"

"About Ethan and Pammy, you mean?"

"About Ethan and you," Charley corrected. There was a moment's silence. Charley listened

as the tape whirred softly inside the tiny recorder. "Tell me about Ethan," she urged gently.

"I told you I didn't want to talk about that
yet."

"I think you do," Charley said.

"Well, you're wrong," Jill snapped. She got
up, began pacing back and forth. "Now, you
want to hear about Wayne or not?"

"Yes. Of course."

Jill took a deep breath and resumed her seat.
She dragged her hair out of its elastic band, then
gathered it roughly behind her head, securing it
so tightly, it tugged on her forehead and pulled
her eyebrows toward her scalp. Her voice, when
she finally spoke, sounded hard. "Like I said,
Wayne wasn't very tall, and he wasn't especially
good-looking either. He had a crew cut and bad
skin but, I don't know, there was just something
about him I liked. Maybe because he was so different from Ethan and my dad." She shrugged.
"I can't remember when we actually met. It was
probably at church. I mean, we were there every
week, and so was he. Pretty soon, we started
hanging out. I'd get out of school, and he'd be
waiting for me at the end of the street. Of course,
at first he wouldn't admit he was waiting for me.
He'd pretend there was some other reason, but
then he'd end up walking me home. Sometimes
we'd go to a movie or out for an ice cream. It
was fun. He never tried anything funny."

"You were friends," Charley stated.

"He was my **best** friend. We'd just talk and talk and talk. I told him everything." She paused. "That was my mistake," she added, a cloud settling over her unlined face.

"How was it a mistake?"

"He started acting different toward me."

"How did he start acting?"

A long pause. "Like Ethan."

"How was he like Ethan?"

"I don't want to talk about it," Jill said stubbornly.

Charley put down her pen. "We're going around in circles here, Jill."

"I know."

"That isn't going to get us very far."

"I know that, too."

"How was Wayne like Ethan?" she asked again.

Another long pause, even longer than the first. "After Pammy got her period," Jill began, "Ethan decided he couldn't keep doing the things he was doing without running the risk of her getting pregnant." She stopped, twisted her lips back and forth, then tugged nervously on her ponytail. Charley recorded each gesture in her notepad. "That's when he started crawling into my bed."

Charley took a deep breath, released it slowly. "How old were you?"

"Nine. Maybe ten."

Charley thought of Franny. In another year, she'd be nine. Dear God, she thought, closing her eyes. "What did he do to you?"

Jill shrugged. "You know."

"I need to hear it from you."

Jill's shrug was bigger the second time. "He made me touch him, use my mouth," she said matter-of-factly. "And he raped me. First with his fingers, then with . . . What's the word your sister always uses in her books? His 'manhood.' " She laughed her girlish giggle. "You know. The standard stuff you see in kiddie porn. It was pretty gross."

The standard stuff you see in kiddie porn, Charley repeated silently, gripping her pen tightly to keep her fingers from shaking. "And this went on until . . ."

". . . until I was fourteen and I finally got my period. I'd been praying for that day for so long, I tell you, 'cause I knew then he'd have to leave me alone."

"And did he?"

"He stopped raping me. But he still made me use my mouth. Said I was better than Pammy or any of the other girls he knew."

Was that a note of pride in Jill's voice? Charley wondered, thinking she'd have to replay that part of the tape.

"Do you like doing that stuff?" Jill asked.

"What?" The word was more exclamation than question.

"Using your mouth. You know. Blow jobs. Do you like doing that stuff?"

"Do you?" Charley asked.

"I asked you first."

Charley considered her response very carefully. She could refuse to answer the question altogether, she thought, but that might make Jill angry, convince her to stop talking. Or she could fudge her reply, say something about all sexual acts being permissible and enjoyable when they took place between two consenting adults. Or that love enhanced every aspect of sex. Except how did she know that, she who'd never been in love? "Yes," Charley finally answered, honestly. "I like doing that stuff."

A slow smile slid across Jill's face, until it reached her eyes. Once again her hand moved to free her ponytail from its tight elastic band. She shook her head, letting her soft blond hair fall loosely across her shoulders. "You know the part I like best about it?" she asked, leaning forward on her elbows. "I like the feeling of power it gives you. You know. He's lying there, all exposed. His thing's in your mouth, for God's sake. He's moaning away. His fate is in your hands." She snickered. "In your mouth, I guess I should say." She traced her lower lip with the tip of her tongue, then leaned back in her chair and closed her eyes, as if remembering. "And you get to decide . . . you get to decide. . . ."

"What?" Charley asked. "What do you get to decide?"

Jill opened her eyes, stared directly at Charley. "Everything."

14

Charley drove home with Jill's words still echoing in her ear, like the refrain of an annoying, but particularly catchy, song. **He made me touch him, use my mouth.** She turned up the radio, began indiscriminately changing the channels in an effort to drown the words out. **He's moaning away. His fate is in your hands.** Her right heel pressed down on the accelerator. The car lurched beneath her, its gears grinding audibly, and picked up speed. **I was nine, maybe ten.** She checked her reflection in the rearview mirror, saw Franny's innocent eyes staring back at her. She looked away, turned up the volume of the radio louder still, and pressed down harder on the gas pedal. **You get to decide. You get to decide.**

What do you get to decide? Charley had asked her.

Everything, had come the cryptic response.

But did a girl who'd been raised by a tyrannical and sadistic father, who'd been raped by her brother when she was all of nine years old, who'd been similarly abused by her first real boyfriend when she was fourteen, and manipulated, then abandoned, by virtually every man she'd met since, ever really get to decide anything?

Charley couldn't help but think of her own formative years, of the remote iceman who was her father, and the damage his coldness had wrought. His wife had sought comfort in the more accepting arms of a woman and fled with her to the other side of the globe, leaving his daughters to seek salvation with a succession of unsuitable men. Emily was not even thirty and already thrice divorced, while Anne, separated from husband number two, relied on the heroines she created in her fiction to find manly perfection and unconditional love. Their brother Bram had sought refuge in drugs and alcohol, their false promises searing his throat and scorching his lungs. And Charley? Charley had babies with disposable men, and chased the glare of the spotlight to keep her warm.

Like Jill, she'd had her first real boyfriend at age fourteen. His name was Alan. Alan Porter, she recalled, a boy as plain as his name. She pictured the tall, skinny boy with the long, reddish hair that was always falling into his pale green eyes, eyes that had seemed so mysterious at the time, but were merely vacant, she realized now. The real mystery was **why** she'd found him so appealing. Like Wayne, he wasn't especially good-looking. His attractiveness lay solely in the fact he was attracted to her.

At fourteen, Charley had yet to peck her way out of the hard, stubborn shell of adolescence. A good head taller than most of the boys in school, her body was still more square than round, her broad shoulders her most prominent feature. It would be another year before her breasts became a source of interest, and her eyes a source of power. In the meantime, boys routinely ignored and overlooked her. Except for Alan Porter who, perhaps overwhelmed by the sight of his studly reflection in her shyly upturned eyes, or more likely acting on a dare from some of his classmates, deigned to saunter over to her locker one morning and say hello.

Within weeks, they were hanging out together, and within weeks after that, they were officially an item, although she couldn't remember that they went on any actual dates. A few parties, perhaps, that were really communal make-out sessions, boys lying on top of girls on an assortment of uncomfortable sofas and chairs in somebody's basement, teenage torsos grinding impotently against one another, furtive hands slipping under skirts and beneath bra straps, fingers fumbling with zippers, low moans and high squeals, the occasional "don't," followed by the plaintive, "let me."

Alan had been relentless in his pursuit of her virginity, and just as relentless in his efforts to distance himself from her once he'd accomplished his goal. "Call me sometime," he'd said afterward, hastily climbing back into his jeans, and choosing to ignore the blood on the gray carpet of Charley's rec room floor. Charley worked at it, but even after repeated washings, the telltale stain remained. Not that it mattered. Her father never noticed.

Charley snapped back into the present, not sure at what point she'd realized that the low wail she was hearing wasn't part of an extended guitar riff on KISS-FM, but rather a police siren. Nor was she able to recall the precise moment she understood that the flashing lights behind her were meant specifically for her. But suddenly a police cruiser was passing her on her left, then quickly cutting in front of her, and signaling for her to pull over. "Damn it," she muttered, coming to a stop at the side of the busy turnpike and reaching into her purse for her license and registration, then opening her window and handing it to the officer before he had a chance to ask for it.

"Any idea how fast you were going?" he demanded, as she'd known he would, although she was surprised by the ferocity of his tone.

Was he really as angry as he sounded? she wondered, lifting her eyes to his and biting down on her lower lip in a gesture meant to convey both vulnerability and regret. The helpless female, overwhelmed by circumstance, and intimidated by such a virile display of competence. This approach had gotten her out of two speeding tickets already this year. "I'm so sorry," she whispered breathily, batting her eyelashes in a furious effort to produce tears. "I didn't realize . . ."

"I clocked you at ninety-five miles an hour."

Charley managed to squeeze out a few tears. The officer looked remarkably unmoved. "Are you sure?" she asked him, genuine disbelief breaking through the artificial girlishness of her voice. Could she really have been going twenty-five miles over the limit? "I never go that fast."

"You can fight it in court, if you want," the officer said, before retreating to his cruiser to run her data through the computer.

Charley watched as his stocky form grew smaller in her rearview mirror, trying to think what approach might work better with the obviously grumpy, middle-aged man. Clearly, he was at the end of his shift and in no mood to play nice, no matter how many tears her big blue eyes managed to produce.

"Look, I'm really sorry," she told the officer upon his return, deciding to simply tell the truth. "I've just had a very upsetting after-noon."

"Think how even more upsetting it would have been if you'd killed somebody," he countered, handing Charley back her license and registration, as well as a speeding ticket for four hundred dollars.

"Four hundred dollars! Are you kidding me?"

"And three points."

"I'm going to lose points?" This time the tears that filled her eyes were genuine.

The expression of the officer's face immediately softened. He looked toward the ground, let out a deep breath.

Charley thought maybe he was reconsidering, that he'd take back the ticket, reduce the speed sufficiently so that, at the very least, she wouldn't lose any points. Accordingly she tucked a few hairs behind her ear and lowered her eyes submissively.

The officer patted the side of her car. "Drive carefully," he told her.

"Shit," she cursed when he was out of earshot, stuffing the ticket into her purse that sat, like an uninterested passenger, on the seat beside her. "Three points! Four hundred dollars! This is all your fault, damn it!" she continued, thinking of Jill, and wondering if she could write the ticket off as a business expense. Research, she thought, waiting for a break in the traffic to pull back onto the highway. "Four hundred dollars!" she wailed again, careful to keep her eye on the speedometer. What a waste. Think what she could have done with four hundred dollars. She could have paid next month's mortgage or purchased a sleeve of an Oscar de la Renta blouse. **You can fight it in court**, the officer had suggested. Maybe I should, she decided, thinking of Alex Prescott, and wondering if he'd charge her to take the case or do it for free. "He'd charge me," she said out loud, thinking that her charm had worked about as well on the young attorney as it had on the middle-aged policeman. "Definitely losing my touch," she muttered, as once again Jill's words brushed up against her own, like a cat against a bare leg. **He made me touch him.** "Shut up." **Use my mouth.** "Go away." **And he raped me. First with his fingers, then with . . . What's the word your sister always uses in her books? His "manhood."** "Yeah, that's a real man for you," Charley exclaimed, hearing someone shouting something about "bitches" on the radio and realizing it was the song she was listening to. Immediately she changed the station. This time, a woman was singing mournfully about her cheating husband, praying he'd come to his senses and come back to her, announcing she'd wait forever, if necessary, for him to return. "Idiot," Charley yelled at the wailing woman. "Better a bitch than a doormat." She snapped off the radio, thinking it was too bad she didn't have any tapes of case law to listen to, as Alex had done on her previous visit to Pembroke Pines.

This was the second time her thoughts had drifted to Alex in as many minutes, she realized. What was that all about?

Do you think he's cute?

What?

Alex? Do you think he's cute?

I hadn't really noticed.

Yeah, sure.

There **was** a tape she could listen to, she knew, glancing again at her purse, and picturing the tiny tape recorder inside it. **Wow. That's a lot better than the tape recorder I had**, she heard Jill say.

I should never have agreed to do this book, Charley thought, knowing she didn't actually have to replay the tape in order to remember any of the things Jill had told her. The young woman's words were seared on her memory, like a branding iron on flesh. Charley doubted she'd ever forget them.

Something else she knew: She was in way over her head.

She could smell her mother's chicken roasting in the oven as soon as she opened her front door.

"Charley, is that you?" her mother called out

as James ran toward her, grabbing her by the knees and almost knocking her down.

"Mommy! Grandma's making mashed potatoes, and I'm helping."

"Yes, I can see that." Charley wiped a spot of something soft and white from the tip of his nose. She hoped it was food.

Franny appeared in the doorway to the kitchen. "I set the table," she said with quiet pride.

"I don't know what I would have done without them," Elizabeth Webb said, coming up behind Franny and draping her arms around the child's shoulders. For the first time, Charley noted an undefined, yet unmistakable, family resemblance between them.

"I feel the same way," Charley said.

"Grandma says I should be a chef when I grow up," James announced.

"That's certainly something to consider."

"Can you be a chef and own a nightclub at the same time?"

"Own a nightclub?" Elizabeth asked.

"Glen owns a nightclub," James said, nodding for emphasis.

"Who's Glen?"

"He's Mommy's friend, and he took me to Lion Country Safari."

"Something I should know about?" Elizabeth asked, glancing hopefully at Charley.

"I'm sure there's lots you should know about," Charley told her. "But why start now?"

Tears immediately sprang to her mother's eyes, and she turned away, swiped at them with the back of her hand.

"You made Grandma cry!" James said accusingly.

"I'm sorry," Charley apologized immediately. What was the matter with her? Her mother had been nice enough to baby-sit, even to make dinner. "I didn't mean . . ."

"No, no, that's quite all right," her mother said. "Your mother didn't make me cry, sweetheart. I just got something in my eye."

"What? Can I see?"

"I'm going to be a writer when I grow up," Franny announced.

It was Charley's turn to get teary-eyed.

"Do you have something in your eye, too?" James asked, his own eyes narrowing.

"A writer is a wonderful thing to be," Elizabeth Webb said.

"I'm going to be a writer, too," James agreed. "**And** a nightclub owner."

"What happened to the chef?" Charley asked.

"What's happening to my mashed potatoes?" Elizabeth cried out in mock dismay.

"Uh-oh." James raced back into the kitchen, followed more slowly by Franny.

"Mom," Charley whispered. "I'm really sorry."

"It's all right."

"It's not all right."

"Tough afternoon?" her mother asked, tucking a few stray hairs into the soft bun at the nape of her neck.

"That's no excuse."

Her mother smiled, although the smile was bracketed by tiny frown lines that brought a slight tremble to her lips. "I love you, Charley," she said simply. "I've always loved you. I hope you know that."

Charley nodded, although what she was thinking was, If you loved me, why did you leave me? How could you just walk out the way you did? I know it wasn't easy, living with my father, but how could you make your escape and leave your children behind? What kind of mother does that? I could no more abandon Franny and James than I could cut out my heart. Do you really think that all you have to do is show up twenty years later and cook chicken and mashed potatoes, and all will be forgiven? Is that what you think? That love is that easy?

"I could use a hug," her mother said, taking a tentative step forward.

Instinctively Charley took a step back.

"Grandma!" James shouted from the kitchen. "Where are you?"

"Coming," Elizabeth said, her eyes still on Charley.

The two women stood looking at each other for several more seconds, neither moving.

"Grandma!"

"You better go," Charley told her, a dull throb filling her chest, as her mother turned and left the room.

"So what was it like, being with another woman?" Charley asked her mother after the children were asleep, and the two women relaxed in the living room, finishing off the last of an inexpensive bottle of Bordeaux. Charley sat on the floor, her back against a chair, her legs stretched out carelessly in front of her, while her mother perched at the end of the couch, legs crossed primly at the ankles beneath her long pleated skirt.

Charley waited for her mother to push back her shoulders indignantly and change the subject, but instead Elizabeth Webb took another sip of her wine and responded, "It was a little strange at first. But then it was rather nice."

"Rather nice?"

"How can I put this?" The question was directed more at herself than at Charley. Several long seconds passed with no answer.

"You don't have to worry," Charley told her, misinterpreting her silence. "This conversation is strictly off the record."

"I'm not worried about that at all. Feel free to reproduce it verbatim, if you'd like."

Could she write about it? Charley wondered. **My mother, the lesbian.** Or how about, **My mother, the switch-hitter?** That ought to be good for a few testy e-mails.

"What is it exactly you want to know?" her mother asked.

"I'm not sure, **exactly**."

"Are you asking what it was like, physically?"

Dear God. Was she? "I guess that's part of it."

"Physically, it's strange. At least, at first," her mother answered with disarming candor. "I mean, you have to adjust to a whole new variety of shapes and smells and tastes. It takes a bit of getting used to. It's easier to be on the receiving end, I have to admit. Much easier to just lie there, close your eyes, and enjoy. But that's rather selfish, and eventually you have to become proactive, as it were. Then it turns into something of an adventure. But it's hard to separate the physical from the emotional. One thing just kind of flows into the other. It's not as if I was born that way." She stopped for a sip of wine. "I know that isn't exactly the politically correct thing to say, but in my case—and I can only speak for me and from my own experience—I never considered myself a lesbian. Still don't. On the contrary, I was always—and still am—very interested in men. I've always enjoyed sex with men, even your father. He was actually quite an accomplished lover. Surprisingly." She smiled at Charley. "Are you all right, darling? You're looking a little pale."

Charley took a long sip of her wine and tried to picture her parents making love. But it was impossible to think of her father being passionate about anything.

"Unfortunately, being a good lover wasn't nearly enough," her mother continued. "Although for a time, it was. At any rate, I was so busy popping out babies, I never really stopped to think about how unhappy I was. We hardly spoke at all outside the bedroom, and eventually nothing was happening there either. Maybe it was me. I don't know. It just seemed as if I couldn't do anything right. Your father was very demanding, as you know, very much a perfectionist about everything, and I was such a slob." As if on cue, she wiped a bit of wine from the bottom of her glass, and brushed several bread crumbs from the elastic front of her white peasant blouse. "Well, it's hard to be anything else when you're looking after four small children, but he didn't understand that. He was always at me about something. So critical. Nothing I did was ever right; nothing was ever good enough. Not my cooking, not my housekeeping. Certainly not my parenting skills. He disapproved of my friends, the books I read, the movies I wanted to see. Not that I'm making excuses for myself—or maybe I am," she amended quickly. "I was just so lonely." She picked up the bottle of wine, emptied what was left of it into her glass. "There's nothing lonelier than an unhappy marriage."

"When did you meet Sharon?" Charley heard herself ask.

"It was about six months after Bram was born. I literally walked into her in the grocery store, ran my cart right over her foot, and promptly burst into tears. Imagine—she's the one who's injured, and I'm the one who's crying. She was very sweet about it. We started talking. Something just clicked. She was from Australia, which was somewhere I'd always wanted to go. But your father wasn't one for traveling. Anyway, she was spending the year in New Haven, working on her Ph.D. in anthropology. I thought she was fascinating. I used to love to listen to her talk. That wonderful Australian accent. And she was so passionate about everything. And so nonjudgmental. So unlike your father. I developed this little crush on her. There was nothing physical. At least, not in the beginning.

"She was gay. I knew that. She made no secret

of it. Said she'd been gay all her life, one of those people who'd known from a very early age she preferred women. I said I wasn't, and she accepted that. We became very close friends. I just wanted to be around her. She made me feel safe.

"And then, one night, I had a fight with your father about something trivial, and it escalated, as these things do, and next thing I knew I was sobbing on Sharon's shoulder, and she was comforting me, kissing my hair and telling me everything would be all right, and then . . . I don't know. It just happened."

"These things don't just happen," Charley said, with more conviction than she felt.

"No, maybe they don't," her mother concurred with surprising ease. "Maybe I went over there knowing what would happen. I don't know. I only know that for the first time in a long time, I felt loved. And it didn't matter that Sharon was a woman. What mattered was the way she made me feel."

"And your children?" Charley asked coldly, the camaraderie of the evening instantly evaporating. "Didn't they matter at all?"

"I will regret leaving you until the day I die," her mother said.

At that moment, a key turned in the lock, and both women's heads snapped toward the sound. "Hello?" Charley called out, scrambling to her feet.

"Hey, Charley, how's it going?" her brother asked, his lanky body suddenly filling the doorway between the foyer and the living room. "Oh, sorry. I didn't realize you had company." He stared at the woman on the sofa, the realization of who she was slowly creeping into his psyche, and then hitting him, full force, like a bullet between the eyes. And then another bullet, this one aimed directly at his heart. Charley watched Bram's skin turn ghostly white as his hand reached for his chest and his breathing stalled.

"Bram," Elizabeth Webb exclaimed, the word a sigh as she jumped to her feet and ran around the sofa toward him. "My sweet boy. . . ."

"Don't," he warned, his arm extended between them like a sword, his index finger pointed accusingly at her head. "Don't you dare." He shuffled back toward the door, then ran down the front walk to his car, which was parked directly behind their mother's mauve Civic.

"Bram," Elizabeth called after him.

Charley watched her brother pull the old MG away from the curb and disappear down the street in a cloud of exhaust. She watched her mother's shoulders slump and her body sink to the floor, her brother's name, more prayer now than sigh, still hovering on the tip of her tongue. Charley pictured herself walking toward her mother and taking her in her arms, kissing her hair, as Sharon had done all those years ago, and telling her everything would be all right.

But instead she stayed rooted firmly to the spot, listening to her mother cry and wondering how it was that family members ever survived one another.

15

"Are you all right?"

Charley stood facing her brother on the other side of his screen door. The screen was torn in several places and the duct tape that had been carelessly applied had come loose and now hung down in a series of ineffectual strips.

Behind the screen, Bram appeared gray and grainy, like a character in an old black-and-white TV show. He kicked the door open with his bare foot. "I'm not hungover, if that's what you're asking. And I'm not stoned either," he said, anticipating her next question, and tucking the bottom of his white T-shirt into his low-slung jeans.

Charley stepped inside Bram's airless, one-bedroom apartment. "God, it's hot in here."

"It's hot outside."

She surreptitiously sniffed at the air for any leftover scent of marijuana, and eyed the rectangular glass coffee table in the center of the room for half-filled glasses of booze. But all she smelled was the scent of freshly brewed coffee, and all she saw on the table was an empty mug and half a buttered bagel. She exhaled, realizing in that instant that she'd been holding her breath all morning, that she'd pretty much been holding it since her brother had fled her house the previous night. What had she been expecting? she wondered, trying to get a handle on the situation, to figure out what her brother was really feeling behind the placid exterior of his beautiful face. She'd lain awake all night, anticipating a call from the police informing her that her brother had been arrested for driving drunk. Or worse. That there'd been an accident on I-95, and they needed her to identify the body. Or that they'd found him lying in an alley, like yesterday's garbage, a dirty needle still protruding from his outstretched arm. Had she driven down here this morning half-expecting to find him lying comatose in his bed, the victim of a fatal, self-administered overdose? "Don't you have a fan?"

"It's in the bedroom."

"You could bring it in here."

"I could."

"Are you all right?" she asked again.

"I'm fine." He shrugged. The shrug said, not so fine. "How are you?"

"Okay."

"Feel like a cup of coffee?"

"Sounds good."

It took only a handful of strides for Bram to reach the small space at the far end of the main room that served as a kitchen. It was perhaps twelve feet by three feet, and was separated from the living area by a high countertop, on which sat a small TV.

Charley sank down on the brown corduroy sofa across from the television, dropping her purse to the floor. She noted that the apartment was clean and tidy, and that the beige-and-brown shag rug that covered most of the living room floor appeared to have been newly vacuumed. While the off-white walls could stand a fresh coat of paint, the colorful prints Bram had chosen to hang on them were bright and cheery. There was a Jim Dine lithograph of a series of pastel-colored bathrobes, another of an orange-and-yellow Calder mobile, and a poster from the Museum of Modern Art in New York of a Picasso nude, the woman's body a series of sharp angles and intersecting arches. There were also three paintings Charley didn't recognize. She pushed herself off the sofa to get a better look, her eyes searching the vibrant swirls for a signature.

"Hope you like your coffee black," her brother said, checking the refrigerator. "I seem to be out of cream and sugar."

"Black's fine. Who did this painting?"

Her brother came up behind her. "Like it?"

"Very much. Where'd you get it?" She took the steaming cup of coffee from Bram's hands.

"I did it," he said, plopping down on the sofa, clearly enjoying the surprised look on his sister's face.

"**You** painted this?"

"Your son's not the only one with artistic talent, you know."

"When did you do it?"

"Last year. Another art course. I did those two as well." He indicated an abstract, pink and green rendering of a landscape, and another painting of a seemingly chaotic bunch of bright red twisting lines that, upon closer inspection, settled quite neatly into the face of a clown.

"These are wonderful, Bram."

"I wish you wouldn't sound quite so surprised."

"Why haven't I ever seen these before?"

"Probably because I just got around to hanging them last night."

"Last night?"

"I did some cleaning up. Part of the new me. Celebrating ten whole days of sobriety. I even decided to take a drive up to Palm Beach and visit my sister, tell her the good news." He smiled ruefully. "Guess that'll teach me to call in advance."

"It must have been quite a shock for you, seeing our mother like that."

"I guess it was bound to happen sooner or later."

"How'd you know it was her? You haven't seen her in . . ."

". . . twenty-two years?" Bram asked with a sardonic grin.

"Yet you knew right away who she was."

"Yeah, I did. Is that what they call maternal instinct? Oh, wait. That's what the mother is supposed to have."

"Bram . . ."

"The funny thing is that when I saw that purple Civic parked outside your house, I thought to myself, What kind of person drives a purple car?"

"She insists it's mauve," Charley said, returning to the sofa and sitting down beside Bram, taking a sip of her coffee. "This is delicious."

"Another one of my specialties."

"You're just full of surprises, aren't you?"

"As are you. Driving down to Miami on a Thursday morning just to check on little old me. Shouldn't you be at work?"

"You don't think this is work?" Charley asked.

"So how did the lady with the purple car react to the fleeting vision of her son?" Bram asked after a lengthy pause.

"She was pretty shaken up."

"Bet she got over it pretty quick though, didn't she?"

"I'm not so sure."

"I am."

"The last time she saw you, you were in diapers."

"Well, there you go. Haven't changed a bit."

"**She** has."

"The only thing that's changed is circumstance. She's older now and all alone. The minute something—**someone**—better comes along, she'll be out of here, and you know it."

"I don't know it."

"Yes, you do. Why are you defending her?"

"I'm not defending her."

"How can you even stand to be in the same room with her?"

"She's our mother."

"Bullshit! You were more of a mother to me than she ever was."

"She's really sorry, Bram."

"She's a selfish bitch. I don't understand how you can just forgive and forget."

"Trust me, I haven't forgotten."

"But you **have** managed to forgive?"

"Yes. No," she corrected immediately. "I don't know," she amended further. "I'm trying."

"Why?"

"Because as angry as I was, as I still am, that's

how sorry she is, how much she wants to make things right."

"Yeah, well, she's a few decades late for that."

"If you'd just see her, talk to her. . . ."

"The last thing I intend to do is talk to that woman."

"That woman is your mother."

"Yeah? Well, maybe I don't need a mother anymore. I've gotten pretty used to life without one."

"If you'd just give her a chance. Give **yourself** a chance. You don't have to love her. You don't even have to like her."

"Good. 'Cause I hate her guts." He laughed, the hollow sound chipping at the air, like a pick through a block of ice. "That sounded very mature, don't you think?"

"What I think doesn't matter."

"What does?"

"**You** do."

"You're saying this is one of those 'You can't truly make plans for the future until you make peace with the past' kind of deals?"

"It's not as trite as you make it sound."

"Yeah? 'Cause it **does** sound kind of trite."

"Bram . . ."

"Look. I coped pretty well last night, didn't I? I didn't leave your house and head straight for the nearest bar. I didn't call my friendly neighborhood dealer. You know who I **did** call?

I called my sponsor," he continued, then smiled shyly. "Did I forget to mention I joined AA?"

Charley burst into a flood of grateful tears.

"Oh, no. Don't cry. Come on, Charley. It's okay." He took the cup of coffee from her shaking hands and wrapped his arms around her. "Please don't cry. I'm useless when a woman cries."

"Why didn't you tell me?"

He shrugged. "I wanted to see if I could make a go of it. And you gotta try not to get too excited about it. Ten days is not a big deal."

"It's a very big deal."

"There are probably going to be relapses. I'm going to try really hard, but I can't make any more promises I can't keep. It's like they say— one day at a time."

"One day at a time," Charley repeated.

There was a long pause. "I'm just not ready to deal with her yet," Bram said finally.

"I understand."

"Maybe one day."

"Whenever you're ready."

"You can tell her I'm all right," he said. "Tell her I didn't freak out or anything."

"I will." They sat together in silence for several minutes, Bram's arms encircling his older sister, their bodies rocking gently back and forth. Eventually, Charley's eyes drifted back to the paintings on the wall. "Those are really amazing, you know that?"

"You think only the Brontë sisters have talent?"

Charley squeezed her brother's hand. "Anne sent me a copy of her book."

"Really? I had to buy mine."

"You actually went out and bought it?"

"It was on sale at Costco."

"Did you read it?"

"Yeah."

"And?"

"I liked it," he admitted sheepishly. "What can I say? I'm a romantic."

Charley kissed her brother's cheek. "God, you're sweet."

A loud wolf whistle cut through the airless room.

"What the hell is that?" Bram jumped to his feet.

"Relax. It's just my cell phone." Charley was laughing as she reached into her purse and retrieved her phone. "Hello?"

"Charley?" the woman's voice asked tentatively. "Is that you?"

Charley hunched forward in her seat and lowered her voice. "Jill?"

"Am I getting you at a bad time?"

Charley looked at her brother, who was regarding her with a mixture of curiosity and concern. "No, it's fine. Is everything all right?"

"Everything's great."

"Good."

"Can you talk?"

Again Charley looked at her brother, thinking she should probably conduct this conversation in private.

Understanding her need for privacy, he whispered, "Why don't you go into the bedroom? It's cooler in there anyway."

"Be right back," she mouthed, pushing herself off the couch and heading toward the small room to the right of the kitchen. "Okay," she said as she sank into the blue comforter that covered the double bed. A soft breeze from the fan in front of the window blew gently on her neck.

"Are you at work? It sounds like I'm getting you away from something," Jill said.

"No. Actually, I'm at my brother's."

"Oh, that's nice. How is he?" Jill asked, as if she and Bram were old acquaintances.

"He's fine."

"Does he remember my sister?"

"Yes, of course. He told me they went out a few times."

"Did he like her?"

"We didn't really get into it."

"Well, say hi to him for me. Tell him I'm really excited to be collaborating with his sister."

"Has something happened, Jill? Is that why you're calling?"

"Oh, no. Is that what you think? That I'm in some sort of trouble?"

"Are you?"

"No. Everything's great."

Everything's great, Charley repeated in her head. The second time Jill had said that. Charley thought it an odd choice of words to describe living on death row.

"I mean, considering," Jill amended, as if understanding Charley's silence. "No, I'm just calling because they said I could use the phone this morning, and you said if I ever wanted to talk, or anything . . ."

"Of course." Charley glanced around the room for a pen and some paper so that she could take notes. But there was nothing on top of the bureau that stood against the far wall except a hairbrush and a spray can of deodorant, and the only things on the lone nightstand beside the bed were a photograph of Franny and James, and a copy of Anne's book, **Remember Love**. Charley thought of the small tape recorder that was sitting on her own bureau in her bedroom at home. **Don't leave home without it**, she told herself, catching sight of her pronounced frown in the mirror over the bureau before opening the

single drawer of the nightstand and absently rifling through it. "What did you want to talk
about?" She located a pencil, but its point was
broken, and she tossed it back inside the drawer.
There was no paper, nothing at all to write on.

"Well, it's just that after you left yesterday, I
started thinking."

"About . . . ?"

"The things I said. And especially about some
of the stuff I wrote in my last letter."

"It wasn't true?" Charley noticed a photograph lying facedown at the rear of the drawer
and decided she could write on the back of it,
presuming, of course, she could find something
to write with.

"Oh, no. Everything I've told you was the
God's honest truth," Jill replied, and Charley
pictured the young woman's eyes opening wide
as her hand reached up to pull at the elastic in
her hair. "It's just that I'm afraid I might have
given you the wrong idea."

"How so?" Charley was about to return to the
living room to get her purse when she discovered
a ballpoint pen lying next to an old pipe. She automatically lifted the pipe to her nose, inhaled
the stale odor of hashish. **Stale**, she reminded
herself, putting it back, then clicking open the
pen and balancing the phone on her left shoulder as she began scribbling on the back of the
photograph: **Phone call from Jill at 10:45** A.M.,

Thursday. Afraid she gave me the wrong impression during our meeting.

"Well, I think I painted a pretty negative picture of my family."

"It wasn't that way?"

"It wasn't **all** that way," Jill qualified.

"Well, yes, you told me there were some good times. The trip to Disney World when your father called you 'cupcake.'" And your brother raped your sister in the next bed, she added silently.

"Yeah. Like that. I mean, my father's not exactly Mr. Softie or anything, but he has his moments, you know. My mother always called him a 'diamond in the rough.' You know what that means?"

A diamond in the rough, Charley managed to write down before the pen started running out of ink. "I believe it takes a lump of coal several thousand years to turn into a diamond," Charley said, searching the drawer for another pen, and locating one underneath a second photograph. She removed both the pen and the photo from the drawer, and found herself staring at a picture of a grinning, dark-skinned boy, about six years old. Who was he? she wondered, flipping over the picture she'd been writing on and seeing the wide smile of a little girl, her round, brown face framed by an avalanche of cornrows, each secured by a small, bright red bow. "I'm sorry. Did you say something?" she asked, realizing Jill had been speaking.

"I said, are you suggesting my daddy's like a lump of coal?" Jill repeated, laughing.

Who were the children in these photographs? Charley wondered, flipping over the picture again, and waiting to write. "It means he needs some polishing to really shine."

Jill laughed again. "That's a good way of putting it. Anybody ever told you you should be a writer?"

"What about your mother?"

"My mother?"

"Tell me more about her. I know she has MS. . . ."

"My mom is great. Don't start on my mom."

"I wasn't."

"She did the best she could."

"I'm sure she did."

Why are you defending her? Charley heard Bram say.

"I mean, it couldn't have been easy for her, what with my dad's temper and Ethan being just like him. And like I told you, I was a handful. There wasn't much she could do. She was always trying to keep the peace, make everybody happy."

"Did she know about what Ethan was doing?"

"What do you mean?"

"Did she know what he was doing to you and your sister?"

A slight pause, then, "We never told her, if that's what you're getting at."

"It's not."

"You're saying you think she knew?"

"I don't know. I guess I'm asking what **you** think."

"I think I'm beginning to feel sorry I called."

"Don't be. I'm really glad you did."

"Why do you have to ask so many stupid damn questions? Why can't you just listen, for a change?"

Very defensive about her mother, Charley wrote, underlining **very** several times. "I'm sorry. I won't ask anything else."

"I think even if she **did** know, there wasn't a damn thing she could do about it."

"I'm sure you're right."

"How can you be so damn sure about everything?"

"I'm really not."

"Especially when you don't know shit."

The line went dead.

"Okay," Charley said, sitting very still. "Okay." After several minutes she pushed herself off the bed and returned to the living room.

"Everything all right?" her brother asked.

"Apparently I don't know shit."

"I could have told you that."

"Thanks. Anyway, I have to get back to work. Oh, I wrote on the back of these." She held up the two photographs. "Is that a problem?"

Bram squinted toward the pictures. "Nah. They're just some neighborhood kids I was thinking of painting."

"Cute kids," Charley said, dropping the pictures inside her purse, and walking toward the screen door.

"Thanks for coming by," Bram said, leaning over to kiss her cheek.

"Will you at least think about seeing our mother?" Charley asked.

"Thanks for coming by," Bram said again, as the screen door shut firmly in Charley's face.

16

WEBB SITE

My mother and I recently engaged in a freewheeling discussion about nature versus nurture. More specifically, which n-word is responsible for one's sexual preferences. The accepted wisdom of the day, of course, holds that one's sexuality is as innate as the color of one's eyes. But is it as simple as that? Think of the thousands of men and women in prison who turn to the same sex for a little comfort and relief—or power and intimidation, as the case may be—only to revert immediately to the opposite sex upon release. (What's that old saying?

"If you can't be with the one you love, love the one you're with"?) And what of choice? Do we have no say in the matter at all?

My mother says we do. At least she says that **women** do. And before I get a barrage of e-mail from religious fundamentalists seeking to recruit her in an effort to save these poor, misguided sapphists from themselves, let me state that for a long time, my mother also chose to be gay. She argues—quite convincingly, I might add—that people are more than what they choose to do with their genitals, and that while there are lots of lesbians, possibly even the majority, who are, in fact, born to love other women, there are also many who, whether by chance or design, **decide** to love other women. They've been abused or mistreated, overlooked or shunned. For whatever reason, they've had it with men. They're looking for a little warmth, and if the body that comes with it looks suspiciously like their own, well, it might take a little getting used to, but ultimately, that's okay. Women are used to getting used to things. We're good at adapting to circumstance.

While it now seems my mother has chosen to revert to the straight and narrow, for twenty years she boldly chose to be gay. She also chose to be absent from her children's lives, which won't exactly win her any prizes for mother of the year. But what exactly makes a good mother anyway? Again, it comes down to the choices we make.

I'm reminded of a story a neighbor told me a while back. She was on a plane coming back from somewhere, and she had the misfortune to be seated next to a big bear of a man and his young son. Soon after takeoff, the boy started squirming, and his father told him gruffly to sit still. The boy protested that his father's wide girth was spilling over onto his seat and not leaving him enough room. The father told him to "shut up unless he wanted his ass kicked." The son, proclaiming he knew his rights, then threatened to call 911. At that point, the father walloped him. My neighbor called the stewardess and requested a seat change. The boy's mother, who, it turned out, was sitting in the row directly behind, quickly agreed to change seats. As they made the switch, my neighbor overheard the boy's mother pleading with her son to listen to his father.

Is this a nurturing mother? Is it part of a woman's nature to placate and make nice? True, she didn't abandon her son, at least not physically, but what message is she giving him? That it's okay to bully and berate someone because he's smaller and more defenseless than you are? That might is right? She would undoubtedly argue that she had no choice, that she was as defenseless as her son, that to stand up to her husband at that moment meant a beating later on. But the truth is that she did have a choice, as all adults do, and it's a mother's job to protect her children, even when it means putting herself in harm's way.

I've been thinking a lot about child abuse these days, and I just can't get my head around it. Why have children if you're going to mistreat them? It's not as if we don't have options. We can choose from multiple forms of birth control, or we can choose to abort or put unplanned babies up for adoption, give those innocent children the chance for a stable and loving home. Instead, too often we choose to bring children into unloving and downright hostile environments, with parents who are too poorly equipped, or just too emotionally unavailable, to care for them.

I'm not talking here about teenage mothers on welfare, who have been maligned enough. Most of these girls are only looking for someone to love and love them in return, and many are the products of abuse themselves. The majority of these young women try really hard to be good mothers for their babies, but their choices are limited at best. The approval they've been seeking all their lives has been transferred from errant boyfriends to needy offspring, and when that child cries all night, it's easy to hear those cries as a rebuke. "You're not a good mother," those cries repeat over and over again, confirming their worst fears. Sometimes, it's easy to strike out.

So what stops one person from lashing out and drives another to pick up that screaming infant and shake it so hard its neck snaps? Are some people just more violent by nature, or have they been raised in households where violence has been nurtured? Abuse is a communicable disease, one that gets transferred from one generation to the next. It can turn deadly at any time.

I could argue that my mother may have abandoned me, but hey, at least she didn't beat me. You could counter that while your mother might have beaten you, hell, at least she was there. The debate is as endless, and ultimately as pointless, as the debate over nature versus nurture. What matters ultimately is **how** we choose to live our lives. We don't get to choose our parents. We **do** get to choose the kind of parents we will be. And as bystanders, we also have a choice: to stand up to injustice whenever and wherever we witness it, or just change seats and do nothing.

The knocking on Charley's door was as ferocious and insistent as it was unexpected. It was barely nine o'clock on a Sunday morning, too early for anyone to come calling. Charley put down her coffee cup, pushed aside the morning paper she'd been perusing—she always liked to get a feel for the way her col-

umns read in actual newsprint—and made sure
the belt on her blue terry-cloth bathrobe was
secure, then left the kitchen table and walked
down the hallway toward the front of the
house. "Who is it?" she asked, glancing toward
the children's bedroom, where Franny and
James were playing a new board game her
mother had bought them.

"It's Lynn," came the angry response. "Open
the door. I have a bone to pick with you."

Charley closed her eyes, took a deep breath,
forced a smile onto her lips, and opened the
door. It was "déjà vu all over again," she thought,
seeing Lynn Moore standing on the single outside step, waving today's paper in her face, the
crystal studs in her long, red fingernails flashing
before Charley's eyes like tiny squares in a revolving disco ball. Her dark hair had been
stuffed into a lopsided twist at the top of her
head, threatening at any moment to burst loose
of its many bobby pins. "Another one?" Charley
asked wearily.

"Don't you have anybody else to torture?"

"You didn't like my column," Charley stated
rather than asked.

"What is it you have against me anyway?"

Charley felt her shoulders slump. "Would you
like to come inside?"

"No, I don't want to come inside."

"I've made some fresh coffee."

"I don't want any coffee. I don't want anything from you except to be left alone."

"And yet, here you are," Charley pointed out.

"It wasn't bad enough that you've already
portrayed me as some pathetic sex maniac . . ."

"I never said . . ."

"Now, I'm irresponsible as well."

"What are you talking about?"

"What was I supposed to do?" Lynn continued, as if Charley hadn't spoken. "I was squeezed
into my seat beside this big brute of a guy whose
entire demeanor screamed 'Don't mess with me,'
and what am I supposed to do when he starts
slapping his kid around? I called the stewardess
over, told her what was going on, and she advised me to change my seat. So, I'm asking you,
what was I supposed to do?"

"I don't know."

"The hell you don't," Lynn exclaimed, waving
the morning paper in Charley's face. "According
to little Miss Know-It-All, I was supposed to
stand up to the injustice I was witness to, forget
about the fact I'm crammed into a confined
space thirty-seven thousand feet above sea level,
and nobody else on the damn plane has witnessed the abuse."

"I wasn't specifically referring to you," Charley hedged.

"You most certainly were. Who else told you
that story?"

"I was trying to make a point."

"Oh, you made it all right. 'As bystanders, we have a choice. To stand up for injustice or just change seats and do nothing.' Tell me, don't you ever get tired of passing judgment on people?"

"I wasn't trying to pass judgment."

"No, you don't have to try. It comes naturally to you. You're a real piece of work, you know that?"

"Mommy?" a frightened voice said from behind her.

Charley turned around to see Franny swaying unsteadily in the kitchen doorway, her eyes wide with trepidation. "It's okay, sweetie. Mrs. Moore's just upset."

"At you?"

"It's all right, Franny," Lynn told the child. "I'm going now. Just do me a favor," she said to Charley. "Stop using my life as fodder for your column."

"Thanks for coming by," Charley whispered, echoing Bram's words as she closed the door, then turned back toward her daughter.

"Why doesn't anybody like you?" Franny asked.

"What? Who says nobody likes me?"

"Everybody's always yelling at you."

"No, they aren't."

Franny looked unconvinced. "I heard Elise talking to Daddy."

Charley knelt down in front of her daughter, smoothed some stray hairs away from her forehead. "What did she say?"

"She said that the only person you care about is yourself." Tears began forming in the corners of Franny's eyes, as if she sensed she was being disloyal to her mother merely by repeating the things Ray's wife had said.

"What else did she say?"

"That you were 'selfish beyond words.'"

"Wow. Beyond words."

"What does that mean?"

Charley gave the expression a moment's thought. "It means there are no words to describe how selfish she thinks I am."

"But you aren't. Are you?"

"No, I'm not," Charley agreed. Was she?

"Are you a real piece of work?"

Charley laughed. "Let's just say I'm a work-in-progress."

"What does that mean?"

"It means I still haven't got all the kinks out. But I'm trying my best."

"I don't think you're selfish beyond words."

"Thank you, darling. I appreciate that."

"What do you 'preciate?" James asked, running into the hallway and throwing himself against his mother and sister with such force, it knocked all three of them over.

Charley quickly scooped her two children into her lap. "I 'preciate my two beautiful angels."

"I'm not an angel, silly," James said, laughing.

"He's a work-in-progress," Franny proclaimed with a shy smile.

"I love you both so much," Charley told them, kissing them repeatedly until they'd had enough and squirmed out of her reach.

"How much?" James squealed, running down the hall backward.

Charley threw her arms out to her sides, stretched her fingers out as far as they would go. "This much." Laughing and crying at the same time, she watched her children disappear inside the bedroom. Beyond words, she thought.

An hour later, the doorbell rang. "Dear God," Charley muttered. "What now?" She approached the front door cautiously. "Who is it?"

"It's Glen McLaren."

Charley pulled open the door. He really **does** look like a gangster, she couldn't help but think. Had he come to collect on the debt of gratitude she owed him? What exactly was he expecting? "Well, this is a surprise."

"A not unpleasant one, I hope. Is this a bad time?"

Correct use of the double negative, she thought, stepping aside to let him enter. "Coffee?" she asked, although it meant making a fresh pot. After Lynn's visit, she'd downed three hot cups in quick succession, burning the roof of her mouth.

"No, thanks." He made no attempt to move farther inside than the foyer, his eyes flitting between the interior of the house and his silver Mercedes on the street. "Where's James?"

"Playing Monopoly with his sister," Charley said, signaling toward the bedrooms. "You want me to get him?"

"No. It's you I came to see." He glanced back at his car. Was he afraid someone might vandalize it?

"Oh?"

"I was hoping to collect on that debt you owe me."

Charley glanced nervously toward the bedrooms. "Now?"

"Now seems like a good time to me."

"What exactly is it you have in mind?"

"Do you like dogs?" Glen asked.

"Dogs?"

"Specifically, little white mutts named Bandit that don't shed and aren't yappy, but **are** housebroken, and will be **heart**broken, if they have to stay in a kennel for the next three weeks."

"You have a little white dog named Bandit?"

"He was a gift from a rather misguided former girlfriend."

"Of course he was."

"But I promise you he's fully trained, and he won't be any trouble."

"You're asking me to look after your dog for three weeks?"

"I'm going to North Carolina to be with my son while his mother takes her belated honeymoon, and the person who was supposed to be looking after Bandit, well, let's just say we had a slight disagreement, and she never wants to see me or my dog again."

"Interesting."

"It isn't really. But Bandit is. Trust me, you'll love him so much you won't want to give him back."

Charley wasn't sure how to respond. "It's not that I'm saying I won't do it," she hedged, "but I'm not exactly a dog person. I've actually never had a pet in my entire life. I wouldn't know the first thing . . ."

"The first thing is to remember to feed him every morning and give him fresh water. And then, just repeat the same thing at night. Take him for a few walks in between. He's still a puppy, so it's probably a good idea to take him out every few hours to do his business. You just plop him down on a spot of grass and tell him to 'do busy,' and he does."

"**Do busy?**"

"I know it sounds silly. . . ."

"It really **does** sound silly."

"It also really works."

"But I'm not even home most of the day."

"When you're not home, he stays in his crate and sleeps. He sleeps in there at night too, and he never cries. I promise. Honestly, he pretty much takes care of himself."

A dog, Charley thought, almost wishing it had been Lynn at her door again, and not Glen. What was she going to do with a dog? For three weeks! Still, he'd taken her son to Lion Country Safari without so much as a grumble. . . . "Is he okay with children?"

"Are you kidding? He loves children."

"James can be pretty rambunctious."

"He loves rambunctious."

"Well, all right," Charley conceded. "I guess we can manage for three weeks."

"Thank you, thank you, thank you." Glen was already opening the front door. "I'll go get him."

"What?"

"He's in the car."

"You left him in the car?" Charley followed Glen outside and down the front walk.

"Don't worry. I left the windows open. See how good he is?" he asked, as they reached his Mercedes.

A little, white furry head popped into view. A tail began wagging furiously.

"It's okay, buddy," Glen said as the dog jumped up and down on the black leather seat. "See? I told you I'd be right back." He opened the door and lifted the excited furball into his arms. The dog immediately began licking his neck.

"This is killing your image," Charley said.

Glen laughed. "Say hi to Charley, Bandit. She's gonna look after you for the next three weeks." He transferred the squirming dog to Charley's arms. The dog responded by immediately quieting down, burrowing into Charley's neck, and laying his chin across her shoulder. "Well, well, well. Aren't you the lucky one."

"I'm lucky?"

"When a dog lays his head on your shoulder like that, it means he'll bond with you for life."

"We're bonding?"

"For life."

"For three weeks," Charley stressed as Glen removed a large box of Bandit's belongings from the trunk. "What's all this?"

"His crate, his food, his dish, his leash, his toys—the squeaky hamburger is his favorite— the phone number of the vet. . . ."

"Oh, God. I don't think I can do this."

"Are you kidding me? Anyone who can handle Jill Rohmer can surely handle a little dog for a few weeks."

"Who says I'm handling Jill Rohmer?" Charley followed Glen back up the walkway to her house.

"You're not doing the book?"

Charley shrugged as Glen opened the front door and deposited the box of Bandit's things in the foyer. "Truthfully, I'm not sure where things stand at the moment. Last time we spoke, she hung up on me."

"Nice to see you're not losing your touch." A mischievous smile tugged at his lips. "What's she like anyway?"

"I don't know," Charley replied honestly. "I'm not sure what to make of her. One minute she's like this lost little girl, all soft edges and vulnerability—you literally have to pinch yourself to remember she was involved in the deaths of three innocent children—and the next minute she gets this weird look in her eyes, like she's measuring you for a casket, and you believe she could be capable of anything."

"Sounds intriguing."

"I don't know. Her lawyer might be right. He doesn't think I'm the right one for the job."

"Then he's wrong," Glen said. "And who are you going to believe—some high-priced attorney with a handful of impressive degrees or a gangster-wannabe with an adorable white puppy? The choice is pretty clear, if you ask me."

Charley laughed, felt the puppy snuggle in

even tighter against her neck. "You're sure there's nothing wrong with this dog?"

"Are you kidding me? He's in heaven. What guy wouldn't be?"

Charley took a step back, as if to distance herself from the compliment, not to mention the man, who was becoming more attractive each time she saw him. Was this business with the puppy just a ruse to disarm her, a way to seduce and then dump her, to get back at her for the mean things she'd said about him in her column? Just because she wasn't into revenge fucking didn't mean he wasn't. "Well, enjoy your visit with your son."

"Thanks. I intend to."

"Call me as soon as you get back. About picking up your dog," she qualified immediately.

"I'll do that. Bye, Bandit." He walked around Charley in order to give Bandit a peck on his forehead. "Take care," he said to Charley.

Charley found herself half-anticipating a similar peck on the forehead, and was almost disappointed when Glen merely patted her arm before climbing back into his car and pulling away from the curb, his left hand extended out the window in a prolonged wave good-bye. As he turned the corner at the end of the street, she lowered Bandit to the grass, shrugged, and said, "What the hell. **Do busy.**"

The dog sniffed around for several seconds,

found a patch of grass to his liking, then lifted his leg and promptly peed.

"Amazing." Charley scooped the puppy back into her arms just as Gabe Lopez opened his front door and glared in her direction. "Mr. Lopez, good morning," she called out, determining to make a fresh start while waving hello with her free hand.

"Just keep the dog off my lawn," he said, before closing the door and retreating back inside his house.

17

FROM: A new fan
TO: Charley@Charley'sWeb.com
SUBJECT: Great column!
DATE: Mon. 12 Feb. 2007, 9:06:24–0400

Dear Charley: Wow! That was some column in yesterday's paper. Couldn't wait to get to work this morning to thank you for it. As a social worker, I thought your main points were very well taken. My colleagues and I have spent far too much time debating the issue of nature versus nurture, and our final consensus is, what difference does it make? What's important isn't so much causes as results. What's needed isn't argument but tolerance. Maybe if we were all more accepting and respectful of one another's differences, there wouldn't be any such thing as child abuse.

Sincerely,
Kara Stephenson

FROM: Charley Webb
TO: Kara Stephenson
SUBJECT: Thank you
DATE: Mon. 12 Feb. 2007, 9:08:16–0800

Dear Kara: Thanks so much for your kind note. It's nice to be appreciated. I hope you continue to read and enjoy my columns.
  Warmly,
  Charley Webb

FROM: Alarmed
TO: Charley@Charley'sWeb.com
SUBJECT: Your recent column
DATE: Mon. 12 Feb. 2007, 9:14:02–0500

Dear Charley Webb,
  I've always approached your columns with a mixture of glee and trepidation. Who will you be skewering today and why? What have you done to your body now? What thoughts are swirling through that pretty little head? So, imagine my chagrin at your most recent column, which was not only thought-provoking, but thoughtful as well. I hope this doesn't mean you've abandoned your more selfish, pardon me, selfless pursuits, such

as Brazilian waxes and Passion Parties—all in the name of research, to be sure—for more important, but far less entertaining subjects, such as child abuse. While I applaud your, no doubt, deep commitment to social justice, I yearn for the shallower Charley of old. Please don't disappoint me again.

   Arnold Lawrence

FROM: Charley Webb
TO: Arnold Lawrence
SUBJECT: Thanks, but no thanks
DATE: Mon. 12 Feb. 2007, 9:20:20–0800

Dear Alarmed Arnold,

   I've read your letter several times now, and I'm still not sure whether to be flattered or insulted. While it's always nice to be considered attractive, I'm dismayed you consider me little more than a decorative empty shell. And while I'm delighted you enjoy my columns, I'm disappointed you find them shallow. Just because something is entertaining doesn't necessarily make it less worthy, any more than the reporting of a serious subject makes the reporter a person of consequence. Rest assured that I will continue to write about subjects that concern and intrigue me. Likely some will be of a serious nature; others will not. All will strive to provide food for thought and discussion. I hope you'll continue to look forward to them with your usual mixture of glee and trepidation.

Sincerely,
Charley Webb

FROM: Sheryl Volpe
TO: Charley@Charley'sWeb.com
SUBJECT: A personal pet peeve
DATE: Mon. 12 Feb. 2007, 9:32:59–0400

Dear Charley—I've been reading you ever since you started at the **Post**, and I find your columns to be insightful, well written, and timely. Surprisingly, one of the things you have yet to address, although you kind of alluded to it in yesterday's column about the father abusing his son, is my own personal pet peeve: overweight people on airplanes! Is there anything more aggravating than paying full price for a ticket and ending up with only half a seat because somebody who can't control his appetite is spilling over into your space? That alone would have prompted me to demand a seat change! I'd love to see your views on this subject.

Yours truly,
Sheryl Volpe

FROM: An understanding reader
TO: Charley@Charley'sWeb.com
SUBJECT: Your mother
DATE: Mon. 12 Feb. 2007, 9:42:13–0500

Poor, dear Charley: Finally we understand what has made you the way you are! Your mother! What a horrible and disgusting woman she is! She truly needs guidance, as do you, the helpless victim of her amoral indoctrination. There is a reason why God-fearing people everywhere vilify those who would pervert the will of the Lord. God himself decreed that these degenerates should be put to death. Your mother must renounce her evil ways, and until she does, you have no choice but to renounce her. I will pray for your souls.

God be with you,
An understanding reader

Charley was trying to come up with clever responses to the last two e-mails when the phone on her desk rang. "Charley Webb."

"Hi," came the clear, semifamiliar voice.

Charley tried to attach a face to it before the caller spoke again, but was unsuccessful.

"It's Emily," the woman said after a pause. "Your sister," she added, enunciating each word clearly, as if speaking into a microphone.

Immediately the image of a beautiful young woman with strong, elegant features and chin-length, straight blond hair pushed itself before Charley's eyes. "Emily! My God! How are you?"

"Very well, thank you. And you?"

"I'm great. Well, a little tired, I guess. I agreed to look after a friend's puppy for a few weeks, and he's supposed to sleep in his crate, but he was up most of the night crying, until I finally moved him into my bed, where he insisted on squeezing right up against my leg, and I guess I'm just not used to sharing my space. . . ." What was the matter with her? She hadn't spoken to her sister in almost two years. Why was she rambling on about the damn dog? "How **are** you?" she asked again.

"Still very well," her sister replied coolly. "Look, I understand you've spoken to Anne."

"A few weeks ago, yes. Why? Is something wrong?"

"No, of course not. Everything's fine. Her new book is number two on the **New York Times** bestseller list."

"That's wonderful."

"Have you read it yet?"

"I'm hoping to get to it this weekend." Charley's eyes rolled toward the ceiling. "Bram read it, though. He really liked it."

"Was he stoned at the time?"

"No. Why? Is it that bad?"

"Dad says it's execrable twaddle."

"Sounds like something he'd say. What's **your** opinion?"

"Twaddle, but not execrable," Emily pronounced.

"High praise indeed."

"How **is** Bram anyway?"

"Good. He's been clean and sober for more than ten days now."

"Ten whole days. Wow." Emily was clearly less than impressed. "And Franny and James? Everybody well?"

"They're terrific. And Catherine?"

"Growing like a weed. Anne tell you she's letting A.J. have the kids?"

"What do you mean?" Charley remembered A.J.'s threat to sue for custody of Darcy and Tess if Anne refused to pay him alimony. "You're saying she's calling his bluff?"

"No. She's giving him full custody. Says she

travels so much these days, and when she **is** home, she's working, doing interviews, etc., etc. She thinks they'll be better off with him."

"But that's ridiculous."

"No, that's Anne. Or rather, that's Elizabeth. You're still in touch with our mother, I take it."

"She'll be devastated when she hears this."

"Are you kidding? It's a total affirmation of her child-rearing techniques."

"Should I call Anne? Try to change her mind?"

"Oh, that'll go over big, you being so close and all."

"But she's making a huge mistake. You know that."

"Maybe. Maybe not. Anyway, it's not the reason I called."

"What is?"

"It's this **People** thing."

"What people?" Charley asked, still reeling from Emily's announcement. How could Anne even be considering giving up her children after everything they'd gone through themselves?

"**People** magazine. This story they want to do."

Charley vaguely remembered Anne having mentioned something about this. "The whole Brontë thing," she said.

"Right. Apparently they don't normally do authors because they're kind of boring, but

Anne's an exception because of the mess with A.J., and because I'm on TV. . . ."

"I'm really sorry I missed your spot on **Good Morning America**," Charley interjected.

"No big deal. Anyway," Emily continued, "once **People** heard that you're a writer too, and that your name is Charlotte, well, how could they resist? So now they're gung-ho to do the piece, and they want to interview all of us as soon as possible. They were thinking that since Anne is going to Palm Beach as part of her speaking tour, we could all meet there."

A million questions raced through Charley's mind. Only one emerged. "When?"

"The date still hasn't been finalized. But probably sometime in the next couple of weeks. I'll have to get back to you with the exact time and place."

"You really think this is a good idea?" Charley asked. The three sisters hadn't been in the same room together in too long to remember.

"Are you kidding? You can't buy publicity like this. Think of the exposure, not to mention where it could lead. **Good Morning America** is already considering doing a segment about us. Anything's possible. Even **Oprah**."

A story in **People** certainly wouldn't hurt her chances of interesting publishers in her book on Jill Rohmer, Charley recognized. They'd be lining up, dangling huge advances in front of her eyes. An appearance on **Oprah** would probably land the book on everybody's must-read list. She'd be rich and famous, not to mention sought-after and respected. All she had to do was say yes. "What about Bram?" she said instead.

"Bram? What about him?"

"Well, aside from the fact he's our brother, he's also a very talented painter. Will he be involved?"

"He doesn't exactly fit the story," Emily said, "but I'm sure he'll get some sort of mention."

"He gets more than a mention," Charley insisted with surprising force.

"We don't get to control the content, Charley."

"What about our mother?" Charley side-stepped.

"She has nothing to do with this." Emily's well-trained, mellifluous tones turned hard and cold.

Charley could see her sister biting the side of her bottom lip, the way she used to do as a child, whenever she was upset about something. "She has everything to do with this," Charley told her. "There wouldn't be three sisters named Charlotte, Emily, and Anne if it weren't for her."

"Just what are you getting at?" Emily asked impatiently.

What **was** she getting at? "I'll do the interview on two conditions."

"Two conditions," Emily repeated incredulously.

"One, that Bram is an equal part of the proceedings."

"You really think he'll still be sober by then?" Emily interrupted to ask.

". . . and two, that you and Anne agree to meet with our mother while you're here."

"What? No way."

"Then I'm not interested."

"You're crazy. This story could put you on the map. It's the chance of a lifetime."

"There'll be other chances." Would there be? What was she doing?

There was a long pause. "I'll have to get back to you." Emily hung up before Charley could say good-bye.

Charley replaced the receiver, then stared at her computer screen in shock. What the hell had she just done? Had she really put the biggest opportunity of her career in jeopardy with her unreasonable set of demands? Who was she to dictate anything to anyone? Her sisters had chosen sides, just as she had. Who was she to tell them they owed their mother a second chance? Emily was right. She **was** crazy.

Charley absently scrolled down the list of new e-mails that had come in while she was on the phone, bringing the latest one up on her screen.

FROM: A person of taste
TO: Charley@Charley'sWeb.com
SUBJECT: Your recent column
DATE: Mon. 12 Feb. 2007, 9:53:01–0400

Dear Charley,
   It seems some people never learn! After I wrote you last time, I thought there was a chance, just a chance, mind you, that you might actually consider what I had to say, and do something to mend your ways. Your column about excess spending was a definite move in the right direction, and gave me reason to be hopeful. But sadly, it appears I WAS WRONG!!! You are as STUPID and FOUL-MOUTHED as ever! How dare you rub your mother's SICK and PERVERTED behavior in our faces. That she likes to EAT PUSSY is DISGUSTING enough, but the joy you take in reporting it is almost too much for any DECENT individual to bear. I can no longer feel even a modicum of sympathy for you. **YOU DE-SERVE TO DIE!**
   P.S.: Don't fool yourself that your children will be spared. They won't be.

   "Oh, no," Charley whispered into the palm of her hand. She immediately forwarded copies of the e-mail to both Mitchell Johnson and Michael Duff, then sank back in her chair and read the letter again and again until she could recite it by heart. "You sick bastard. How dare you!" She reached into her desk, found the card Officer Jennifer Ramirez had given her, and called her cell phone. But the policewoman was unavailable, and Charley could only leave a message on her voice mail. "Damn it! Damn it!" she railed, getting up and turning in helpless circles behind her chair.

The phone rang. Charley pounced on it. "Hello? Officer Ramirez?"

"Alex Prescott," the man answered. "Is this a bad time?"

Charley took a few seconds to catch her breath and try to calm herself down. "No, it's . . . I just had a rather unpleasant e-mail."

"What do you mean, unpleasant?"

"The usual: I'm stupid and disgusting and deserve to die."

"That definitely qualifies as unpleasant."

"You ever get e-mail like that?"

"Occasionally. My favorite ones are the ones that quote Shakespeare. You know the line about, 'First, we kill all the lawyers'?"

"Really?" Charley realized she was smiling, and wasn't sure why she should be taking so much comfort in the fact that Alex's life had been threatened, too. "So you don't think I have anything to worry about?"

"I'm sure it's just an empty threat."

"It also threatened my children," she said, hearing her voice break.

"Then I think you should phone the police."

"I've done that. I was just waiting for them to call back."

"I'll call you another time," he offered.

"No, that's okay. What's up?" Had Jill contacted him, told him she was upset about their little spat, and that she wanted to bring in another writer?

"Jill's sister, Pam, has agreed to meet with you."

"Really? When?"

"Unfortunately it has to be this weekend. Her father and brother will be out of town, and she'll only talk to us when they're not around."

"I'll see what I can arrange."

"You'll let me know as soon as possible?"

"Absolutely." Charley hung up the phone. It rang again immediately. "Officer Ramirez?"

"Not quite," her sister replied, each word a block of ice.

"Emily?"

"I've talked to Anne," she said. "You've got a deal."

18

You look tired," Alex said as Charley climbed into the front seat of his car. A light rain was falling, so the top on his convertible was up.

Charley waved good-bye to her mother, who was watching from the living room window, and tried not to bristle at Alex's assessment. She'd actually spent considerable time getting ready for this trip—more than she would have devoted to an actual date—and she thought she looked pretty damn good. She'd selected her wardrobe carefully, eliminating a pale pink blouse for being too girlish, and discarding a bright floral print for being too loud, before ultimately selecting a mauve silk jersey top over a pair of classic black pants. The outfit was sophisticated without being imposing, alluring but not overtly sexual. "Who are you trying to impress?" her mother had asked.

Who **was** she trying to impress? Charley

wondered as Alex pulled the car away from the curb. Not Jill's sister, Pam, that was for sure. And certainly not Alex, who was dressed casually in jeans and a checkered shirt, and who had obviously made no effort at all to impress **her**. "I haven't been getting a lot of sleep."

"More threatening e-mails?" Alex turned north toward Okeechobee, heading for I-95.

"No, thank God. Just a puppy with a tiny bladder."

Alex looked surprised. "I never would have pegged you for a dog lover."

"Just doing a favor for a friend." Charley quickly explained the situation with Glen McLaren.

("It's Glen's dog," Charley had told her mother earlier. "What could I do? I owed him."

"He wouldn't settle for a blow job?" had come her mother's instant response.)

"Glen McLaren," Alex repeated now, twisting the name around his tongue, as if it were familiar.

"You know him?"

"The name rings a bell."

"He owns a nightclub in Palm Beach."

Alex shrugged, as if he'd already lost interest. "I'm sure it'll come to me. Was that your mother watching us from the window?"

"That was my mother."

"Very attractive from what I could see."

"Definitely one of a kind."

Alex smiled. "Aren't they all?"

"Sounds like you speak from experience," Charley observed.

"I'm sure we all have our 'mother' stories to tell."

"Tell me one of yours."

For an instant, Charley thought she might have pushed the familiarity button too far, that Alex might opt out of the conversation altogether and revert to the safety of his legal tapes, but he only smiled and said, "My mother is one of those people who never uses one word when a thousand will do. She can take a whole day to tell you what she had for breakfast."

"Sounds fascinating."

"It isn't. But what can you do?"

"What **do** you do?"

"I listen. It's not the end of the world."

"And your father?"

"He stopped listening when I was two years old. To make my mother's very long story short, he walked out the door one day and never came back."

"You're saying you never saw him again?"

"I saw him off and on until he got married again, started a new family. After that, I didn't see him much. Haven't heard from him at all in about five years now. I think he moved to California."

"Do you miss him?"

"Can't say that I do. Although I have a couple of half-brothers I'm a little curious about," he continued, unprompted.

"You could contact them," Charley suggested.

"I could," he agreed. "If I'm remembering what Jill said correctly, you have a brother and two sisters."

Charley's shoulders stiffened. She was still angry at being given the brush-off by Jill earlier in the week. She'd driven all the way to Pembroke Pines, only to be told that Jill wasn't feeling well and wouldn't be able to see her. "If she pulls that stunt one more time," Charley said now, without bothering to elaborate, "I'm pulling the plug."

Alex didn't try to pretend he didn't know what she was talking about. "She told me to tell you how sorry she is about the way she acted."

"She has to understand that no question is off limits."

"She understands that."

"This book was her idea," Charley reminded him. "I'm not here to be jerked around."

"She swears it'll never happen again."

"Well, she's right about that," Charley said, determined not to forgive Jill so easily. The week had been a busy one, what with trying to organize her next column and trying not to obsess over her latest threatening e-mail.

"I'll need that list," Officer Ramirez had reminded her, and Charley had spent several
hours jotting down the names of everyone
she'd ever offended, starting with Lynn Moore
and Gabe Lopez, and going all the way back to
grade school. She'd even included her father
and sisters on that list, ignoring the look of
surprise that flashed through Jennifer Ramirez's
dark eyes.

"My sisters are actually coming to Palm Beach
in a couple of weeks," Charley heard herself confide.

"That's nice." Alex paused, turned his head
toward her. "Isn't it?"

"I guess we'll find out." They didn't speak
again for several minutes. Alex turned on the
radio, and the sound of "easy rock" filled the car,
Josh Groban crowing mellifluously, if more than a
touch melodramatically, about being "raised up."

"What kind of music do you like?" Alex
asked.

"I guess I should say classical," Charley responded after a moment's thought.

"Why should you?"

"I don't know. So you won't think I'm shallow, I guess."

"I don't think you're shallow."

"You don't? Because I am," she said, and was
grateful when he laughed. "Country," she admitted after a pause. "I like country."

"Really? Any artist in particular?"

"I like them all," she admitted. "Garth Brooks, Vince Gill, Tim McGraw."

"No women?"

"Faith Hill, Alison Krauss. Dolly Parton, of course."

"Of course. Everybody likes Dolly."

"What kind of music do **you** like?" Charley asked in return, realizing she was asking because she was interested and not just because she felt obligated.

"Classical," he deadpanned. "Just kidding. Actually, I'm kind of partial to country myself." He switched the station to WIRK. The Judds were singing "Mama, He's Crazy." "I even play a pretty mean guitar."

"That doesn't surprise me. Well, actually, I'm a little surprised you play the guitar, but not at all surprised you play it well, if that makes any sense."

"I think it might."

"I used to play the piano," Charley said.

"You don't anymore?"

"I stopped when I was twelve. My father said my playing gave him migraines."

"You were that bad?"

"I was that **good**," Charley corrected. "Took a lot of dedicated practicing to give that man a headache."

Alex was clearly intrigued, although he

stopped short of asking her to elaborate. "What's your favorite food?" he asked, perhaps seeking safer ground.

"Italian."

"Thought you might say that. Ever eaten at Centro's?"

"No. Where's that?"

"A little strip mall not far from Pembroke Correctional. Maybe we'll go there after we see Jill on Wednesday."

Was he asking her out on a date? Charley wondered, sidestepping the question of dinner. "I didn't realize you'd be joining us," Charley said, referring to Wednesday's meeting with Jill.

"I thought it might be a good idea, in light of what happened. Plus, I have an appointment in Fort Lauderdale in the morning. I can meet you at the prison. Unless, of course, you have any objections. . . ."

"No. No objections."

"Good."

There was another brief lull in the conversation. The Judds were replaced by the group, Alabama. "All I really got to do is live and die," they sang lustily.

"Just how much do you know about what happened?" Charley asked Alex.

"What do you mean?"

"You know that Jill was sexually abused by her brother," Charley stated.

"Yes."

"And that her father abused her as well."

"He beat her, yes."

"Did he abuse her sexually?"

Another pause. "You better ask Jill about that."

"I'm asking you."

"I don't feel comfortable discussing it."

"What if Jill says it's okay for you to talk to me about it?"

"Then I'll talk to you about it."

Another silence. The final chorus of Alabama drifted off, followed by the news: a six-year-old boy had drowned in a boating accident on the Intracoastal; a local politician was the subject of a police investigation regarding Internet porn; there was renewed fighting in Afghanistan. "How'd that case go that you were working on?" Charley asked.

"Which one was that?"

"You know. The world against mother . . ."

"Oh, that one," he said with a sly grin. "I won."

Dania was just north of Hollywood, a short drive from the Fort Lauderdale airport.

Jill was right about the place, Charley thought, glancing from one side of the deserted main street to the other, noting the boarded-up storefronts. A good many of the buildings were empty and looked as if they'd been that way for some time, their exteriors dull and lifeless, the paint peeling from their sides in large, dry strips, the lettering on the front windows chipped and occasionally illegible, the windows themselves dark and streaked with grime.

"From what I understand," Alex was saying, "this used to be something of a hub. Now, there are only a few stores still in business."

"Isn't 'collectibles' spelled with an **i**?" Charley asked, as they passed an empty store advertising ANTIQUES AND COLLECTABLES.

"Maybe you can spell it either way."

"Are you a collector?" Charley asked.

"I used to collect baseball cards when I was a kid. You?"

Charley shook her head no. "My mother had this fabulous collection of dolls from all over the world. At least a hundred of them. I used to sneak into her room to play with them."

"She still have them?"

"My father threw them out after she left. I came home from school one day, and they were all gone. At first, I thought maybe she took them with her. . . ." Charley's voice drifted off. She waited for him to ask the obvious questions about her family, but either he was reluctant to pry or he wasn't interested.

"What about antiques?" he asked instead.

"What about them?" Why wasn't he interested?

"Do you like them?"

"Not especially." Hadn't he sort of asked her out on a date? Was he miffed because she hadn't answered him? "What about you?"

"Never understood the appeal. I prefer being the original owner."

"Which would explain your choice of automobiles."

Alex laughed. "Believe it or not, this car was brand spanking new at one time. I paid cash, money I'd been saving up for years. I'd always wanted a convertible. Still can't quite bring myself to part with it." He turned right at the end of the street, then left, then left again. Before long, they were away from the main area and heading toward the less-populated part of town. "The Rohmers live down here," he said, a mile and several turns later. He pointed toward a modest gray, wood-framed bungalow at the end of the block.

Charley reached for the tape recorder inside her purse, clicking it on, and speaking softly into it. "The house is small, maybe twelve hundred square feet, one floor, looks like all the other houses in the area, almost deliberately nondescript. Painted gray with white trim, paint looks reasonably fresh, well-tended front lawn, curtains in front window drawn. Gate around back.

Single-car garage." She dropped the recorder back into her bag, removed a small digital camera. "Is it okay if I take pictures?"

"Do it discreetly," Alex advised, pulling the car into the driveway.

Ignoring the steady drizzle, Charley was out of the car and snapping pictures before Alex could turn off the engine.

"This way," he said, taking her elbow and escorting her toward the front door. He rang the doorbell, then waited. After ten seconds, he rang it again.

"She does know we're coming, doesn't she?" Charley asked, wishing she'd brought an umbrella, as her mother had suggested.

"She knows."

Another ten seconds passed. Charley could feel the rain penetrating her silk jersey top. In another ten seconds, her clothes would be soaked right through and her hair would be pasted to her head, like a cloche. Not my best look, she was thinking as Alex rang the bell a third time. "Maybe it isn't working," she suggested. But even as she was saying the words, she could hear the chimes echoing throughout the interior of the house.

Alex knocked on the door. Still no response. "Wait here," he said, going around the side of the house and unlocking the gate to the back-yard.

"This is fun," Charley said to herself, feeling someone watching her. Slowly, she turned in the direction of the house next door.

A woman was standing at her open front door, half-in, half-out of her house. She looked about sixty, although her long gray hair might have made her look older than she was. She was slightly overweight and wearing a red velour tracksuit that spelled JUICY GIRL across its zippered front. "What do you want?" she called over.

What's it your business? Charley was tempted to respond, but she didn't. It was probably not a good idea to alienate the neighbors. She might want to talk to them eventually, especially if Pam had changed her mind about cooperating. In fact, it might be a good time to talk to them right now, Charley decided, impulsively cutting across the Rohmers' front lawn to the neighbor's house, covertly clicking on the tape recorder in her purse. "I came to see Pamela Rohmer. Do you know if she's home?"

"Haven't seen her." The woman's voice was rough and raspy, probably the result of too many cigarettes over too many years. Her yellow-stained fingers confirmed this impression, as did the stale odor of ash clinging to her tracksuit. "What do you want with Pam?"

"I have an appointment," Charley hedged, glancing around for Alex, and seeing nothing but rain. "Alex?" she called out. Where had he gone? "Alex?"

"You might as well come inside for a minute," Juicy Girl said. "You're getting soaked."

Charley took another glance around before stepping inside the woman's small foyer, papered in brown and gold stripes. She wiped her feet on an old sisal mat, and shook some of the water out of her hair with her hand. "Thank you, Mrs. . . ."

"Fenwick. You're . . . ?"

"Charley Webb."

"You're a reporter?"

Charley tried not to appear either too surprised or flattered. The woman was clearly more sophisticated than she looked, and had better taste than the brown leather bean bag propped against the living room wall on her left would indicate. "Yes. You read the **Palm Beach Post**?"

"Why would I read the **Palm Beach Post**?" Mrs. Fenwick scoffed.

"I just assumed. . . . How did you know I'm a reporter?"

"What else would you be?" Mrs. Fenwick rolled watery blue eyes toward an overhanging light fixture that looked vaguely like a crown of thorns. "I would have thought you people would have had your fill by now. There's not much meat left on the bones."

"I'm not sure I understand."

"Bunch of vultures," Mrs. Fenwick elaborated. "Isn't it enough Jill's sitting on death row? You gotta pester poor Pammy to death as well?"

"I'm not trying to pester anybody, Mrs. Fenwick."

"You're not here to interview Pam about her sister?"

"I'm here at Pam's invitation."

"Really? Then why isn't she answering her door?"

Charley forced her lips into a smile, felt a drop of rain fall from the tip of her nose into her mouth. She glanced back outside, looking for Alex, but he was still nowhere to be seen. "Look. I'm writing a book. . . ."

"A book? My, my. Aren't we ambitious?"

"It was Jill's idea. I assure you she's cooperating fully."

A strange look passed across Mrs. Fenwick's face.

"Maybe I could ask you a few questions," Charley broached, her reporter's instincts sensing a shift in the woman's attitude, and deciding to take advantage of it.

"Such as?"

"To start with, how long have you lived next door to the Rohmers?"

"Twenty-five years."

"So you've known Jill . . ."

"All her life. Pammy, too. Lovely girl, Pammy. Takes wonderful care of her mother."

"And Jill?"

Mrs. Fenwick shook her head, picked some invisible tobacco from her tongue with her fingers. "Polite, respectful, eager to please. Hard to believe she did those awful things," she added without prompting.

"Hard," Charley repeated, hearing a qualifier in Mrs. Fenwick's voice. "But not impossible?"

There was a pause. "Not impossible," Mrs. Fenwick concurred.

"Charley!" Alex suddenly called out. "Charley, where are you?"

Charley opened the front door, although she still couldn't see Alex. "Be right there." She turned back to Mrs. Fenwick. "Why not impossible?"

The woman reached into the pocket of her sweatpants, pulled out a loose cigarette and a book of matches. "I don't know."

"I think you do."

"Why should I tell you?" Mrs. Fenwick put the cigarette in her mouth, lit it, and inhaled deeply before slowly releasing the smoke into the space between them.

"Because I think you want to."

Mrs. Fenwick shook her head. "The last thing I need is more trouble with Ethan."

"More trouble?"

"Pammy's the sweetest girl in the world. I'd do anything for her. And her mother is, well, you know, she's been in that wheelchair for years, and getting worse every day. But that husband of hers, and that Ethan. Always angry about something. One time I complained his car was blocking my driveway. Next thing I knew, the front of my lawn was covered with trash. Another time, he threw eggs at my front door."

"Charley?" Alex called again.

"What can you tell me about Jill, Mrs. Fenwick?" Charley asked, ignoring him.

"It's probably nothing. Just a feeling I had. . . ."

"Tell me."

"This goes back a long time, maybe eight, nine years," Mrs. Fenwick began. "We had this bird's nest in one of our trees out back, and the eggs had just hatched. Don't ask me what kind of birds they were. Probably just sparrows. Not very interesting really, but I used to love watching them. They were all scrawny, their mouths always open, crying to be fed. I showed the nest to Jill, and she seemed quite intrigued. Anyway, one afternoon, I came home from work. . . ."

"Charley!"

"Over here!" Charley called back impatiently as Alex materialized on the Rohmers' front lawn. "What happened when you came home from work, Mrs. Fenwick?"

"I really don't know why I'm telling you this."

"What was Jill doing when you came home from work that day?"

A moment's hesitation, then: "She was in my backyard, standing at the foot of the tree, the nest on the ground, the poor little birds lying dead at her feet. She was crying, said a cat must have gotten to them. I comforted her. We buried them together. I didn't think too much about it until later on, when I looked out my bedroom window, and I saw her sitting on the grass, her back against her house, playing with this big, long stick, and staring up at my tree with this weird little smile on her face. That was when I knew it wasn't a cat that got to those poor little birds."

"Charley!" Alex ran up the front walk.

"Can we talk again?" Charley asked her.

Mrs. Fenwick shook her head. "No. I've said quite enough. You should go." She opened her door, all but pushed Charley into Alex's arms.

"What's going on?" Alex asked.

"I'll tell you later. Did you find Pam?"

Alex pointed through the rain toward the Rohmer house. The curtains in the front window had been pulled back. Pamela Rohmer stood between the panels, watching them approach.

19

The front door of the Rohmer house opened directly into the living room. The room was a small, perfect square, completely dominated by a large plasma TV that took up most of one cream-colored wall. A well-worn, beige chesterfield was pushed against the wall at right angles to it, between two brown leather La-Z-Boy loungers. A real guy's room, Charley thought, surprised by a vase of fresh-cut flowers on a glass side table beside the archway leading into the tiny dining room, the only indication a woman might also live here. Charley noted that the table was already set for dinner. She checked her watch. It was barely two o'clock.

Pamela Rohmer was standing by the large front window. She was taller than her sister, with the same dirty blond hair and heart-shaped face, but while her eyes were a similar brooding shade of brown, they lacked Jill's vitality. They were faded, like a photograph left too long in the sun, and void of curiosity, as if she already knew the answers to all life's questions, and found them to be both useless and uninteresting. She was wearing jeans and a white blouse with a Peter Pan collar, and her freshly washed hair hung straight to her shoulders. "Charley's kind of a strange name for a girl," she said before Alex could formally introduce them.

"It's actually Charlotte." Charley decided to wait until later to request a photograph.

"Charlotte Webb." Pamela nodded as she absorbed this information. "Guess your parents thought that was cute."

"You have no idea."

Pamela smiled. "Can I get you something to drink?"

Charley shook her head.

"Sorry about keeping you waiting for so long. I was busy with my mother and couldn't get to the door."

"Is she all right?" Charley asked.

"She's asleep. For the moment." Pamela's voice was as deep as it was distracted, almost as if she were speaking to you from another room. Charley wished she could jot that observation down before she forgot it. "Have a seat." Pamela indicated the sofa with a wave of her hand.

Charley sank down, a vaguely musty smell rising from the cushions to compete with the scent of citrus air-freshener. Pamela perched on the edge of the sofa's far end, crossing one ankle neatly over the other, and folding her hands primly in her lap. Alex walked to the window, pretending to be looking out at the rain. "Thanks for agreeing to see me," Charley began.

Pamela shrugged. "It's what Jill wants."

"Have you talked to her?"

"She called last week, asked me to cooperate."

"Well, I appreciate it." Charley looked to Alex for a nod of encouragement, but he was still looking out the front window, seemingly engrossed in the growing downpour. She glanced back at Pamela, who was staring at her without expression. What am I doing here? Charley wondered. I have no idea what to ask this woman, no clue where to start. She tried to dredge up the list of questions she'd been tossing back and forth in her head all week, but her mind was as blank as the look on Pamela's face. What do I say to this woman to get her to trust me? "Listen, before I forget," Charley heard herself say, "my brother said to say hello."

"Your brother?"

"Bram Webb?" Charley asked, as if she wasn't sure. "Apparently you knew each other a few years back?" Again, the sentence emerged as a question. Charley bit down on her tongue. She'd always hated people who attached question marks to the end of obvious statements. Didn't they know what they were talking about?

"Bram's your brother?"

"I understand you took some classes together."

"Art classes, yes. He's very talented."

"He said the two of you dated for a while."

"We went out a couple of times, yeah. Bram and Pam, we used to joke. A perfect match. How's he doing?"

"Great. He's doing great." I hope, Charley added silently. She hadn't heard from her brother since she'd called to tell him a family reunion was in the offing.

"Please tell me I'm hallucinating," was all he'd said.

"I always thought he had such an unusual name. Obviously your parents . . ."

"Obviously," Charley repeated, with a roll of her eyes.

"Bram Webb," Pam said, shaking her head in wonderment. "Wow. Small world, huh?"

"Small world," Charley agreed, reaching into her purse and bringing out her tape recorder, setting it on the cushion between them. A flash of fear interrupted Pam's blank stare. "If you don't want me to tape this," Charley said quickly, "I can just take notes." She quickly withdrew a small pad from her purse, began rifling around for a pen.

"No, I guess it's all right."

"You're sure?"

Pam nodded, smoothed down the sides of her hair, almost as if she thought the tape recorder was a camera.

Charley realized the recorder was still running from her encounter with Mrs. Fenwick, and wondered if Pam could hear its gentle hum. "I was talking to your neighbor," she said.

"Mrs. Fenwick?"

"She's a big fan of yours."

Pam absorbed this latest piece of information without any noticeable change to her expression. "She's a nice lady."

"She says you take very good care of your mother."

Pam shrugged. "I do my best."

"Okay. So, are we ready?" Charley asked.

"I guess."

"Do you have anything you want to say before we start?"

"Like what?"

Like, do you think your sister is a cold-blooded killer of little children? Charley thought, deciding it would probably be more prudent to take a slower, gentler approach. "Look, why don't we start with some background information, kind of ease into this."

"Background information?"

"You're how old exactly?"

"Twenty-five on May sixteenth."

"And you're not married."

"I'm not married," Pam repeated.

"Divorced? Engaged?"

"Single."

"Have you always lived at home?"

"Yes."

"Do you work? Outside the home, I mean?"

Pam shook her head. "My mother's kind of a full-time job."

Charley noted this was said without rancor. "It must be hard for you."

"She's my mother." Again Pam shrugged. "What would you do?"

Charley cleared her throat, moved the tape recorder several inches to the right, although it had been perfectly fine where it was. "There's nobody to help you?"

"Well, there was Jill, but . . ."

"Jill told me that at one time you wanted to join the Peace Corps."

"She remembered that? It was so long ago."

"She also said you talked of becoming a nun."

Pam grimaced. "Kind of hard to be a nun when you're not Catholic."

"She said your father was very upset by that, that he hit you so hard you lost partial hearing in one ear."

Reflexively, Pam raised her hand to her left ear. "That was an accident."

"An accident he hit you?"

"An accident he hit me so hard," Pam qualified. "It wasn't like I didn't deserve it."

"You think you deserved to be beaten?"

"I never said I was beaten."

"Weren't you?"

Pam's eyes narrowed. "I thought you were
going to ask me about Jill."

"Well, I'd like to know about both of you,"
Charley sidestepped. "I find it interesting that
siblings often have such different memories of
their childhood. Sometimes you'd never suspect
they'd grown up in the same house."

"Is that true of you and Bram?"

"Well, it's certainly true of me and my sisters," Charley acknowledged.

"Alex says your sisters are pretty famous."

"Yes, they are."

"Are you close?"

"Not so much."

"Why? Are you jealous?"

The question caught Charley by surprise.
"Jealous? No. Well, maybe a little," she admitted
after a pause. Then, "Maybe more than a little."
Was she? Or was she just saying that to disarm
Pam, worm her way into her confidence? "Were
you jealous of Jill as a child?"

"Yes," Pam said simply. "I hated her."

"That's a pretty strong word."

"I guess. She was just so pretty and angelic-looking, and everybody was always making such a fuss about her. I resented her for that. The way all she had to do was smile and everybody let her do whatever she wanted. My father used to call her his 'little cupcake.' Even Ethan let her get away with murder." Pam stopped abruptly, perhaps caught off guard by her choice of words. "It was the same way at school," she continued after several seconds. "The boys hovered like flies. I was pretty jealous of that. I was always shy, nervous around guys. One time, I asked for her advice about this boy I liked, his name was Daniel Lewicki, and she laughed and said, 'You gotta treat 'em mean to keep 'em keen.' But I could never do that. Jill said I was hopeless. She said I didn't deserve to have a boyfriend, that she was gonna get Daniel to ask her out. And she did."

"She stole your boyfriend?"

"Well, we'd never actually gone out."

"But you liked him. Jill knew that."

"It was no big deal. Besides, she was right— she treated him like dirt, and he just kept coming back for more."

"What about Wayne Howland?" Charley asked.

"The preacher's son? What about him?"

"I understand he and Jill were close."

"They were friends. But then they had some sort of falling out, and he stopped coming around."

"Do you know what caused the falling out?"

"No. But Jill was stubborn like you wouldn't believe. It was either her way or no way at all. Maybe Wayne wasn't quite so 'keen' after awhile."

Charley tried to reconcile the picture Pam was painting of Jill with Alex's view of his client as a young woman who'd been abused and manipulated by every man she'd ever met. Of course it was entirely possible that Pam's animosity toward her sister was coloring her recollections. "What are your feelings for Jill now?"

"I feel sorry for her."

"Because she's in jail?"

"Because she's in pain."

"What makes you think she's in pain?"

"How could she not be?"

"Because of what she's done?"

"Nobody's blameless," Pam said cryptically.

"What do you mean?"

There was a long pause. "There were things that happened to Jill," Pam said slowly, "things I could have prevented, things I should have done."

"Such as?"

Pam shook her head slowly from side to side, said nothing.

"What things could you have prevented?"

Pam fidgeted in her seat, looked as if she was considering bolting from the room.

"Jill told me about Ethan," Charley said slowly. "About what he did to her." She reached across the cushions for Pam's hand, cupped it inside her own. "About what he did to you."

Pam pulled her hand away, as if she'd been burned, then folded one arm under the other across her chest. She began swaying back and forth.

"How old were you when the abuse started?"

"I don't want to talk about that."

"Okay." Charley pretended to be reading from her notes. "Can you just confirm a few things for me?"

Pam said nothing, continued rocking back and forth.

"Jill said you went to Disney World for your tenth birthday. . . ."

"I really don't want to talk about this."

"And that she shared a room at the motel with you and Ethan, Ethan in one bed, you and Jill in the other. Is that right?"

Pam nodded, her entire body starting to tremble.

"And in the middle of the night, Ethan moved her into his bed, then crawled in beside you. She said she heard you crying and telling him to stop, and that the next morning, there was blood on the sheets."

"I can't do this," Pam said.

"Would it be easier if I weren't here?" Alex asked.

Charley jumped at the sound of Alex's voice. She'd forgotten all about him.

"Maybe you could go check on my mother. If you wouldn't mind." Pam motioned toward the rooms at the back of the house. "Through the dining room. The last door on the right."

Alex glanced briefly at Charley as he left the room. Go easy, the glance warned.

"I'm sorry to have to dredge up such painful memories," Charley began.

"You keep thinking it'll get easier with time," Pam said, speaking as much to herself as to Charley. "What's that saying? Time heals all wounds?"

Charley nodded.

"Well, it's not true. Some wounds never heal."

Charley recalled watching her mother pack for Australia, along with the hollow sensation that filled her chest, as if she'd been stabbed repeatedly and was slowly bleeding out. She remembered discovering the empty cabinet that once held her mother's extensive doll collection, and the way her body had collapsed in on itself, as if she'd been sucker-punched. She experienced anew the numbness that had overtaken her body as she stood waiting by the front door, night after night, for her mother to come home. Pam was right, she thought—some wounds never healed.

"I'm sorry to be such a baby," Pam said.

"Please don't apologize."

"I want to cooperate. Jill says it's important."

"What else did she say?"

"That she doesn't want me to hold anything back, that she wants me to tell the whole story."

"Do you think you can do that?"

"I don't know."

"I think you can."

"It's not easy. Everybody has his own truth. Nobody ever thinks he's the bad guy. We all have our own elaborate system of justifications and rationalizations for the things we do. I know Ethan does."

"Have you ever talked to him about what happened?"

Pam laughed, a sharp, hollow sound, like a tree branch snapping in two. "I tried to once. After his wife kicked him out and he moved back here. But he denied everything, said I was just trying to make trouble for him. He insisted he never touched me, that I'd imagined the whole thing."

"What about your father?" Charley asked.

Whatever color had been left in Pam's face quickly disappeared. Her fingers reached for her left ear. "Sometimes he gets a little rough."

"Is it true he shot the family dog?"

"The dog was old and sick. Shooting him was an act of kindness more than anything else."

"You really believe that?"

"What difference does it make? It happened a long time ago."

"Some wounds never heal," Charley reminded her.

Pam moaned audibly.

"Did your father molest you, too? Did he molest Jill?"

"Look," Pam said, her voice a plea. "I want to help my sister. I really do. But what you're talking about happened a long time ago. It's one thing for Jill to make these accusations public, but I still have to live in this house."

"No, you don't. You can go to the police. They'll arrest Ethan and your father."

"And what about my mother? What would happen to her? I don't have any money. How can I possibly look after her if they put my father and brother in jail?"

Charley paused, suddenly remembering her phone conversation with Jill. "Do you think your mother knew about the abuse?"

"My mother was as much a victim as Jill and I were."

"But did she know what was going on?"

"I don't know. She was sick a lot. Besides, what could she have done?"

"She could have protected you, gotten you away from this house."

"You think it's so easy to just walk away?"

Charley thought about her own mother. How easy had it been for her?

Pam suddenly reached over and snapped off the tape recorder. "This interview is over." She stood up. "I think you should go now."

"Wait, please." Charley jumped to her feet. "Just a few more questions."

Pam cocked her head to one side, waited for Charley to continue.

"Do you think Jill murdered those children?"

"The evidence was pretty overwhelming."

"That's not what I asked."

"That's still my answer."

"Do you think she acted alone?"

"Maybe. Maybe not."

"So, you think someone else might have been involved?"

"It doesn't really matter what I think, does it?"

"That depends. Do you think that someone else was Ethan?" Charley pressed, wishing she could turn the recorder back on.

"The police didn't seem to think so."

"But you disagree?"

"Not necessarily. Ethan may be a miserable son of a bitch, but I can't see him killing a bunch of little kids."

"Pamela!" a woman's voice called weakly from the other room. "Pamela, where are you? What's going on?"

"I have to go," Pam said, moving toward the bedrooms in the back as Alex reappeared in the archway.

"I'm sorry," Alex apologized. "She woke up, saw me in the doorway. I didn't mean to scare her."

"Pamela!"

"I'll be right there."

"Can we talk again?" Charley asked, gathering up her tape recorder from the sofa.

Pam shook her head vehemently from side to side.

"Take my card," Charley began, stuffing it into Pam's reluctant hand. "If you think of anything. . . ."

"I won't," Pam said. "Tell Jill I'm sorry." She stopped at the entrance to the dining room. "And please remember to give your brother my regards. Those were good times," she said. And then she was gone.

20

"Damn it. What's wrong with me?" Charley was ranting as she bolted through her front door, letting it slam behind her.

"Charley?" Her mother approached from the direction of the bedrooms, Bandit at her heels. "You're home early. Is everything all right?"

Charley stomped into the living room and plopped down on the sofa, dropping her purse to the floor, and throwing her head back against a pillow. The dog was immediately on the sofa beside her, jumping up and down against her shoulder and licking her face with excitement. Charley struggled to keep Bandit's tongue away from her lips. "Yes, hello, hello. Now leave me alone. I'm not in the mood. No, things aren't all right," she told her mother in the same breath. "Where are the kids?"

"In their room, changing their clothes. They've been cooped up all day because of the rain, so I promised to take them to McDonald's and a movie. We weren't expecting you home till much later. What happened, darling? Your interview didn't go well?"

"That's an understatement. Jeez, Bandit! You stuck your tongue right in my mouth!" she wailed as the dog continued his frantic welcome.

"He's just happy to see you. He needs a little hug."

A hug, Charley thought. The dog needs a hug. What about what I need? Which is what, exactly? she wondered, gathering the squirming ball of white fur into her hands. Immediately Bandit burrowed into the crook of her neck, then went completely still.

"Amazing," Elizabeth Webb uttered.

Charley felt the muscles in her neck and shoulders instantly relax as Bandit's warmth quickly penetrated her skin.

"You have a real way with him," her mother said.

"I didn't do anything."

"You don't have to. That's the wonderful thing about dogs. They love you no matter what you do."

"Unlike people," Charley remarked.

"People are harder to please." Her mother sank into the seat beside her. "What's the matter, darling? You left the house with such enthusiasm."

"That was before I realized what a lousy reporter I am."

"Who says you're a lousy reporter?"

"I do," Charley admitted. "I'm way out of my depth here, Mom. Looks like I'm as shallow as everyone seems to think."

"Who thinks you're shallow?"

"I don't know how to talk to people," Charley continued, as if her mother hadn't spoken. "Worse—I don't know how to get them to talk to me. I don't know what questions to ask. I don't even know whether I should be asking questions at all, or just letting them ramble on. I don't know what's important and what isn't. I don't know **who's** important and who isn't. I don't know what I'm doing. Period." She felt her mother's hand reach over to caress her hair.

"You sound just like you did when you were a little girl. And don't say, How would you know?" her mother said just as Charley was about to. "I may not have been around for all of your childhood, but I **was** there for the first eight years, and I know that anytime you tackled something new, whether it was a game of Chutes and Ladders or a project your teacher had assigned, you'd get yourself all in a flap, convinced you couldn't do it."

"This is a little different."

"Somehow you always managed to pull it off."

"Give me one example," Charley challenged.

Her mother gave the matter several seconds thought. "All right. I remember when you were about four years old, and you just had to have this yo-yo. You were so insistent, even after the salesman told you you were too young to manipulate it properly. You were so positive you could master it that I gave in and bought it for you. And, of course, you couldn't do it. You couldn't even get it to go up and down, let alone all that fancy stuff. And you cried and carried on, made yourself so miserable I finally told you to throw the damn thing out. But you didn't. You stuck with it. You kept at it until one day you were handling it like a pro."

Charley hunched forward in her seat, eyed her mother skeptically. "Are you making this up?"

"Yes," her mother admitted with a sigh. "How did you know?"

"Because I hate yo-yos. I still can't work them properly."

"All right, so that wasn't the best example, but it was all I could think of on such short notice. The point I was making is still valid."

"Just what point would that be?"

"That it's natural to get upset and anxious when you're tackling something new, but that you're a bright, talented young woman who will succeed at anything you set your mind to. And if you don't know the appropriate questions to ask right now, you'll figure them out soon enough. So stop worrying, and stop being so hard on yourself. Do you want to know what Sharon claimed was the secret to happiness?"

Charley tried not to flinch at the casual reference to her mother's deceased lover. "By all means."

Her mother pulled her shoulders back and pushed her ample chest forward. "Lower your expectations," she said.

"Lower your expectations? That's it?"

"That's enough. Sharon was the happiest person I ever met. Now, why don't you go change into something more casual and come with us to McDonald's and the movies?"

Charley's head was spinning. Was her mother right? Did she demand too much of herself? Of everyone? Was happiness just a matter of not expecting quite so much? "Would you be mad if I said I'd rather not? I'm just pooped."

"Then I have another idea," her mother said. "Why don't you let me take the kids to my place for the night? I'll bring them back in the morning, and we can all go to TooJay's for breakfast. How does that sound?"

"Sounds great."

"Good. Then it's settled." Elizabeth jumped to her feet, strode into the hall. "Franny, James. Pack up your overnight bags. You're spending the night at Grandma's."

Charley smiled at the sound of her children's excited whoops of glee. The dog, perhaps stirred into action by the sudden commotion, began furiously licking the underside of her neck. At least one male thinks I'm desirable, she thought, trying not to think about Alex Prescott. "See you Wednesday," he'd said as he dropped her off in front of her house. No mention of going anywhere later for a drink to commiserate with her about the aborted interview with Pamela. Not another word about dinner at Centro's this Wednesday night. In fact, he'd barely spoken to her at all on the drive back from Dania, probably disgusted by her so-called interviewing technique, but too polite to say so. "I imagine you want to write things down while they're still fresh in your mind," he'd said, but Charley suspected he was happy to see her stew in her own juices. I knew you weren't the right person for this job, his silence had rebuked her throughout the long drive home. So Charley had concentrated on recording her impressions of the Rohmer house and the people who lived there, when what she really wanted to do was hurl her notebook at his head. **Two sisters**, she'd scrawled across the top of one page, **raised by the same parents in the same environment, both battered, both sexually abused. One becomes a caregiver, the other one a killer.**

Why?

She had no answer.

"Do you remember what I was like as a baby?" Charley asked her mother now. "And don't make it up."

"I don't have to make it up. Of course I remember what you were like as a baby. You were lovely," Elizabeth said. "A little intense, maybe, but very sweet, very curious. Did everything right on schedule."

"What about Emily and Anne?"

"Emily was more of a prima donna. A gorgeous child, of course, but she cried every night for four hours, like clockwork, from the age of six weeks till the age of three months. Irritable crying, Dr. Spock called it, said it would last exactly six weeks, and he was right. After that, she settled down, although once Anne was born, she had a harder time than you did adjusting. The middle child syndrome, I guess. And it didn't help that Anne was the best baby on earth. A real gift. She never cried, never fussed. Always smiling. Toilet-trained herself at thirteen months. Really quite remarkable. Bram, of course, was the exact opposite," she continued. "He cried all the time. And it didn't matter if you picked him up or rocked him or took him for a drive in the car. He screamed constantly. And when he finally stopped screaming, he became a head-banger, slamming his head against the side of the crib for hours on end when he didn't get his own way. One time he actually knocked himself unconscious. I lived in fear he was going to kill himself." She sighed. "I guess not much has changed, when you think about it."

"I think things are about to," Charley told her.

"What makes you say that?"

Charley told her mother about her conversation with Emily.

"Your sisters are coming here?" Elizabeth's eyes filled with tears.

"The date hasn't been finalized, but it should be sometime in the next couple of weeks."

"And they've agreed to see me?"

"I thought maybe we'd have dinner here," Charley sidestepped. "Bram will come, too."

Elizabeth looked as if she were about to faint. She leaned against the far wall for support, crying softly. "I never expected this."

"What did you say the secret of happiness is?" Charley asked rhetorically, thinking she should probably go over and take her mother in her arms, but unable to get her body to cooperate. Two years might have passed since Elizabeth's return, but a span of two decades still occupied the space between where Charley sat and her mother stood. It was too great a distance to cross.

"Mommy!" James raced into the room, throwing himself in Charley's lap.

"Why is Grandma crying?" Franny asked from her grandmother's side.

"I'm crying because I'm so happy to be your grandma," Elizabeth said.

"That's silly," shouted James. "You don't cry when you're happy."

"Sometimes you do," Charley said, trying to get her son to sit still long enough to kiss his cheek.

"Grandma's taking us to McDonald's and a movie," Franny said, her voice wary, as if she was afraid Charley might object.

"Are you coming too?" James asked.

"Not today, sweetheart. This time Grandma's got you all to herself."

"I packed my Superman pajamas."

"Then I guess you'll have a super sleep." Charley watched her son climb off the sofa and wrap himself around his grandmother's knees.

"Is it going to rain all weekend?" Franny asked her mother, as if Charley were somehow responsible for the inclement weather.

"I think it's supposed to clear up for tomorrow."

"And I think we should get going, if we don't want to be late," Elizabeth said.

Charley followed her mother and children to the front door, the dog wrapped around her neck like a shawl. "See. It's stopped raining already," she told Franny, who studied the gray sky and looked doubtful. "Good-bye, gorgeous things. Go easy on your grandmother." Charley knelt down for a final hug, but James was already running down the front walk toward Elizabeth's mauve Civic.

"Come on," he shouted, creating wide circles with his arms as he urged them forward.

"You'll take good care of Bandit?" Franny asked her mother. "You won't forget to feed him and take him for a walk?"

"I won't forget," Charley said.

"Bye, Bandit." Franny kissed the dog's wet nose. Bandit responded by shellacking her face with his tongue.

"Call me if it gets to be too much," Charley advised her mother as Franny joined her brother by the side of the road.

"I can't thank you enough, darling. I know it was you who convinced the others to see me."

"No thanks necessary."

"I love you very much. You know that, don't you?" her mother asked, as she always did.

"I know. Have fun," Charley said. She watched her children buckle up in the backseat of the car, and stood there waving until they were out of sight. She lowered the dog to the grass. "Do busy," she commanded gently.

Immediately, Bandit lifted his leg. "Would that everything were so easy," Charley said, as she picked up the dog and reentered her house, closing the door behind her.

* * *

The first time Tiffany Lang saw Blake Castle, she knew her life had changed forever, Charley read. She reached for the bottle of wine on the coffee table, filled the wineglass almost to the top, and took a good, long sip. "Fortification," she said to Bandit, who was curled up on the cushion beside her. **It wasn't just that he was the handsomest man she'd ever seen, although that was undeniably true. It wasn't the blueness of his eyes or even the way they seemed to look right through her, as if he were staring straight into her soul, as if he could read all her most secret thoughts.** "You can do this. I can do this," she told the dog. **Nor was it the insolent way he occupied the center of the room, his slim hips tilted slightly forward, his thumbs hooked provocatively into the pockets of his tight jeans, the pout on his full lips issuing a silent invitation, daring her to come closer. Approach at your own risk, he said without speaking.** "See, that part's not half-bad." Bandit cocked his head to one side. "I kind of like that last sentence, **Approach at your own risk, he said without speaking.** That's not so awful." She took another sip of wine, started reading again with fresh resolve. "This is the number-two best-selling book in America," she informed the dog. "It'll probably be number one next week, and not only will I read it, I will enjoy it. And I will call Anne when I'm finished to tell her how **much** I enjoyed it. I will not be condescending and superior, like certain lawyers I could mention." What was with Alex Prescott anyway? Charley continued silently. One minute he was suggesting dinner at some little Italian bistro; the next minute he was giving her the cold shoulder. "And I assure you, I'm not used to getting the cold shoulder from men," Charley told the dog, whose emphatic bark served as an exclamation point. "He's not even that good-looking. He's just kind of cocky, you know what I mean?" Bandit barked again, as if he did. "And I've always been a sucker for arrogance. I even wrote a column about it once. I don't suppose you read it. Tell me," she instructed the dog, "if nobody out there is reading my columns, how come I'm so popular?" Bandit jumped off the sofa, began spinning around in circles. "I'm so damn popular, I'm home alone drinking on a Saturday night. How's that for popular?" In response, Bandit barked three times in rapid succession, then ran for the door, where he spun around and barked again. "No, we already went for a walk."

Bandit began scratching at the door.

"All right, all right. I get the point." Charley pushed herself off the sofa, took another long sip of her wine, then decided to take the glass with her. Maybe the fresh air would do her some good, clear her head of unwanted thoughts, and allow her sister's stellar prose to get the attention it no doubt deserved. "We're just going to the corner, that's it." She opened the door.

The man standing on the other side wasn't very tall, but what he lacked in height, he made up for in muscles, his taut biceps bulging with impressive menace beneath his sleeveless black T-shirt.

Charley gasped, her wineglass falling to the floor, the dog scooting out between the man's black leather, pointy-toed boots. Shock mingled with fear as she tried to slam the door in the man's face, but he was too strong and too quick, and within seconds, without touching her, he'd managed to maneuver her back into the house and into her living room, until she was stretched backward over the sofa and he was almost on top of her, looming over her like an enraged grizzly. Was this the nutcase who'd written her those e-mails? The man who'd threatened her and her children? Thank God they weren't here, she was thinking as her eyes skirted the area for something she could grab, her hand stretching for anything she could throw at his head. Was he here to kill her? Would her mother and children find her lifeless body sprawled across the living room floor when they returned the next morning? Would this lunatic still be here, waiting? Charley's fingers knocked against the bottle of wine on the table. Could she grab hold of it?

"Don't even think about it," the man said.

Charley's hand fell limp at her side. "Who are you?" But even as she was asking the question, Charley realized she already knew who the man was. "You're Ethan Rohmer," she said, as a strange calm enveloped her.

"Pleased to meet you," Ethan said, smiling as he took a few steps back, allowing her room to stand up straight.

"What do you want?" she asked, although again, she already knew the answer.

"I want you to stay away from Pamela. I want you to stay away from my mother. I want you to stay away from my house."

Charley said nothing. She was already trying to gather together the words to describe him in print: dark eyes framed by girlishly long lashes; a nose that had obviously been broken more than once, yet still managed to suit the perfect oval of his face; thin lips that smiled with perverse ease; chin-length hair blonder than both his sisters'; a torso that was noticeably long in proportion to his legs.

"I come home tonight, and I know right away something's wrong," Ethan said. "Takes me awhile, but pretty soon I worm it out of them. Turns out my psycho sister's hotshot lawyer has brought some skanky reporter around, trying to dredge up dirt for a book she's writing, telling vicious lies, and getting everybody all upset. I don't like it when strangers upset my family."

"You're saying Jill's lying?"

"I'm saying she's a psycho bitch."

"Which doesn't mean she's lying."

"What'd she tell you? That I helped her kill those kids?"

"Did you?"

"Kids aren't my thing."

"You raped her when she was eleven years old," Charley reminded him.

"The hell I did." He gave a short laugh of derision, pushed the hair away from his face. "I assure you that anything that happened between Jill and me was at her instigation."

"And Pamela?"

"Pamela wants you to stay away from her. She's afraid if you keep poking your nose into other people's business, you're liable to get hurt."

"Are you threatening me?"

Ethan smiled. "Just looking out for your welfare."

"I think you should leave now," Charley said, upset by the slight tremor she heard in her voice.

"As long as we've got an understanding here. You stay away from my family. You got that?"

Charley saw a shadow flit against the wall

behind Ethan. She heard something click, a dog barking, and sirens rounding the corner.

"Don't move," Gabe Lopez said as Ethan turned to see a rifle pointed at his head. "I'll blow your fucking face off."

"Hey, man," Ethan said, raising his hands into the air as Bandit scrambled into Charley's arms. "This is all a misunderstanding. Put the gun away, man."

"I was on my porch when I saw this guy go inside and your dog run out," Gabe explained. "When you didn't run after him, I knew something was wrong, and I called 911."

"Thank you," Charley said, as Bandit licked at the tears that were just starting to fall.

"What's this I hear about you raping an eleven-year-old girl?" Gabe Lopez released the safety catch on his rifle.

"It's a lie, man. I never raped anybody."

"Tell it to the judge," Gabe Lopez said with a laugh. He was still chuckling as the police were pushing Ethan's head inside the police cruiser some fifteen minutes later. "I always wanted to say that," he said to Charley. Then, propping his rifle against the living room wall, "Is there any wine left in that bottle? I could use a drink."

21

"Tell me about Tammy Barnet," Charley instructed before Jill could sit down. Charley was sitting beside Alex at the interview table in the small airless room at Pembroke Correctional, her back stiff, her tape recorder already running. After last week's debacle, after being unceremoniously escorted off the premises when Jill refused to see her, she was determined to dictate the course of their session, to show Jill who was in charge.

"Hi, Alex," Jill said, ignoring Charley's directive as she pulled out her chair. "That's a nice blouse, Charley. Pink really suits you."

"Please answer the question."

"I didn't hear one."

"How did you meet the Barnet family?" Charley rephrased, feeling the ground already starting to slip beneath her feet.

"Come on, Charley. Be nice. You could at least

ask how I'm feeling. Tell me you're glad to see me. Something. **Any**thing. Girls like a little fore-play before the main event. You know that."

"I'm in no mood for games, Jill. You've wasted enough of my time."

Jill leaned forward, her elbows on the table, the playfulness vanishing from her eyes. "Then let's not waste any more. I'm sure you've already talked to the Barnets."

Charley had indeed spent most of yesterday afternoon interviewing Tammy Barnet's mother. She and her husband were in the midst of a painful divorce, their daughter's murder having proved too great a hurdle for them to surmount together. ("He blames me," Mrs. Barnet had ex-plained tearfully.) Mr. Barnet had refused to meet with Charley, but Mrs. Barnet had been co-operative, even eager to talk, although she was still in shock, two years after the event, that the seemingly sweet young woman she'd hired to baby-sit her little girl could have so brutally snuffed out her life. "I'd like to hear your ver-sion," Charley told Jill now.

Jill smiled sweetly at her lawyer, as if Charley hadn't spoken. "I wasn't expecting you today, Alex."

"I thought I'd sit in, make sure things went smoothly," he said.

"Why wouldn't they? I've already apolo-gized to Charley several times for my behavior

last week. You got my letter, didn't you, Charley?"

Clearly this meeting was going to proceed at
Jill's pace and discretion, or not at all. There was
no point in fighting it, Charley realized. "I got it,
yes. Thank you." Jill's formal letter of apology
had arrived on Monday, along with twenty-four
pages of tightly written ramblings about everything from her mother—**I honestly don't know
whether she knew what was happening or
not, but I really can't blame her even if she
did. There was nothing she could have done
to stop it**—to her favorite singing group—**I
really like Coldplay, and am still upset that
Chris Martin married that scrawny bitch,
Gwyneth Paltrow. What does he see in her
anyway?**—to her fear of closed-in spaces—**Any-
place where I can't stand up straight puts
me in a total panic. What do you suppose
that means?**

"So, we're okay, then?" Jill asked.

"We're okay. We just have a lot of ground
to cover, and I'd like to get started. I'm sorry
if I was so abrupt," Charley lied.

"And I'm sorry about what happened with
you and Ethan."

"You heard about that?" Charley glanced accusingly at Alex. She'd called him right after the
police left, but he hadn't been home. He'd returned her call first thing the next morning to

express his concern and dismay. Then he'd asked if she wanted to abandon the project, said he'd understand completely if she'd changed her mind and wanted out of their agreement. She'd told him she'd see him on Wednesday afternoon, as planned.

"Are you kidding?" Jill was saying now. "The guards couldn't wait to tell me what happened."

"How did they know?"

Jill shrugged. "You can't believe how fast this sort of news travels through the system. It's like they have some sort of psychic newsletter or something. They said my brother had been arrested for breaking into your house and threatening you. They thought it was pretty funny. I called Alex right away, but he was tied up and obviously too busy to get back to me," she said pointedly.

Alex ignored the mock hurt in Jill's voice. "Not much to say. Your father posted bail. I doubt Ethan will get more than a slap on the wrist, considering he didn't actually break into Charley's house, and no real threats were uttered, other than those of an irate neighbor with a loaded rifle who threatened to blow Ethan's face off."

"Never thought I'd be grateful to the NRA," Charley said, rubbing her forehead at the memory of Gabe Lopez coming to her defense. Who'd have thought? she asked herself, recalling the scene that followed: the police rushing in, arresting Ethan, taking him away, the neighbors gathering outside her house, some venturing inside to find out what had happened, finding Gabe Lopez and Charley sharing a bottle of wine, then returning to their homes to fetch bottles of their own, the whole thing turning into an impromptu street party, Lynn Moore offering tipsy hugs of forgiveness along with home-baked chocolate chip cookies, the already surreal evening ending with half the street cavorting in Doreen Rivers's backyard pool.

Officer Ramirez had called yesterday to tell Charley that there was no hard evidence linking Ethan to the threatening e-mails she'd received, although they'd keep an eye on him. Nor could they charge him with rape unless Pamela came forward to back up her sister's allegations, the word of a convicted child killer sitting on death row apparently considered something less than totally reliable.

Charley had no doubt that Ethan had sexually abused both his sisters. She was less convinced of everything else Jill had told her, and even less sure that she was smart enough to figure out where the lies stopped and the truth began. Was it possible that Jill herself didn't know?

After Sunday brunch at TooJay's, Charley had spent most of the day drawing up a list of the people she needed to interview—the Barnets, the Starkeys, Wayne Howland, who'd joined the army and was rumored to be fighting in Iraq, Gary Gojovic, whose testimony against his former girlfriend hadn't exactly helped her case, Jill's former teachers, her classmates, her childhood friends, the arresting officers, the various detectives, the prosecutors themselves, the members of the jury, even Alex. How was she supposed to know what to ask any of them?

"You're a bright, talented young woman who will succeed at anything you set your mind to," her mother had told her. "And if you don't know the appropriate questions to ask right now, you'll figure them out soon enough."

With a little bit of professional help, Charley recognized, managing to contact Dr. John Norman, the psychologist who'd interviewed and then testified against Jill at her trial, first thing on Monday morning. "I need your help," she'd begun after introducing herself and explaining her predicament.

"I have a patient coming in at ten o'clock," the man replied in clipped, even tones. "You can't really expect me to give you a lesson in abnormal psychology in twenty minutes, can you?"

Charley imagined the man she was speaking to was middle-aged and balding, rather like the psychiatrist on **Law & Order**, although he could just as easily have been young, with a full head of hair. Voices were as deceiving as everything else, where people were concerned.

"You've read my report, I assume?"

"Yes. In it, you describe Jill as having a 'borderline personality disorder,' meaning . . ."

"Meaning that she's intensely narcissistic and lacks the basic human emotions, including empathy."

"How does something like that happen?" Charley asked.

"Current theory holds that borderline personality disorder is the result of three main factors," Dr. Norman told her patiently. "One's genes, one's upbringing, and one's environment. In the case of someone like Jill Rohmer, the fact she was brutalized as a child obviously contributed to her brutalizing others later on."

"But not everyone who was abused as a child goes on to become a cold-blooded killer. Her sister, for example."

"Ms. Webb, if I were capable of predicting who would grow up to be a killer, I'd be more famous than Freud. The important thing for you to remember is that Jill Rohmer is nobody's fool. She's a very manipulative and clever liar."

"So, how do I deal with someone like that?"

"Very carefully," the psychologist replied.

"I met Mrs. Barnet in the park," Jill was saying now, suddenly answering the question

Charley had almost forgotten she'd asked. "The park was a couple of blocks from our house, and I used to go there when I wanted to be by myself."

"That would be Crescent Park?"

Jill looked genuinely surprised. "I don't know. I didn't realize it had a name."

"Go on."

"Well, one day I was sitting on one of the swings—there were three of them—and Tammy came running over. Her mom was right behind her. You could see how crazy she was about Tammy, just by the look on her face. How come you want to talk about this now?" Jill asked Charley. "Are we finished talking about **my** childhood?" She seemed mildly put out.

"I thought we'd take a break from that for a while," Charley answered.

"How come?"

"Well, you've already given me a lot to digest, what with your letters and our previous conversations. I just thought we might tackle something else today. Unless you have something specific you'd like to share with me."

Jill leaned back in her chair, looking skeptical as she twisted the ends of her hair between her fingers. "Something I'd like to **share**? Now you sound like a psychiatrist."

"Your letters are quite remarkable," Charley said, sensing hostility, and trying to maintain control of the situation. (Dr. Norman had stressed that it was important never to let Jill have the upper hand. "If anyone's going to do the conning, it should be you," he'd said.) "You have a real flair for writing," Charley elaborated. "A gift."

Jill's smile was immediate and proud. "You think so?"

"Absolutely. Those letters tell me a lot about you."

"Such as?"

"That you're a very bright and talented young woman," Charley said, borrowing her mother's words, and wondering whether her mother had been similarly insincere. "That you can succeed at anything you set your mind to."

"Honestly? You're not just saying that?"

Charley shook her head. "It's true."

"That's so nice. It really means a lot to me that you think that."

What are mothers for? Charley thought. "So, you met Tammy and her mother at the park," she reiterated.

"Tammy wanted the swing I was sitting on. Said it was her favorite because it went higher than the others. I said okay. I even offered to push her. One thing just kind of led to another. I guess I must have given Mrs. Barnet my phone number, 'cause she called a few days later, asked if I could baby-sit on Saturday night. I said, sure. Turned out that the Barnets liked to go out every Saturday night, so I lucked into a regular job. Of course, that didn't sit too well with Gary. You talk to him yet?"

"Not yet."

"Yeah, well, when you do, watch out. He lies like a rug." Jill laughed. "My father used to say that all the time. 'Man lies like a rug,' he'd say. I didn't know what he meant for the longest time. But once I figured it out, I had the best laugh."

"Gary didn't like you baby-sitting on Saturday nights?"

"At first he thought it would be okay, because he just assumed I'd let him come over and we could, you know, make out and stuff. He especially liked the idea of doing it in the Barnets' bed, but that didn't sit too well with me. I mean, what if they came home early or Tammy woke up? So after awhile I wouldn't let him come over anymore. He was pretty mad. Then I started baby-sitting for the Starkeys on Friday nights, and he got really upset, said, 'What kind of girlfriend spends her entire weekends baby-sitting a bunch of brats?'"

"It **is** a bit unusual for a girl your age, especially one with a boyfriend—you would have been how old?"

"I was nineteen when I started baby-sitting Tammy."

"Gary was probably unhappy to be spending so much time alone."

"He was unhappy 'cause he wasn't getting his dick sucked as often as he liked. At least, not by me," Jill said.

Right, Charley thought. "You must have really enjoyed baby-sitting," was what she said.

"Oh, I did," Jill said with such enthusiasm it was impossible not to believe her. "I loved those kids. Tammy was so cute, with her red hair and her little black patent leather shoes. She had the cutest little button nose. And this weird little giggle. I used to love making her laugh."

"And the Starkey twins?"

"They were the sweetest things. Blond hair, blue eyes. Noah had this little scar above his right eyebrow where he'd picked the scab off a chicken pox. I used to kiss it all the time. You just wanted to eat him up. His sister, too. Really sweet."

Yet you slaughtered them! Charley wanted to scream. These sweet little children with the cute button noses and kissable scars are dead because of you. How can you sit here and discuss them so calmly, so **lovingly**? Take it easy, her reporter's voice cautioned. Keep her talking. Ask direct questions. Stay in control, the way Dr. Norman had advised. Go slow, or you'll lose her. "You met Mrs. Starkey in the park as well?"

Jill's eyes narrowed in thought. "No. I met her in the mall. I was in the bookstore, buying a present for Tammy, and she came in with the twins, and she asked me what book I was buying, and I told her. It was **The Paperbag Princess**, which is a really good book. I said I couldn't recommend it highly enough, so she bought a copy. And we ended up taking the kids for ice cream, and it just kind of took off from there. Kind of like with Mrs. Barnet. I'm very good with people," Jill said. "They really like me."

Charley nodded, searching for even a small trace of irony in Jill's voice, hearing none. "What sort of things did you do with the kids?"

"The usual. I read to them, we watched TV, we played Barbie and hide-and-seek."

"Ever play doctor with them?" Charley asked casually.

"What?" Jill's eyes widened. She glanced warily at Alex. "What's that supposed to mean?"

"Just that kids sometimes like to play doctor," Charley said.

"I'm not a kid."

Charley marveled at Jill's indignation. She seemed genuinely perturbed at Charley's suggestion. "Did they ever ask you questions of a sexual nature?"

"Like what?"

"Like, where do babies came from, or how are they made?" Charley elaborated.

Jill hesitated. "Sometimes Noah would say

something like, he had a penis and Sara didn't. Stuff like that."

"They ever get on your nerves?"

"No. They were good kids," Jill said.

"So, you never hit them or anything?"

"Of course not."

"How did you discipline them?"

"I didn't have to."

"You never had to send them to their rooms for a time-out?"

"No, they were great. They never gave me any trouble."

"Did you ever take them swimming?" Charley asked, shifting gears.

"Swimming?"

"The Barnets had a pool, didn't they?"

"Yeah. Tammy and I went swimming together a couple of times."

"Bathing suits can be tricky for little kids. You ever help Tammy get out of her wet suit?"

"I guess I did."

"So you saw her naked."

"Maybe. So what?"

"Did that turn you on?"

"Did **what** turn me on? Seeing a little girl without her clothes? How sick do you think I am?"

The question proved too much for Charley. "Jill, I have to remind you that you're on death row for the sex slayings of three young children. Can you really be so outraged by my question?"

"I'm not sexually turned on by children," Jill said emphatically. "I don't even like sex, for God's sake."

"You don't?"

"It's a real pain, if you ask me."

Interesting choice of words, Charley thought. "Do you like pain?"

"What?"

"Do you like inflicting pain?" Charley clarified.

"No. Of course not."

"It wouldn't be all that abnormal though, given your upbringing."

"It wouldn't be abnormal?" Jill sputtered.

"A psychiatrist might argue the fact that being brutalized as a child led you to brutalize others," she said, proferring Dr. Norman's assessment.

"Might he now?"

"How would **you** explain what happened to those children? How would you explain the bite marks and the cigarette burns, the sexual assaults and the . . ."

Jill covered her ears with her hands. "Stop it. Stop it."

"Tammy and the twins were tortured before they were killed. They were suffocated with plastic bags, their dying screams recorded on a tape recorder found in your bedroom. Your voice was on those tapes. Your DNA was on their bodies."

"There are reasons. . . ."

"Tell me."

"I can't."

"Then what am I doing here?"

"You don't understand."

"Then help me to understand."

"It wasn't my idea. I never wanted to hurt those children. I loved them."

"Whose idea was it?"

Jill bit down on her lower lip, her eyes moving from Charley to Alex, then back to Charley. She pulled at her hair, fidgeted in her seat, buried her face in her hands. "It was Jack's," she said finally.

Charley inched forward in her chair, tried not to look too eager. "Jack?"

"My boyfriend."

"I thought Gary was your boyfriend."

Jill giggled. "So did he."

The giggle was unsettling. Was Jill playing with her? Charley wondered. "Jack who?"

Jill shook her head. "Jack Splat, could eat no fat . . ."

"I believe that's **Sprat**," Charley barked, in no mood to be toyed with.

"Yeah? Well, it should be **Splat**. You know, like when you squish a bug, and it goes splat!"

Jill tossed her hair from one shoulder to the other with a flick of her head.

"Tell me about Jack," Charley urged quietly.

Jill's eyes got that dreamy, faraway look. A small smile played with the corners of her mouth. "He's the best."

Charley cocked her head to one side. Just like Bandit, she thought, as she waited for Jill to continue.

"And I don't mean just that he's good in bed. Which, of course, he is. He's the best. He does this thing with his tongue that sends me into total spasms."

Reflexively, Charley crossed one leg over the other. "I thought you didn't like sex," she interrupted, looking over at Alex, who was staring into his lap. Probably wishing he'd stayed in Palm Beach Gardens, Charley thought.

"I don't. At least I didn't. Until Jack."

"What makes him so special? Aside from his tongue." Charley uncrossed her legs, crossed them the other way.

"Everything. He's sweet and smart and funny and considerate." Jill shrugged. "I don't know. He's just different from any other guy I've ever met."

"And it was this sweet, smart, funny, considerate guy's idea to kidnap and murder three helpless children?" Charley asked before she could stop herself.

"You're sounding very judgmental, Charley," Jill chastised.

"Sorry. I'm just having a hard time reconciling the adjectives with the actions."

"I don't understand."

You're not the only one, Charley thought. "It was Jack's idea to kidnap Tammy Barnet and Sara and Noah Starkey?"

"He said it would be fun."

"Fun?"

"He said we'd take them on an adventure they'd never forget. I honestly never thought . . ." Jill's voice drifted off.

"Tell me what happened."

Jill looked to Alex, her eyes questioning whether she should proceed. He nodded.

"I went over to Tammy's. She was playing in her tree house in the backyard. I knew she played there every day. Her mother would watch her from the kitchen while she was getting dinner ready. So I snuck around the back of the house and I got her attention, and I put my fingers over my mouth, you know, telling her to 'ssh,' and waved her over, like it was supposed to be a big secret. And I told her to come with me, that we were gonna surprise her mother. And she got all excited and took my hand, and we got into Jack's car, which was waiting around the corner, and away we went."

Charley barely suppressed a shudder. "And

you honestly never thought any harm would come to her?"

"I honestly didn't."

"What about Noah and Sara Starkey? You had to know what was going to happen to them."

Jill stared into her lap. "Jack said it would be different."

"But it wasn't, was it?"

"No."

"And you just went along with him. You helped him. . . ."

"I did as I was told."

"Why?" Charley asked, incredulously. The image of Gabe Lopez suddenly popped into her mind. "Did he have a gun to your head?"

"He didn't need one."

"What does that mean?"

"He had this power over me. It was like I had no choice. What's that old nursery rhyme?" Jill asked. **"Jack and Jill went up the hill to fetch a pail of water. Jack fell down and broke his crown . . ."**

No choice, Charley was thinking as she silently finished the rhyme.

And Jill came tumbling after.

22

So what do you think? You really think there's a Jack?" Charley asked Alex.

"I think there's a guy. Whether or not his name is Jack, I couldn't say."

"She honestly never told you?"

Alex shook his head, lifted up his fork, and stabbed at his salad.

It was a few minutes after five o'clock in the afternoon. They were sitting in the small back room at Centro's, an unassuming Italian restaurant located in an even more unassuming strip mall a few miles east of Pembroke Pines, drinking an exceptional Shiraz, and trying to pretend the dinner they were about to eat was strictly business. Was it? Charley wondered. What was this dinner really about? "Jack and Jill," she mused. "Seems almost too perfect."

Alex raised one eyebrow as he directed a forkful of mixed greens into his mouth, somehow managing to look appealing even with a hint of salad oil glistening at the side of his lips. "You don't like your carpaccio?" He indicated her barely touched appetizer with his chin.

"No, it's delicious." Charley lifted a slice of the raw meat to her mouth, lowered it again almost immediately. "It's just so frustrating," she continued. "One minute I'm convinced Jill and I are making real progress; the next minute she completely shuts down."

"You were getting too close."

"To what?"

"The truth, obviously."

"The truth is anything but obvious," Charley corrected.

"The truth is that Jill didn't act alone. The truth is that someone else was calling the shots."

"That someone else being Jack **Splat**?" Charley leaned back in her chair as Alex speared another forkful of his salad. "What am I doing here, Alex?"

"Not eating your appetizer, by the look of things."

Charley chuckled, once again brought her fork to her lips. "I meant . . ."

"I know what you meant."

"What am I doing with Jill? Or maybe I should say, what's Jill doing with me? Is this all an elaborate game to her? Is she playing with me? Like she played with Tammy Barnet and the Starkey twins before she . . ." Her voice drifted off, her eyes falling on the hand-painted map of Italy on the wall behind Alex's head.

"I really don't think so," Alex said. "I honestly think she wants to cooperate, that she wants the truth to come out. I **know** she thinks the world of you."

"Is that supposed to make me feel better? That a child-killing psychopath thinks I'm ter-rific?"

"It's hard for her, Charley. She's never talked about some of these things before. To anyone."

"Not even to you?"

"Not even to me." He finished the last of his salad. "At least not in the kind of detail she talks about them with you. I knew about Ethan, of course. And I have my suspicions about her father."

Charley ran her fingers along the edge of the white paper tablecloth. "Such as?"

Alex hesitated.

"Come on, Alex. I know Jill gave you permis-sion to talk to me about this."

"Yes, she did. It's just that I'm used to **keep-ing** client's confidences, not revealing them to reporters. It's a hard habit to break."

Charley found herself oddly stung by his casual reference to her as a mere reporter. Don't be ridiculous, she castigated herself silently, pushing the carpaccio into her mouth and chewing furiously. That's what you are, isn't it? A reporter. Trying to do her job. To ferret out the truth. To write a thought-provoking, best-selling book about a heartless, bone-chilling sociopath, and in the process, to become rich, famous, and respected, not necessarily in that order. What else **but** a reporter would you be to him?

What else would you like to be? she found herself wondering, biting into another piece of raw meat. "So, what suspicions do you have regarding Jill's father?" she asked, trying not to notice how distinguished Alex looked in his navy suit, or the way the color underlined the deep blue of his eyes. What was the matter with her?

"I think he may have sexually abused Jill, along with Ethan. Isn't that what you think?"

Charley sighed. "I think the Rohmers manage to make the Webbs look almost normal."

Alex laughed. Charley waited for him to ask the obvious questions about what her family was like, but he didn't.

Clearly he doesn't care, she thought. "How come you didn't raise any of this at Jill's trial?"

"Any of what?"

"The abuse, the family history, the mysterious Jack Splat."

"I wanted to."

"Jill wouldn't let you?"

"She refused to testify," he said simply. "Said

she'd deny everything if I so much as raised the possibility of abuse or an accomplice."

"Because she was protecting someone or because she was afraid?"

"Probably a bit of both." He finished the wine in his glass, looked around for the waiter. "I guess this book will be her testimony."

"A little late, wouldn't you say? She's sitting on death row."

Alex squirmed in his seat, pushed his salad plate into the middle of the table, almost knocking over the small vase of brightly colored plastic flowers. "I'm painfully aware of where my client is sitting, Miss Webb," he said.

"I'm sorry. I didn't mean to . . ."

"No, I'm sorry," he apologized immediately. "I didn't mean to snap at you like that. Do you think we could talk about something else? **Anything** else. At least for a little while?"

"Of course."

There was silence.

"So, what made you decide to become a lawyer?" Charley asked, then rolled her eyes. Of all the dumb questions to ask, she was thinking, feeling like a teenage girl on her first date. Why was she so nervous?

"Will you excuse me for a minute?" he asked as if she hadn't spoken, then left the table before Charley had a chance to respond.

She watched him disappear into the washroom

at the back. "Well, this is going very well," she said under her breath. Then, to herself, Where did you think it was going to go? It was obvious the man wasn't remotely interested in her, that he'd taken her to dinner—at five o'clock in the afternoon no less, when the place was filled with seniors there for the "early bird" specials—because he felt obligated. And now he couldn't wait to get away from her. That was why he'd been so eager for her to finish her appetizer. Not because he wanted to impress her with the quality of the food, but so that the waiter could serve them their main course and they could get out of here. Since she had her own car, he wouldn't even have to suffer her company on the long drive home. They could go their own merry—and separate—ways.

Wasn't that what she wanted as well? When had she started to think of Alex Prescott as anything other than a means to an end? He wasn't even that attractive, she decided, watching as he exited the washroom and began zigzagging through the other tables toward her. **It wasn't the blueness of his eyes or even the way they seemed to look right through her, as if he were staring into her soul, as if he could read all her most secret thoughts,** Charley recited silently, as he stopped to talk to the waiter. **Nor was it the insolent way he occupied the center of the room, his slim hips tilted**

slightly forward, his thumbs hooked provocatively into the pockets of his tight jeans, the pout on his full lips a silent invitation, daring her to come closer. Approach at your own risk, he said without speaking. "Shit," Charley said out loud, downing what was left of her wine in one prolonged gulp.

"Something wrong?" Alex asked, pulling out his chair and sitting down.

Charley held up her empty glass. "Out of wine."

"I've asked the waiter to bring us each another glass. So," he said, leaning forward on both elbows. "What made me decide to become a lawyer? Was that the question?"

She shrugged. "Small talk 101."

He smiled. "Well, let's see. My mother always said I could argue anyone under the table. An old girlfriend complained I always had to have the last word. And the idea of justice as a goal always fascinated me."

"What do you mean?"

"People are always trying to make things right," he explained. "Something bad happens, you immediately look for the good you hope will come out of it. Something gets broken, you instinctively try to fix it. Someone gets hurt, you want to kiss it better. A family falls apart, you look for somebody to blame. Innocents get slaughtered, you cry for the blood of the guilty.

Somebody has to pay. People want justice," he concluded. "They think it will make a difference."

"You're saying it doesn't?"

"I'm saying I haven't given up on the idea entirely, which is why, to answer your earlier question, I became a lawyer."

"An idealist and a cynic all in one sentence," Charley said, not without admiration.

"I like the structure the justice system provides," Alex continued, again as if she hadn't spoken. "Just the putting of those two words together—justice and system—the notion that you can have a **system** of justice, I find that fascinating. I like that you have this whole institutionalized procedural—arrests, arraignments, grand juries, indictments, trials, sentences, appeals. I like that people come to me because they think I can help them. I like that sometimes I'm able to do just that. I'm glad that I can put my ability to argue anybody into the ground to good use, and that sometimes my last word is strong enough to keep someone from going to jail. Occasionally I even get to make things right."

"You kiss it better," Charley said, and smiled.

Alex suddenly pushed himself out of his chair, leaned across the table, and kissed her on the lips. Then he sat back down, watching the colors shift on her face as the waiter approached with two fresh glasses of wine. "I'm sorry. I shouldn't have done that," he said as soon as the waiter departed.

Charley said nothing. If she spoke, the words might dislodge the pleasant tingles that lingered on her lips. What had just happened?

"Can we pretend I didn't do that?"

"Why did you?" Charley asked.

"Because, obviously, I'm an idiot."

"I don't think you're an idiot."

"You don't?"

Charley shook her head. Alex leaned forward and kissed her again. This time Charley kissed him back.

"Well, this is a surprise," Alex said, as the waiter returned with their dinners.

"It certainly is," Charley agreed.

"I'm sorry," the waiter said. "You didn't order the lasagna?"

"No, I did," Alex said. "I definitely ordered the lasagna."

"And I'm the ravioli special." The waiter placed the ravioli in front of Charley, the steam rising from her plate partially obscuring her view of the man sitting across from her. Who was he? she found herself wondering. More to the point, who was **she**? "I feel like a character in one of my sister's books," she admitted.

"And how does that feel?"

"Pretty good actually."

They laughed.

"What exactly happened there?" Charley asked.

"I kissed you. You kissed me back," he said.

"But why did you kiss me? I didn't think you even liked me."

"You didn't think I liked you?" Alex repeated incredulously. "That's why I keep making this incredibly boring drive down here, because I don't like you?"

"I assumed you were just looking out for Jill's interests."

"It was more a case of looking out for yours."

"Really?"

"Don't you ever look in the mirror?" Alex asked. "God, the first time you walked into my office, I just about fell off my chair. And then you opened your mouth, and it got even better. You were smart and feisty and full of pee and vinegar, as my mother used to say, and I thought, Shit, man, you're in trouble here."

"You sure had me fooled."

"God knows I tried."

"I thought you were an arrogant son of a bitch. Which isn't necessarily a bad thing," Charley qualified immediately. "I have a soft spot for arrogant sons of bitches."

He laughed. "I kept telling myself to keep my distance, keep everything nice and professional, try not to notice how nice your hair looked, or how pretty you smelled. But then you were sitting across from me, not eating your carpaccio, and making small talk 101, and you said something about kissing it better. . . . And so I did."

"So, what happens now?"

"That's up to you."

"Well, I'm not really very hungry," Charley said, pushing her plate away. "I don't usually eat this early."

"We could always get a doggie bag," Alex suggested. "Eat later."

"Later?"

"After."

"After?" she repeated. "As in 'happily ever'?"

He smiled. "As in after," he said.

It was almost ten o'clock before they finally got around to eating their dinner. "I'm so starving," Charley said, tearing into her ravioli, and watching some of the spicy tomato sauce drip down the front of Alex's pale blue shirt. "Oh, no. Look what I did."

Alex reached across the round glass table to wipe up the spill, his fingers brushing up against Charley's bare breast beneath. "It's an old shirt."

They were sitting in the small eating area off the large kitchen in his one-bedroom condo off PGA Boulevard in the heart of Palm Beach Gardens. The seventh-floor apartment looked out over an artificial lake beyond which was a new plaza full of upscale restaurants and specialty stores. The fabulous Gardens Mall was right next door. The ocean was less than ten minutes away. I could live here, Charley found herself thinking, then instantly dismissed such thoughts from her head. One night does not a lifetime make. Just because Alex Prescott was good in bed—make that **great** in bed—didn't mean their relationship would last longer than any of her others. She took another mouthful of ravioli, hoping he'd be around at least long enough for her to finish her research.

"You're frowning," he said.

"Am I?"

"Having second thoughts?"

She shook her head. "Just wondering how this will affect our working relationship."

"It doesn't have to affect it at all. We're both professionals."

"Yeah, but I'm a girl," Charley reminded him with a laugh. "We don't compartmentalize as easily as you guys do."

"Somehow I doubt that." He took one forkful of lasagna, then another. "How come you never got married?" he asked. Then, "Don't answer that. It was a stupid question."

"No, it wasn't. I mean, I **do** have two children after all." Whom her mother had graciously consented to look after until she got home.

"You have a date?" Elizabeth had inquired when Charley called her from the restaurant.

"It isn't a date."

"Of course it isn't. Have a good time, darling."

"Marriage was just never a high priority," Charley told him. "I guess because of how miserable my parents' marriage was." She shrugged. "How about you?"

"I came close once. A few years back. Didn't work out."

They ate in silence for the next several minutes, Charley naked beneath the shirt Alex had been wearing before they made love. He was now bare-chested above a pair of jeans. She thought of asking him why his close call hadn't worked out, then decided against it. The fact was he probably didn't know. Who could really say why a relationship didn't work? Weren't there two sides to every story? Reality was subjective, truth a matter of opinion. The bottom line was that relationships either worked, or they didn't.

"So, what's next on the agenda?" he asked. "With regard to Jill's book."

"**My** book," Charley corrected.

He smiled. "Sorry. **Your** book."

"I thought I'd interview Jill's old boyfriend."

"Gary Gojovic," Alex stated, carefully enunciating each hard syllable.

"You're not a fan?"

"Gary's testimony pretty well guaranteed Jill a seat on death row."

"It was pretty damning," Charley agreed. "That stuff about seeing Jill torturing a kitten . . ."

"Which she's always denied."

"Alex," Charley reminded him, "she murdered three little children. Why would she have any problem torturing a cat?"

Alex tossed his fork to his plate. "Speaking of animals, how's your little dog?"

Charley found herself suddenly smiling from ear to ear. "He's great. So sweet. I come home, he's waiting at the door. I sit down, he jumps into my lap. I leave the room, he follows me. If I disappear for two seconds, he's so glad to see me when I get back, you'd think I'd been gone for years. I'm trying not to get too attached."

"Sounds like you're already hooked."

"Yeah, well, there's something very appealing about unconditional love. But I just have to keep reminding myself that he's not my dog, and that pretty soon I'll have to give him back."

"To Glen McLaren," Alex stated, tapping his fingers restlessly against the glass tabletop.

"Is there a problem?" Charley asked, sensing there was.

"How well do you know this guy?"

"Glen? Not very. But I consider him a friend," Charley said. "I repeat, is there a problem?"

"I don't know. Maybe."

"What are you trying to say, Alex? It's not like you to be so circumspect."

"You have to understand that I wasn't trying to pry. It was just that I thought his name sounded familiar, so I did a bit of snooping around. Turned out that, at one time, Glen McLaren had a financial interest in a couple of clubs in the Lauderdale area."

"I know that. So?"

"So, did you know that one of the people who used to hang out at one of those clubs was a small-time drug dealer by the name of Ethan Rohmer?"

"What?"

"I found out Ethan was arrested one night trying to sell drugs to an undercover cop, although a smart lawyer got the charges dismissed."

Charley tried to process what she was hearing. What did it mean? "Are you trying to tell me that Glen and Ethan are somehow involved?"

"I'm not trying to tell you anything. The truth is they might not know each other at all."

"Just because Ethan was a regular at a club in which Glen had a financial stake says nothing other than . . ."

". . . Ethan was a regular at a club in which Glen had a financial stake," Alex agreed.

"It's entirely possible the two men never met, that they weren't even aware of each other's existence."

"Absolutely."

"Kind of coincidental though, you have to admit."

"It could be nothing. It's **probably** nothing."

"But you don't think so," Charley stated.

"I don't know what to think," Alex admitted. "Shit."

"It's probably nothing," Alex repeated.

Charley nodded.

"Just be careful, that's all." He came around the table, put his hands on her shoulders, began gently kneading the muscles at the back of her neck. "Can you stay the night?"

She shook her head. "No. I should be getting home."

"I'll follow you in my car," he offered when she was dressed and at the door.

"No, that's hardly necessary."

"I insist."

"Alex, really, I'll be fine."

"Don't argue," he said.

Charley smiled. She didn't say it out loud, but this was one argument she was only too happy to lose.

23

Her mother was sitting on the sofa, sound asleep, **Remember Love** open on her lap, Bandit dozing at her feet, when Charley tiptoed into the living room. "Mom," she whispered gently, as the dog woke up and began jumping up and down with excitement. "Yes, hello, Bandit, hello. I'm glad to see you, too," Charley said, realizing she was. "Mom," she whispered again, slightly louder the second time, her right hand reaching toward her mother's shoulder, stopping before she made contact. "I'm home."

"Darling," her mother said, opening her eyes and straightening her back. "How'd it go?"

"Good. Everything's good."

Her mother smiled, twisted her neck from side to side. "I must have dozed off. What time is it?"

"Almost eleven. You can sleep here tonight if you want."

"Oh, no." Elizabeth put the book on the coffee table, then pushed herself to her feet and stretched her arms high above her head, her fingers straining toward the ceiling. "I should get going." She grabbed her bright red shawl from the back of the sofa, wrapping it across her shoulders as she walked toward the front door.

Charley thought she should probably try to convince her mother to stay, or at the very least, spend a few minutes with her inquiring about her day, but what she said was, "I'll call you tomorrow." Bandit stood at her feet, barking his good-byes as her mother climbed into her mauve Civic and drove off. "You have to do busy?" she asked the dog.

In response, Bandit ran to the nearest shrub and lifted his leg.

"Amazing," Charley marveled, as she always did. "Amazing," she repeated, thinking it the perfect word to describe the day's events. Not to mention the evening's. She scooped the dog into her arms and walked down the hall toward her children's bedroom, opening the door and peeking inside. "Sweet dreams, my beautiful angels," she whispered before closing the door and continuing on to her room.

She undressed, remembering the measured way Alex had removed each item of her clothing, feeling his hands gentle on her breasts and buttocks, the touch of his lips on the side of her neck, the gentle probing of his fingers between her legs, the expert exploration of his tongue. God, if he was half as good in the courtroom as he was in the bedroom, he'd be as well-known as Clarence Darrow, she thought, recalling the law books that were stacked along the bottom of his living room walls, competing with an impressive collection of old movie classics. Otherwise, the condo wasn't very different from the apartments of most men who lived alone, its elaborate stereo system pretty much overwhelming everything else—the brown leather sofa and matching chair that sat on the Mexican tile floor, a large TV and DVD player, along with an outdated VCR for those classic old movies. The paintings on the walls were more decorative than artful: a generic landscape, a bowl of green apples, a harbor full of sailboats.

The bedroom was another matter entirely. Here, gorgeous black-and-white photographs dominated the walls: a fully clothed couple lying on a stony beach, embracing behind a large umbrella, by Henri Cartier-Bresson; an exuberant sailor kissing a young woman in Times Square on D-day, by Robert Doisneau; a magnificent orchid in bloom by Robert Mapplethorpe; a Diane Arbus photo of two young sisters staring blankly into space; another picture of two women laughing exuberantly, their heads thrown back, their mouths open. "This is quite a collection," she'd whispered, her eyes falling on the guitar that leaned against the side of the desk opposite the bed, the moon shining through the side window reflected in the glass of his computer screen. "Maybe you'll play it for me later."

"Later," he'd said.

"After," she'd whispered.

And they'd laughed.

Ultimately, Alex had begged off playing for her, claiming it was his ace in the hole, a way to guarantee she'd be back. Not much to worry about there, Charley decided now, groaning softly. "Amazing," she whispered again, washing her face and brushing her teeth, then crawling into bed. Immediately Bandit folded his warm little body into the crook of her knees, and she fell sound asleep.

She dreamed she was chasing a large black umbrella across a field filled with flowers, Ethan Rohmer in hot pursuit, as several men in sailor suits stood on the sidelines cheering him on. She felt Ethan's hot breath on the back of her neck, his fingers grabbing for her hair. She felt herself falling, saw Ethan's shadow looming over her as he dragged her to her feet. "What do you want?" she pleaded as he began wrapping her in a bright red shawl. Except the man was no longer Ethan. He was Glen McLaren.

Charley woke up with a start, gasping for air. Bandit was immediately on his feet, licking the perspiration from her face and neck. "It's okay. It's okay, Bandit," Charley told him, patting his head, trying to reassure them both. Already the dream was disappearing, evaporating like morning dew. She'd been chasing after something, she remembered, although she could no longer recall what that something was, and a group of sailors had been watching. Was that right? And then Ethan had grabbed her. Except it wasn't Ethan. "It was Glen," she stated out loud.

Glen McLaren had a financial interest in several clubs in the Lauderdale area.

So?

So, did you know that one of the people who used to hang out at one of those clubs was a small-time drug dealer by the name of Ethan Rohmer?

So? So what? What did it mean? Did it mean anything?

Charley lay awake, flipping from her left side to her right, then onto her back, where she stared up at the slowly spinning ceiling fan for the better part of an hour, trying to rid her mind of all conscious thought. Eventually she gave up on sleep altogether and went into the kitchen, Bandit following after her, where she made herself a cup of herbal tea. She carried it into the living room and plopped down on the sofa, wondering if Alex was awake, if he, too, was having trouble sleeping. She saw her sister's novel on the coffee table and picked it up. Hell, she was living the damn thing, she thought. She might as well find out what to do next. Besides, the book had put her mother to sleep. With any luck, it would do the same thing for her.

Instead, Charley was up all night reading it. By 7 A.M., she was on the final paragraphs.

Tiffany watched Blake leave. As always, she was struck by the steadiness of his gait, the sureness of his footing. She wondered where such confidence came from, and whether she would ever be able to experience it on her own, without Blake at her side, guiding her every move. Would he look back? she wondered, arranging her features into a brave smile in case he did. Would he remember the days they'd spent laughing, the nights they'd spent loving, the hours, the minutes, the seconds when she'd embraced him with every fiber of her being? Would he be haunted, as she knew she would be, by the memory of the love they'd once clung to, yet tended to so recklessly, and abandoned so carelessly?

"Remember, love," she whispered as his shadow was absorbed by the night sky, and he disappeared from her sight forever. "Remember love."

Charley snapped the covers of the book shut, wiping away a tear. "Oh, please. Tell me you're not crying. Tell me you weren't actually moved by that ridiculous nonsense. What's happening to you?"

"Mommy?" Franny asked from the doorway. She was wearing a lilac-colored nightgown sprinkled with tiny pink ribbons, and sleep had styled her hair in an appealing array of tangles. "Is Grandma still here?"

"No, sweetie. She went home last night."

"Then who are you talking to?"

Charley made a face. "Myself."

Franny sank down on the sofa beside her mother. Bandit immediately jumped into her lap. "What about?"

"Your Auntie Anne's book." She tossed it on the cushion beside her.

"Is it good?"

"If I tell you something, will you promise never to tell another living soul?"

Franny nodded earnestly.

"I liked it."

"Well, that's okay, isn't it?"

"I'm not sure."

Franny nodded, as if she understood. "Grandma says Auntie Anne and Auntie Emily are coming to visit soon."

"That's right."

"Will I get to see them?"

"Absolutely. We're all going to have dinner together."

"Will Grandma make her famous chicken?"

"I hadn't thought about that yet. But we could ask her."

"I think you should tell Auntie Anne you liked her book."

"You do?"

"You always like it when people say nice things about your columns."

"You're right. How'd you get so smart anyway?"

"Elise says I take after Daddy," Franny answered seriously.

"Does she," Charley stated wearily. "What else does she say?"

"That she thinks I'm pretty."

"Well, she's certainly right about that."

"And that you've done a really nice job with me."

Charley couldn't disguise the surprise in her voice. "She told you that?"

"I heard her talking on the phone to one of her friends. She said that you've done a really nice job with me and James, and she hoped she could do as good a job with Daniel."

Once again, tears filled Charley's eyes.

"Are you crying?"

Charley quickly wiped the tears aside with the backs of her hands. "I'm just tired."

"I'll take Bandit out to do busy," Franny volunteered.

"Thank you, sweetheart. I'd appreciate that."

Franny wrapped her arms around her mother's neck, gave her a kiss on the cheek. "I love you."

"I love you, too."

Remember love, Charley thought, and couldn't help but smile.

"Ms. Webb's residence," the housekeeper announced.

"Can I speak to Anne, please. It's her sister. Charley," Charley added quickly, glancing at the clock beside her computer in her office at the **Palm Beach Post**, and noting that it was not quite nine thirty. Was Anne up this early? Did she work in the mornings? Would she be disturbing her? Was her sister even home, or had she already left on her tour? Charley grimaced, realizing how little she really knew about her sister's life.

"Charlotte?" Anne asked seconds later. "Is everything all right?"

Why was that always the first question any of them asked each other, as if the only possible reason for calling was that something might be wrong? "Everything's great. I read your book."

"You did?"

"I liked it. I stayed up all night actually. Couldn't put it down."

"You sound surprised," Anne remarked.

"No. Well, maybe yes, actually. But very pleasantly."

"That's good, I guess."

"How are the kids?" Charley asked.

"Fine. Emily told you I'm letting A.J. have custody?"

"Do you really think that's wise?"

"I guess we'll find out in twenty years, when they write their tell-all books."

"Are you sure about this, Anne? You told me A.J. was just using the kids to blackmail you for more alimony."

"Yeah, well, I guess that plan didn't work out the way he thought it would."

"I really think you should reconsider. . . ."

"And I really think this is none of your business."

"Since when aren't you my business?"

"Since a long time ago," Anne reminded her.

"We're still sisters," Charley reminded her back.

"Okay, spare me the sentiment. This really isn't like you, Charley. What's going on?"

"Nothing's going on. I just don't want you to do anything you'll regret. Like Tiffany in **Remember Love**," she added, rolling her eyes. Had she actually just used her sister's book as a reference point?

Anne laughed, as if reading Charley's

thoughts. "Look, there's nothing for you to be concerned about. A.J.'s a great father. He's much better with the kids than I am. He'll take good care of them."

"Like Dad took care of us?"

"Dad **did** take care of us, Charley. I mean, he might not have been the warmest person in the world . . ."

"Warm?" Charley interrupted. "He wasn't even tepid!"

"He did the best he could."

"He did the **least** he could."

"You didn't give him much of a chance."

"I gave him every chance in the world. I'm not the one who cut off contact."

"He felt betrayed, Charley."

"How did I betray him? Because I agreed to see our mother after twenty years?"

"You're still seeing her."

"Why shouldn't I? Why should I have to choose between them?" Charley asked.

"Because that's the way it is."

"It doesn't have to be."

"You didn't give him any choice."

"That's ridiculous. We all have choices."

"Right. You've made yours. He's made his. And I've made mine. Can we just leave it at that?"

"Could you please just think about things a little more before you finalize anything?"

"Trust me, I've given the matter plenty of thought. I'm not abandoning my children, Charley. It's not as if I'm running off to Australia," she said pointedly.

Twenty years of sadness filled the space between.

"Okay," Charley conceded.

"Please don't worry about me. Everything's terrific. My book is selling like hotcakes. I've just signed a multimillion-dollar deal for three more. My speaking tour's a smashing success. Four hundred people turned up in Kansas City last week, which is, like, amazing."

Amazing, Charley repeated, seeing Alex smile at her from a corner of her mind.

"And almost as many in Atlanta on Monday. I'm off to Denver tomorrow, then on to L.A. and San Francisco."

"When will you be in Florida?"

"Looks like I'll be in Palm Beach a week from Saturday, which I think is March the third. I'm probably also going to do a signing that afternoon, and my publicist is trying to nail down Sunday for the interview with **People**. And if you say 'what people?' I may have to shoot you."

Charley scribbled the dates down. "Okay, so we'll do dinner Saturday night?"

Silence.

"Anne? Dinner at my place Saturday night?"

"Fine," Anne said curtly. "I'll speak to you next week."

"Take care," Charley told her sister.

"You, too."

Charley waited until her sister had disconnected before hanging up. She sat staring at the picture of her children on her computer screen for several minutes, trying to imagine voluntarily giving them up. It was impossible, she decided.

Her fingers pressed the appropriate keys, and a blank page instantly filled the screen. WEBB SITE, she typed at the top of the page, then scrolled down to begin the first paragraph. **I've been thinking a lot about families lately,** she began. **My own. Other people's. And I've concluded that they are wondrous things indeed. Sturdy patchwork quilts, held together by the most delicate, the most tenuous, of threads. The slightest snag, they risk fraying and falling apart. Yet some are strong enough to survive generations of such snags. Why some, and not others?**

She stopped. Pressed DELETE. Too pompous, she decided, the words immediately vanishing. She began again. **I've been thinking a lot about families lately. As regular readers of this column know, my mother abandoned me and my siblings when we were little. My sister is now considering doing the same thing to her**

children. Tradition! **I can hear Tevye belting from his rooftop perch.**

Delete. Too judgmental.

I've been thinking a lot about families lately. I've spent a good part of the past several weeks interviewing Jill Rohmer about hers. Jill was physically beaten by her father, sexually molested by her brother, emotionally abandoned by her mother. She is currently awaiting execution for the grisly sex slayings of three helpless children. Can anyone really be too surprised?

Delete. Too unpleasant. What else had she been thinking about?

I finally got laid last night. Hooray!

"Problems?" Mitch Johnson asked from the entrance to her cubicle. Charley immediately pressed the DELETE button and turned around.

"Mitch. I didn't realize you were there."

"Thought I'd check in on my star reporter, since I haven't seen a whole lot of her around here lately."

"I've been in and out."

"Mostly out, I gather. How is Jill Rohmer anyway? As sexy as her photographs?"

"You find Jill Rohmer sexy?" Charley couldn't decide if she was more curious or horrified.

"In a perverted, psycho kind of way." Mitch smiled. "Don't you?"

"Can't say that I do, no."

"Too bad. It's an intriguing image—the two of you girls together."

"I should get back to work," Charley said testily.

"What do you and the child-killer talk about anyway?"

"I guess you'll have to wait and read the book."

"Only if I get a free copy."

Charley turned back to her computer.

"Sunday's column is due on my desk by four o'clock," she heard Mitch say on his way out.

"Asshole," she muttered when he was gone.

I owe my sister an apology, she began typing. **She's written six bestselling novels, and until last night, I hadn't read a single one.**

The phone rang. "Charley Webb," she said absently, trying to formulate her next sentence.

"This is Gary Gojovic," the voice said. "I understand you've been trying to reach me."

"Yes, hello, Mr. Gojovic. Thank you for returning my call."

"Do I know you?"

"I don't think so. I'm a reporter with the **Palm Beach Post**." The line went dead in her hands. "Hello? Mr. Gojovic? Hello?" Charley hung up, checked her address book for his phone number, then dialed his office.

"Hartley and Sons Plumbing and Installation," the receptionist announced.

"Gary Gojovic, please."

"One moment. I'll connect you."

"Gary Gojovic," came the voice seconds later.

"This is Charley Webb. Please don't hang up." Again the line went dead in her hands. "Great. That's just great." She pressed REDIAL.

"Hartley and Sons Plumbing and Installation," came the now-familiar voice.

"I've been thinking of installing a new shower," Charley improvised. "And a friend of mine recommended Gary Gojovic."

"Yes, Gary's our top installer. Do you have anything specific in mind?"

"I was hoping for a whole new look."

"That's always very exciting. Where are you located?"

Charley gave the woman her address.

"I could have Gary there tomorrow morning between ten and twelve, if that's all right."

"It's perfect."

"May I have your name?"

Charley's mind went completely blank. She stared at her computer screen. **I owe my sister an apology**, she read. **She's written six best-selling novels, and until last night, I hadn't read a single one.** "Tiffany," Charley heard herself say, borrowing the name of her sister's latest heroine. "Tiffany Lang."

24

"Mrs. Lang?" the young man asked, smiling when he saw her. He was maybe thirty, short and somewhat stocky, with close-cropped blond hair and pale green eyes, and when he smiled, the edges of his mouth turned down instead of up. "I'm Gary Gojovic, from Hartley and Sons."

Charley stepped away from her front door to allow him entry, Bandit rushing forward to greet him. "You'll have to excuse my dog," she said, surprised by her unintended use of the possessive pronoun. "He thinks everybody's here to see **him**."

Gary bent down to rub behind Bandit's ears, lowering the handful of brochures he was carrying to the floor. Bandit's tail wagged so hard, his entire body shook. "Easy, little guy. You're gonna fall over if you aren't careful. What kind of dog is he?"

"I think he's a combination of things. You obviously like dogs." Charley touched the tiny tape recorder inside the pocket of her denim shorts, shifting her weight from one bare leg to the other. Nothing like a small dog and a little skin to stimulate conversation, she was hoping, surreptitiously checking the cleavage revealed by her scoop-neck white T-shirt. Not too much. Just enough to get the testosterone flowing and the tongue wagging.

"Oh, yeah, I love dogs. I have three of my own."

"Three? My goodness." **My goodness**? Charley repeated silently. Maybe she really **was** Tiffany Lang. "What kind are they?"

"Dobermans."

"Ouch." Charley automatically took several steps back.

"Dobermans are great dogs. Don't believe that nonsense you read. You're good to them, they're good to you."

"Like people."

"Exactly." Gary picked up his brochures and pushed himself back to his full height, which Charley estimated to be maybe five feet seven inches. "Sorry I'm late. I had a little trouble finding the place."

"It can be a bit tricky." Charley tried picturing Gary standing next to Jill. They were an easy fit, she decided, studying the slope of his shoulders, the thrust of his hips, as Jill's image arranged itself around him.

"Yeah. I turned too soon. Ended up having to make a circle around the Convention Center."

"Happens to people all the time. Can I get you a cup of coffee?"

"No, thanks. I'm all coffeed out."

"Some orange juice?"

Gary shook his head, glanced toward the back of the house. "So, you're thinking of putting in a new shower?"

"I'm thinking about it." Charley led him toward her en suite bathroom, carefully exaggerating the wiggle in her walk, as Bandit raced ahead. She guided Gary around her freshly made bed into the all-white bathroom.

"Not too much room in here," he observed, eyes bouncing from the ceiling to the floor, from the window to the mirror over the sink. "Limits your options a bit." He examined the combination shower-bath, pushed back the white plastic shower curtain, and sat on the side of the tub, running his blunt fingers along the square white tiles lining the shower wall. "You been having problems with these tiles?"

"Not that I know of. Why?"

"Well, these aren't really bathroom tiles. They don't absorb moisture very well. I'm surprised they haven't started popping off the wall." He knocked against them, as if to illustrate what he was talking about. "Hear that?"

Charley leaned forward. "It's kind of hollow."

"Could be a real problem. Floor tiles, too." He kicked at the floor with the heel of his black boot.

"You're kidding." The tiles on her floor and shower weren't suitable? They were going to start popping off? She was going to have to retile her bathroom?

"So, the first thing I'd recommend is replacing all of them with something more appropriate. And then I'd suggest going with a shower door instead of a curtain. They're just better at containing the water. We have a variety of designs that would fit in easily along the top of the tub. I can show you a few I think would work well in here." He tapped the brochures in his lap. "And then you might consider going with a bigger shower head. Unless, of course, you want to replace the whole shebang, tub and all. But I don't think that's necessary. Tub looks okay, and like I said, you don't have a whole lot of room to work with."

"How much are we talking about?"

"Well, that'll depends on what you select. The prices for a shower door vary from just under five hundred dollars to more than two thousand."

"Two thousand dollars for a shower door?"

"Top of the line. Labor included."

"Can I see the brochures?"

"Of course." He handed them over.

Charley flipped through the pages of the first brochure, wondering if there was any way she could subtly shift the conversation from bathroom plumbing to child murderers. "You know, I could really use a cup of coffee." She walked out of the bathroom before Gary Gojovic had time to react. "Sure I can't get you some?" she asked, walking into the kitchen and dropping the brochures on the table, pouring herself a cup of the coffee she'd brewed just before Gary's arrival.

"Maybe half a cup. Cream, no sugar." He sat down at the kitchen table, pointed toward James's painting of the alligator and the snake that was taped to the refrigerator door. "Who's the artist?"

"My son, James. He's five." Charley handed Gary his coffee, her fingers brushing up against his. "I also have an eight-year-old daughter."

"Get out. You don't look old enough to have an eight-year-old daughter." Gary smiled shyly, as if he knew the line was weak.

"Why, thank you. I'll take that as a compliment."

The smile grew bolder. "It was meant as one."

"What about you?" Charley took a sip of her coffee, the steam carrying the rich aroma high into her nostrils. "Any kids?"

"Not unless you count my Dobermans."

"A wife?"

"Nope. Never married."

"Interesting. Me neither."

Gary looked intrigued. "I find that very hard to believe."

"Why is that?" Charley leaned forward to deposit a plate of shortbread cookies on the table in front of Gary, feeling his gaze fall into her cleavage.

"Well, look at you. You're gorgeous." He paused, his eyes lifting toward hers. "But you know that, don't you?"

What was she doing? Charley wondered. Although this wasn't the first time she'd flirted with a man in order to extract information, it was the first time she felt guilty about it.

Gary lifted one of the cookies to his mouth. "Shortbread. My favorite. How'd you know?"

Charley sat down, removing her tape recorder from her pocket and placing it between them in the middle of the table. It was time to end this charade. "I know shortbread cookies are your favorite because Jill Rohmer told me they were."

The cookie dropped from Gary's hand. "What the hell?" He jumped from his chair, as if he'd just received an electrical shock. The coffee sloshed around in his cup, spilled over the sides, and ran down his hand. Bandit began to bark.

"Please sit down, Gary. I just want to talk to you."

"What's going on here? Who the hell are you?"

"My name is Charley Webb. We spoke on the phone yesterday."

Gary's eyes narrowed. "The reporter from the **Palm Beach Post**?"

"I need to talk to you about Jill Rohmer."

"I'm out of here." Gary lowered the mug to the table, dropping the cookie beside it, and started from the room, his own voice following after him. **Well, look at you. You're gorgeous. But you know that, don't you?** Gary stopped, turned back, stared at Charley accusingly. "What? You're gonna play that for my boss? Get me fired? Is that the idea?"

Was it? Could she really do something like that? Could she even threaten it? "I just have a few questions."

"I gave all my answers in court. The case is over. I have nothing left to say."

"I'm writing a book about Jill," Charley explained, "and I'm trying to cover all sides of this story, yours included."

Gary shook his head. "You two make a great team."

Charley tried not to be stung by the comparison. "Please, sit down, Gary. I could really use your help."

He looked toward the floor. "Do I have a choice?"

Charley reached over, pressed a button on the

tiny tape recorder, erased their entire encounter, then waited.

Gary stood very still for several seconds, his hands forming fists at his sides. Then he walked from the room.

"Shit," Charley muttered, bracing herself for the sound of the front door slamming shut.

It never came.

"What is it you want to know?" he asked, returning to the kitchen moments later.

Charley expelled a deep sigh of relief. "Thank you so much."

"Spare me the thanks. Just get me another cup of coffee." He sank into the high-backed wooden chair. "And make it quick. I have a pretty full afternoon."

Charley jumped to her feet, poured him a fresh cup of coffee, added cream. "Do you mind . . . ?" She indicated the tape recorder.

"On the contrary. I insist. Guess we don't have to do a test," he added.

"I'm really sorry about that."

"I'm sure you are." He grabbed a cookie from the plate, popped it into his mouth. "Great cookies, by the way."

"Your name is Gary Gojovic?" Charley began. "Am I pronouncing that correctly?"

"Gojovic," he repeated. "You're saying it just fine."

"What kind of name is that?"

"Slavic. My grandparents are from the Ukraine."

"But you were born in the U.S.?"

"Second generation Floridian."

"That's unusual."

"So I'm told. What's this got to do with Jill?"

"Just trying to provide some context. How old are you, Gary?"

"Twenty-nine."

"How long have you been working for Hartley and Sons?"

"Going on three years."

"They're located in Juno Beach?"

"Yep."

"And before that?"

"Before that I worked for Jennings Hardware in Dania."

"Is that where you live?"

"Used to. I live in Jupiter now."

"But Dania's where you met Jill Rohmer?"

"I met her when she came into the store to buy a toaster."

"Tell me about her."

He shrugged. "What's there to tell? I thought she was cute. We started talking. I asked her if I could call her sometime. She said, no, she'd call me."

"Interesting."

"Jill's nothing if not interesting."

"How old were you at the time?"

"Twenty-four . . . twenty-five, maybe."

"And Jill was seventeen?"

"I **thought** she was eighteen."

"So you started dating?"

"In a manner of speaking."

"What manner?"

"What is it you want me to say?"

"I just want you to tell me about your relationship with Jill. In as much detail as you're comfortable with."

"I'm not comfortable with any of this."

"I know this isn't easy."

"You don't know shit." Gary bit into another cookie, some powdered icing falling to his chin, like flakes of snow. "Do you have any idea what it's like to find out that someone you actually considered marrying is a homicidal maniac? That the girl you thought might one day be the mother of your children murdered three little kids? I mean, what does that say about me?"

"It says you can be fooled."

"Oh, I'm a fool all right," he agreed. "You certainly proved that this morning."

"Anybody can make a mistake, Gary."

"Yeah? How many psychopaths have you fallen in love with?"

"So, you were in love with Jill?" Charley asked, returning the question to him.

Gary leaned back in his chair, looked toward the backyard. "I guess."

"Tell me about her."

He made a sound that was half-laugh, half-snort. "What can I say about Jill that hasn't been said already?" He smiled, almost in spite of himself. "She was this really neat combination of innocence and mischief. All soft one minute, hard as a rock the next. Satin and steel. And cute as hell. She had that whole girl-next-door thing going on. What is it they say—a lady in the living room, a whore in the bedroom?"

"Jill was a whore in the bedroom?"

Gary's smile grew wider. "There was nothing she wouldn't try."

"Okay. We're getting a little ahead of ourselves. Can we go back to your first date?"

"That was our first date," Gary said, and laughed.

"She slept with you on your first date?"

"Didn't even have to take her out for dinner first. She was waiting for me that night when I finished work. I walked outside to the parking lot, and there she was, standing beside my car. I asked her how she knew it was mine, and she said she'd been watching me for a couple of weeks. Next thing I knew she was riding me in the backseat. It was pretty intense."

"Go on."

"Well, we started seeing each other regularly after that. Two, three times a week. Of course, I was seeing other girls, too. At least at first. Till Jill found out about it."

"She asked you to stop?"

"Not exactly. She went straight to the source. Beat up one of the girls pretty bad. Broke her nose."

"What's this girl's name?"

"Susan. Susan Nicholson. She still lives in Dania, I think."

"And the other girls?"

"There was just one other. Christine Dunlap. Jill put a water moccasin in her parents' swimming pool."

"What!"

"Of course, no one could ever prove it, and Jill always denied it," Gary added. "But I knew. Everybody did."

"Do the Dunlaps still live in Dania?"

"Are you kidding? They sold the house three months later. I think they moved to Tampa."

"What did you think about all this?"

"Well, this here's the really awful part about the whole thing. The truth is . . . I was flattered. Can you beat that? Stupid me, I thought it proved how much she loved me. Just goes to show you what a great blow job'll do to your brain. I mean, I can really sympathize with Bill Clinton on that one."

Do you like doing that stuff? Charley suddenly heard Jill ask.

"So, you stopped seeing these other girls?" she asked.

"Didn't have much choice in the matter."

"And Jill became your girlfriend."

"Started seeing her pretty much every night."

"For how long?"

"About a year, give or take."

"What sort of things did you do together, other than the sex?"

"Went to movies, went dancing, drinking. The usual."

"Did Jill have a lot of friends?"

Gary shook his head. "Not so many. Her sister was her closest friend, I guess."

"You ever meet her brother?"

"Ethan? A real asshole. I kept as far away from him as possible."

"Did Jill ever talk to you about him?"

"She said he molested her when she was a kid."

"What about her father?"

"Said he used to beat her, that he shot her dog. She cried about that something fierce. That's why I was so shocked when I saw what she did to that stray kitten."

"What did she do?"

"She was holding it. It was squirming around

like crazy. At first I thought she was just tickling it. But then it started making these godawful sounds, more like shrieks than squeals, and so I went over to tell her to let it go. That's when I saw she was stabbing at it with a penknife. I grabbed it away from her. It took off like a bat out of hell."

"What did Jill do then?"

Gary shrugged. "Laughed. Said she'd never liked cats. I swear, that's what she said. She'd never liked cats."

"Was that the end of your relationship with her?"

"Pretty much. I mean, we kept seeing each other off and on. Hey, I'm not proud of it, but it's just hard to let go when the sex is so good. But it was never really the same. That's when she started baby-sitting pretty much every weekend. And I kind of had suspicions she was seeing somebody else."

"Any idea who it was?"

"Not a clue. Except I don't think it was a local guy. I think I would have heard about it if it was."

"When was the last time you saw Jill?"

"At her trial. We done yet?"

Charley reached over and turned off the recorder. "Can I call you if I think of any more questions?"

Gary pushed the brochures across the table. "Only if they concern shower doors and bath-room tiles." With that, he popped another cookie into his mouth and walked from the room.

The flowers—a beautiful arrangement of pink roses and white daisies—arrived at exactly twelve o'clock noon. **Are you free tomorrow night?** the card read. Signed, **Alex.**

"What do you have in mind?" Charley asked, balancing the phone between her shoulder and her ear as she filled a tall vase with water.

"How's dinner at Taboo sound?"

"Sounds great. The kids are with their fathers this weekend, so you can pack a toothbrush, if you'd like."

"Consider it packed," Alex said immediately.

"The flowers are extraordinary."

"Last night was extraordinary."

Charley felt herself actually blushing. "It **was** pretty amazing," she agreed.

"What time will you get home from seeing Jill tomorrow?"

"About five. Thanks for getting me the extra time with her."

"No thanks necessary. How about I pick you up at seven thirty?"

"Sounds perfect."

"See you tomorrow night."

"Bye." Charley arranged the flowers in the vase and carried them into the living room. It was only when she caught her reflection in the living room window that she realized she was smiling from ear to ear.

25

Jill was frowning when she walked into the interview room. "You're late."

"I got held up in traffic." Charley glanced at the fistful of papers in Jill's hand. "There was all this construction I wasn't expecting."

"You should have left your house earlier."

"I wasn't at home. Are those papers for me?"

Jill held firmly to the crumpled sheets. "Maybe." She slid into the chair across from Charley, her lips a pout, clearly not ready to forgive Charley for being ten minutes late.

"I'm really sorry, Jill. It won't happen again."

Tears formed in Jill's eyes, a few falling the length of her cheeks. "I thought maybe you weren't coming, that you were mad at me about something."

"What would I be mad about?"

"I don't know. Where were you anyway?"

"In Dania."

Jill's eyes widened. "You went back to talk to Pam?"

"No. I went to see Susan Nicholson."

"Who?"

"The name doesn't ring a bell?"

"Should it?"

"Apparently you broke her nose a few years back."

A slow smile crept into the corners of Jill's mouth. The tears disappeared from her eyes. "Susan Nicholson. God, I'd forgotten all about her."

"She hasn't forgotten you."

"I'll bet. How's her nose looking these days?"

"Like somebody broke it in three places."

"Yeah, well, she deserved it. You don't go messing with another woman's boyfriend."

"The way I heard, it was the other way around."

"Yeah? Sounds like you've been talking to Gary, too."

Charley nodded.

"So he told you about Susan, did he? What else?"

"He says you put a poisonous snake in Christine Dunlap's swimming pool."

Jill waved aside the accusation impatiently. "He's full of shit. I never did that. I mean, it's Florida, for God's sake. There are snakes. Sometimes they slither into people's pools. I didn't have anything to do with that. Stupid jerk." She slammed the papers she was holding against the desk. "I don't know what I ever saw in him."

"He says he saw you torturing a kitten."

"Yeah, he said that on the witness stand, too."

"Was it true?"

"Stupid thing scratched me. I was just trying to get it off me."

"By stabbing it?"

"It worked, didn't it? Damn thing took off running."

Charley pointed to the papers in Jill's hand. "What's that?"

"Some stuff I wrote down."

"Looks like a lot."

"Sixty pages. I wrote it yesterday."

"You wrote sixty pages in one day?"

"There's not a whole lot else to do around here." She released the papers, pushed them toward Charley.

Charley straightened out the edges, began thumbing through them. They were packed tightly with Jill's handwritten scrawl.

"It's pretty much everything I could remember from my childhood. Stuff I liked, stuff I didn't. My favorite movie actors, rock stars, models, TV shows. I even rated them. You know—thumbs up, thumbs down. It was kind of fun."

Charley removed her tape recorder from her purse, placed the papers carefully inside. "I'll read these later."

"There's other stuff there, too. Stuff about some of the things that go on in here."

"You ever know a guy named Glen McLaren?" Charley asked, recalling the possible connection between Glen and Jill's brother, Ethan.

"Glen who?" Jill asked, her shoulders stiffening almost imperceptibly.

"McLaren."

Jill shook her head, stared at the wall behind Charley's head. "Don't think so. Who is he?"

"He owns a couple of clubs. Your brother might know him."

"Yeah? I'll be sure to ask him the next time he comes to visit." She laughed. "My father was here a couple of days ago. Did you know that?"

Charley fought to keep the surprise from registering on her face as she snapped the tape recorder on. "No, I didn't. How'd that go?"

Jill sank back in her seat, crossed one arm over the other. "Not very well."

"Why not?"

"He doesn't want me talking to you, doesn't want me to do this book. Says it's not good for my mother, that Ethan's already in a shitload of trouble because of it."

Charley said nothing, waited for Jill to continue.

"I told him it was too late, that I was doing it anyway."

"What'd he say to that?"

"That I'm an ungrateful bitch, that it was a good thing I'm on death row, or he'd kill me himself."

"Charming."

Jill giggled. "That's what I should have told him."

"What **did** you tell him?"

"That I was sorry." She started to cry. "Can you beat that? I apologized to him!"

"What for?"

"For not being the daughter he wanted me to be. For hurting my mother. For embarrassing him. For bringing shame to our family."

"He's not exactly blameless here, Jill."

"I know that."

"He should be apologizing to you."

"I know that, too. Not that he ever will." She shook her head vehemently, her ponytail slapping against her neck. "What's your father like?"

Charley felt her breath catch in her throat, so that she had to push the next words out. "He's very brilliant. A scholar. Professor of English literature at Yale. A phenomenal lecturer. Very much in demand."

"Not to mention, very demanding," Jill added, as if she knew.

"That, too," Charley agreed.

"Didn't you write in one of your columns that the two of you no longer speak to each other?"

"Yes. That's right."

"Why not?"

"Guess I'm not exactly the daughter he wanted me to be, either."

Jill nodded. "Guess we have something in common."

"Guess we do."

"I think we have a **lot** in common."

"So you've said before," Charley said, recalling Jill's initial letter.

"I don't just mean our bra size," Jill said. "We both carry around a lot of anger."

"You think I'm angry?"

"Aren't you?"

"Are **you**?" Charley asked, turning the question around.

"I asked you first." Jill sat back in her chair, folded her arms across her chest.

"I'm not angry."

"You're lying."

Charley scoffed. "Why would I lie?"

"You tell me."

"There's nothing to tell."

"You're not angry with your mother for running off and leaving you when you were a little girl? You're not angry with your father for being a brilliant scholar but a lousy human being? You're not angry with your sisters for being less talented than you are, but way more famous and successful? You're not mad at your brother for being a total screw-up? You're not angry with your neighbors for, I don't know, whatever it is that neighbors do to piss each other off? You're not angry with your friends? Wait, I forgot. You don't have any friends. Why? Because they make you so angry."

"Okay, Jill. I think you've made your point."

Jill laughed. "That's the problem with writing the kind of column you do, Charley. People learn to read between the lines. That's where all the good stuff is."

Charley nodded, pretended to be checking on the tape recorder when what she was really doing was trying to buy some time, to get her breathing back under control so that she could speak without screaming.

"The difference between you and me," Jill continued, "is that you have a positive outlet for all your anger. You have your writing," she continued before Charley could ask. "You get to vent, to channel all that rage into words. I only discovered that when I started writing to you. I realized how cathartic it is to get that stuff out. Cathartic—is that the right word?"

Charley nodded.

"And yesterday, well, I started writing and I just couldn't stop. The words were pouring out of me like rain. The more I wrote, the better I felt. Maybe if I'd had that kind of outlet, those poor children wouldn't have had to die." A fresh flood of tears began spilling from Jill's eyes.

Charley reached into her purse, handed Jill a tissue.

"Thank you." Jill dabbed at her eyes, although the tears continued to flow unabated. "I'm not a monster, you know."

"I know."

"I loved those kids."

"I know you did."

"I never meant for anything bad to happen to them. You have to believe me."

"I do."

"I never wanted them to die."

"What happened, Jill?"

"I don't know. I don't know." Jill began rocking back and forth in her chair.

"Yes, you do. You do know."

"Jack said it was going to be fun. He promised he wouldn't really hurt Tammy."

"What did he do?"

"He used one of those stun guns on her. What do they call them—Tasers?"

Charley nodded, unable to speak.

"It kind of knocked her out. Then we drove out to this deserted old garage. I think it used to be a gas station or something. Tammy was starting to wake up, so Jack put a blindfold over her eyes and tied her hands behind her back.

She was crying, saying she wanted to go home. Jack didn't like that. He said we were just getting started. That's when he told me. . . ." She broke off.

"Told you what?" Charley's voice was a strained whisper.

"He told me to take her clothes off. I said, no. I didn't want to."

"But you did it," Charley stated.

"I had to. It was what Jack wanted."

"Then what?"

"You know. It's in Tammy's autopsy report."

"You burned her with cigarette butts and penetrated her with a bottle?"

"I tried to fake it. But Jack was too smart. He wouldn't let me."

"Did you ever think of saying no?"

Jill looked at Charley as if Charley had completely lost her mind. "I could never do that."

"But you could torture a helpless child."

"Tammy wasn't so helpless."

"What?"

"She could have made a run for it. I kept whispering for her to run. But she was such a stubborn little thing. She wouldn't move. Kept crying at me to take her home. But how could I do that? Jack was standing right there, operating the camera and telling me what to do, like he was this big-shot Hollywood director or something. I told her to stop making such a fuss, but she just kept screaming. I finally had to put that plastic bag over her head to keep her quiet."

Charley fought back the impulse to throw up. She sat on her hands to keep from wrapping them around Jill's neck.

"You're disgusted with me. I can see it on your face," Jill said.

"It's not easy listening to this, Jill."

"I know that. Just think how hard it was for me at the time."

"How hard it was for you?" Charley repeated without inflection.

"I tried to help Tammy as much as I could," Jill said. "I made a few pricks in the plastic with my nails, so that she could breathe. But I guess they weren't big enough. I don't know. I tried to help her. I really did."

"And the Starkey twins?"

"Double your pleasure," Jill said, and tried to smile. "Sorry. I shouldn't have said that. It was just something Jack used to sing. **Double your pleasure, double your fun. . . .** I think it was an old jingle for some chewing gum or something. I'm sorry. I shouldn't have said it. It was really insensitive of me."

"Tell me about the Starkey twins," Charley said, too numb to say anything else.

"It was basically the same thing. Times two. Oh, except this time Jack suggested the twins do things to each other. You know . . . sexually. But they weren't very good at it, and Jack made me show them how."

"This is all on videotape?"

Jill closed her eyes. "I don't know what Jack did with those tapes, so there's no point in asking. I asked him to destroy them, but I don't think he did."

"Who is Jack? Where can we find him?"

Again, Jill's eyes filled with tears. "He's long gone."

"Leaving you to take the blame for everything, to rot in jail until your execution," Charley pointed out, hoping to goad Jill into revealing her former lover's identity.

"Can't come too soon for me," Jill surprised her by saying.

"You really want to die?"

"I deserve it, don't I? After what I did."

"You didn't do it alone," Charley said, when what she really wanted to say was, Yes! You deserve to die! I'll happily pull the switch myself! "Why are you protecting him?"

"I have no choice."

"I don't understand. What could he possibly do to you now?"

"I don't want to talk about this anymore."

Charley let out a deep breath. She didn't want to talk about it anymore, either. The truth would come out soon enough. Every time she talked to Jill, Jill revealed more and more. She actually had a confession now, what had happened to those children in their killer's own words. In time, Jill would reveal Jack's true identity. Charley was sure of that.

"So, how are Franny and James?" Jill asked, as if this was the most natural of questions.

"What?"

"I asked how . . ."

"I heard what you said."

"Why are you looking at me like that?"

Charley realized she was glaring across the table at Jill. She averted her eyes and tried to soften the set of her jaw. "I don't want to talk about my kids."

"I'm just making conversation."

"Talk about something else."

"You sound really angry."

"I don't want to talk about my kids," Charley repeated forcefully.

"Okay. Whatever. Take it easy." Jill pushed herself away from the table, walked to the door, and knocked for the guard. "I think we've accomplished all we're going to today, don't you?"

Charley turned off the recorder and returned it to her purse, glancing at the sixty pages of Jill's handwritten musings inside. "I guess this should keep me occupied for a while."

Jill paused in the now-open doorway, the female prison guard looming over her, waiting. "Charley. . . ."

Charley forced her eyes to Jill's.

"I had no choice. Please tell me you understand. I had no choice."

Charley nodded. "I'll see you next week."

"Holy fuck!" Charley shouted once she was safely inside her car. "Crap, shit, fuck, goddamn son of a bitch!" She slapped the steering wheel, banged on the side window, then pummeled the seat beside her. "Shit, fuck, fart!"

Shit, fuck, **fart**? she thought, the words echoing throughout the small space. Charley burst out laughing. "What are you? Five years old?"

Like James?

Like Tammy Barnet.

"Shit," Charley said again, then burst into tears. "Goddamn it." How could Jill have done such horrible things? How could she talk about them so matter-of-factly? What was the matter with her?

She can do it because she has no conscience or empathy, Charley thought, recalling Dr. Norman's assessment. Because the only person's pain she can truly feel is her own. And whether she was born that way or whether that empathy had been beaten out of her as a child no longer mattered. What mattered was that three innocent children were dead. What mattered more was that the person who'd orchestrated those grisly deaths was still out there. What mattered most was that more children were at risk.

Every day.

Everywhere.

She thought of the nasty e-mails threatening Franny and James. She'd kill anyone who tried to harm them.

We both carry around a lot of anger, Jill had told her.

She was certainly right about that.

Her cell phone whistled. Charley fished through her purse until she found it. She checked caller ID, but the number was unfamiliar. "Hello? Hello?" she said again, when no one answered. Charley waited three more seconds, then flipped the phone shut and tossed it back inside her purse. "Idiot," she said, as the phone began ringing again. "Hello?"

"Charley?" The word was slurred, the voice unrecognizable.

"Who is this?"

"Charley." This time the word was more a sigh than a name.

Charley felt a sinking sensation in the pit of her stomach. "Bram, is that you?"

"How's it going, Charley?"

"Goddamn it, Bram. Are you drunk?"

"I don't know. Am I?"

"Where are you?"

"Please don't yell at me, Charley. My head is killing me."

"Where are you, Bram?" Charley repeated.

"I'm not altogether sure."

"Shit!"

"You shouldn't swear. Mother wouldn't like it."

"Is there anybody else there? Someone I can speak to?"

"There's this girl." He snickered. "I can't seem to remember her name, but she's coming out of the bathroom, and she's not wearing any clothes. Uh-oh. She doesn't look happy."

"Give me that," Charley heard a woman say. "Hello? Who is this?"

"I'm Bram's sister. Who are you?"

"My name don't matter. What matters is your brother's been here all night and he owes me two hundred bucks. You gonna take care of that or am I gonna have to take care of him? You get what I'm saying?"

Charley closed her eyes and rubbed her forehead. "Just tell me where you are," she said, scribbling the address on the back of one of Jill's pages. "I'll be there as soon as I can."

26

Took you long enough to get here." The woman in the doorway was the color of thick, dark molasses. She wore a magenta polyester top with a deep V-neck that exaggerated the fake fullness of her breasts, and a short lime-green skirt over a pair of thigh-high, brown suede boots. A dense mass of dark ringlets framed her round face, accentuating the lines around her wary brown eyes and collagen-plumped lips.

It was the face of a woman who'd seen it all, and been disappointed by most of it, Charley thought, stepping inside the run-down apartment that reeked of quick sex and spilled beer. "I got here as fast as I could. There's a lot of construction on the roads."

"Spare me the details. Where's my money?"

"Where's my brother?"

"Sleepin'." The woman hitched her thumb

toward the bedroom in the back, then held out her hand.

Charley extracted the money from the rear pocket of her jeans, and deposited it in the woman's waiting palm. The woman made a point of counting out the ten twenty-dollar bills Charley had retrieved from a nearby ATM machine, then tucked them into her cleavage before leading Charley through the darkened living room. There were no lights on and the drapes were pulled, but even so, Charley had no trouble making out the empty bottles of alcohol lying scattered across the cheap shag carpet. **Man lies like a rug**, she heard Jill say, as the scent of marijuana wafted toward her nose. "What drugs has he been doing?" she asked as the woman opened the bedroom door.

"Don't know nothin' about no drugs." The woman pointed to the figure lying supine across the bed. "Just get him out of here, will you? I gotta get back to work."

Charley moved closer to the bed. Bram's white shirt was unbuttoned, and the fly of his jeans was zipped only halfway up, as if the effort to dress himself had proved too great a task, and he'd passed out from the exertion. If he'd been wearing a belt, it was missing. Still, both shoes were on. "Can you give me a hand with him?"

The woman waved long, fake fingernails in

the air. "Sorry, honey. Can't risk breaking these babies. They cost a bundle."

Charley took a deep breath, holding it inside her lungs in a concerted effort not to inhale the collection of stale odors emanating from the bedsheets, and grabbed Bram's right arm, throwing it across her shoulder and trying to hoist him to his feet. It was like trying to pull the trunk of an ancient oak tree up by its roots. "Come on, Bram. Wake up."

Bram didn't move.

"Come on, Bram. I'm getting really sick of this." After several minutes, Charley succeeded in dragging him off the bed. He collapsed with a thud on the fake bearskin rug, and promptly curled into a fetal position. "Bram, I'm warning you. In another minute, I'm just gonna leave you here."

"That ain't an option," the woman said from the other side of the room.

"Then I'm afraid you're going to have to help me."

"Jesus," the woman muttered, kicking at Bram's legs. "Can't you get nothin' up?" Once again, her boot connected with Bram's leg.

"Ouch." Bram grabbed the woman's ankle, although his eyes remained closed.

"Let go of my foot, if you know what's good for you," the woman said.

Bram opened his eyes. "Katarina, my angel."

"Katarina, my ass. Go on. Get the hell out of here."

"Bram. . . ." Charley said, trying to pull her brother to his feet. "Come on. Get up."

Bram smiled his most beatific smile. "Charley, what are you doing here?"

"Rescuing you. For the last time," Charley said, hoping she meant it. He was obviously in no condition to drive, which meant she'd have to take him back to his apartment, which meant she'd be late getting back to Palm Beach and her date with Alex, which she'd been looking forward to all day. Damn her brother anyway. Why couldn't he get his act together? "Where's your car?" she asked when they reached the front door.

Bram looked slowly up and down the street, then back at Charley. "I'm pretty sure it was here last night."

"For God's sake, Bram."

"For God's sake, Charley."

"Charley, Bram. . . . Who named you people anyway?" Katarina said, pushing Charley and her brother outside, then slamming the door shut.

"Honest to God, Bram," Charley said, stuffing her brother into the front seat of her car, then securing him with the seat belt. "If we can't find your car, we're going to have to call the police and file a report. . . ."

"That's probably not a good idea," Bram said, leaning his head back against the seat. "In case you hadn't noticed, this isn't the best area, and I'm not in great . . ."

Charley waited for her brother to finish the sentence. **I'm not in great shape, I'm not in great humor, I'm not in great . . .** whatever. But he didn't, and Charley understood, without having to look, that he was already asleep.

"So, how's he doing?" Alex asked as Charley returned to the living room and sat down beside him on the floor in front of the sofa, Bandit following at her heels and sniffing at the packages of Chinese takeout that sat opened and half-eaten on the coffee table. Immediately Alex's arms wrapped around her.

Charley snuggled against him as Bandit curled into her lap. "Sleeping like the proverbial log."

"Well, that's good anyway."

"Yeah. He needs his rest, because as soon as he wakes up, I'm going to kill him."

Alex laughed. "That's my girl."

Charley smiled. Was that what she was? His girl? "Thanks for being so nice about everything."

"No thanks necessary. We can do Taboo another night."

"I was really looking forward to it."

"Me, too. But these things happen."

"Yeah, well, they happen way too frequently for my liking."

"Any idea what set him off?"

"It's probably my fault," Charley conceded. "I called him the other day, after I spoke to Anne, told him the date of our little family reunion, said I expected him to be there with bells on."

Alex nodded. "It was probably the bells that pushed him over the edge."

"I should never have mentioned those damn bells," Charley agreed with a laugh. "Thanks for talking to the police about the car."

"They'll still have to speak to Bram," Alex reminded her.

"Any hope of getting it back in one piece?"

Alex shrugged. "There's always hope."

"I'm beginning to doubt that. At least as far as my brother is concerned."

Alex reached for a deep-fried wonton, dipped it in the sweet orange sauce, and took a bite. "Try not to be too hard on him, Charley. Aren't slipups like this part of the recovery process?"

"They're part of the disease," Charley corrected. "And I know I should be sympathetic and supportive, just like I would be if he had any other awful illness, but part of me keeps saying there's an element of choice involved here, a luxury that people with diseases like cancer or Parkinson's don't have. You can't choose not to have cancer or Parkinson's. He **can** choose to stop drinking and doing drugs."

"It may not be that easy."

"I'm not saying it's easy. I'm saying it's necessary."

Alex kissed away the tears that were now trickling down Charley's face.

"I'm sorry. I didn't mean to yell at you," Charley said. "God, you're the last person I should be angry at."

"You're not angry. You're just passionate."

Charley smiled. "I like that word much better."

"Feel free to use it whenever you'd like." He kissed the side of her mouth.

Charley tasted the sweet wonton sauce as it transferred from his lips to hers. "Jill says I carry around a lot of anger."

"Oh, she does, does she? What else does the charming Miss Rohmer say?"

"That we're a lot alike."

"Can't say I see the resemblance."

"I **do** have a lot of anger."

"Passion," Alex corrected.

"You had to hear her this afternoon, Alex," Charley said, remembering. "The casual way she discussed killing those children. Then in the same breath, she asked about Franny and James, and couldn't understand why I got upset."

"Sociopaths are experts at compartmentalizing."

Charley pulled back slightly. "That's the first

time I've ever heard you refer to Jill as a socio-path."

"Look, I read Dr. Norman's report, too, and just because I'm a lawyer doesn't mean I'm an idiot," Alex said with a smile. "It's a bit like what you were saying about Bram and his addictions. I know Jill was beaten and abused and manipulated, that she never stood a snowball's chance in hell for a happy, well-adjusted life. And I feel very sorry for her. I really do. I sympathize with her. Hell, sometimes I even like her. But I also know what she did to those kids. And I know that normal people don't do things like that, no matter how badly they've been treated, or how expertly they've been manipulated. Clearly, this guy Jack sensed a kindred soul in Jill, or he would have looked elsewhere."

"So you're really convinced she had a partner?"

"Aren't you?"

Charley stroked the top of Bandit's head in contemplation. He immediately rolled over onto his back for her to rub his stomach. "I'm not sure. One minute I'm absolutely positive she's telling me the truth; the next minute, I'm just as sure she's making everything up, that the whole thing's nothing but a big game to her."

"To what end?"

"To no end. For her own amusement. Something to do. I don't know. I imagine things can get pretty boring on death row."

"Think she's been playing with me, too?" Alex asked.

"I think she'd like to," Charley teased. "She gets this little sparkle in her eyes every time she says your name. It's kind of cute actually."

"Bite your tongue."

"Can I bite yours instead?"

He leaned his lips toward hers. "Be my guest."

Charley's mouth opened to welcome him. The subsequent kiss was deep and tender. She never wanted it to end.

"I thought I smelled Chinese," a voice said from somewhere above Charley's head. Bare feet shuffled into the living room, stopping beside the coffee table.

Immediately Charley pulled out of Alex's embrace, Bandit jumping from her lap to the floor to greet Bram. "I thought you were asleep," Charley told him.

"I was. Then the unmistakable odor of chicken with cashews came whispering in my ear."

"I'm not sure odors can actually whisper," Alex deadpanned.

"Who are you?" Bram asked.

"This is Alex Prescott. Alex, this is my brother, Bram."

"Nice to meet you, Alex."

"You, too, Bram."

"Do you mind if I join you?" Bram indicated the food on the table. "I see you have lots left."

"You're sure your stomach can tolerate it?"

"I'm fine, Charley."

"I'll get you a plate," Alex offered.

"Why, thank you, Alex. Who **is** this guy?" Bram whispered to Charley as Alex left the room.

"He's a friend of mine."

"More than just a friend, by the look of things when I walked in here. And, by the way, what **am** I doing here?"

"You don't remember my coming to get you?"

Bram shook his head. "I have a vague recollection of a pair of torpedo-shaped breasts."

"I assure you those weren't mine."

"Whose were they?"

"That would be Katarina."

"The hurricane?"

"The hooker. And that was Hurricane **Katrina**, by the way."

"And who's this Alex again?"

"A friend."

"Are you pregnant?"

"Are you crazy?"

"I get drunk, you get pregnant," Bram explained as Alex reentered the room. "I have blackouts, you have babies," he continued, not quite under his breath.

"Enjoy," Alex said, handing him a fork and a plate.

Bram surveyed the remaining food. "Chicken with cashews, deep fried wontons, sweet and sour pork, honey garlic spare ribs, sesame shrimp in a tangy lemon sauce, not to mention this intriguing vegetable thingy over here. Good choice, people. You done good." He piled large portions of each on his plate, then plopped down on the sofa. "Don't suppose there's any wine left over?"

"Don't suppose you'd like to sleep out on the sidewalk tonight?" Charley asked in return.

"Oh, come on, Charley. Where's your sense of humor?"

"Same place as your car."

"My car?"

"Your beloved MG that got swiped from in front of Hurricane Katarina's love nest."

"Shit," Bram said, dropping his head to his chest.

"Alex has already spoken to the police. But you'll have to file a report in the morning."

"Shit," Bram said again.

"I believe the word you're looking for is 'thank you.'"

"I believe that's two words."

"Don't be a smart-ass."

"I really loved that car."

"Then you should have taken better care of it."

"Yes, I should have," Bram snapped, jumping to his feet. "Thank you, Mother, for pointing that out."

"Okay, Bram, take it easy. I don't need Chinese food all over the floor."

"And I don't need a lecture."

"Well, you sure as hell need something." Charley was on her feet now as well, her patience gone, along with her goodwill and better intentions. "What's the matter with you, anyway? How many times is this going to happen? What's it going to take to get you to straighten out?"

"I don't know, I don't know, I don't know," Bram shouted as Bandit began barking and jumping at his feet. "Where did this fucking dog come from?"

"Take it easy, Bram," Alex said.

"Take a hike, Alex." He shoved the plate of food at Alex's chest, forcing Alex to take it.

"Bram, stop it right now. I mean it," Charley warned.

"Or what? You'll ground me? Take away my car? Oh, I forgot. Somebody already took it."

"For God's sake, stop being such an asshole."

"You mean for **your** sake, don't you?"

"How about for **your** sake?"

There was silence. Bram swayed forward on

the balls of his feet, then swayed back again. "I'm fine, Charley. You don't have to worry about me."

"You're my brother. How can I **not** worry about you?"

"I'm sorry."

"Being sorry isn't good enough."

"Yeah, but it's **all** I'm good at," Bram said, sinking back into the sofa.

Charley was right beside him. "That's bullshit, and you know it. You're good at lots of things." The dog jumped into Bram's lap, licked at his face.

"Jesus Christ, can you call the damn dog off?"

Charley lifted Bandit off her brother's lap and put him on the floor. "Come on, Bram. . . ."

"Come on, Charley," he countered. "Look at me. I've failed at everything I've ever tried."

"Then try something else."

Bram looked from his sister over to Alex, a slow smile filling his handsome face. "She's really something, isn't she?"

"She really is," Alex agreed.

"What happened, Bram?" Charley asked. "You were doing so well."

"I don't know. I really don't. I was watching TV last night and this stupid show came on, **Entertainment something-or-other**, with this horribly perky woman talking about all these dumb celebrities I've never even heard of, and then suddenly, there was Anne's picture, and this cheerful voice was talking about Anne's decision to give up her children, and I started shouting at the TV, and my neighbor started banging on the walls, and next thing I knew, I was at some bar talking to a pair of torpedo-shaped breasts. And the rest, as they say, is . . . a total blur. Is Anne really letting A.J. have the kids?"

Charley put her arm around her brother's shoulders. "Apparently."

"Figures. What's the expression? History teaches us that history teaches us nothing?"

"Maybe you can change her mind at dinner next week."

"Yeah, sure." He glanced over at Alex. "And speaking of dinner, give me back my food."

"I should probably get going," Alex said to Charley, returning Bram's plate.

"No. Don't go."

"Yeah, it's better if I do."

"Please don't leave on my account," Bram said.

"Nice meeting you, Bram."

"You, too."

Charley followed Alex to the front door. "I'm so sorry about the way things worked out."

"Don't be. This way I'll be super-prepared for my case on Monday."

"Will you call me?"

Alex took Charley's face in both his hands, kissed her tenderly on the lips. "Are you kidding?" He opened the door, stepped into the cool night air.

"Don't forget your dog," Bram called after him.

Charley closed her eyes and did the only thing she could do under the circumstances: she laughed.

The phone rang at just after midnight.

Charley groped for it in the dark, picked it up in the middle of its second ring. "Hello?"

"Hi," the voice said. "It's me."

"Jill?" Charley pushed herself up in bed. "It's so late. Is something wrong?"

"How are Franny and James?"

"What?"

"I thought I heard them crying for their mommy."

"What?" Charley said again, louder this time, and then again, until she was shouting, "WHAT? **WHAT?**"

"Charley," another voice interrupted. "Charley, wake up."

She felt a hand on her shoulder.

"Charley, wake up. It's okay. You're having a nightmare."

Charley opened her eyes, saw her brother

perched on the side of her bed, the dog licking his hand. "Oh, God. That was awful."

"Dreaming about me again?"

Charley shook her head, tried to smile. "No. You're off the hook this time."

"I'm gonna get my act together, Charley," Bram said. "I'm gonna call my sponsor first thing in the morning. I promise. This won't happen again."

"That would be nice."

"I'm sorry I ruined your evening."

"I'm sorry I woke you up."

"I'm glad I was here."

"So am I. I love you, Bram."

"I love you, too."

27

The phone rang at exactly nine o'clock the next morning. "Can I please speak to Charley Webb?"

Charley tried to put a face to the unfamiliar male voice. Was she having another nightmare? She gulped at her coffee, grateful when she felt it burn her throat. It meant she was awake. "This is Charley Webb."

"My name is Lester Owens. I'm a senior editor with Pinnacle Books in New York. I apologize for calling so early, especially on a Sunday. . . ."

"That's quite all right."

"It's just that I finally got around to reading your proposal last night, along with the columns you sent, and I wanted to touch base with you as soon as I could, to tell you that I find the idea of this book enormously exciting. I love the way you write. Your style is so accessible and engaging. Please tell me you haven't already signed with another house."

"I haven't signed anything as yet," Charley said, holding her breath. Okay—so not a nightmare, she was thinking. But a fantasy for sure.

"Good. Do you have an agent?"

"I have a lawyer," Charley qualified. Did she? Would Alex be prepared to negotiate on her behalf? Was she getting ahead of herself? Calm down, she told herself. Calm down. She gave Lester Owens Alex's name and phone number.

"I'll be in touch," Lester Owens said instead of good-bye.

Charley returned the phone to the kitchen counter and took another gulp of her coffee. "He'll be in touch," she told the dog at her feet. Bandit cocked his head from side to side as the phone rang again. "He's changed his mind," she wailed, raising the phone gingerly to her ear. "Hello?"

"I just wanted to tell you how much I enjoyed this morning's column, darling," her mother said. "Your sister will be very pleased, I'm sure. You said such nice things about her book. And I think you're so right about this elitist attitude toward women's fiction."

"Mom, I think I may have my own book deal," Charley squealed, filling her mother in on her conversation with Lester Owens.

"Oh, darling, congratulations. That's such good news."

"Well, it's not a done deal yet, but . . ."

"What's not a done deal?" Bram said, shuffling into the kitchen and pouring himself a cup of coffee, as Bandit rushed over to greet him. "And what's with this dog?" he asked, sitting down at the kitchen table.

Charley quickly said good-bye to her mother. "How are you feeling?"

"Tired and cranky. Who's been calling so early anyway? It's like Grand Central Station around here. What are you smiling about?"

"I might have a book deal," Charley told him, trying to keep from jumping up and down.

"You're writing a book?"

"About Jill Rohmer."

"About Jill Rohmer," Bram repeated, a worried look furrowing his brow. "When did all this happen?"

"About a month ago. She wrote me a letter. You remember. We were in Glen's office. . . ."

"Who the hell is Glen?"

"Glen McLaren. Owner of Prime."

Bram's eyes narrowed in concentration. "The one who hit me?"

"That's the one. Bandit is Glen's dog, by the way."

Bram raised his hand to his forehead, as if he had a sudden headache. "You know, I think it's better when I'm drunk. Things seem to make more sense that way."

"Very funny."

The phone rang again. Charley picked it up. "Hello."

"I just had a very intriguing conversation with a Mr. Lester Owens in New York," Alex said. "Apparently he's quite interested in a projected book by a gorgeous newspaper columnist and first-time author whom I'm apparently repre-senting."

"Are you mad? Is that okay?"

"Are you kidding? It's fabulous. He's going to get back to me in a couple of days with an offer. Congratulations."

"Thank you. I can't believe how excited I am."

"You should be. How's your brother?"

Charley glanced over at Bram. "Looking pretty good actually. We're just having some coffee. Want to join us?"

"I better not. Rain check?"

"Of course."

"I'll call you later."

"Alex Prescott, I presume from the smile on your face," Bram said, as Charley replaced the receiver and sat down across from her brother.

"He's going to negotiate my book deal." Char-ley's smile widened, threatened to spill off her face.

"He's an agent?"

"A lawyer. Jill's lawyer, actually," she added, her smile disappearing.

"Jill Rohmer's lawyer," Bram repeated.

"He's very good."

"You're dating the man who defended Jill Rohmer," Bram said incredulously.

"It's not as crazy as it sounds."

"That's good, 'cause it does sound kind of crazy. Was this book thing his idea?"

Charley scoffed. "Hardly. He didn't want me involved."

"Good. Neither do I."

Bram's vehemence caught Charley by surprise. "What? Why?"

"Oh, I don't know. Wait, I **do** know. Jill Rohmer's a lunatic. She'd just as soon slit your throat as look at you. How's that?"

"I thought you didn't know Jill."

Bram pushed his hair away from his face with his free hand, slumped back in his chair. "I don't. Not really."

"Not really? What does that mean?"

"It means I met her once, and believe me, once was enough. She scared the hell out of me."

Charley got up from the table and ran quickly into her bedroom, returning with her tape recorder. She put it in the middle of the table, pressed RECORD. "Tell me."

"Is that thing really necessary?"

"It is. Talk."

"It's nothing." Bram lifted his hands in the air in a gesture of surrender. "Okay. One night Pam and I went out for some pizza after class. All of a sudden, Jill shows up—'funny seeing you here, what a coincidence, etc., etc.'—plops herself down next to her sister, helps herself to Pam's pizza, flirts with me pretty brazenly."

"What did Pam do?"

"Just sat there, didn't say anything. I got the feeling she was scared of her sister. When Jill left, she 'accidentally' knocked over Pam's Coke, spilled it all over her. Pam was totally humiliated. Next time I asked her out, she said no."

"And that was the only time you ever met Jill?"

"The only time."

"You're sure? You never dated her, never slept together?"

"I think I would have remembered that," Bram insisted.

"And there's nothing else you have to tell me?"

"That was the first, last, and only time I saw her."

"So why didn't you tell me this before?"

"I didn't think there was anything to tell. Why didn't you tell me you were writing a book?"

Why **hadn't** she told him? "I guess I was waiting to see how things played out. So far all I've been doing is research."

"Meaning you've already met with Jill?"

"A number of times, yes."

"She say anything about me?"

"No. She didn't mention meeting you at all."

"She probably doesn't remember."

"Somehow I doubt that."

"Well, it explains why you're having nightmares anyway."

The phone rang again. Charley stood up, returned to the counter. "Hello?"

"Charley, this is Lynn Moore," her neighbor's voice announced. Charley pictured the woman sitting at her kitchen table, surrounded by dildos and fur-lined handcuffs. "I just wanted to tell you that I agree totally with what you said about women's fiction in your column this morning."

"Thank you," Charley said, turning back to her brother. But all she saw was the fading trail of steam from his coffee as he walked from the room.

Well, this day certainly hadn't turned out the way she'd been expecting, Charley thought as she dropped Bram off at his sponsor's apartment and headed toward the turnpike. She was supposed to pick James up from his father at five o'clock, and it was already after four. There was no way she'd make it up to Boynton Beach in time, which meant she'd also be late picking up Franny in Lantana, and Elise would be waiting with that patented Elise-look-of-reproach on her face that made Charley want to punch her into the ground.

This wasn't exactly the way I'd seen myself spending Sunday either, she argued silently. I was supposed to be spending the day in bed, making mad, passionate love to one of the world's great lovers, a man who actually understood the way a woman's body worked, who knew just the right amount of pressure to apply, and where and when to apply it. Instead, she'd spent the day with her brother, driving him back to Miami, where they'd passed the bulk of the afternoon filling out police reports. The next stop had been Coral Gables to see his sponsor, a middle-aged man with brown hair and a graying beard, who'd smiled kindly at Charley and advised her she might benefit from calling Al-Anon. She'd told him she'd try to do that as soon as she could find the time, and he'd nodded patiently and told her she sounded a lot like her brother, which made her want to punch him to the ground as well.

We both carry around a lot of anger, she heard Jill say.

"I'm not angry," Charley said out loud. "Horny, maybe. But not angry." Besides, the day hadn't been without its share of good news: the call from Lester Owens in New York, a potentially lucrative book deal in the offing. She had much to celebrate, she was thinking, as she continued north along the turnpike. Maybe she'd take the kids out to dinner. Maybe she'd persuade Alex to join them. No, that wasn't a good idea, she decided immediately. It was way too early to introduce him to her kids. Wasn't it? What was she thinking?

James was sitting beside his father on the outside steps of Steve's narrow trailer in the relatively upscale trailer park in Boynton Beach where he lived. "Mommy!" James shouted, jumping up as soon as he saw her car, and throwing himself at her feet as she walked across the small patch of lawn toward him. "Guess what? Guess what? Daddy's getting married!"

Steve studied his boots self-consciously, running his right hand through his long blond hair. "Thought we were gonna wait a few seconds before springing that on your mother," he said, looking up and blushing noticeably. "Sorry, Charley."

"You're getting married?"

"We haven't set a date yet, but . . ."

". . . you're getting married."

"Yeah." Steve smiled at her expectantly.

Charley wanted to smile back, but she

wasn't sure how she felt. Not that she hadn't assumed Steve would get married one day. Certainly not that she had any interest in him herself anymore. Just that everything between them had been relatively easy and uncomplicated up until now, just as things had been simple and smooth between her and Ray before Elise entered the picture. "Well, congratulations," she heard herself say. "You look really happy."

"I am. Thanks."

"Her name is Leo and she's a Laurie," James announced proudly.

"What?"

"He means her name is Laurie and she's a Leo," Steve corrected. "That's her sign. She's into that sort of thing," he added sheepishly.

"I guess there are worse things she could be into." Charley thought of her brother.

"Would you like to meet her?"

"She's here?"

"She's waiting inside."

"In that case, I'd love to meet her." Charley's body tensed as Steve knocked on the trailer door.

It opened seconds later, and a very pretty girl with waist-length brown hair and a mouthful of blindingly white teeth stepped into the late afternoon sun. "I'm really pleased to meet you," she said, extending her hand. "I've been reading your columns over the Internet ever since Steve told me who you are. They're really good. You're a Pisces, aren't you?"

Uh-oh, Charley thought. A total flake. What she said was, "How did you know?"

"I swear I didn't tell her," Steve said proudly.

"It's just so obvious. You're creative, intuitive, sensitive. It's all there in your writing."

Well, maybe not a **total** flake, Charley amended. "Are you an astrologer?"

"No. It's just a hobby. I'm a Leo. We like that sort of thing."

"Laurie's a dental technician," Steve volunteered. "That's how we met."

"I thought he had the nicest teeth." Laurie giggled.

"He does have lovely teeth," Charley agreed.

"Do I have nice teeth?" James demanded loudly, pulling his lips away from his gums with his fingers, and opening his mouth as wide as he could.

"You have the best teeth of all," Laurie said just as Charley was about to. James wrapped his arms around Laurie's knees as Laurie instinctively caressed the top of his head.

Charley felt her body immediately relax. So what if Laurie was a bit of a flake? She was sweet and kind and she obviously adored her son.

What more could she ask for? "Will you be living here?"

"We're hoping to find a house," Laurie said. "If we can find one we can afford."

"We're trying to save up," Steve added.

"You'll do it."

"I hope you'll be able to come to the wedding," Laurie said.

Charley hadn't anticipated this. "That's very sweet of you."

"I'm going to be the ring-grower," James announced proudly.

"Ring-**bearer**," his father corrected.

"It's just going to be a small wedding," Laurie continued, "but we'd love it if James's sister could be the flower girl."

"I'm sure she'd be thrilled."

"And if you want to bring a date . . ."

"That's really very kind."

"So, what do you think?" Steve asked after Laurie had gone back inside the trailer and James had been secured in his car seat.

"I think she's lovely. You're a very lucky man."

"I always have been." Steve leaned in to kiss her cheek. "Thanks, Charley."

"Take care."

"You, too."

Minutes later Charley was heading up Military Trail toward Lantana. It was only when she looked in her rearview mirror to check on James that she realized she was crying.

"Well, well, well. Look who decided to show up," Elise said, opening the front door of her small, split-level home before Charley had a chance to knock. Her dark curls were piled on top of her head like a wayward bow, the baby attached to her right hip straining to untie it.

"Sorry," Charley apologized. "Hi, Daniel. How are you, sweetie?"

"Sweetie is teething and miserable. He kept us up all night. Franny! Your mother's here," Elise called into the house. "She and Ray are building a fort out of Legos. They've been at it all weekend. Franny! Your mother's waiting! You want to come inside?" she asked reluctantly.

Charley looked toward her car. James had fallen asleep in his car seat about five minutes before they'd reached Lantana, and she didn't want to wake him up. "I better not."

Inside the house, the phone rang, once, twice, three times. "Damn it. Isn't anybody going to pick that up?" Elise demanded of no one in particular. "Do I have to do everything around here?" The phone continued to ring. The baby started to cry. Elise looked as if she was about to do the same.

"Why don't you let me take Daniel while you get that," Charley offered.

Elise immediately thrust the baby into Charley's hands and disappeared inside the house.

"Well, hello there, sweetheart," Charley said to the baby, who was eight months old, a hefty twenty-five pounds, and staring at Charley as if she had three heads. "Are your teeth giving you a hard time? I think I might know a dental technician who could help you."

The baby reached for her nose, grabbed hold of its tip, squeezed hard.

"Those damn telemarketers," Elise was muttering upon her return. "Ray, for God's sake, enough already with the stupid fort. Charley's waiting."

"Be right there," he called back.

Elise shook her head. "Honestly. He's worse than the kids." She looked at her baby in Charley's arms. "Careful he doesn't drool all over you."

"That's all right. It's an old shirt." Daniel's chubby little hand moved from her nose to her ear.

Elise sighed, leaned against the door frame.
"Are you okay?"

"I'm pregnant," Elise said with a weary shrug.
"Oh."

"Ray's ecstatic, of course."

"You're not?"

"I'm exhausted. Ray! Franny! Get out here!" She stared into the darkening sky. "It's not that

I'm not happy about the baby. I am. It's just that my whole life has changed so drastically in the last couple of years. I got married, became a stepmother, then a mother myself. Now I'm gonna have another baby. And sometimes it all feels like too much, you know? Like I just want to yell 'stop,' and slow everything down."

"Is there anything I can do?" Charley asked, surprising them both. "I mean, if you ever need somebody to look after Daniel for an afternoon or something. . . ."

"You'd do that?"

Would she? "Why not? Franny's here a lot, and you've been nice enough to look after James a couple of times. . . ."

"Is this supposed to make me feel bad because I wouldn't take him the last time you called?"

"What? No, of course not."

"I'm sorry," Elise apologized quickly. "I'm just a crab apple. That's what Ray calls me these days: his 'little crab apple.'"

Charley tried to smile. She had no desire to learn what terms of endearment her former lover called his present wife. Still, she understood what Elise was talking about. Her world had also changed dramatically in the two years since her mother's return. In the last few weeks alone, there'd been seismic changes: she was embarking on a new phase of her career; she'd met a man who might prove more than a temporary diversion; her sisters and brother had agreed, however reluctantly, to a family reunion; she'd patched things up with her neighbors. She even had a dog, for God's sake, albeit only temporarily. And now Steve was getting married, and Ray was about to have another child. Nothing ever stayed the same. There was no time to look back, only forward. And the only thing she could see was more changes ahead.

"Does this mean you want to be friends?" Elise was asking nervously.

"God, no," Charley said quickly. There was change, and then there was insanity.

Elise gave a big sigh of relief. "Good. 'Cause I don't think that would be such a hot idea. Because of Ray and everything."

"I don't want to be friends," Charley said emphatically.

"Okay. So, great." She took the baby from Charley's arms. "Franny! Hurry up! Your mother's waiting."

Franny appeared quietly in the doorway, reached for her mother's hand. "See you," Charley waved as Ray came to stand behind his wife, a protective hand on her shoulder.

"Drive safe," they called out in unison as Charley backed out of the driveway. They were still waving as Charley turned the corner and headed for home.

28

I understand you have a book deal. Congratulations," Jill said as she entered the interview room.

Charley's posture stiffened. There was something about the tone of Jill's voice that advised caution, as did the fact Jill was almost fifteen minutes late for their session. Charley turned on the tape recorder that was already in position, and adjusted her notepad on the table in front of her. "You've been speaking to Alex, I take it."

"I called him this morning. He seemed very pleased with himself."

"He should be. He did a wonderful job with the negotiations."

"How long has this been going on? These . . . negotiations."

Charley decided to ignore the not-so-subtle implications of Jill's remark—what exactly had Alex told her?—and simply answer the question as asked. "Just since yesterday morning. A pub-lisher made an offer; Alex made a counter-offer. It went back and forth a few times, and they came to an agreement late this morning. Alex called me just as I was leaving my office to give me the good news."

"I guess I must have phoned him right after that."

"I guess so."

"I had a feeling something was going down."

"You seem a little put out," Charley ob-served.

"Why would I be put out?"

"I don't know. Are you?" Was she imagining it?

"He get you a good deal?" Jill pulled out her chair, although she remained standing.

"I think so. Considering this is my first book and everything."

"And everything," Jill repeated.

"Is there a problem, Jill?" Charley undid the top button of her white blouse, adjusted the del-icate gold chain at her throat. "I mean, this is what we were hoping for, isn't it?"

"I guess."

"Then why the attitude?"

"What attitude?"

"I don't know. I'm just sensing. . . . You're tell-ing me everything's okay?"

"Suppose you tell me."

"Everything's great with me," Charley said.

"As it should be. You have a new book deal, a new boyfriend. . . ."

"A new boyfriend?"

"How long's that been going on anyway?"

"How long has what been going on?"

"Oh, please, Charley. I'm not stupid."

"I don't think you're stupid."

"Then don't treat me like an idiot."

"What exactly did Alex say to you?"

"Alex? Mr. I'm-afraid-that's-confidential? Him, say anything? Are you kidding me?"

"Then where are you getting this?"

"Are you denying it?" Jill asked.

Could she? Charley wondered.

"You think I need somebody to tell me there's something going on between you and Alex? You think I don't have eyes? You think I can't see for myself? You think I don't notice the way he looks at you, that I can't hear the pride in his voice when he so much as mentions your name? You think I can't tell from the look on your face? So, go ahead, Charley. Lie to me. Tell me you're not sleeping with him. Go on. Make it convincing. I might even decide to believe you."

"This is really none of your business," Charley said instead, softening her tone in an effort to soften the sting of her words.

"You're fucking my lawyer, and it's none of my business?" Jill demanded. "I mean, isn't there something just a tad unethical about that?"

"There's nothing unethical going on."

"You're not fucking my lawyer?"

"He's not **my** lawyer."

"He's not negotiating your book deal?"

"That happened after . . ." Charley broke off when she saw the sly smile tugging at the corners of Jill's lips. "There's nothing unethical about my seeing Alex."

"So, you **are** seeing him? He was mine first, you know."

"Yours?"

"**My** lawyer. **My** friend," Jill said, her voice rising. "He didn't even want me to do this book thing. He said he thought it was a bad idea. And he sure as hell didn't want you involved. Thought you were too shallow, too lightweight."

"I know what he thought." Charley was amazed the words still had the power to sting.

"He didn't even think you were all that pretty. 'She's okay,' is what he told me after you first went to his office. 'Are you sure you don't want to try for somebody with more credentials?' And then, suddenly he stops trying to get me to look elsewhere, and his voice turns to mush whenever he says your name. That's when I knew there was something going on. Probably even before you two jerk-offs did."

"I'm sorry you're so upset." Clearly Jill considered Alex her personal property, and Charley the unwanted trespasser.

"Alex is a serious guy," Jill scolded, tears filling her eyes. "He doesn't need his heart broken."

"Who says I'm going to break his heart?"

"Aren't you?"

"I don't know what's going to happen."

"He really likes you. I can tell."

"I really like him," Charley said.

"Well, whoop-dee-doo. Where does that leave me?"

"Alex isn't about to desert you, Jill."

"Oh, yeah? As it is, he hardly comes to see me anymore."

"I know he's been working on your appeal."

"Which he'll lose."

"Maybe not. Once you tell everyone what really happened, once the authorities know who else was involved. . . ."

"You're saying this book will save my life? That I should accept Charley Webb as my lord and savior?"

"You know that's not what I'm saying."

"But you **do** want to know who Jack is," Jill stated.

Charley leaned forward in her seat as Jill stopped pacing. She knew Jill was trying to provoke her, and that anything she said at this point would be wrong.

"What if I decide not to tell you?" Jill asked.

Charley forced the expression on her face to stay as passive as possible, as if Jill's threats didn't affect her one way or the other. "Obviously that's your prerogative."

"Obviously." Jill arched her back and stretched her neck from side to side, as if preparing for a fight. "What happens to your precious book deal then, huh? What happens if I decide I've told you more than enough already?"

"My book deal would be unaffected. I already have plenty of information, not to mention your confession on tape. Anything more would just be icing on the cake."

"Icing on the cake," Jill repeated, then laughed. "I'm not sure how Jack would take to being called 'icing.' " She sat down in her chair and pushed her legs out in front of her, staring at the far wall. "Although he is very delicious." She ran her tongue across her lower lip, looked back at Charley.

"Obviously, on a personal level," Charley continued, trying a different tack, "I'd be very disappointed if we stopped now."

"On a personal level? What personal level would that be exactly?"

"I thought we had a relationship."

"Are you saying you consider me a friend?"

Does this mean you want to be friends? Charley heard Elise ask.

"No," Charley admitted. "We aren't friends."

"What happens to our weekly sessions after you have everything you need?" Jill asked, tears forming anew. "Am I ever going to see you again?"

"Of course you'll see me."

"Where? In the newspapers? On TV? How about 'in my dreams?' "

"I don't know what's going to happen."

"I do," Jill said, tugging at her hair and wiping the tears from her eyes with the back of her hand. "I know that once you're finished with this book, you won't have any time for me anymore. You'll be busy with other projects, and with Alex. Maybe the two of you will even get married. You gonna invite me to the wedding?"

"Whoa. You're getting way ahead of yourself here."

"You won't come back," Jill insisted, shaking her head from side to side. "And then who'll ever come to visit me? You think Jack will come?"

Charley's breath caught in her lungs. "I don't know. Has he visited you before?"

Jill released a deep breath, her eyes moving restlessly around the room, eventually settling on the tape recorder in the middle of the table. "When are you supposed to have this book finished by, anyway?" she asked.

"The end of the year."

"So, like, theoretically, I could keep stringing you along for another ten months."

"Is that what you're doing? Stringing me along?"

"Maybe."

"Is that why you didn't tell me you'd met my brother?"

"You never told me you were screwing my attorney," Jill countered.

"I won't be played with, Jill. I told you that the first time we met."

"And I won't be tossed aside like a used Kleenex."

Charley reached across the table to turn off the recorder.

"What are you doing?"

"We're going around in circles here, Jill." Charley stood up, dropped the recorder into her purse.

"What do you mean? Stop. You're not going, are you?"

"I think you need some time to think things through, decide if you want to proceed."

"I want you to sit down. I want you to talk to me."

"That's not why I'm here, Jill. I'm here so that you can talk to **me**."

"All right. So, okay. I'll talk. Just sit down. Don't be so impatient, for God's sake. Where's your sense of humor?"

"It's waiting to hear something funny," Charley said, sitting back down and returning the tape recorder to the middle of the table.

"You want to hear funny?" Jill asked. "My father was here again yesterday. That's pretty funny."

Charley waited for her to continue.

"He says my mother's getting worse. That it's getting harder and harder for him to look after her at home."

"It seemed to me as if your sister was the one doing most of the looking after."

"Yeah, I guess that's the funny part. What's poor Pammy gonna do now? Guess the joke's on her."

"What joke?"

Jill shrugged. "Pammy's the joke."

"You don't like your sister very much, do you?"

Jill smiled her sweetest smile. "What are you talking about? I love my sister. Don't you love your sisters?"

Charley ignored Jill's question. "Is that why you made it a habit of trying to seduce her boyfriends?"

"I didn't have to try very hard." She paused. "Ask your brother, if you don't believe me."

Once again, Charley tried hard not to react, although her eyes betrayed her. "You're saying something happened between you and my brother?"

"I'm saying to ask him."

"I already did."

"Then you already know."

"He says nothing happened."

"Then he must be telling you the truth." Her smile grew wider. "Brothers and sisters never lie to one another, do they?"

"I believe my brother."

"That's good. I think you should."

"Why don't you like your sister?" Charley asked, trying to keep her voice steady.

"I never said I didn't like my sister. You did."

"Is it because you could never measure up?"

"To what?"

"Pam was always the good girl, the studious one, the thoughtful one."

"The martyr," Jill interjected.

"The one who looked after your mother, who kept the family together. . . ."

"Yeah, that turned out really well, didn't it?"

"According to your own notes, she walked you to school every day when you were small, made you your lunch, finished your homework assignments so you wouldn't get in trouble. . . ."

". . . Breathed a big sigh of relief when Ethan started coming into my bed instead of hers," Jill snapped. "Oh, yeah. She was just great. She really looked out for me, didn't she?"

"What could she have done?"

"I don't know. Tell somebody, maybe? She was the good one, remember? The one everybody listened to, the one they believed. Me—I was the liar, the troublemaker. You think anybody was going to believe I was being diddled by my brother and . . ."

"And?" The single syllable floated across the table, hung suspended in the air between them.

"Do I really have to spell it out for you?" Jill asked.

"Your father was molesting you?"

"He was sodomizing me!" Jill shouted. "And you want to hear really funny? You want to hear something that'll push that sense of humor of yours right over the edge? He said he was doing it for **my** benefit. So I wouldn't have to worry about getting pregnant. Wasn't that thoughtful of him?" Jill pushed aside another onslaught of tears. "And now he comes to visit me, and he pretends like nothing ever happened, like I had the most normal childhood in the world. And what do I do? I go along with the whole stupid charade."

"You've never confronted him?"

"You ever confront **your** father?" Jill asked.

"What?"

"You ever confront your father for the things he did?"

"My father never molested me."

"No? What **did** he do?"

"Nothing. That was the problem."

"Sounds a lot like my problem with Pam."

There was silence.

"Interesting, isn't it?" Jill continued. "I can ignore what my father and Ethan did, and yet I can't get past what Pammy and my mother **didn't** do. And you've managed to forgive your mother for deserting you, but you can't bring yourself to forgive your dad. For nothing."

"What an absolute pile of bullshit," Charley was still fuming hours later, as she stormed down the third-floor corridor of the **Palm Beach Post** toward her cubicle, Jill's words reverberating in her brain. "Don't let her get to you. Don't let her get to you."

"Charley?" Michael Duff called from his office as she was marching past. "Got a minute?"

"Sure." Charley took a few seconds to calm herself down, then walked back to Michael's office.

"I understand congratulations are in order," he said as she entered the room.

"Congratulations?"

"I got a call from a friend of mine in New York this afternoon. Apparently one of my star columnists has a book deal."

"It just happened this morning. I meant to tell you," Charley stammered.

"The publishing business is pretty incestuous. News travels fast."

"I got sidetracked. I'm so sorry."

"No apologies necessary. But remember, I'm counting on first serial rights."

"You've got them," Charley promised as she exited Michael's office and continued on toward her own.

"Congratulations," one of the support staff called as she turned the corner.

"Thank you," Charley called back, thinking, News travels fast indeed.

Mitchell Johnson was sitting at her computer.

"Mitchell?" Charley asked, as he spun around to face her, his face flushed. "Something I can do for you?"

He jumped to his feet. "Michael told me your book deal came through. I came over to congratulate you, but you weren't here."

"So you made yourself at home?"

"Just waiting for you to come back."

Charley motioned toward her computer. "Find anything interesting?"

"Not really." He laughed, though the sound was hollow, forced. "A book and a weekly column. You don't think you're biting off more than you can chew?"

"I think I can handle it."

"Atta girl."

"I also think you should leave."

Mitchell's lips squeezed together in an unattractive pout. "As you wish."

"And in the future, if I'm not here," Charley told him as he brushed past her, "neither are you." She watched his back stiffen slightly, and then he was gone, although the cloying scent of his aftershave remained. "Damn it," she said, straightening the various items on her desk that he might have touched: the notepads and black felt pens, the glass paperweight in the shape of an apple, the monthly calendar from a local realtor, the chunk of purple crystal that was supposed to be good luck. "I should probably spray every-thing," she said, wondering if Mitchell had been trying to access any of her files. He had a well-deserved reputation for snooping, and it probably wasn't the first time he'd been in here without her knowledge. She leaned across her chair and opened her e-mail, hoping there was nothing of any urgency. It was after five o'clock. It had been a very long day, and she was eager to get home.

FROM: Lester Owens
TO: Charley@Charley'sWeb.com
SUBJECT: Welcome Aboard!
DATE: Wed. 28 Feb. 2007, 2:10:17–0800

Dear Charley,

  I can't tell you how thrilled I am that we've been able to reach a deal, and that you will be joining the Pinnacle Books family. That's truly what I be-lieve we are—a family! Welcome! Of course, I'll be speaking to you shortly, and even hope to meet with you in person in the not-too-distant future. But

I just wanted to take this opportunity to welcome you aboard, and to extend my good wishes for a long and prosperous partnership. If there's anything you need, or any assistance I might offer, feel free to let me know. I'm at your disposal. I eagerly await your first chapters.

  Sincerely,
  Lester Owens

FROM: A worried fan
TO: Charley@Charley'sWeb.com
SUBJECT: Your recent columns
DATE: Wed. 28 Feb. 2007, 2:32:15–0400

Dear Charley, as a longtime reader of your column, I've grown alarmed at your most recent endeavors. They're much too thoughtful and conciliatory. Where's the Charley of old? The one who would have torn a piece of crap like **Remember Love** to shreds, then consigned it to the garbage pile where it belongs. Could the fact the author is your sister have influenced your review? From past columns about your family, I thought you were above such obvious partisanship. Guess I was wrong. I write this in hope that this Sunday's column finds you back in peak form. Perhaps another visit to the waxing salon is warranted. It should be about that time. Fondly, a worried fan.

FROM: Elated
TO: Charley@Charley'sWeb.com
SUBJECT: You're the best!
DATE: Wed. 28 Feb. 2007, 3:10:10–0500

Dear Charley,

Just wanted to drop you a note to tell you how much I've enjoyed your columns of late. Not only have they been entertaining, as they always are, but they've been insightful as well. I especially liked what you had to say about your sister's book, and am glad that your family seems to be getting back on track. In today's world, nothing is more important than family. Good luck to you all.

FROM: Glen McLaren
TO: Charley@Charley's Web.com
SUBJECT: Bandits and Other Strangers
DATE: Wed. 28 Feb. 2007, 3:28:05–0800

Hey, Charley. This is one of those good news, bad news kind of letters. First, the good news: I've been very busy with my son, who is terrific, by the way, and I've also been meeting with possible investors who are interested in my opening some clubs here in the Raleigh area. Which brings me to the bad news: I may have to stay on a few days longer than originally intended, and hope that won't be a problem for you as far as Bandit is concerned. I know I'm impinging on our friendship—is it too presumptuous of me to call us friends?—and I hope you'll forgive me and let me take you out to dinner when I get back. Please tell the little mutt I miss him, and give him a big hug and kiss from me. (You can have one too.) Bye for now. With thanks and appreciation, Glen.

"No!" Charley cried out loud, the realization that she didn't want to give Bandit up hitting her with surprising force. In the short time she'd been looking after him, he'd managed to become an integral part of her life. He shared her days, her nights, even her bed. "Do busy" had become a natural part of her lexicon, and Bandit's sweet head resting on her shoulder was as comforting to her as a soft pillow.

And now she had to give him back.

"No. I can't do that. He's mine. Mine, mine, mine." She was about to answer his e-mail, tell Glen there was no way on earth she could give Bandit back, beg him if she had to, when she noted there was still one e-mail remaining. She clicked it on.

FROM: A person of taste
TO: Charley@Charley'sWeb.com
SUBJECT: Your children
DATE: Wed. 28 Feb. 2007, 4:02:55–0400

Dear Charley,
   I'm coming. Soon.

29

"Franny, James, where are you?"

The silence that answered Charley was almost oppressive. Charley walked purposefully from her bedroom into the living room, then continued back through the kitchen and down the hall to the children's room, her steps quickening, Bandit at her heels. "Franny? James?" They'd been immersed in a noisy game of Twister when she'd decided to do some tidying up before her sisters arrived, and now they were . . . where? She checked the bathroom and the closets before returning to the kitchen and stepping onto the back patio, her eyes scanning the perimeter of the small property. No one was there. "Franny? James?" Charley's voice rose in urgency as her eyes jumped the wood fence into her neighbor's yard. But Doreen Rivers's pool was mercifully empty, and besides, Charley assured herself, her children would never go for a swim without first asking permission. They wouldn't go anywhere.

So where were they?

"Problems?" a voice asked from somewhere above Charley's head.

Charley raised a hand to her forehead, shielding her eyes from the bright afternoon sun as she stared up at Gabe Lopez's newly tiled roof. The worker in the yellow hard hat was looking down at her, shadows and perspiration mingling on his handsome face. "Have you seen my kids, by any chance?" Charley asked.

He shook his head. "Not since this morning."

Charley nodded without speaking, afraid if she said anything else, she might start screaming. Where were they, for God's sake? Hadn't she given them strict instructions not to so much as open the door without her, even to let Bandit out to pee? She stepped back inside the kitchen, pulling the patio door shut behind her, and narrowly missing clipping Bandit's back legs. "Okay, calm down. Calm down. Think for a minute. Where would they go?"

And then she heard it, a squeak, then a twittering, followed by the unmistakable sound of muffled giggles, all coming from down the hall.

"James? Franny?" Once again Charley marched down the hall to her children's bedroom and peeked inside. Once again, she saw nothing. Bandit suddenly scooted over to the first of the two twin beds, his nose disappearing under the bed skirt, his tail wagging furiously.

"Go away, Bandit," a small voice whispered, wiggly fingers appearing to brush the curious dog aside.

Bandit's tail wagged so hard, it threatened to knock the little dog off his feet. He barked three times, backed up, then barked again.

"Okay, kids, enough is enough. Get out from under there." Charley's tone made it clear she wasn't happy.

Franny was the first to emerge from her hiding place under the far bed. Her freshly brushed hair was a mess of stray strands, and her newly ironed white shirt was covered in dust.

"Oh, God, look at you," Charley wailed, torn between wanting to shake her and hug her. "What have you been doing? I've been calling you for five minutes."

"We were playing hide-and-seek," James announced, slithering out from under the other bed and scrambling to his feet.

"Yeah? Well, next time, let me in on the game, would you?"

"Are you mad?" Franny asked. "You sound mad."

"The word is **angry**, and yes, I'm angry. You scared me half to death."

"Why were you scared half to death?" James

picked Bandit up and began vigorously rocking him back and forth.

"Because I didn't know where you were, that's why," Charley snapped, stopping when she saw tears spring to her daughter's eyes. "I'm sorry," she said quickly. "I didn't mean to yell. It's okay. It's okay." It's **not** okay, she continued silently. There's some nutcase out there threatening to hurt you. Someone whose last e-mail said he was coming soon. And the cops don't seem to have the first clue what to do. According to their expert, the e-mails are coming from different computers, making the sender almost impossible to find. So all I can do is be extra vigilant, and what if that isn't enough? **What if it isn't enough?** Charley thought about Jill Rohmer's chilling confession, about how many crazy people were out there, about how easy it was to snuff out the lives of the innocent. "It's just this project I'm working on," she said. "It's making me a little jittery."

"What's jittery?" James asked.

"Nervous," Charley explained. "Edgy."

"What's edgy?"

"It means she should stop working on it," Franny said simply, walking from the room.

"Can we take Bandit for a walk?" James lowered the squirming dog to the floor.

"Later. After Grandma gets here. Then I'll go with you."

"Can we do finger painting?"

"Sorry, sweetie. Not today. Remember, Mommy's sisters are coming to visit, and I'm not sure what time they'll be here."

"What **can** we do?"

The doorbell rang.

"I'll get it," James said, running out of the room.

"Don't open it without me," Charley called after him.

But the door was already open by the time Charley and her children reached the front hall. "I keep forgetting I have a key," Elizabeth Webb said apologetically, her smile immediately twisting into a frown. "What's wrong?"

"Mommy's edgy," Franny announced.

"And I'm bored," James said.

"And what are you?" Elizabeth asked Franny.

Franny glared at her mother. "I'm **mad**," she said.

"My goodness," Elizabeth said. "Looks like I've come just in time."

"Are you going to make dinner for the sisters?" James asked.

"I certainly am. The groceries are in the car. Think you can help me carry the bags inside?"

James was halfway out the door when he stopped and turned around. "Can we?" he asked his mother.

Charley nodded her consent as the phone

rang. "Just keep an eye on them," she whispered to her mother.

"Of course."

"You look really nice," Charley added, noting her mother's bright red blouse and flowing black skirt. Her mother patted the neat chignon at the nape of her neck and smiled with girlish pleasure, the shine in her eyes highlighted by just a hint of mascara. Charley went to the kitchen and answered the phone as her mother all but danced toward the front door. She barely had time to say hello.

"Charlotte, it's Emily," her sister said.

Charley knew instantly something was wrong. There was a tightness to her sister's voice that went beyond the formal use of her name. But she pushed such thoughts aside, overwhelming them with a torrent of words. "Emily, thank goodness. I've been trying to reach you and Anne all week. Where are you? Did you just get in? Do you want me to come pick you up?"

"Charlotte. . . . Charley. . . . Wait. Listen to me."

"Mom just got here with the groceries. She's making her famous chicken. I don't know if you remember it, but it's the best . . ."

"Charley, we aren't coming."

"What? Don't be silly. You came all the way here and now you won't come to dinner?"

"We're not in Florida."

"What?"

"Careful with that bag, James," Elizabeth called out as James raced into the kitchen, followed by his sister and grandmother. "There are some bottles in there we don't want to break." Elizabeth helped James lay the bag gently on the counter as Franny deposited several more bags on the kitchen table. "Okay. Off we go again. There's lots more. I think I overdid," she said with a wink to Charley as the trio headed back outside.

"What do you mean you're not in Florida?" Charley whispered angrily into the phone.

"Anne decided to cancel her speaking engagement."

"What are you talking about? When did she decide this?"

"A couple of days ago. She called me from Atlanta, told me she was having second thoughts."

"Second thoughts," Charley repeated dully. "Which she didn't bother sharing with me, of course."

"She didn't want it to turn into a whole big thing."

"You mean she didn't want me trying to change her mind," Charley corrected.

"I don't think you could have. She's been traveling back and forth across the country for weeks now. She's exhausted."

"So she randomly decides to omit Florida?"

"Not randomly, no."

"You couldn't talk some sense into her?"

"Why would I? I agree with her. If anybody needs a dose of common sense, it's you."

Charley shook her head in anger and disbelief. "What about the interview with **People**?"

"It's been rescheduled for sometime next week. In New York. Of course you're more than welcome to take part."

"I don't think so."

"Don't be so stubborn, Charley. You ever hear of cutting off your nose to spite your face?"

"Is that what you think I'm doing?"

"Isn't it? I heard you got a book deal. What better time for you to come to New York?"

I'm coming. Soon.

"I just can't get away right now."

"No? Well, I guess it doesn't really matter. The article's mostly about Anne anyway. Someone from the magazine will probably contact you in the next week or so, for a quote or something. Anyway, I should get going. . . ."

"You should have come to dinner."

"We don't always do what we should. But hey, it's done. There's no point beating it into the ground."

"She'll be so disappointed," Charley said as her mother reentered the kitchen, deposited more bags of groceries on the counter.

"She'll get over it. Anyway, say hi to the kids, and I'll talk to you anon."

"Anon," Charley repeated, chewing on the word as the line went dead in her hands.

"Who'll be disappointed?" her mother asked, as Franny and James bounded into the kitchen and started emptying the plastic bags.

"That was Emily," Charley told her mother, watching the enthusiasm fade from her face, and hoping she wouldn't have to say more. But her mother continued to stare at her expectantly, as if she actually needed to hear the words for them to count. "Apparently Anne had to cancel her Florida engagement, so they won't be coming."

"The sisters aren't coming to dinner?" James asked.

"Come on, James," Franny said, her eyes traveling warily between her mother and grandmother. "Let's go play Twister."

"Does that mean you're not making your famous chicken dinner?" James persisted.

Elizabeth pulled back her shoulders, and took a deep breath. "Of course I'm going to make my famous chicken dinner. I just need a few minutes to catch my breath, that's all."

"You can finger paint, if you want," Charley said to the children.

James immediately reached under the sink to gather the supplies.

"Anne **had** to cancel her Florida engagement?" Elizabeth asked as the children began arranging the paints on the outside patio, Bandit racing back and forth across the lawn.

"Did we really expect them to come?" Charley asked for both of them.

Elizabeth sank into one of the kitchen chairs, pushed a bag of groceries aside. "I guess I must have."

"I'm sorry."

"I just keep hoping. . . ."

"I know. I keep hoping, too."

"What about Bram?"

"I don't think I'd count on him showing up either," Charley said. She'd called Bram several times this morning without success. He hadn't returned any of her messages.

"I bought so much food."

"So I noticed."

Elizabeth smiled sadly, her bottom lip trembling. "What about that young man you're seeing? Think he'd like to try some of my famous chicken dinner?"

Charley was about to say no—hadn't she already decided it was too early to introduce Alex to her family?—but then she decided, what the hell? Having Alex around might keep the evening from being a total disaster. So she called him, explained what had happened.

"What time do you want me?" came his immediate response.

"He'll be here at six thirty," Charley told her mother.

"In that case," Elizabeth said, pushing herself to her feet and glancing at the clock on the microwave oven. "We'd better get this show on the road."

"That was quite possibly the best chicken I've ever had in my entire life," Alex said, polishing off the last of the food on his plate.

"And that was definitely the best wine," Elizabeth said in return. "Thank you for bringing it."

"Can I try some?" James asked.

"I think you should stick to milk for a while," Charley told her son, smiling at the small group gathered around her kitchen table. Her instincts had been correct. Inviting Alex had been a great idea. He got on well with the kids and her mother, and seemed to have taken at least some of the sting out of Bram's failure to appear. Unlike his sisters, Bram hadn't even had the decency to call. Charley had phoned his apartment again just as her mother was serving dinner, listened to the now-familiar instructions on his voice mail to leave a detailed message after the beep. She hadn't needed to go into a lot of detail. Her message had been clear and succinct: "Asshole," she'd said before slamming down the receiver.

"What's your sign?" James demanded suddenly of Alex.

"My what?"

"Your sign," James repeated with mock exasperation. "Franny's a Gemini. Grandma and me are Taurus, and Mommy's a Pisces."

"He's developed an interest in astrology," Charley said.

"My dad's marrying a Leo," James said, as if this explained everything.

"Well, then, let's see. My birthday's November fifth," Alex said. "What does that make me?"

James gave the date a moment's thought. "A Virgo. No, wait. A Scorpio."

"Mommy's birthday's next week," Franny announced.

"It is?"

"March tenth," she elaborated.

"One of the happiest days of my life," Elizabeth said softly.

Charley's eyes welled up with tears. She fought the urge to get up from her seat and take her mother in her arms, kiss her warm, soft cheeks. Instead, she got up from the table and began noisily clearing away the dishes.

"In that case, we'll have to do something special to celebrate," Alex said.

"Can we go to Disney World?" James began bouncing up and down in his seat.

"James . . ." Charley cautioned.

"We've never been to Disney World," Franny said.

"Franny . . ."

"Nor have I," Elizabeth chimed in.

"Mother . . ."

"Me neither," Alex concurred. "And actually, I've always wanted to go."

"Can we go, Mommy? Can we? Can we?" Franny and James asked with one voice, Franny jumping almost as far out of her chair as her brother.

"We could drive up on Saturday morning, spend the night, and leave Sunday afternoon," Alex said.

"Please, please, please."

"My secretary can make all the arrangements," he offered. "Come on, Charley. It'll be fun."

"Can we go, Mommy? Please. Can we go?"

"I don't know . . ."

"Where are we going?" came a voice from the front hall. All eyes shot toward the sound.

"Uncle Bram!" James jumped from his seat and raced into the hall. "We're going to Disney World next week for Mommy's birthday! Want to come?"

Charley found herself holding her breath as James dragged her brother into view.

Bram was wearing a gray silk shirt and a pair of neatly pressed black pants, his dark hair trimmed since the last time she'd seen him, his eyes sober and penetrating. Charley thought she'd never seen him look more beautiful. Or more frightened.

What should she do? Introduce them? **Bram, this is your mother. Mother, this is your son.** She wondered if he even realized that neither Emily nor Anne was there, and when he opened his mouth to speak, she felt as if her heart might stop beating, so afraid was she of what he might say.

"Sorry I'm late." Bram avoided his mother's steadfast gaze and focused directly on Charley. "It smells great. Anything left for me?"

Elizabeth Webb was instantly on her feet. "I'll get you a plate," she said, never taking her eyes off her son.

Charley pulled another chair to the table, took her brother's hand, and sat down beside him, not sure who was trembling more.

"Okay, kids, bedtime. Say goodnight to everyone," Charley announced at just past eight o'clock. Dinner was over, dessert had been served, and Bram was lingering over his third cup of coffee. Neither he nor their mother had touched much of their peach pie.

James hugged both his mother and grandmother, then looked hopefully at Alex. "Are you really taking us to Disney World?"

Alex glanced over at Charley, raised one eyebrow. When you can't beat 'em . . . she thought, and smiled her agreement.

"Yay!" James cried. "We're going to Disney World! We're going to Disney World!"

"Goodnight, James," Alex said. " 'Night, Franny."

"Goodnight, Alex," Franny said shyly. "It was very nice meeting you."

"Nice meeting you, too."

Franny shook his hand, then kissed her mother and grandmother.

"Can Uncle Bram read us a story?" James was already pulling on Bram's arm.

Bram offered no resistance. He'd said little at dinner, other than to the kids and occasionally to Alex, whose presence had undoubtedly served as a buffer, keeping long-festering resentments at bay. The only words Bram had spoken to his mother all night were to inquire—without actually looking at her—how she was, and Elizabeth had answered simply that she was fine. When she'd ventured to add that she was so grateful he'd been able to join them for dinner, Bram had muttered something about always being happy to see his niece and nephew, then spent the rest of the meal horsing around with James. "I guess I can read you a story or six," Bram said now, allowing himself to be dragged down the hall.

"Lights out in twenty minutes," Charley called after them.

"They're great kids," Alex told her.

"Charley's a wonderful mother," Elizabeth said.

"And you're a wonderful cook. Thank you for a remarkable dinner," Alex told her.

"That sounds suspiciously like an exit line." Charley watched Alex rise to his feet. "You're not going, are you?"

"I think it's probably a good idea." He took her hand, led her toward the front door. "I suspect the three of you have a lot to talk about."

"You really think that's wise?"

He kissed her tenderly on the lips. "I think it's time," he said.

30

Okay, Bram, I think that's enough stories for one night." Charlie pushed open the door to her children's room half an hour later, surprised to find the room in darkness. It took her eyes several seconds to adjust, and when they did, she saw her children asleep and Bram perched on the side of Franny's bed, staring into space, an open book on the bed at Franny's feet.

"They fell asleep during story number three," he said quietly, without looking over.

"How long ago was that?"

"Ten, fifteen minutes."

"And you've just been sitting here ever since?"

"I got up to turn off the lights."

"Then you sat back down," Charley stated.

"I did. It's nice in here. Quiet. Not too crowded. Did I hear somebody leave a little while ago?"

"Alex."

"Wrong answer."

"She's not going anywhere, Bram."

"Couldn't you have left a few travel brochures lying around? Some nice picture books of Australia to make her homesick?"

"She **is** home."

"For now."

"She's been back two years," Charley reminded him.

"Which is exactly how old I was when she left. There's a kind of nice symmetry to that, I suppose."

"She's really sorry."

"So am I." Bram released a deep breath, as if he was struggling with a heavy weight. "She's a stranger to me, Charley. I look at her, and there's no connection at all."

"Which is strange, because you look just like her," Charley remarked. "The dark hair, the shape of your face, your eyes, even the way you move your hands when you talk."

Bram immediately folded his arms across his chest, tucked his hands beneath his armpits. "You're seeing things."

"No. Emily and I look more like Dad. You and Anne look just like . . ."

"You're seeing what you want to see," Bram interrupted.

"Maybe."

"I shouldn't have come tonight."

"I'm glad you did. It took a lot of courage."

He laughed. "Yeah. That's why I've been hiding in here for the last half hour."

"She won't bite, Bram."

"She doesn't have to."

Charley walked slowly toward him, held out her hand. "Come on. She's not getting any younger."

Bram grabbed her hand and held on tight, although he didn't move. "Why is it I feel as if **I** am?"

Charley smiled, understanding exactly what he meant. "Come on," she said again. "She's waiting."

They sat grouped around the coffee table in the living room, like the last three pawns in a not-so-friendly game of chess, Charley on the sofa, her mother and Bram on the two oversize rattan chairs across from her. Charley's eyes flitted nervously between her mother and brother, afraid to linger. Her mother stared anxiously toward Bram, afraid to look away. Bram stared at the floor, clearly wishing he were somewhere else.

"I know this isn't easy for you," Elizabeth said to her son.

"You know nothing about me," Bram countered.

"I know you're angry, that you have every right to be."

"That's very big of you, to approve of my anger."

"Bram," Charley warned, leaning forward in her seat, as if preparing to leap across the coffee table and separate them, should the discussion get out of hand.

"I'm sure there are a good many things you'd like to say to me," Elizabeth broached.

"On the contrary," Bram said. "There's absolutely nothing I have to say to you. I was taught never to talk to strangers."

A spot of pink materialized on Elizabeth's cheek, as if she'd been slapped. "I'm your mother," she said, her lower lip trembling.

Bram laughed, the harsh sound stopping abruptly as his eyes connected with Charley's. "Sorry. I assumed that was a joke."

"I know I wasn't there for you in any meaningful way for a very long time. . . ."

"Try 'no way at all for twenty-two years,' " Bram amended.

"And words can never adequately express how sorry I am for that. . . ."

"No words are necessary because I'm not interested in hearing them."

"I thought about you every day. . . ."

"Well, that's very interesting, because I didn't think about you at all." Bram looked toward the vase of red-and-yellow silk tulips on the bamboo table against the far wall. "Well, no, that's not exactly true. I probably thought about you initially. I was two years old, a baby, for God's sake, and babies need their mothers. So, I must have cried. Is that right, Charley? Did I cry?"

"We were all very sad," Charley acknowledged.

"And I'll carry that sadness with me for the rest of my life." Elizabeth's eyes filled with tears, the faint blush in her cheeks sweeping across her face.

"Nobody's asking you to carry anything," Bram snapped. "Trust me—it's not necessary. Because one of the neat things about being two years old is that you forget everything. Can you get your head around that? **I forgot you even existed.** So you can cry and say you thought about me every day for twenty-two fucking years, but the truth is that I have no memory of you whatsoever. None. Nada. Zero. Zippo. Zilch. I look at you," he continued, really looking at his mother for the first time all night, then having to turn away again almost immediately, as if blinded by a painful flash of light, "and I see this attractive older woman who looks a little bit like me, I guess, but who means absolutely **nothing** to me. And I'm sorry if that sounds harsh. I'm sorry if it makes you sad. But what did you expect after all this time? I'm not Charley. Charley was eight when you left. She has memories. You left before I was old enough to process any, and for that, I'm actually very grateful. But I have no interest in picking up where we left off, or in picking up the pieces. I have no interest in getting to know you, in establishing any kind of relationship. I have no desire to **bond**. It's too late. I don't want you. I don't need you."

"I think you do," Elizabeth said with quiet conviction.

Bram jumped to his feet, began pacing back and forth behind his chair. "Well, then I guess that's all that matters. What **you** think, what **you** want, what **you** do. You're the center of your universe, just as you've always been. God, I could use a drink."

Elizabeth was suddenly on her feet, her arms reaching out to stop Bram's pacing. He recoiled at her touch, raised his arms in front of him, as if warding off evil spirits. "You can tell me you have no memory of me," Elizabeth said, taking several steps back. "You can tell me I'm a stranger to you, that I'm just a selfish old woman who means nothing to you, that you don't want anything to do with me, and I'll have no choice but to accept that. But don't tell me you don't need me because I know you do. And I know that until you deal with me, your problems with alcohol and drugs are going to continue."

"You think my problems with drugs and alcohol are your fault? God, is there no end to your power? You know, I really **could** use a drink." Bram's eyes began skirting the room, as if searching for an errant bottle of wine.

"Bram. . . ." Charley cautioned.

"I think you've been taking your anger at me out on yourself, that the drugs and alcohol . . ."

". . . are expressly so that I don't have to listen to this kind of shit." Bram ran his hand through his hair, then looked to the ceiling, as if appealing for help.

". . . are your way of dulling the pain."

"Really? Which pain is that? The pain of discovering my mother is a dyke, or the pain of knowing she's a selfish bitch who thinks she can pop in and out of my life whenever it suits her?"

"Bram . . ."

Bram marched into the kitchen. Charley heard the sound of the fridge door opening and closing. "You don't have one goddamn beer?" Bram demanded, returning to the living room and throwing his hands in the air, as if he were tossing out confetti. "No white wine? You didn't buy any champagne to celebrate Emily and Anne coming to town? Oh, wait. I forgot. They didn't come. They had the good sense to cancel at the last minute. Thanks for telling me, by the way."

"We could go to a therapist," Elizabeth offered her son. "Together."

"A therapist? I don't want to go to a fucking therapist. I want to go to a fucking bar."

"Okay, Bram, that's enough fucking for one night," Charley said.

Bram laughed. "Okay, Mommy." He laughed again, pointed an accusatory finger at his mother. "Did you hear that? Charley was more of a mother to me than you ever were."

"I know that, and . . ."

"And what? You're sorry? We get that. You're sorry. Now get this—big fucking deal!"

There was a shuffling sound. Charley turned to see Franny standing in the doorway, James by her side.

"Uncle Bram used the **f**-word," James exclaimed, sleep-filled eyes opening wide.

"We heard yelling," Franny said.

"It's okay, sweetheart." Charley rushed to their side. "Uncle Bram was just excited."

"About going to Disney World?" James asked.

"Absolutely," Bram agreed. "Sorry for all the noise."

"You're coming, too, aren't you, Grandma?" Franny asked cautiously, as if afraid of the answer.

Elizabeth smiled, but said nothing.

"It's Mommy's birthday," Franny said.

"She's a Pisces," James embellished.

"Of course your grandmother's coming," Bram said. "You think she'd miss your mother's birthday? Perish the thought," he added under his breath.

"Come on," Charley told her children. "Off to bed."

"I'll tuck them in," Elizabeth volunteered, hurrying the children out of the room.

"Are you all right?" Charley asked her brother as soon as they were gone.

Bram shook his head. "I'd feel a lot better with a drink."

"Maybe you should call your sponsor."

"You ever hear such a load of crap?"

"I don't know. Maybe a therapist wouldn't be such a bad idea. We could all go."

"Maybe **I** should go before Dr. Phil comes back." He walked quickly toward the front door.

"Bram . . ."

"Don't worry about Disney World. I have no intention of tagging along and ruining everybody's good time. It's not really my thing anyway." His hand reached for the doorknob.

"Bram. . . ." This time the voice that stopped him wasn't Charley's, but his mother's. Bram reluctantly released his grip on the door handle and slowly turned around. "Please," Elizabeth said. "There's something I need to say to you."

"Apology accepted," Bram decreed preemptively. "Can I go now?"

"This isn't another apology." Elizabeth pulled her shoulders back, clasped her hands together in front of her, and took a deep breath, as if she were about to deliver a speech in front of a crowded auditorium.

"Well, then," Bram said. "You have something to say? Then, by all means, spit it out."

Charley watched her mother take another deep breath, then took the next one along with her. It felt as if an eternity passed before her mother spoke again.

"I know you don't believe me, but I really do understand your pain."

"Of course you do."

"And I understand your anger. I even sympathize with it. It was a terrible thing I did, running away to Australia, leaving you and your sisters in that house. And I will regret it till my dying day."

"You've said this already."

"But there's nothing I can do about any of that now," Elizabeth continued as if Bram hadn't spoken. "What's done is done. I made my choices. Right or wrong, I made them, and I can't go back and unmake them. I may be every bit as selfish and awful as you seem to think. I may be guilty of every horrible, neglectful thing you accuse me of. But you can only blame your mother for so long. Eventually you have to accept some responsibility for the way your life turns out. You're not two years old anymore, Bram. You're all grown up, and what happens to you from now on is **your** choice. You can choose to stay stuck in the past, to drink and dope yourself into oblivion, and it's still not going to change what happened. It's time to move forward, time to make a real life for yourself. With me or without me. I didn't give you a choice when I walked out on you all those years ago. But you have one now. I want to be a part of your life more than anything in the world. But I can't spend the rest of my life apologizing. It doesn't do either of us any good."

"You're telling me you messed up, but it's my problem now? Is that what you're saying?"

"I know it's not fair, but . . ."

"Well, you're certainly right about that. Anything else you want to say?"

"Just that I love you."

Bram nodded, his hands forming fists at his sides. "Okay. So, I can go now?"

"Bram, please," Charley cautioned as her brother opened the front door. "Don't do anything stupid."

"Bye, Charley. Thanks for dinner." He walked quickly toward the nondescript, white rental car that was parked at the corner. "Happy birthday," he called out, climbing inside and waving as he pulled away from the curb. "And in case I don't see you next week, many happy returns of the day."

*   *   *

It was almost midnight when Charley climbed into bed and picked up the phone. He'd still be up, she was thinking. He always stayed up late, catching up on his reading until well past twelve o'clock. She'd been debating whether to call him ever since her mother left, her mother's words to Bram still bouncing around in her brain, like pebbles tossed against a window pane. **I made my choices. . . . I can't go back and unmake them. . . . I may be guilty of every horrible, neglectful thing you accuse me of. . . . Eventually you have to accept some responsibility for the way your life turns out. . . . You're all grown up, and what happens to you from now on is your choice. . . . You can choose to stay stuck in the past. . . . It's time to move forward, time to make a real life for yourself. . . . You can only blame your mother for so long.**

"Or your father," Charley said aloud, pressing the appropriate numbers before she could change her mind, and listening as the phone rang once, then twice, before being picked up.

"Robert Webb," the elegant voice said, without a hint of fatigue.

Charley heard the rustle of paper, and wondered which one of the three daily newspapers he read every night—**The New York Times**, **The Washington Post**, and **New Haven Register**—she was taking him away from. "Dad, it's me. Charley." There was silence, and for an instant, Charley wasn't sure whether or not her father had hung up the phone without so much as a word. "Dad?"

"What can I do for you, Charlotte?"

Charley felt her breath escape her chest in a series of short, painful spasms. Her father's voice betrayed not a hint of what he might be feeling, which didn't surprise Charley, who'd often wondered whether he had any feelings at all. Still, it was almost midnight and she hadn't spoken to him in almost two years. Did he have to sound so matter-of-fact? "How are you?" she ventured meekly.

"Fine."

He obviously wasn't going to make this easy. "I'm sorry to be calling so late. I remembered you rarely go to sleep before one."

Silence. Then, "Is there a reason for this call, Charlotte?"

"Not really. I mean, there's nothing wrong or anything like that. The kids are great. I'm not in any trouble. It was more an impulse kind of thing."

"More an impulse kind of thing," he repeated. Charley could almost see him wince as he dissected her grammar.

"I was just wondering how you are, what you've been doing. . . ."

"I'm fine. I'm basically doing the same thing

I've always done. Teaching, going to meetings, reading."

"Have you seen much of Emily and Anne?"

"They keep in touch."

"Anne's book is doing really well."

"So it would seem."

"Have you read it? It's pretty good, actually. I mean, it's not high art or anything," she found herself equivocating, sensing his disapproval, "but I was surprised how much I enjoyed it. I couldn't put it down. That should count for something."

"Should it?"

Charley could feel him glancing at the clock beside his bed. She took a deep breath. "I've actually just made a deal with a publisher to do a book. Nonfiction. About Jill Rohmer. She killed three little children she used to baby-sit. . . ."

"Sounds like something you'd be interested in."

Charley tried to ignore the dismissiveness in her father's voice, but it pierced at her heart, like the sting of a wasp. "You always talked about writing a book," she said. "Whatever happened to that?"

"Serious literature demands a great deal of time and thought. It's not something one can toss off in one's spare time. Something of which I have perilously little, I'm afraid."

"Sometimes you just have to **make** time," Charley said.

"I'll bear that in mind. Anything else?"

"No. **Yes**," Charley corrected, continuing on before she lost her nerve, the words pouring from her mouth like water from a tap. "You're my father. We're family. And we never see each other. We never speak. And it doesn't have to be this way. I'm sorry if I've disappointed you. I really am. I know I'm not the perfect daughter. Far from it. But you've disappointed me as well. There are all sorts of ways I wish you were different. But you're not. You're who you are, and I have to accept that. Just as I hope you can accept me for who I am. We're human beings. We make choices, and we make mistakes. But that's part of what being an adult is all about, isn't it? Accepting responsibility for one's choices, learning to accept the choices of others, and moving on, moving forward?"

"And the point of this little diatribe is . . . ?"

"The point is that whether or not I choose to have a relationship with my mother shouldn't affect my relationship with you. One doesn't negate the other. My seeing her again doesn't cancel out the things you did for me, or the education you provided me with, or the fact you were there when she wasn't. But because she left us doesn't mean she ceased to exist, just like her coming back doesn't mean you've ceased to matter. She's my mother. You're my father. I shouldn't have to choose between you."

There was a pause. For the second time, Charley wondered whether her father had disconnected the line. "Are you finished?" he asked finally.

Charley nodded, then realized she needed to say the word out loud. "Yes."

"Well, that was quite the speech. Aside from a few lapses in grammar, and an unfortunate tendency toward the trite, it was reasonably succinct and well-delivered. I have no doubt you're as sincere as you are misguided."

"Misguided?"

"Please allow me the same courtesy I allowed you, and let me speak without further interruption."

"I'm sorry," Charley mumbled. "Go on."

"You talk about choices. Well, I made my choice twenty-two years ago when your mother walked out and sued for divorce. I made the decision to be angry and bitter and unforgiving for the rest of my life."

"But that's . . ."

"Crazy? Ridiculous? Maybe it is. But it's still my choice," he said loudly, biting off each word. "I have no interest in forgiving your mother, or in making things easier for you. This is the way things are for **me**, the way I have **chosen** to live my life. Your mother betrayed me. She betrayed all of us. And I consider your subsequent embrace of her to be a betrayal of me. So if you want to forgive her, then you're right, that's your choice, and I have to accept it. But I don't have to like it. I don't have to approve of it. And I certainly don't have to welcome a traitor back into my midst."

"A traitor? Dad, for God's sake. . . ."

"I thought I made it perfectly clear during our last conversation that I wouldn't tolerate such treachery. Maybe you shouldn't have to choose between your mother and your father, but you do. And you've made your choice. Unless, of course, you've changed your mind. In which case, things can return to the way they were before. Is that why you've called, Charlotte? To tell me you've changed your mind?"

There was a long pause. "I haven't changed my mind," Charley said.

This time the silence of the line going dead in her hands was unmistakable.

31

WEBB SITE

Families. You gotta love 'em. Right?

Take mine, for example. I have two glorious children, whom I adore. I also have a mother I'm just starting to get to know, a father who refuses to talk to me, two sisters I rarely see, and a brother who is usually too preoccupied to see anything.

Which brings me to last weekend.

For whatever reasons—and I'm sure at least one of them made sense at the time—I decided it was time to reunite my siblings with their mother. The past is past, I reasoned. It was time to live and let live. So I essentially blackmailed my sisters and bullied my brother into accepting my invitation for dinner, persuaded my mother to make her famous chicken, then bathed the kids, brushed the dog, and prayed we'd all find a way to get along. After all, we're family. Right?

Tell that to my sisters, who canceled at the last minute, or my brother, who refused to look at his mother all night, no matter how many times—and how sincerely—she apologized for abandoning us as children. So much for forgiveness. So much for the past being past. No one, it seems, is ready to let go. We have too much invested in the way things were to try to change the way things are.

The sad truth is that the past is never really past. It's always with us. Sometimes it's strong and supportive, pushing us toward the future like a friendly wind at our backs. But more often than not, it's wound tightly around our shoulders like a shroud, its weight dragging us down, tethering us to the ground, occasionally even burying us alive. The strange thing is that given the opportunity to rid ourselves of these deadly wraps, we often cling to them instead.

"You're not two years old anymore," my mother told my brother in exasperation at the conclusion of our meal. "Everything you say about me may be true, but you're all grown up, and it's your problem now." I'm paraphrasing and condensing here, but the message is clear: You're an adult. Shit happens. Deal with it.

It wasn't just my brother, I realized in that moment. I'm an adult, too, with problems of my own. My father, for example, to whom I hadn't spoken in far too long. He'd chosen to interpret my acceptance of my mother as a rejection of him. I needed to make peace, for my sake as much as his. So I picked up the phone and called him in New Haven. I apologized for the lateness of the hour and any hurt I might have caused him over the years and, burying my pride, all but begged him not to make me choose between my mother and him any longer. He turned me down cold. Word for word, this is what he said: "Twenty-two years ago I made the decision to be angry and bitter and unforgiving for the rest of my life."

Huh?!

l anyone make the con-
to be angry and bitter
ng for the rest of his life?
ately, actively, and even
nhappy? Does this make
l? Apparently it does. At

read-   You're either with me or
ritten   is saying. Deal with it.
ave to   n dealing with it, Dad.
, she'd   at some people aren't
itchell   it takes to love them,
see it?   ust be valued as well as
loesn't   hat if this is how you
article   your life, then you'll
without me. As a child,
itterness made me feel
!" She   lone. You were callous
hand-   and careless in your
ailored   tened me. You frighten
r cubi-   ow. I have children of
lid you   ust be protected from
eption-

ge you   say I've given up on
u. Am I   ether. I'm still hoping
r and sisters over for
d Sun-   so that we can enjoy
chicken and, if not
t least put it in its
erful, as   for now, I'm leaving
ighbor for the week-

end, packing up my kids, my mother
and the new man in my life, and we'r
heading off to Disney World to cele
brate my birthday.

It seems I've finally come of age.

Charley stared at her computer screen
ing and then rereading the column she'd
for this Sunday's paper. She'd probably
cut out the word **shit**, but what the hell
leave it in there for the time being, give M
something to edit. Would her sisters
Bram? Her father? Probably not. "It
matter," she said out loud, forwarding the
to Mitchell's e-mail.

"What doesn't matter?"

Charley spun around in her seat. "Gle
jumped up, her eyes absorbing the darkl
some man in the white silk shirt and
black pants standing at the entrance to h
cle. What was he doing here? "When
get back to town? And why didn't the re
ist page me?"

"I got in last night. And she didn't p
because I told her I wanted to surprise yo
interrupting anything?"

"No. As a matter of fact, I just finish
day's column."

"So how've you been? You look wond
always."

"I feel pretty good." Had he come to tell her he wanted Bandit back as soon as possible? "How was your visit with your son?"

"Fabulous. Best kid in the world."

There was something about the tone in Glen's voice that gave Charley pause. "Problems?"

"Not really. Can we talk about this at lunch?"

"Lunch?"

"I made a reservation at Renato's."

Charley felt the color drain from her face. "Oh, my God. Did we have a . . . ?"

"A date? No. I'm just being my usual smug and presumptuous self. What do you say? Are you free?"

Charley checked her watch. It was almost noon, and she had her interview with Jill at two o'clock. "Well, normally I'm quite partial to smug and presumptuous, but I have to be in Pembroke Pines by two. How's coffee . . . ?"

"Coffee's good."

"There's a cafeteria on the main floor."

"Lead the way."

"It's not exactly Renato's," she apologized as they entered the large room minutes later. It smelled of tuna casseroles and gravy, and was already pretty crowded. All eyes shot immediately in her direction.

"Just like high school," Glen remarked, following Charley through the rows of long tables toward the coffee machines at the back.

"Hi, Jeff. . . . Anita," Charley greeted two of her coworkers. They looked vaguely stunned by her acknowledgment. "So, what's the problem with your son?" she asked as she and Glen settled into two chairs at a small table near the back wall several minutes later, coffees in hand.

"There's no problem with Eliot." Glen looked toward the recessed ceiling. "It's my ex-wife. . . ."

"She's giving you a hard time?"

"It's not that."

"You still love her?"

"God, no."

"What then?"

"It's her husband. I don't know. I guess I'm afraid . . ."

"You'll always be Eliot's father, Glen," Charley told him.

Glen took a sip of his coffee. "You always finish other people's sentences for them?"

Charley smiled sheepishly. "Just being my usual smug and presumptuous self."

He laughed. "There. See, I knew we were kindred spirits. So, how's your book coming along?"

Charley told him about her book deal and her interviews with Jill. "Did you know that Ethan Rohmer used to deal drugs out of one of your clubs in Fort Lauderdale?"

"Really? Who told you that?"

"Is it true?"

Glen looked annoyed as he took another sip of coffee. "I wouldn't know. It didn't happen on my watch."

"You ever meet him?"

"Not that I remember. Why?"

"Just curious."

"I don't hang around with drug dealers, Charley."

"I wasn't suggesting you did."

"Weren't you?"

"No. Of course not. Hey, I let you take my son to Lion Country Safari, remember? I wouldn't have done that if I didn't think you were a decent guy."

"You barely knew me," he reminded her.

"Yeah, but my instincts told me I could trust you."

He raised his cup to hers. "Let's hear it for instincts." He finished off the rest of his coffee. "So, how's Bandit? He didn't give you too much trouble, I hope."

"No. No trouble at all."

"Yeah, he's a good little guy, isn't he?"

"You can't have him back," Charley said, more forcefully than she'd intended. Several heads turned toward them.

"What?"

"I can't do it. I just can't do it," Charley continued. "Talk about presumptuous, but I just can't give him back. Remember when you first brought him over, and he put his head on my shoulder, and you said that meant he would bond with me for life. . . ."

"Charley . . ."

"Well, what you forgot to mention was what would happen to **me**—that I would bond with him, too. And that's what's happened. I am so attached to that little dog, it would break my heart to lose him. And I know it's not fair, that an old girlfriend gave him to you and everything, but I can tell you were never that crazy about her anyway, and you're so busy, and I'll take such good care of him. You can visit him whenever you want. . . ."

"Charley. . . ."

"Please don't make me give him back." Charley's eyes filled with tears.

There was a moment's pause. "I can visit him whenever I want?"

Charley flew from her chair into Glen's arms. "Oh, thank you, thank you."

"How does Saturday night sound?" he asked as she quickly resumed her seat. "To visit Bandit, I mean. We can order pizza and . . ."

"I'm taking the kids to Disney World for the weekend."

"Disney World. I like Disney World. Feel like company?"

"I'm also taking my mother."

"I like mothers."

"And my boyfriend," Charley added.

"Not so fond of boyfriends," Glen said with a sad smile. "Sorry. I didn't realize you were seeing anybody."

"It's pretty new."

"And pretty serious?"

"I'm not sure. I think it could be."

"Well, that sucks," Glen said, and laughed.

"Can I still keep Bandit?" Charley asked, only half-jokingly.

"He's all yours." Glen pushed himself to his feet. "I think it's time for me to get out of your hair."

"You don't have to go yet."

"Yeah, I do." He reached over, cupped her chin in his hand. "Take care of yourself, Charley."

"You, too."

Charley sat very still in her chair, the imprint of Glen's fingers lingering on her skin, as Glen walked out the door without looking back.

"You're very quiet today." Jill leaned back in her chair and smiled across the table at Charley.

"I'm supposed to be listening," Charley reminded her. Jill had been talking for the better part of two hours, mostly mundane recollections of her high school years. As a result, Charley's thoughts kept drifting back to Glen, and the surprisingly gentle touch of his fingers on her skin.

Jill glanced at the tape recorder in the middle of the table. "How many hours of tape have you got so far?"

I think it's time for me to get out of your hair, she heard Glen say. "Sorry. What?"

"I asked how many hours of tape you have."

"I'm not sure. A lot."

"Have you listened to any of them yet?"

"No."

"How come?"

Because I can't bear to, Charley thought. What she said was: "I thought I'd get all my research done first. Then I'll start putting everything together."

"That'll be fun," Jill remarked, the dreamy quality in her voice matching the faraway look in her eyes. "You'll get to relive it all again."

Charley felt her stomach turn over. "Like you did with the tapes they found under your bed?" She tried to make the question as casual and off-hand as possible. She looked away, brushed some invisible lint from her gray pants.

"You shouldn't do that," Jill said.

"Do what?"

"Look at the floor, pretend to be uninterested. It's a dead giveaway."

"A giveaway?"

"In cards, they call it a 'tell.'"

"I'm not following."

Jill released a deep sigh, as if her star pupil was being insufferably obtuse. "You ever play poker?"

"No."

"Okay. Let me see if I can explain it. A 'tell' is like, every time you get a good hand, you touch your nose, or every time you're bluffing, you scratch your neck. You don't even know you're doing it. But anybody watching you can figure it out pretty quick."

"You're saying I do this?"

"All the time. Whenever you don't want to look too interested in something I've said, you look at the floor or study your nails. And you're forever dusting off your clothes." Jill laughed. "You're as easy to read as one of your sister's books."

Charley bristled, although she tried to disguise her annoyance with a smile.

"Now you're angry. You get this tight little smile on your face whenever you don't want me to know how you really feel."

"You think you understand me pretty well," Charley said.

You think you know me.

"Am I wrong?"

"Why would I pretend to be uninterested in anything you've said?"

"You're probably afraid I'll clam up if you

sound too eager. Like before, when we were talking about the tapes, and I said 'you'll get to relive it all again.' We both know that's a pretty provocative thing to say. It promises all sorts of juicy revelations. So you pretend to be all nonchalant, thinking stupid me doesn't have a clue, and will just keep blabbing away, spilling my guts out, trying to impress you."

"Is that what you're doing—trying to impress me?"

Jill shrugged, rolled her head along the top of her spine from one shoulder to the other. "I have a bit of a crick in my neck. Must have slept on it funny."

"Why did you keep those tapes under your bed?" Charley was growing impatient with being psychoanalyzed by a psychopath. Was she really as easy to read as one of her sister's books?

"Pretty obvious, isn't it?" Jill asked.

"Apparently not."

Jill rubbed the base of her neck. "I didn't want anybody to find them."

"Did you ever listen to them?"

"Why would I do that?"

"To relive them," Charley said, echoing Jill's words.

"Why would I want to relive them?"

"Why make them in the first place?"

"That was Jack's idea."

"And yet you're the one who kept them."

Jill shrugged, raised her eyebrows in a silent dare.

"Is it possible you got a kick out of listening to those tapes?" Charley probed.

"A kick?"

"A sexual charge."

"A person would have to be pretty sick to get sexually aroused by that kind of thing."

Charley refrained from stating the obvious: that a person would have to be pretty sick to have done such things in the first place. She lowered her voice, tried to muster as much sympathy as she could. "We can't necessarily control what turns us on."

"That's very generous of you, Charley." Jill raised both arms above her head, stretched out her back. "What impulses can't you control, I wonder?"

"We're talking about you."

"Aw, come on, Charley. Humor me. Tell me what gets you hot."

"I don't have time for this, Jill."

"Does fucking my attorney make you hot?"

"Okay, I'm out of here." Charley jumped to her feet.

"Oh, sit down, for Pete's sake. Enough with the histrionics. Do you want to know who Jack is or don't you?"

Charley remained standing. "To tell you the truth, I'm not sure there really is a Jack."

Jill looked genuinely shocked. "You don't believe me?"

"I'd like to. I'd really like to think I haven't been wasting my time driving down here every week, that everything you've been telling me isn't total bullshit. But I'm not sure anymore."

"Jack would be very hurt to hear that you doubt him."

Charley sat back down, stared directly into Jill's eyes. "Then tell me who he is."

"Very good, Charley," Jill exclaimed. "That was really good. No 'tell' there at all. It was really intense."

"Who is he, Jill?"

"You'll find out."

"When?"

"Soon enough."

"I'm running out of patience, Jill."

"Next week. How's that? It'll be my birthday present to you." Jill smiled. "What? You're surprised I know it's your birthday? You don't remember that column you wrote about how you never got to celebrate your birthday after your mother left, and how you make a really big deal out of birthdays now that you have kids of your own? I could relate because we never celebrated birthdays around our house either, and I always thought, if I ever have kids . . ." She broke off, her eyes losing their mischievous sparkle.

"Doesn't look like that's going to happen any time soon."

"You're saying you'd like to have children?"

"Isn't that every girl's dream?"

"You're not exactly every girl."

The sparkle suddenly returned to Jill's eyes. "That's true. So, what've you got planned for lucky number thirty-one?"

"We're going to Disney World," Charley said quietly, remembering Jill's horrifying visit to the Magic Kingdom, and wondering how she'd react.

"Oh, that's great," Jill said with unabashed enthusiasm. "The kids will love it. Have you been before?"

A moment to process Jill's reaction. "No. This will be my first time."

"I absolutely loved the teacup ride," Jill said. "I mean, I know most people love Space Mountain and Pirates of the Caribbean the best, but my favorites were the teacup ride and It's a Small World. **It's a small world after all**," she began singing. "You want to know what happened to us inside Small World? It was the funniest thing ever. You have to hear this." She squirmed in her seat, leaning forward, and speaking directly into the recorder. "Here we all were in these little boats that supposedly sail around the world, and all these dolls are singing that stupid song over and over again for like, twenty minutes, and I'm singing along, of course. I think it's the greatest thing ever. My father looks like he's about to start ripping the heads off everything in sight, and Ethan is threatening to jump ship. Finally the ride is almost over. We can literally see the light at the end of the tunnel. We have, like, thirty seconds left to go. And suddenly, the whole thing stops dead. The lights go out and nothing is moving. Except the dolls. They're still singing. And we sit there for, like, another twenty minutes, listening to those stupid dolls sing that stupid song over and over again, until even I'm getting sick of it, and then suddenly, just when everybody's about to start screaming, the lights go on and the boats start moving again. Except instead of moving forward, they're going backward. Another twenty minutes to get back where we started! And all the while, the dolls are singing. **It's a small world after all.**" Jill was laughing now. **"It's a small world after all.** It was so funny." She wiped a few happy tears from her eyes. "Talk about reliving it all." She sat back, released a deep sigh. "Wish I could go with you."

With those words ricocheting in her head, Charley turned off the recorder, stuffed it in her purse, and stood up, almost knocking over her chair. "How about I tell you all about it when I see you next week?"

"I'll look forward to it."

Charley walked to the door and knocked for the guard.

"Charley?"

Charley turned around.

Jill was on her feet, a crooked little half-smile playing with her lips. She lowered her eyes coquettishly. "Happy birthday," she said.

32

She first heard the noise as part of a dream. She was looking for a pair of shoes to match the black-and-white dress she was planning to wear to dinner at Renato's, only all she could find were ugly old pumps in purple and green. In frustration she began tossing the shoes to the floor. One bounced back and hit her in the middle of her forehead. She felt the wetness of the blood as it dripped between her eyes. Which was when she woke up.

Charley opened her eyes to find Bandit licking her face. "What are you doing up so early?" she asked the dog, sitting up in bed and checking the clock on the bedside table. It was 6:35 A.M. "We have another twenty-five minutes before we have to get up." She sighed, lay back down. Which was when she heard the noise again.

Bandit jumped off the bed and ran to the

bedroom door, then turned back toward Charley, as if exhorting her to join him. Reluctantly, Charley climbed out of bed and threw a pink cotton robe over her white T-shirt and boxer shorts. Probably just one of the kids, too excited about today's trip to sleep, she was thinking as she crossed the hall to their room and opened the door. But both kids were still asleep, their overnight bags packed and waiting beside their beds.

She heard Bandit barking with excitement, and quickly exited her children's room, closing their door behind her. Someone was in her kitchen, she realized, trying to make sense of what was happening. Was it a burglar? But what kind of burglar breaks into a house at almost seven o'clock in the morning? she thought, deciding she was probably still dreaming. Which was when she heard the voice.

"Ssh!" it cautioned. "Not so loud. You'll wake everybody up."

Charley pushed herself toward the kitchen. The man was wearing jeans and a green-and-white Hawaiian print shirt. He was standing beside the counter, every cupboard door in the room wide open. "Bram!"

Bram spun around. "Happy birthday, Charley."

"What are you doing here?"

"Did I wake you up?"

"It's six-thirty in the morning. What do you think?"

"I think I woke you up. You were always really grouchy in the morning."

"What are you doing here?" Charley asked again.

"Making blueberry pancakes. Or **trying** to," Bram said in exasperation. "I bought the pancake mix, I bought the blueberries. I relied on you for a Mixmaster. Which seems to have been a colossal error on my part."

"You're making pancakes?"

"Trying to."

"Are you drunk?"

"Are you?" he countered.

"Of course not."

"Neither am I. Now where's your Mixmaster?"

Charley pointed to the Cuisinart on the counter beside the coffee maker.

"Shit," Bram said. "Couldn't see it for looking."

"What are you doing here, Bram?" she asked a third time.

"Making you blueberry pancakes for your birthday," he answered, taking her in his arms and kissing her on the cheek. "I wanted to make sure I got here before you took off. I'm coming with you, by the way."

"You're coming to Disney World?"

"Is that a problem?"

"Mom's coming," Charley reminded him, convinced now this was all a dream.

There was a moment's silence. "I know that."

"And you're okay with it?"

Another pause, longer than the first. "I guess we'll find out."

"Oh, Bram." Charley surrounded her brother with her arms. If this was a dream, she definitely didn't want to wake up. "Thank you. This is the best birthday present ever."

"Glad you like it, 'cause you can't take it back. What time are we leaving?"

"Mom and Alex should be here before eight."

"Oh, I forgot about Alex."

"Is that a problem?"

"Just means we'll have to take two cars. Which isn't a problem because . . ." Bram led Charley toward the front door and opened it. "Ta dum! They found mine." He pointed to his freshly washed sports car at the curb in front of the house. "By the way, we probably should send Katarina flowers and a thank-you note," he said as Bandit ran outside and peed, then raced back in again.

"The occasion being . . . ?"

"If it hadn't been for her, my car wouldn't have been stolen, and I wouldn't have had a message from the police waiting for me when I got home from your place last week telling me they'd found it. In one piece, no less. So how could I get plastered when I had to go reclaim my car? And more good news—whoever stole it also stole the stash of weed and other assorted goodies I had in the glove compartment, along with my cell phone, so not only couldn't I get stoned, I couldn't call my dealer. And by the time I got back to my apartment, I was so exhausted, I couldn't be bothered doing anything but crawl into bed. So here I am a week later. Clean, sober, and ready for the Magic Kingdom."

Charley didn't know whether to laugh or cry, so she did both.

"Oh, please don't cry. I'm useless when a woman cries."

"I'm just so happy. I was so afraid when I couldn't reach you . . ."

"I just needed some time to be alone and think things through."

"And what conclusions did you reach?"

"I concluded that it's time for you to get dressed and let me get started on birthday pancakes for six."

"You promise you won't change your mind, that you'll be here when I get back?"

"I'll be here when you get back."

By the time Charley returned, freshly showered and dressed in a crisp white blouse and khaki-colored capris, the kids were up and helping Bram set the table. "Happy birthday," Franny sang out in greeting. She was wearing a pink T-shirt and matching pants, and her hair was brushed and secured at the sides by two pink barrettes in the shape of cupids.

"Happy birthday! Happy birthday!" James echoed. He was wearing a Mickey Mouse T-shirt that was half-in, half-out of his navy blue shorts.

"Uncle Bram's making pancakes," Franny said with obvious pride.

"And he's coming with us to Disney World!" James said.

"I know. Isn't that wonderful?"

In response James ran excited circles around the table, Bandit at his heels.

The front door opened. "Hello?" Elizabeth Webb called from the front hall. "What smells so good?" She appeared in the doorway to the kitchen, stopping abruptly when she saw Bram standing by the stovetop, frying pan in hand.

"I'm making blueberry pancakes," he told her. "Seems you're not the only one in the family with a famous recipe. Of course, in my case, the recipe is Aunt Jemima's. But what the hell?"

"Uncle Bram's coming with us to Disney World," James told his grandmother.

"Is that true?" Elizabeth's eyes were glued to her son's face.

"Isn't that what grown-ups do?" Bram quickly turned away and started spooning batter into the pan.

"I'll make coffee," Elizabeth volunteered.

There was a knock on the door.

"That'll be Alex," Charley said, running to answer it. She pulled open the door. Gabe Lopez stood on the other side.

"Sorry to bother you so early," he began immediately, "but I saw the car pull into the driveway and figured you were up."

"Is there a problem?" Charley asked, as Bandit jumped up and down against the man's shins.

Gabe leaned down to pat Bandit's head. "I just wanted to warn you that the men will be working on the back patio with jackhammers all day, so it might get pretty noisy."

"Actually we'll be in Disney World all weekend, so it won't be a problem. But thanks for the warning."

Gabe Lopez sniffed at the air. "Something smells very good."

"My brother's making blueberry pancakes. Would you like to join us?"

"I shouldn't," Gabe Lopez said, about to turn away. "But I will."

"Good." Charley was surprised to realize she meant it. "Go on in. Everybody, this is my neighbor, Gabe Lopez," she called after him. "He'll be joining us for breakfast." She was about to close the door when she saw Alex's car round the corner.

"Guess who's coming to breakfast," she told him as he bounded up the front walk.

"What's going on?" he asked.

"You'll have to see for yourself."

"Okay. Is everybody ready for a little piece of heaven?" Bram was asking minutes later.

James giggled. "Piece of heaven," he repeated, and giggled some more.

It truly **was** a piece of heaven, Charley thought as she took her seat at the table between her mother and Alex. Franny and James sat on either side of Gabe Lopez. Bram hovered over everyone, loading everyone's plates with pancakes.

"Who wants orange juice?" Alex asked, getting up to pour everyone a glass.

I should get my camera, Charley thought, so I can keep this moment forever, replay it whenever I want, keep the memory of it alive. **Relive it**, she thought with a shudder, seeing Jill's wicked smile in the reflection of the patio door. Go away, she ordered silently. You're not invited to this party.

"Something wrong, darling?" her mother asked.

"No," Charley said quickly, banishing Jill's image from her brain, although a part of her remained, skulking about the room like an evil spirit, winking from the shadows as Charley wolfed down the pancakes on her plate. "I should take Bandit over to Lynn's," Charley said when she was through, hoping the fresh air would be enough to banish Jill's malevolent presence once and for all.

"And I should get going as well," Gabe Lopez said, standing up and bowing his head in appreciation. "Thank you so much."

"I'm glad you could join us," Charley said, walking Gabe to the front door.

"It's a pleasure to have such nice neighbors," he told her.

"It is indeed."

Gabe Lopez cut across the lawn to his house just as several workers pulled their truck into his driveway. The man in the yellow hard hat was not among them.

Charley secured Bandit's leash. "Kids, come say good-bye to Bandit."

Franny and James ran toward the door, scooped Bandit into the air, and smothered him with kisses. "Bye, Bandit," they said together.

"Be a good boy," James added solemnly.

"I'll be back soon." Charley picked up the paper bag full of the things Bandit would need for the weekend and led the dog outside.

Lynn was waiting at her front door, long red fingernails gripping the handle of a steaming mug of coffee, when Charley arrived. Even this early in the morning, she was fully made up, her hair teased into a bouffant ball, her bare feet squeezed into three-inch platforms. "How's my little furball?" she cooed as Bandit licked her toes and Charley handed over the bag of his belongings.

"Everything should be there. His food, his dish, his favorite toy." Charley pulled a rubber hamburger from the bag and squeezed it. It made a squeaky sound that caused Bandit to snap to attention. "The vet's number's in the bag if there's an emergency. . . ."

"There won't be. Will there, big guy? No, there certainly won't be." She picked Bandit up, pushed her red lips forward to be kissed. Bandit obliged by sticking his tongue directly into her mouth. "Oh, my goodness. You're a fast one. Yes, you are. You're a fast one. I wasn't expecting that. No, I wasn't."

"I really appreciate this, Lynn."

"Not at all. What are neighbors for?"

Charley began to smile, but a sudden sharp pain in her stomach stopped her cold.

"Something wrong?" Lynn asked.

"I think I ate one too many blueberry pancakes."

Lynn patted the bulge at her tummy. "Tell me about it. You want some Pepto-Bismol?"

"No, I'll be okay." But by the time Charley got back home, her stomach was cramping so badly she could barely stand up straight.

"We're trying to decide whose car to take," her mother said as she walked in the front door. "Alex's is a little bigger, but mine is newer. . . ."

"And purpler," Bram added.

"And purpler, yes," Elizabeth said with a smile. "As well as safer. And I already have a car seat for James installed, and . . ."

"We'll take your car," Alex said easily, carrying the first of the overnight bags to the mauve Civic in the driveway, followed closely by James. "Are you okay?" he asked Charley upon his return. "You look a little pale."

"My stomach's giving me a hard time," Charley acknowledged quietly. "Guess I'm just not used to such a big breakfast." She felt another twinge, and looked away in order to hide her growing discomfort. She was immediately overcome with dizziness, and grabbed the wall to keep from keeling over.

"What's the matter, dear?" her mother asked.

"Nothing. It's nothing."

"You're sure you're okay?" Alex asked. "We don't have to leave yet."

"No, I'll be fine. Really."

"You don't look very good," Franny said.

"Is there a problem?" Bram asked.

"Come on, everybody," James yelled from the side of the car. "Let's go."

"I'm fine," Charley insisted, as a strong spasm shot through her insides.

"You're not fine," Alex said. "Come on. You're sitting down for a few minutes." He led her into the living room, sat down beside her on the sofa. "You think you're going to be sick?"

"I don't know."

"Take deep breaths."

Charley did as she was told but felt no better.

James bounded back into the room. "Come on!" he urged. "We're gonna be late."

"Mommy isn't feeling well," Franny told him.

"But it's her birthday!"

"I'm fine," Charley said, determined not to ruin the weekend. She tried to stand up, but the pain was like a powerful jab to her solar plexus, and she collapsed back onto the sofa.

"Okay, that's it," Alex said. "I'm sorry, kids, but it doesn't look like we're going anywhere today."

"No!" James cried. The disappointment in that single word was both overwhelming and heartbreaking.

"Of course we're going," Charley insisted.

"Charley, you can barely move," Alex said.

"I'll be okay in ten minutes."

"Then we'll go in ten minutes," Alex said. "Okay, look. Here's a suggestion. Bram and your mother can drive the kids up, check into the motel, get started on the Magic Kingdom, and you and I will meet them there as soon as you're feeling better. We need two cars anyway. How's that?"

"Can we, Mommy? Can we? Can we?"

"I don't know."

"What do you say? Think you can manage without us for a few hours?" Alex asked Charley's mother and brother.

"I think we can," Elizabeth said hopefully. "What do you think, Bram?"

"I think we should probably get started." The forced enthusiasm in Bram's voice was almost enough to mask the panic in his eyes.

"We'll finish packing up the car," Alex told them, "and you and the kids can be on your way." He helped Bram tote the rest of the bags outside, James right behind them.

"I'm not sure this is such a good idea," Charley said when they were gone.

"It's a wonderful idea," her mother told her. "It gives your brother and me a real chance to connect. Are you sure you're not faking this whole episode . . . ?"

"Trust me, I'm not faking."

"Are you gonna be all right?" Franny asked.

Charley nodded, the motion making her feel even worse. "Mom, get my cell phone, will you? It's in my purse."

Her mother quickly located the phone in

Charley's bag. "Here it is, darling. Do you want me to call the doctor?"

"No. I want you to take it with you."

"What? No. I hate these things."

"Mom, you have to take it. Bram's phone got stolen, and I have to be able to reach you. I can't let you go without it."

"But I'm useless with these things."

"You can handle it. I promise. Just remember, it doesn't ring. It whistles."

"Of course it does." Her mother tossed the phone reluctantly into her purse.

"Franny, Grandma, come on!" James yelled from the front lawn. "We're going."

Franny touched her mother's hand tenderly, then ran from the room.

"You know the name of the motel. . . ." Charley said to her mother.

"I know everything, sweetheart. Not to worry."

"Then go on," Charley urged. "I'll call you as soon as I'm feeling better. If you don't hear from me before you get there, you call **me**."

Instead of leaving, Elizabeth sank down in the cushion next to Charley and tenderly took her in her arms, rocking her gently. Charley felt the warmth of her mother's embrace, the touch of her lips as they brushed against her forehead. A part of her instinctively moved to push her mother away, but another part of her, the part that had been waiting for this moment for twenty-two years, held firm and held on tight. How fitting this should happen on her birthday, she was thinking, as she buried her head against her mother's breasts and cried like a newborn baby.

"My beautiful girl," her mother whispered, kissing the top of her head. "My sweet, beautiful girl. I love you so much."

"I love you, too," Charley told her, crying harder now.

"Okay, the car's all packed." Alex reentered the room with Bram at his side. "The kids are buckled in and raring to go."

Charley loosened her viselike grip on her mother's waist as Elizabeth kissed her forehead. "Don't you worry about a thing, darling. You just get better."

"Fast," Bram added.

Charley nodded, feeling worse.

The sound of jackhammers came pounding through the walls. "Oh, God," Charley moaned as Bram leaned close to kiss her good-bye.

"Don't let the kids out of your sight for a minute," she warned.

"I'll watch them like a hawk," Bram said.

"Drive carefully," Charley heard Alex call out as her mother's car pulled out of the driveway seconds later. Seconds after that, Alex was back at her side. "Do you really think that was such a good idea?" Charley asked him.

"I think it was a great idea. You need to rest."

"I sure need something."

"Maybe I should take you to emergency."

"What? No. This is hardly an emergency."

"It could be your appendix."

"It's not my appendix. It's those damn blueberry pancakes."

"They **were** pretty rich," Alex agreed. "Can I get you anything? Some tea maybe?"

"No. I think if I can just sleep for a few minutes." As if on cue, the jackhammers started up again, the vibrations slicing through Charley's body like an electric saw. "Oh, no."

Alex's head jerked toward the sound. "What the hell is going on over there?"

"Whatever it is, they'll be doing it all day."

"Well, then, we certainly can't stay here." He reached down and dragged Charley to her feet, placing one of her arms over his shoulder and gripping her firmly by the waist.

"What are you doing? Where are we going?"

"To my apartment. The sooner, the better. To be honest, I'm starting to feel a little peculiar myself."

"We make quite a pair," Charley said, trying to smile.

Alex stopped at the front door, kissed her gently on the cheek. "I think I like the sound of that," he said.

33

Charley woke up to the sound of a door closing in the distance. She opened her eyes and sat up, trying to orient herself to her surroundings. She was quickly overwhelmed with dizziness and sank back down. Slowly, carefully, she glanced toward the wall to her right, recognizing the series of beautiful black-and-white photographs that hung there. She was in Alex's bedroom, she reminded herself, although she had only the vaguest memory of the drive over, and only a slightly stronger recall of the elevator ride up to his apartment. She remembered being half-carried, half-dragged into his bedroom, then tucked underneath the bedcovers, Alex collapsing beside her. But Alex wasn't there now, she realized, feeling the indentation where his body had been. "Alex?" she called out, her voice disappearing even before it made contact with the air. Where was he?

What time is it? she wondered, turning her head gingerly toward the clock on the end table beside the bed. It took several seconds for her eyes to focus, and several more for her to convince the numbers to make sense. Could it really be almost eleven o'clock? Was that possible? Had she really lost almost the entire morning?

Her family was most likely in Kissimee by now, she realized. Maybe even checked into the motel. What was the name of it? she wondered, panicking when it refused to come. Something cutesy, she thought. The Castle of the Sleeping Dwarfs. . . . Sleeping Beauty's Inn. . . . "Beautiful Dreamers Motel," she murmured, nodding her head in confirmation, then having to close her eyes when the room nodded back. What the hell was going on? She'd been fine when she woke up this morning. Now she felt as if she'd been run over by a truck. Could the flu strike so quickly and violently?

"I have to call my mother," Charley said, although no sound reached her ears. Had she even said the words out loud? Her mother was probably worried sick, she thought. No doubt she'd been trying to reach her, and would have no idea where she was, or how to get ahold of her. She'd likely called the house half a dozen times by now, only to get Charley's voice mail, which would have confused her no end. "I have to call her," Charley said again, once more forcing her body into a sitting position, then sitting very still until the room stopped spinning.

Her eyes traveled slowly across the bed from one end table to the other, looking for the phone. But it was missing from its holder. And Alex was nowhere in sight. "Alex?" she called again, pushing the word from the back of her throat along with a mouthful of bile. Hurling herself toward the marble en suite bathroom, Charley threw up in the toilet bowl, then collapsed on the floor, laying her head on the cool tile, and wondering what the hell was happening to her. She'd had stomachaches before, as well as morning sickness during both pregnancies. But nothing like this. Was it possible Alex had been right? That her appendix was attacking? Where was he anyway?

Charley took a series of deep breaths, eventually swallowing enough air to push herself to her feet. "Now what?" she asked her ashen-faced reflection in the mirror over the sink.

Find a phone, her reflection told her.

Charley shuffled out of the bathroom, through the bedroom, and down the hall into the living room. The portable phone was sitting on the coffee table in front of the sofa. Charley grabbed it just as her legs gave way and she fell to the floor, like a discarded marionette. Supporting her back against the sofa, she stabbed at the numbers and waited for the familiar ring.

I'm sorry, a robotic voice informed her seconds later. **The number you have dialed is not in service.**

"Bullshit! What are you talking about?" Charley tried the number again, but her fingers had lost their power, and she watched them slide helplessly across the face of the phone, so that she had to stop and do it again. She listened as the phone rang once, twice, three times, before finally being picked up.

"Hello?" the girl said, amid a rush of giggles.

"Franny?"

"Margo, where the hell are you? Everybody's waiting."

"Margo?" Charley repeated.

"Stop fooling around," the girl said. "You're really late."

"Who **is** this?"

"What?"

"I need to speak to Bram," Charley said.

"Who?"

Charley hung up the phone. Clearly she'd called the wrong number. "Shit. What's the matter with you?" She tried her number again, this time with a deliberateness that would have been comical in other circumstances. The phone rang four times before being transferred to voice mail.

This is Charley Webb, her own voice informed her. **I'm sorry I can't take your call**

right now, but if you'll leave your name, phone number, and a short message, I'll get back to you as soon as I can.

"Mom, it's me," Charley said. "Where are you? I'm at Alex's. His number is . . ." What the hell was his number? She had no idea. "You'll have to look it up. Alex Prescott in Palm Beach Gardens. Call me." She disconnected the line, then dropped the phone to the floor, where it bounced underneath the coffee table. Who was she kidding? Her mother would never figure out how to access her messages. Maybe Bram would have the sense to figure it out. Although Bram had never been known for his good sense, she thought, and might have laughed had it not been for the heaviness in her head. Flu or no flu, she was thinking as her eyes fluttered to a close, one thing was certain: she'd never eat blueberry pancakes again. An instant later she was asleep.

She dreamed she was in a china store, shopping for teacups. "I'm a collector," she told the saleswoman in the long peasant skirt.

"In that case," the woman told her, "you should see these." She led Charley into a back room filled with giant cups in a variety of pastel colors.

Glen McLaren was sitting in the cup closest to the door.

"Glen!" Charley exclaimed. "What are you doing here?"

He laughed. "It's a small world."

Which was when the fire alarm sounded.

"You need to get out of here," Glen said as the ringing grew louder and more insistent.

Charley opened her eyes. The ringing continued. The phone, she realized, taking a deep breath and trying to locate it, her fingers groping along the floor. How long had she been asleep this time? She noticed the watch on her wrist as she reached under the coffee table, and tried to figure out what it said. It was either ten minutes after eleven or five minutes to two, she decided, unable to detect any difference between the small hand and the large. She grabbed the phone, pressing one button after another before stumbling onto the right one. "Hello?" she whispered into the receiver as the connection was made. "Mom, is that you?"

You have a collect call from . . . the voice announced as the recording paused for caller identification.

"Jill Rohmer," a voice pronounced clearly.

Will you accept the charges? the recording continued.

"What?" Charley shouted. What was happening?

Will you accept the charges? the recording repeated, as if it understood.

Charley fought to regain control of her senses. Could Jill Rohmer really be on the other end of the line? Surely she was still dreaming. Surely this was all part of a prolonged nightmare that had started with a batch of blueberry pancakes and was ending with a collect call from a killer. But whatever it was, reality or illusion, Charley understood she had no choice but to see it through to its conclusion. "Yes," she heard herself say. "I'll accept the charges."

There was a second of silence, and then Jill's voice. "Alex?"

"Jill," Charley said. "Is something wrong?"

Another silence. "Charley?"

"Yes. Is something . . . ?"

"What are you doing there? I thought you were going to Disney World."

"I'm not feeling very well."

"What are you doing at Alex's apartment?"

"It's a long story," Charley said, hoping she wouldn't have to tell it.

"I've got lots of time," Jill said, as if reading her thoughts.

Charley closed her eyes, fought the urge to succumb to unconsciousness. She had neither the strength nor energy required to deal with Jill. "Look, Alex isn't here right now."

"I need to speak to him. They're threatening to cut back on my privileges. Where is he?"

"I don't know. Can I give him a message?"

"What—now you're his secretary?" Jill asked.

"I'll tell him you called."

"I'll tell him myself. He's **my** lawyer."

"I'm sorry, Jill. I'm just not up for this conversation right now."

"You're not **up** for it?" Jill repeated angrily. "What is this? I'm being dismissed?"

"I don't feel very well."

"What **are** you up for, pray tell?"

"Good-bye, Jill."

"Are you up for finding out who Jack is?"

Charley leaned forward, pressed the receiver tightly to her ear. "What?"

"Feeling better all of a sudden, are we?"

"Enough, Jill. I'm not in the mood for your games."

"Really? You're not in the mood?"

"I told you, I don't feel well."

"How **do** you feel exactly? Like you got run over by a truck? Like your insides are on fire?" She held on to the last word just long enough to get Charley's full attention. "Like you had too many blueberry pancakes for breakfast?"

There was a loud swishing sound, as if all the air in the room had just been sucked out. Charley realized it was the sound of her body, gasping for breath. "What did you say?"

"Those pancakes are a real killer, aren't they?" Jill continued, flippantly. "I try to avoid them myself. All those calories. It's hardly worth it."

"How did you know I had pancakes?"

"How do you think I know? It's the only

thing he can make, for God's sake. I tried to tell him he should expand his horizons, but what can you do? The man may hate his mama, but he sure loves his Aunt Jemima."

The words bounced painfully from one side of Charley's brain to the other, refusing to settle down long enough to make sense. "What are you talking about?"

"Oh, come on, Charley. Do I really have to spell it out for you?"

"Yes. You really do," Charley said forcefully. "You need to spell it out."

"Well, let's see then. How do I spell Jack? Oh, I know: B . . . R . . . A . . . M."

Charley pushed herself to her feet as the letters smacked her right between the eyes, threatening to knock her back to the floor. "I don't believe you."

"What is it you don't believe, Charley? That Bram is Jack, or that you're not nearly as smart as you like to think you are? Who do you think suggested I contact you in the first place? You think it was a coincidence that I just happened to know the brother of the woman I asked to write my story? That's 'know' in the very biblical sense of the word, by the way."

"You're lying," Charley protested weakly.

"Poor, stupid little Charley, playing house with my attorney, while her brother is . . . where?

Wait, let me guess. He's in Disney World. Isn't that right? And he's not alone, is he? He's with your children." She snickered, an obscene sound emanating from somewhere low in her throat.

"You're crazy."

"And you're such a fool. You deserve whatever happens." The sneer in Jill's voice was audible. "You won't forget to tell Alex I called, will you? Oh, and happy birthday, Charley. Many happy returns of the day."

The line went dead in Charley's hand.

"Jill! Jill!" Charley screamed. Then, "Noooooo! It can't be. It can't be." Her body began convulsing in a series of painful dry heaves, folding in on itself as she fell back against the sofa, frantically pressing in the numbers on the portable phone. "Please, Mom. Pick up. Pick up the phone," she yelled as once again her own voice reached her ears.

This is Charley Webb. I'm sorry I can't take your call right now . . .

Charley pushed the button to disconnect, located the REDIAL button, and jabbed at it repeatedly. "Pick up the phone," she commanded. "Pick up the damn phone."

This is Charley Webb . . .

Charley threw the phone across the room, only to watch it bounce against the wall and fall into Alex's collection of classic old movies, sending several spinning across the floor. It was at that moment she heard someone calling her name.

"Charley," the voice was yelling from the outside corridor. "What's going on in there? Are you all right?" The door opened and Alex rushed inside, a small bag of groceries in his arms. He promptly dropped the bag to the floor and ran to Charley's side. "What happened? I could hear you screaming all the way down the hall."

"It's Bram!" Charley shouted, clutching the sides of his arms in an effort to stay upright.

"What?" Alex's eyes flew across the room. "Where?"

"He's got my kids!"

"I don't understand. Of course he's got the kids."

"He's Jack!"

"What are you talking about?"

"My brother. He's Jack! He's Jack!" Charley started sobbing.

Alex guided her back to the sofa, sat down beside her. "Charley, calm down. You're not making any sense."

"We've got to call the police."

"We will," Alex said soothingly. "Just as soon as you tell me what's going on."

"Jill called."

"Jill called here? Why?"

"She wanted to talk to you."

"About what?"

"Something about taking away her privileges," Charley said impatiently. "I don't know. All I know is that she told me that my brother is Jack."

"That's ridiculous." Alex began shaking his head from side to side, as if Charley were speaking a language he didn't comprehend. "Okay, start again. You're going to have to talk me through this word for word."

"There isn't time. We have to call the police."

"When did Jill call?"

"A few minutes ago." Charley looked at her watch, the numbers dancing in front of her eyes, refusing to stand still. "I think."

"You think?"

"I was in bed. The phone rang," Charley began, then stopped. "No, that's not right. I was in bed. Something woke me up. You weren't there . . ."

"I went to get us some chicken soup. I thought I'd be back before you woke up."

"I got out of bed," Charley continued as if he hadn't spoken. "I tried to find the phone. . . ."

"I moved it so it wouldn't disturb you."

". . . I threw up in the bathroom."

Alex touched her face. "I'm so sorry."

"Then I came in here, found the phone, tried calling my mother. But she wasn't picking up. I think I fell asleep again. I don't know for how long. What time is it?"

"Almost noon."

"Oh, God. I must have fallen asleep. The phone woke me up. It was Jill."

"You're sure?" Alex questioned. "You're sure you weren't dreaming?"

"I'm not sure," Charley answered honestly. Had it been a dream? "I don't know. I don't know."

"Okay. What exactly did Jill say to you?"

Charley recounted the conversation to the best of her abilities.

Alex listened carefully, then jumped to his feet, looking anxiously around the room. "Where'd you put the phone?"

"I don't know. I threw it. . . ."

Alex was already on the other side of the room, his eyes traveling back and forth along the floor. He finally located the phone against the far wall.

"What are you doing?" Charley asked, watching him.

"Calling the state police."

"I don't understand. If you think I was dreaming. . . ."

"Nobody's dreams make that much sense," he said simply.

Charley burst into tears.

"Hello? Hello? Yes. I need to alert the police in Kissimee," Alex said forcefully. "What? Yes, all right. Please hurry." He put his hand over the receiver. "They're trying to connect me to the right people." He started to pace. "What really pisses me off is that I didn't make the connection before. Of course it was no coincidence she picked you. . . . Hello, hello? Yes, this is an emergency. I need to get ahold of the police in Kissimee. . . . My name? Alex Prescott. I'm an attorney. . . . Yes, Prescott. Two **t**'s. Look. My girlfriend's children are in danger. They're with her brother, and we have reason to believe that. . . . No, don't put me on hold. Shit! They have me on hold again."

"Oh, no. What do we do?" Charley tried to stand up, but her knees refused to hold her weight, and she fell back down again.

"You take deep breaths and try to clear your head. As soon as you feel strong enough, you go into the bedroom and get my cell phone out of my briefcase. Then you keep trying to reach your mother. Hello? Hello? For Christ's sake, where the hell are these people?"

Charley took a succession of deep breaths, trying to reassure herself that everything would be all right. Alex was here now. And there was still a chance, however slim, that this whole stupid day was just a nightmare of epic proportions. She'd wake up to find the kids asleep in their beds, her mother and Alex on their way over, and her brother . . . her brother making blueberry pancakes in the kitchen.

The man may hate his mama, but he sure loves his Aunt Jemima.

"This can't be happening."

"It'll be all right, Charley," Alex assured her. "I promise you everything will be all right."

Charley nodded, Alex's strength pushing her off the sofa and out of the living room. By the time she reached the bedroom, she was out of breath and sweating profusely, and she had to grab the wall for support. It took her a minute to remember why she was there, another minute to locate Alex's briefcase on the floor beside his desk, and yet another minute to figure out how to open it. The phone was immediately visible on top of a bunch of official-looking papers, and she grabbed for it, the motion sending the contents of the briefcase flying out of her hands, the official-looking papers scattering like so much debris. "Oh, God. What am I doing?" She quickly tapped in the number of her cell phone. "Please pick up. Please pick up," she prayed, falling to her knees and trying to corral Alex's papers inside her shaking hands.

This is Charley Webb. I'm sorry I can't take your call right now . . .

"No! No!"

Alex came running into the room, pulled her to her feet. "Charley, what are you doing?"

"I spilled all your papers. . . ."

"It doesn't matter. None of that matters."

"Nobody's answering my phone."

He sat her down on the bed. "Okay, listen to me. Are you listening to me?"

Charley nodded, although his words were blurry and indistinct, as if he were underwater.

"I talked to the state police. They promised to send somebody to the motel in Kissimee."

"Thank God," she sighed before her panic returned. "What if they're not there?"

"Then they'll turn Disney World inside out. I'm going to drive up there now and meet with them. . . ."

"I'll come with you." Charley tried to stand up.

"You're staying put. You can barely move."

"What about you? You were sick, too."

"Not half as sick as you are."

"Oh, God, Alex. If he hurts my children. . . ."

"He won't."

"You promise?"

"I promise." He kissed her. "Now I'm going, and I'm taking my cell phone so that you can contact me as soon as you reach your mother."

"I don't know your number."

"I'll write it down. Okay? I'll leave the number on the coffee table in the living room. You keep calling your mother, and as soon as you reach her, you call me. Have you got that? Charley, I need you to focus. Have you got that?"

"I'll keep calling my mother."

"And you'll phone me as soon as you reach her."

"I'll phone you as soon as I reach her."

"I'll leave the number on the coffee table," he reiterated.

"You'll call me as soon as you get there?" she pleaded.

"I'll call you as soon as I get there."

She followed him back into the living room, watched as he jotted the number for his cell phone on a piece of paper and left it on the coffee table.

"I'm leaving it right here," he told her, moving toward the door. "You keep trying to reach your mother."

She nodded, hanging on to the wall and crying so hard she could hardly see him anymore.

He opened the door, then hesitated, turned back. "You'll be all right? Maybe I should take you to the hospital."

"No. No hospital. Not until I know the kids are safe."

"Promise me you'll call 911 if you start to feel worse."

"I promise."

"You're sure you're all right?"

"I'm sure. Please hurry."

They stared at each other for several more seconds. Charley waited until Alex was gone before collapsing to the floor.

34

For the next hour, the only part of Charley that moved was the thumb of her right hand as it pressed, and then re-pressed, over and over again, the REDIAL button on the phone.

Press. Ring.

This is Charley Webb. I'm sorry I can't take your call right now . . .

Press. Ring.

This is Charley Webb. I'm sorry . . .

Press. Ring.

This is Charley Webb . . .

Press. Ring.

This is . . .

"Oh, God," Charley cried, her head lolling from side to side. She had to get up. She couldn't just sit on the floor forever. She should get up, wash her face, brush her hair, be ready in case Alex called and she had to leave in a hurry.

Press. Ring.

This is Charley Webb . . .

Slowly, carefully, Charley finally managed to push herself into a standing position, although she had to lean against the wall for support.

Press. Ring.

This is Charley Webb . . .

She followed the wall around the corner to the bedroom, ignoring the legal documents strewn across the floor as she approached the bathroom. Standing over the sink, she tucked her hair behind her ears and splashed some cold water on her face, then found an old toothbrush in the medicine cabinet, and brushed her teeth. "That's better," she said, although it wasn't really.

Press. Ring.

This is Charley Webb. I'm sorry . . .

She returned to the bedroom, trampling several legal-size sheets of paper beneath the soles of her sneakers as she walked. Lowering herself slowly to the floor, as if she were sliding through a vat of thick honey, she began gathering the papers together, returning them to Alex's brief-case. **Pinnacle Books,** she read, the words pulsating off the page like a strobe light. **Charley Webb.** Her book contract, she realized, knowing how elated seeing this would have made her even a few short hours ago.

Press. Ring.

This is Charley Webb. I'm sorry . . .

She was sorry all right. Sorry she'd ever met with Jill Rohmer. Sorry she'd allowed herself to be seduced by thoughts of riches and fame. Sorry she'd lent a sympathetic ear to Jill's admittedly horrifying history of abuse, while all the while Jill had been laughing behind her back, plotting with her brother—her beloved brother, was it possible?—to do her children harm.

How could it be?

Press. Ring.

This is Charley Webb . . .

Charley returned to the living room, moving marginally faster now, and retrieved the bag of groceries from the floor near the front door. She carried the bag to the kitchen and removed the several cans of chicken soup, deciding maybe a little soup would make her feel better. Somehow she managed to get the can open and the soup into a cup. Then she put the cup in the microwave oven and turned it on, watching the automatic timer count down the seconds until the soup was ready.

Press. Ring.

This is Charley Webb. I'm sorry . . .
This is Charley Webb. I'm sorry . . .
This is Charley Webb. I'm sorry . . .

She carried the soup into the living room and sat down on the sofa, the aromatic steam drifting toward her nostrils. She took a tiny sip of soup, felt it hot against the back of her throat. If she could only manage to keep it down, she was thinking, as she tried her number yet again.

Press. Ring.

This is Charley Webb . . .

"Where are you, for God's sake? Why aren't you picking up?"

She pictured her mother looking around in confusion, wondering where that strange wolf whistle was coming from. Damn it. She should have changed it to a traditional ring. Why hadn't she changed it?

She pictured her children: sweet, sensitive Franny with her big, sad eyes and sharp, analytical mind; rambunctious, carefree James, with his boundless energy and enthusiasm. How could anyone think of hurting them?

She thought of the e-mails she'd received.

I'm coming, the last one had stated ominously. **Soon.**

Had Bram sent them?

She remembered the photographs of children she'd found in the night table beside his bed. **They're just some neighborhood kids I was thinking of painting**, Bram had told her. Was that what they were? Potential portraits? Or were they potential victims? "No. Please, no."

Her beautiful, lost brother, who'd spent much of the past decade in a drug-fueled haze—was he really capable of hurting anyone other than himself?

Press. Ring.

This is Charley Webb. I'm sorry . . .

How many times had she let him down? How many times had she disappointed him, scolded him, turned her back on him? He was the youngest, the most beautiful, and by far the most vulnerable of the four Webb children. His sisters had somehow managed to channel the pain of their childhood into something productive, but Bram's pain had been relieved only by alcohol and narcotics.

Charley remembered her mother showing her how to hold Bram when he was an infant. She recalled the instructions to rock him gently, never imagining hers would soon be the only arms to do so. She pictured him hanging on to the indifferent skirts of a succession of nannies, the tears in his eyes glazing over, then eventually drying up altogether. She remembered the cruel taunts of the other children that chased him home from school, the crueler admonishment from his father to "take it like a man."

Press. Ring.

This is Charley Webb. I'm sorry . . .

She'd abandoned him, too, Charley acknowledged silently. Fled to Florida upon her graduation from college, determined to make a name for herself, her total self-absorption allowing little time to worry about her dissolute younger brother. Eventually Bram had sought her out, driving his ancient MG down to Miami, where he'd rented an apartment and, when he wasn't too stoned, attended a few art classes. In one of those classes, he'd met Pamela Rohmer. And through Pamela, her sister, Jill.

Jack and Jill.

Was it possible?

Charley pressed the REDIAL button again, and listened to the ring, bracing herself for the unwelcome sound of her own voice.

"Hello?" she heard her mother say instead. "Hello? Is somebody there?"

Charley's breath caught in her throat. She'd reached them. They were safe.

"Nobody's saying anything," her mother continued. "I don't think I'm doing this right."

"Mom!" Charley yelled, the word an explosion. "Mom? Listen to me!"

"Charley?"

"Where have you been? I've been calling you for hours."

"We were at the Magic Kingdom. It was so crowded there, I guess I didn't hear you whistling. I tried calling you earlier, but I kept getting your voice mail."

"Is that Mommy?" Charley heard a small voice ask.

"Franny?" Charley cried. "Is that Franny?" Her daughter was there. She was unharmed.

"Well, of course it's Franny. Here. I'll let you talk to her. I have to lie down for a few minutes. My stomach's been acting up off and on all day."

Charley heard the phone exchanging hands. "Where are you, Mommy?" Franny asked. "Are you almost here?"

"Not yet, sweetie. But Alex will be there soon. So I need you and James to sit tight, and not go anywhere until he gets there. . . ."

"James isn't here," Franny interrupted.

Charley felt her body turn to stone. "What?"

"James isn't here," Franny repeated.

"Where is he?"

"With Uncle Bram."

Charley had to bite down on her lower lip to keep from screaming. "Where are they?"

"They're still at the Magic Kingdom. James wanted to go into Pirates of the Caribbean, but the line was so long, and Grandma wasn't feeling well."

"Let me speak to her again."

"She's pretty sick, Mommy. . . ."

"Franny, put your grandmother on the phone," Charley snapped.

"What's the matter?" Franny started whimpering.

"What is it, darling?" Charley heard her mother ask Franny.

"I think Mommy's mad at me. . . ."

"Charley?" her mother asked, returning to the line. "What . . . ?"

"You left James with Bram?"

"Is that a problem? They were having such a good time, and I didn't want to ruin it for everyone just because I wasn't feeling well. Franny wanted to keep me company."

"How long ago was that?"

"Not long. Not more than half an hour ago. Why? Is something wrong?"

"Yes," Charley told her. "Something's very wrong. We have to find James. We have to get him away from Bram."

"What are you talking about?"

"I can't explain it to you now. Have you talked to the police?"

"The police? Good God, no. Why would we . . . ?"

"They probably came when you were in the Magic Kingdom. Hopefully they'll be back. . . ."

"Why? What is this about?"

"Alex will explain everything to you when he gets there. In the meantime, don't let Franny out of your sight, and if Bram comes back with James, make sure you don't let them leave."

"You're starting to scare me."

"Don't be scared. Just do it."

"When will Alex be here?"

Charley checked her watch, although it was a useless gesture. The numbers on its face refused to stay still. "In about an hour." Was that right? How long had he been gone? She saw the piece of paper with his cell phone number lying on the coffee table. "I'll call him as soon as I get off the phone. Just keep your eye on Franny. Don't let her out of your sight," Charley said, the same thing she'd told her brother this morning.

I'll watch them like a hawk, he'd replied.

Was it possible he'd been planning all along to kill them?

No, it couldn't be. It couldn't.

Charley pressed the portable phone's OFF button, then immediately pressed in Alex's number. It scarcely had time to ring before Alex picked it up.

"Charley?" he said. "Were you able to reach your mother?"

"I just spoke to her. She's with Franny at the motel."

"Where's James?"

"Still at Disney World. With Bram."

Silence, then, "Okay, listen. At least we know Franny's safe."

"Where are you?"

"I'm almost there. And I'll call the police and fill them in. Did your mother say anything else?"

"Franny said James wanted to go into Pirates of the Caribbean, and that there was a very long line."

"Those lineups can take hours," Alex agreed. "With any luck, they'll still be standing there when the police arrive."

"Do you really think so?"

"I think there's a chance. How are you feeling?"

"A little stronger," Charley lied.

"Good. I'll call you as soon as I know anything."

"Call me no matter what."

"I will. Try to stay calm."

Charley sat on the sofa for at least ten minutes without moving after Alex said good-bye. Everything's going to be all right, she assured herself repeatedly. Franny was safe. Alex was on his way. He'd find James before Bram could hurt him. Everything would be okay.

Except nothing would ever be okay again. Not if it was true Bram had been Jill's accomplice. Not if it was true he'd drugged her in an attempt to separate her from her children. Not if it was true he was as deranged and cold-blooded as Jill.

Could it really be true?

Could it?

It was one thing for Jill to fool her, and quite another to be taken in by someone she'd known literally his entire life. Her own flesh and blood.

Sweet, sensitive, beautiful Bram. Yes, he was troubled. Yes, he was irresponsible. But he was also a loving brother and a wonderful uncle—no way was he a sadistic psychopath. No way could he ever hurt the children he'd doted on since the day they were born. No way would she ever believe that.

And why should she? she asked herself suddenly. Because Jill had said he was? Why would she believe anything Jill said to her?

Because she knew things, Charley reminded herself. She knew about Aunt Jemima and the blueberry pancakes. She knew about Bram's decision to go to Disney World. How would she know any of that unless . . . unless someone had phoned her and provided her with all the pertinent information?

In the next minute Charley was on her feet, pacing back and forth across the room. "It can't be. It can't be." And yet it was the only thing that made sense. Charley raced back into Alex's bedroom, began rifling through his dresser drawers. What was she doing? What was she looking for? "There's nothing here," she said out loud, pulling loose T-shirts and sweaters from the drawers and dropping them to the floor, then careening toward Alex's closet, and pulling open its door as she fell to her knees. "Just a lot of shoes," she said, flinging them aside. It was then that she noticed a large stack of magazines pressed into a corner, and dragged them toward her. "No. Oh, no," she said, staring at the top cover—a naked woman, bound and gagged, her body twisted into an unnatural position, her face contorted in obvious pain. The other magazines were even worse, the inside pictures growing increasingly graphic, the images more horrific with each flick of the page. Charley looked up, saw a shoebox on a high shelf. She knocked it to the floor with one swipe of her hand. Its lid fell open, the contents of the box spilling to the floor. Charley stood there crying as pornographic pictures of children fell about her head like ashes from a crematorium.

She grabbed her stomach, fighting the renewed urge to vomit as she ran into the living room. Her eyes darted toward Alex's collection of classic old movies, a few of which were still scattered across the floor. **White Christmas, Casablanca, An Affair to Remember.** She began tossing aside one cassette after another. What was she looking for?

Any idea where the tapes are?

None whatsoever.

You're sure she didn't give them to you for safekeeping?

Lawyers aren't allowed to hide evidence, Charley.

What if you didn't know what was on the tapes?

What if he did? What if he knew only too well?

"I'm so sorry, Bram. I've been such an idiot."

Which was when she saw it.

It was at the very back of the shelf, squeezed between **Lawrence of Arabia** and **Citizen Kane**. A simple black cassette with three handwritten words printed on its side.

Jack and Jill.

Charley reached for it, her hand trembling, the delicate hairs on the backs of her arms standing at full alert.

Slowly and carefully, she removed the cassette from its carton and put it in the VCR, then pressed PLAY. Then she waited, her face only inches from the giant TV monitor. There followed several seconds of nothing but a blank, brilliant blue screen, and for a moment Charley thought whatever had been on that tape might have been erased. But in the next instant the blank screen was filled with Jill's laughing face. The extreme close-up made a mockery of her normally delicate features, rendering her almost gargoyle-like, as if the camera had somehow managed to penetrate her soul. She was smoking a cigarette and blowing kisses at the lens. "What are you doing? That's not my good side," she was saying, her voice dissolving in a fit of girlish giggles. "I'll show you my good side." She lifted up her T-shirt to expose her naked breasts.

That was when Charley became aware of other sounds. A man's whispered instructions, a child's muffled cries. "Oh, no," Charley moaned as the camera panned slowly to little Tammy Barnet tied to a cot, squirming and whimpering behind the blindfold that covered her eyes. "No. Oh, please, no."

"Okay, Jill," the male voice whispered seductively. "Now take the cigarette and press it against Tammy's thighs."

"Oh, God." Charley covered her eyes.

"Make the brat shut up," the man ordered sharply. "She's starting to get on my nerves."

"I want my mommy," the little girl cried.

"You'll never see your mommy again if you don't stop blubbering."

"Come on, Tammy," Jill urged. "Be a good little girl. It'll all be over soon."

The little girl let out a sudden, bloodcurdling scream.

"That was just a love bite, silly," Jill chastised, laughing.

"My turn," the man said as Charley edged closer to the TV, the man's voice drawing her in like a magnet. She watched Jill take the camera from his outstretched arms.

"Okay, big boy. It's your turn to shine," Jill said, aiming the camera at the man's feet. The camera panned slowly up the man's legs, resting a few seconds on the pronounced bulge at the

crotch of his jeans. It then continued its languor-
ous climb up his chest and neck until it reached
his smiling face.

Alex.

Charley began rocking back and forth, unable
to turn her eyes away as Alex proceeded to place
a plastic bag over the child's head. "This isn't
happening. This isn't happening." She scrambled to her feet, switched off the VCR before she
could see more, then removed the cassette from
the machine, her fingernails digging into the
plastic as she tried to wrap her mind around
what she'd just seen. But there was no time for
trying to put it all together, to add up the hows
and the whys. None of that mattered now. Only
one thing mattered: Alex had killed those children. He was Jill's lover, her accomplice, her
mentor.

He was Jack.

He'd killed those children, and now he was
on his way to murder her son. "Move," she commanded her legs. "Move."

In the next instant she was on her feet and
searching for her purse. She found it on the floor
in the bedroom, and she tossed the cassette
inside it, then fished around for her car keys.
Except she wasn't at home. Her car wasn't here.
And she was in no condition to drive, her stomach reminded her with a sudden surge of nausea.
Clearly Alex had poisoned her. But when? Bram

had made the pancakes; her mother had made the coffee.

Who wants orange juice? she heard Alex ask brightly.

Okay, no time for that now, Charley admonished herself. She had to do something. Alex had obviously been faking when he pretended to call the state police, which meant there were no officers on their way to rescue James. She had to reach her mother, tell her to call the local police. She returned to the living room and grabbed the phone, pressing in the number of her cell.

This is Charley Webb. I'm sorry I can't take your call right now . . .

"Shit!" What was going on? Charley pressed 911.

"What is the nature of your emergency?" an operator asked.

"I need to speak to the police in Kissimee. There's a man on his way to Disney World to hurt my son."

"I'm sorry. You'll have to speak slower. Your son has been hurt?"

"Not yet. But there's a man, his name is Alex Prescott. . . ."

"Your name is Prescott?"

"No. My name is Charley Webb. Listen to me. My son is in danger. He's in Disney World. . . ."

"I'm sorry, but you really should be talking to the state police."

"Fine. Can you connect me?"

"No, I'm sorry. I'm not equipped to do that."

Charley disconnected the line, pressed the number for information.

For what city? the recording asked sprightly.

"I can't do this," Charley muttered, her head starting to spin as once again, she disconnected the line. Somewhere in the back of her brain, a number kept circling. As soon as it settled, she pressed it in. Seconds later, a man answered.

"Glen," Charley cried gratefully. "This is Charley. I need your help."

35

"Okay, Charley. Take deep breaths. Try to calm down."

Charley gulped at the air as if she were drowning and about to go down for the third and last time. Her eyes shot to the road ahead, the cars in the surrounding lanes quickly reduced to a series of colorful streaks as Glen's silver Mercedes sped past them. The way James would have painted them, Charley thought, swallowing a scream. "Can't you go any faster?"

"I'm doing a hundred and twenty," Glen told her. "I want to get us there in one piece."

"Just get us there," Charley pleaded, a fresh onslaught of tears cascading down her cheeks, causing Glen's handsome features to slide up against one another, until they too were transformed into a series of intersecting lines and free-floating shapes, like an abstract work of art. "Tell me again what the police said when you

spoke to them." Charley fought to remember
what Glen had told her, but her brain was like
Teflon, and the words refused to stick. She
vaguely remembered him saying that the police
wanted them to sit tight until they could interview them, but there'd been no way she was prepared to do that. She remembered the frustration
in Glen's voice as he'd repeatedly tried to persuade the state police of the urgency of the situation. She recalled the sudden silence on the
other end of the line when Glen had mentioned
the name Jill Rohmer. "Do you think they believed you?" she asked, as she was sure she'd
asked several times already.

"I don't know," he admitted. "I'm sure they
get a lot of crank calls. Obviously it would have
been better to talk to them in person, show them
the tape."

"We'll show it to them in Kissimee. You told
them that, didn't you?" Charley fought through
the fog in her head to remember the precise words
Glen had used when describing the videotape.

"I told them."

"And they'll meet us at the motel?"

"They said to call when we got there. Why
don't you try calling your mother again?"

Charley grabbed the phone in her lap, placed
the call to her mother.

**This is Charley Webb. I'm sorry I can't
take your call right now. . . .**

"Why isn't anyone picking up? Oh, my God," Charley gasped in the next breath.

"What's the matter?"

"What if Alex is already there? What if he's not letting her answer the phone? What if . . . ?"

"Call the front desk," Glen said, taking control.

"The front desk?" Of course, the front desk! Why hadn't she thought of that earlier? What was the matter with her? "I don't know the number," she wailed, panicking as even the name of the motel eluded her. **The Seven Dwarfs . . . The Sleeping Beauty . . . ?** What was the name of the damn place? "I can't think. I can't think."

"Charley, calm down. You need to be calm."

"I'm so dizzy. My head is spinning. I can't . . ."

"You can," Glen told her steadily. Then again, "You can."

Charley took another deep breath, then closed her eyes, tried conjuring up the picture of the motel as it appeared on its website. The image appeared slowly, like a photograph in developing fluid, revealing itself gradually, faint shadows growing into colorful shapes, the shapes shifting, becoming concrete. "Beautiful Dreamers," Charley said out loud, as a sprawling, white, two-storey building appeared fully formed on her memory screen, its logo floating across the bright blue skyline in cherry-red capital letters. She pressed in 411, retrieved the motel's phone number from information, impatiently agreeing to the additional charge of fifty cents to be automatically connected. "Hurry up. Hurry up."

"Beautiful Dreamers Motel," purred a mellifluous male voice seconds later, as if Charley had aroused the speaker from a deep sleep.

"I need to speak to Elizabeth Webb," Charley directed, as beads of perspiration broke out along her hairline. She leaned back against her headrest, struggling to control her dizziness and stay conscious as, all around her, palm trees spun out of control along the side of the turnpike, as if caught in the eye of a hurricane.

A slight pause, the sound of a keyboard clacking, then, "I'm sorry. We have no one by that name registered here."

"What? Of course you do. What are you talking about?"

Another silence, more clacking. Then, "No. I'm sorry. I'm not showing anyone by that name."

"Wait. Wait," Charley urged, more to herself than to the sleepy young man on the other end of the line. "Try Alex Prescott," she said, almost gagging on the name. To think that just a few short hours ago, she'd been seriously contemplating a lifetime with this man.

Another round of clacking. Then, "Yes, that's better. I'm showing two rooms reserved under that name. Only one is occupied at the moment. Would you like me to connect you?"

"Yes!" **Are you an idiot?** Charley almost shouted as he was transferring her call. The phone rang twice before being picked up.

"Hello?" the child's voice answered.

"Franny. Thank God."

"Mommy! Where are you?"

"I'm almost there, sweetie. Let me speak to Grandma."

"She's asleep. She's so sick, Mommy. I'm really scared."

"Okay, listen to me. . . ." Charley heard a faint knocking in the distance.

"Somebody's at the door," Franny announced.

"What?" Charley lurched forward in her seat, so that her head almost smashed against the car's front windshield. Her seat belt snapped tightly against her chest, securing her firmly in place. "Wait! Don't answer it. Franny, do you hear me? Don't answer it."

"Why not?"

Charley took a deep breath. Maybe it was Bram. Or the police. "Okay, listen, sweetheart. I want you to look out the window and see who it is. Can you do that?"

"Okay."

Charley felt her daughter put down the phone. She watched her in her mind's eye as the child approached the motel room's large front window and parted the curtains. In the next second, Franny was back on the line. "It's okay, Mommy," she said, a smile in her voice. "It's Alex."

"What?! No! Don't let him in! Franny? Franny?"

But Franny was already on her way to the door.

"Don't open the door! Franny, do you hear me? Don't open the door!"

The sound of a door opening. "Hi, Alex," she heard her daughter say.

Then silence.

The blood froze in Charley's veins. She turned to Glen, whose normally healthy complexion had turned a sickly shade of beige. "He's got Franny," she said.

"Okay, listen to me. This is not a crank call," Glen was shouting into his phone at the state police seconds later. "The man's name is Alex Prescott and he's kidnapped a little girl named Franny Webb. She's eight years old."

Charley grabbed the phone from Glen's hand, and quickly provided the officer on the other end of the line with a detailed description of her daughter, then of her son. "Alex is probably on his way to Disney World right now," Charley told the officer, pushing the words out between sobs. "Please stop him before he hurts my children."

The officer offered his sympathies and asked her to repeat the story again for his superior. Once again, Charley recounted the whole horrifying tale. How many times had she said the same thing in the last hour? To how many people? Why were the police so reluctant to believe her? "What if it's too late?" she asked as she was put on hold.

"It isn't," Glen said, although he sounded less than convinced.

"I couldn't bear it if he does anything to hurt them."

"Try not to think that way, Charley."

"You didn't see the tape," Charley cried. "You didn't see the awful things he did to those children." She looked at the purse in her lap, felt the tape burning a hole in its lining, like acid on flesh. "Yes, I'm still here," she said suddenly into the receiver. "What kind of car does Alex drive," she said, repeating aloud the question she'd just been asked. She described the old, mustard-colored Malibu convertible in as much detail as she could remember. "It's about ten years old. No, I'm sorry. I don't know the license plate number. But how many can there be?" She started to shake. Glen took the phone from her hands, spoke softly to the officer on the other end.

"They're issuing an Amber Alert," he told her seconds later.

"Thank God."

"And they're sending an ambulance to the motel. They'll meet us there."

Charley pushed away her tears with the back of her hand, tried to sit up straight. "How much longer till we get there?"

"Maybe half an hour."

"I've been such a fool."

"Just because you were fooled doesn't make you a fool," Glen told her. He reached over, took her hand in his. "We'll get him, Charley. I promise you. We'll get him."

"Before he hurts my children?"

Glen squeezed her hand gently but said nothing.

Twenty-five minutes later, they pulled into the parking lot of the Beautiful Dreamers Motel. Four police cars were already there, as was an ambulance. Charley teetered on wobbly legs toward the entrance, almost colliding with an elderly couple lingering beside the front door. "Where can I find the police?" she demanded of the young man behind the front desk of the ornate gold-and-white lobby. "What room?"

"You are . . . ?" He lifted a nearby phone to

his ear. Charley noted a spray of freckles across the bridge of his nose, and small, light brown eyes behind a pair of square-framed designer glasses.

She all but screamed her name at the young man, who took an involuntary step back and raised his right hand. "Room 221, second floor, to your right. Just follow the pool around back until . . ."

But Charley was no longer listening. She was out of the lobby and down the hall, following the smell of chlorine as she turned one corner and then another, tripping over her feet as she tore down the red-and-gold carpeting, Glen steadying her before she could fall. How long until she started feeling better? How long until she started feeling human again?

When I get my children back, she thought.

"This way," Glen said, pulling on her arm and leading her down another corridor until they reached the large pool area. "Here," he said, guiding her around a trio of youngsters sitting on the steps of the pool's shallow end. "This way," Glen said, guiding her toward the concrete stairs. "Can you manage?"

Charley pushed herself up the steps, then turned left at the landing, where she almost fell into the arms of a waiting policeman. "Charles Webb?" the officer asked, looking at Glen.

"I'm Charley Webb," Charley said with as

much authority as she could muster. "How's my mother?"

"The paramedics are with her now. They've given her something to settle her stomach. She should be all right."

Charley raced down the hall to where another officer stood guard in front of room 221. The normally spacious room was crowded with police officers and medical personnel. It reeked of vomit. Her mother sat on the end of one of two double beds, a red-and-white-flowered bedspread wrapped around her shoulders, her skin the color of ashes, her dark hair wet with perspiration and matted to her forehead. "I'm so sorry," Elizabeth whispered when she saw Charley. "It hit me in the car soon after we left. I tried to ignore it. I didn't want to spoil the trip. What happened?"

"You were drugged," Charley told her, sitting on the side of the bed, and taking her mother in her arms as Glen conferred with the police. "Alex put something in our orange juice."

Her mother's face radiated confusion. "Alex? I don't understand. Why would . . . ?"

"Do you remember anything at all?" Charley interrupted.

Elizabeth shook her head. "I'm sorry. I just remember feeling worse and worse. I vaguely recall crawling out of the bathroom and into bed. I think I remember Franny covering me with the bedspread. And then, nothing. The next thing I knew, the police were bursting through the door, and I was trying to sit up, and everyone was asking a lot of questions and poking at me, and I couldn't see Franny. . . . I'm sorry, darling. I'm so sorry."

"Ms. Webb?" a man asked. He was tall and balding, about fifty years old, wearing a nondescript tan-colored suit and an olive-green tie. Charley assumed he was the person in charge. She pushed herself to her feet. "I'm Detective Ed Vickers with the Florida State Police. I need to ask you some questions."

"What you need to do is find my children before that monster hurts them."

"We'll do the best we can, Ms. Webb. Do you have a picture of them with you?"

Charley reached inside her purse, retrieved her wallet, withdrew the latest school photos of Franny and James.

"Do you remember what they were wearing earlier?"

"Franny was wearing a pink T-shirt and matching pants. . . ."

"And two pink barrettes in her hair, the shape of angels," her mother added.

"Cupids," Charley said softly. "James was wearing a blue Mickey Mouse T-shirt and navy-blue shorts."

"I don't suppose you have a picture of Alex

Prescott," the detective half-stated, half-asked, as he handed the photo of her children to one of the other officers, who in turn relayed their description to someone on the other end of his cell phone.

Once again Charley reached inside her purse, pulled out the cassette labeled **Jack and Jill**, handed it to Ed Vickers.

"What's this?"

Charley told him, watching his brown eyes narrow and his bushy eyebrows sink toward the bridge of his wide nose.

"How did you get this?" Ed Vickers asked as the room grew silent.

"Please," Charley began. "I'll explain everything on the way to Disney World. We have to find my son before Alex does." She braced herself for Detective Vickers's outright refusal, coupled with his gruff assertion that she should stay put, but it never came.

"You can ride with me," he told her. "The paramedics will take your mother to the hospital."

"Not until I know my grandchildren are safe," Elizabeth protested, standing up, and raising herself to her full height, which even slightly hunched forward with pain, was nothing less than impressive. "I'm coming with you."

"Fine," Detective Vickers stated, heading for the door while barking orders at his underlings.

Charley reached for her mother's hand, and together the two women followed the officers outside.

Even without the drugs in her system, Charley suspected Disney World would have proved overwhelming: the crowds, the noise, the rides, the actors disguised as much-loved cartoon characters mingling with their adoring young fans throughout the vast amusement park. Thousands upon thousands of people, Charley realized, her eyes piercing the milling throngs, searching for a streak of pink, a dash of blue. It seemed as if every other little boy she saw was wearing a Mickey Mouse T-shirt, and virtually every little girl was dressed in pink. "How will we ever find them?" she whispered hopelessly, watching as the spinning teacup ride slowed to a stop in front of her, disgorging its happy passengers as a new group of eager and squealing youngsters immediately surged forward to take their place.

"Don't forget that Alex has the same problem," Glen reminded her.

"Except he's had a good head start."

"Bram won't let Alex take James," Elizabeth said, clinging to Charley's side.

Charley squeezed her mother's hand on her arm, realizing she no longer knew who was holding up whom, that it was impossible to tell where her mother left off and she began.

The Amber Alert had been issued. Police were combing the highways, roads, and miles of Disney World parking lots looking for an old mustard-colored Malibu convertible. The theme park was in virtual lockdown. Everyone trying to leave was being screened and scrutinized. If Alex was anywhere in the area, they'd find him, Detective Vickers had assured her. Would it be too late?

A life-size Cinderella in a beautiful white gown floated regally by, pursued by dozens of laughing children. Where were their parents? Charley wondered. Who was looking after them?

"There's the Pirates of the Caribbean." Glen guided her toward the huge lineup that zig-zagged back and forth in front of the popular attraction.

Charley quickly scanned the faces of those waiting. Surely she would easily spot her brother towering over everyone else. But Bram and James were no longer anywhere in line. Not to mention this was undoubtedly the first place Alex had looked. Had he found them?

They continued walking. "There he is," Charley suddenly gasped, breaking away from Glen and her mother and dashing toward a little boy holding a Mickey Mouse balloon. In almost the same second, a number of officers swarmed in to surround the frightened child, but Charley knew even before she saw his sweet but decidedly un-James-like face, and heard the outraged protests of his parents, that she'd made a mistake. "I'm sorry," she muttered, and might have collapsed had it not been for all the people gathered around her. "I'm so sorry."

"It's okay, Charley," Glen said, leading her away. "It's okay."

Suddenly she heard a familiar and disturbing tune. **It's a small world after all. It's a small . . .** "Oh, God."

"What's the matter?" Glen asked.

The song pulled Charley forward like a magnet until she stood in front of the colorful, doll-covered attraction. Again, she studied the faces of those waiting in the fast-moving line to hop into one of the boats. In one end and out the other, she thought, remembering Jill's story about getting stuck when her family was mere feet away from the tunnel's end. "These rides, they all have separate exits, right?"

"Some of them do."

"We should go around the back." Charley was already making her way in that direction. But there were almost as many people behind the attraction as in front of it. Charley stood for a few minutes watching families exit the ride, some still singing along to the relentlessly perky tune.

It's a small, small world.

She saw a door marked PERSONNEL ONLY, and

she pushed it open. "Can I help you?" a man in a Goofy costume asked from inside, and Charley shook her head and retreated quickly.

An officer approached, and for a minute Charley thought he was about to arrest her for trespassing. Instead, he told her, "We may have something."

Whatever else he said was quickly lost in the echo of those four words.

"Bram!" Charley exclaimed, rushing toward the man who was sitting on the ground, his legs stretched out in front of him, his back against the side of a door at the back of Space Mountain.

"Charley!" He tried to stand up, but succeeded only in falling over on his side. "Where's James? What's going on?"

"We found him in there," a policeman said from somewhere beside Charley. He pointed toward another door marked PERSONNEL ONLY.

"I swear I'm not drunk, Charley."

"I know you're not."

"Looks like someone used a Taser gun on him," the officer remarked.

"A Taser gun!" Bram exclaimed, pushing his hair off his forehead and shaking his head. "Shit. I thought I was having a heart attack. Would somebody please tell me what the hell is going on."

"Did you see who did this to you?"

"I didn't see a thing."

"Can you tell us exactly what happened," the officer prodded.

"I'd just bought James this big, stuffed snake. It was supposed to be the snake from **Jungle Book**," Bram began, struggling to get the words out. "And we were walking along, talking about how it looked just like the one he'd painted, when suddenly I felt this awful pain in the small of my back, and next thing I know, my legs were going out from under me, and I'm going down. Then I get tossed inside some dark closet where I get zapped again. I couldn't see a thing. I must have passed out. What time is it?"

"Almost four-thirty," Charley told him.

"I couldn't have been out more than twenty minutes. Where's James?"

"We don't know."

"Jesus. Let me up." Again, he tried to stand up. Again he failed.

"You're not going anywhere until the paramedics have examined you," the officer told him.

"Where's Mom?" Bram asked Charley, sounding as young and defenseless as any five-year-old.

"Right here," Elizabeth said, stepping out from behind Glen and kneeling in front of her son. "I'm right here." She sank to the concrete beside him, took him in her arms. Bram laid his head against her shoulder and closed his eyes.

Charley clutched the memory of that image like a talisman as she hurried back into the center of the surging crowd.

She spotted them coming out of a restroom, a handsome man and a young boy walking hand in hand, the boy wearing a Mickey Mouse hat to match his shirt and carrying a large stuffed purple snake. It was the snake that first caught Charley's eye.

"It's them," Charley said, so quietly she wasn't sure anyone had heard her. It was only when she saw Detective Vickers speaking into his headphones and listened as he alerted the others to their location that she was even able to breathe. Her body lurched forward, but was quickly blocked by the detective's arm.

"Wait," he advised, "until we get everyone in place."

We found him, Charley was thinking. James is here, and he's okay. My baby's okay.

Although Franny was nowhere in sight.

Where was Franny?

"Okay, now listen to me," Detective Vickers was saying. "Are you listening?"

Charley nodded, her eyes glued to her son as, fifty feet away, Alex hefted him over his head, depositing him on his shoulders.

"He has no idea you're on to him, remember, so don't do anything to make him suspicious until we get James away from him. Just smile and wave and pretend everything's all right. Okay? Can you do that?"

Again Charley nodded. "Alex!" she called out, forcing a smile onto her face. "James!"

"Mommy!" James cried happily.

Charley registered the surprise in Alex's eyes, watched his expression freeze, then convert into something approximating joy. If she didn't know better, she might have thought he was actually glad to see her.

"Charley! I found him. He's okay."

"Thank God," Charley said. "Come here, baby. Let Mommy hold you."

"How did you get here?" Alex asked, holding tight to her son's heels.

"I couldn't wait any longer. A friend gave me a lift."

"I want to go down," James said, kicking at Alex's chest.

"Whoa, boy. Hold on a minute."

"Now. I want to go down now." James started hitting Alex on the head with his stuffed snake. "I don't like you. You made Uncle Bram fall down."

Alex grabbed the snake from James's hand and tossed it angrily aside. In that instant, Glen rushed forward and snatched James from Alex's shoulders, transferring him swiftly to Charley's outstretched arms.

Charley promptly smothered her son's face with kisses. Had he ever smelled so good? she wondered, running her hands along his arms, his face, his legs, to make sure he was really there, that he hadn't been stabbed or burned or abused.

"Glen!" James shouted enthusiastically, as Glen retrieved the stuffed snake from the ground and returned it to him. "Are you coming to Disney World with us, too?"

"Charley, what's going on?" Alex appealed to her.

"You used a Taser gun on my brother."

"Only to save your son."

"Was it the same gun you used on Tammy Barnet and the Starkey twins?"

Alex looked stunned. "What are you talking about?"

"I found the videotape," Charley said simply.

Alex said nothing, although his eyes shifted from side to side, as if he were contemplating making a run for it.

"Don't even think about it," Detective Vickers advised, taking two steps forward.

"Where's Franny?" Charley asked.

"I have no idea," said Alex.

"You took her from the motel. What have you done with her?"

A slow smile slithered across Alex's mouth. "If

you've seen the tape," he said, "I would think you'd already know the answer to that question."

Charley clutched her stomach, bit down on her lower lip to keep from screaming. "No," she said instead, her voice a low growl. "There hasn't been enough time. And you like to take your time. Don't you, Alex?"

"You never complained," he told her, clearly enjoying himself.

"Tell us where the girl is," Detective Vickers said, "and maybe I can put in a good word . . ."

"Oh, please, Detective. Do you really think I'm remotely interested in your good words?"

"He hasn't had time to take her anywhere," Charley found herself thinking out loud. "He drove right here from the motel. That means she's still in his car."

"Well done, Charley," Alex said, as his hands were secured behind his back with handcuffs. "If this book thing doesn't work out, you might consider a career as a detective."

Detective Vickers's cell phone rang. He answered it, looked from Charley to Alex and then back again. "They found the car," he told her.

"Franny . . . ?"

"She was in the trunk, unconscious, but okay. She'll be fine."

Two uniformed officers started to lead Alex away.

"Wait," Charley called after them. She ran forward, stopped a foot from Alex's face, then looked over her shoulder at Glen. "Is this how you do it?" she asked, suddenly shifting her weight from her back foot to her front as her right hand curled into a tight ball, and her fist came crashing against Alex's cheek.

36

Charley sat in the small interview room at Pembroke Correctional waiting for the guards to bring Jill down from her cell. Not that she was sure Jill would see her. Even though she had consented to the interview, there was no guarantee she'd keep her word.

And what would Charley do when she saw her—this smiling psychopath who'd dispatched her lover to seduce her, and orchestrated the abduction and would-be murder of the two most precious things in Charley's life?

More than a month had passed since her thirty-first birthday, a month of Charley waking up in the middle of the night in a cold sweat, nightmare visions of children being tortured circling her head like vultures, eager to swoop down to pick at her flesh. Daylight brought little respite. Everywhere she turned, she saw little Tammy Barnet fighting for air inside her plastic bag, and heard the Starkey twins crying for their mother as their flesh was seared repeatedly with the butts of lit cigarettes. She saw her mother, slack-jawed and barely conscious, wrapped in a red-and-white-flowered bedspread, and her brother sitting splay-legged on the ground, his normally luminous gray-blue eyes clouded with pain and disbelief. She saw her son perched un-easily on Alex's shoulders, struggling to be put down, and her daughter lying ashen-faced and limp in a paramedic's arms, and every time she realized how close she'd come to losing them, she groaned out loud.

She couldn't sleep. She couldn't eat. She couldn't write. She'd taken a leave of absence from the **Palm Beach Post**. She'd abandoned work on her book. She drove her children to school each morning and picked them up every afternoon. In the hours between, she sat in her living room and tried not to imagine the tragedy that could have been. Sometimes she was suc-cessful; more often she wasn't.

Her children, on the other hand, were proving to be remarkably resilient. Franny had no recollec-tion of being Tasered; she only remembered open-ing the door to the motel room, and then waking up in her mother's arms. James's only complaint was that his trip to Disney World had been cut short, and he proclaimed to all who would listen that he liked Glen much better than Alex.

Glen called often, usually just to say hi and see how she was doing. Charley knew he was just waiting for her to say the word and he'd be there. But Charley was no longer sure what the right words were. Alex had robbed her of her instincts. He'd played her like a goddamn Stradivarius.

Still, she couldn't blame him for everything. Ultimately, it had been **her** ego, **her** ambition, **her** self-absorption that had put her children at risk. "Looks like my father was right about me after all," she confided to her mother one night.

"Your father is a moron," her mother said.

It was her mother who'd insisted she confront Jill.

At first, Charley had balked at the idea. She told herself that she had no interest in ever seeing Jill again. She had no more questions to ask her. Nor was she eager to hear Jill's answers. The police had already informed her that Jill had initially met Alex through Ethan—Alex had been the "smart lawyer" who'd managed to get the drug dealing charges against him dismissed—and it didn't take a genius to recognize that in Alex, Jill had found her perfect match, a man whose perverse fantasies meshed seamlessly with her own. Did it matter that, separately and individually, these two sociopaths might never have acted on their murderous impulses, that it was only when they joined forces that they became lethal?

Besides, anything Jill told her would probably be lies anyway. And even if Jill wasn't lying, Charley no longer trusted herself to know the difference.

All that mattered was that Alex was in jail awaiting trial, and that he would no doubt soon be joining his paramour on death row. What mattered was that they wouldn't be able to harm anyone else's children ever again.

No, Charley tried to convince herself, she had no desire to give Jill another shot at humiliating her, another chance to manipulate and deceive her. Let her amuse herself at someone else's expense.

"This isn't like you," her mother had said. "Since when do you feel guilty about things, especially things there's nothing to feel guilty for? Since when do you sit around wallowing in self-pity? You're the best mother, the best sister, the best daughter anyone could hope for. You are so much more than I deserve. And you're a wonderful writer. You have a real gift. Don't ever doubt that. Don't you dare let that miserable little twit take that away from you. Don't you dare give her that kind of power."

"Do I have a choice?" Charley had asked.

"You always have a choice."

Could she really do this? Charley wondered now, hearing footsteps stop outside the door. In the next second, the door swung open and a muscular female guard escorted Jill Rohmer into the room. The guard quickly removed Jill's hand-cuffs, then made her retreat. Jill was wearing the mandatory orange T-shirt and sweatpants she always wore, and her hair, longer than Charley remembered it, hung loosely around her face. She scrunched her lips into an unattractive pout, and stared at the wall. "I'm not sure I really want to talk to you," she said.

"I'm not sure I want to talk to you either," Charley heard herself reply.

Charley watched Jill's head swivel toward her, their eyes making contact for the first time in more than a month. "You've lost weight," Jill said.

"You've put some on."

"Yeah? Well, you try living on the crap they feed you in here," Jill said, bristling. "Nothing but starches. How's your hand?" she asked, as if the two thoughts were somehow connected. "I heard you broke a couple of fingers punching Alex's lights out."

Charley flexed her still-sore fingers under the table, said nothing.

"They make it look so easy on television, don't they?" Jill asked. "Guys swinging at each other left and right, beating the crap out of everybody in sight, and nobody ever breaks a sweat, let alone a couple of fingers." She laughed, the laugh dying abruptly in her throat. "I should hate you for what you did, you know that."

"**You** should hate **me**?"

"But I don't hate you. Hell, I actually like you. You're the only friend I've got."

"I'm not your friend, Jill."

"No, I guess not. But it was kind of fun while it lasted, wasn't it?"

"It was many things," Charley told her. "Fun wasn't one of them."

"Ouch. Guess I misread you."

"Guess you did."

"So, what brings you down here today?" Jill sat down across from Charley, leaned forward on her elbows. "You looking for closure, Charley? Is that why you're here?"

"I guess you could say that. I need a final chapter for my book." Charley withdrew her tape recorder from her purse and set it in the middle of the table, pressed the ON button, then sat back and waited.

"Don't you mean **our** book?"

"No. I mean **my** book. The book that's going to make me rich and famous while you sit in here and rot until they strap you to a gurney and stick a needle in your arm." Charley smiled. "Now **this** is fun."

Jill stiffened in her seat. "And where will your precious book be if I decide not to tell you any-thing? What will you do then?"

"I guess I'll have to make it up." Charley

shrugged. "You're not that complicated, Jill. I'm sure I'll think of something."

"You're awfully confident for someone who almost got her children killed."

Charley pushed her chair back and rose to her feet, reaching across the table for the tape recorder when what she really wanted to do was reach for Jill's throat.

"Oh, sit down. Don't get your panties all in a knot," Jill said. "Your confidence is what I've always admired about you."

Charley slowly sank back down, waited for Jill to continue.

"It's really interesting the way things work out, isn't it? I mean, I'm not much of a reader. I never read the papers. Unless, of course, I'm in them." Jill giggled, looked to Charley for a smile, then continued when none was forthcoming. "Anyway, this one Sunday, Pammy was sitting at the kitchen table reading your column out loud to our mother, and she mentioned how she went out with your brother a couple of times. So I started listening—it was the one about how you decided to have kids without getting married—and I thought it was funny and kind of cool, and I thought your picture was great. Like you were telling everyone they could go eat shit. So I started reading your columns pretty much every week after that. And I learned all about your sisters and your mother and your kids. I learned what you liked and didn't. I got to know you pretty well actually, and I decided that if I ever got famous, I was gonna get you to write my story. That's when I met Alex." She smiled, her eyes sparkling with the memory. "You want to know how we met?"

"I already know how you met."

"Yeah? You want to hear about our first date? I'll tell you if you promise not to get jealous."

"I'm not the jealous type."

"You're lucky." Jill shook her head in wonderment. "I'm **so** the jealous type. I was fit to be tied when you started seeing Alex. Not that I didn't know what was going on. I helped plan it, for God's sake. But it's one thing to plan something, and another to actually do it. The idea of him kissing you, of you putting your hands on him, it just made me sick. I was going crazy thinking about the two of you together. I'd picture the two of you making love, and it made my skin crawl. No offense," she said, giggling again.

"It makes my skin crawl, too," Charley said.

Jill laughed. "Maybe now, yeah. But not at the time, I bet. I mean, wasn't he the best lover ever? I told you he was. I sure as hell didn't lie about that."

"You were telling me about your first date," Charley said, trying to steer the conversation away from herself.

"It's actually not that interesting a story. He took me to this cute little Italian restaurant. Alex likes Italian. But you know that, don't you?"

Charley winced, looked at the tape recorder.

"The only really interesting thing that happened is that I sucked him off in the men's bathroom."

"You're a class act," Charley said.

"And you're a real prude, aren't you, Charley? Despite the trail of discarded lovers and two bastard kids, you're a prude at heart. That's a laugh."

"Glad I amuse you."

"Oh, you do. You do. Alex and I used to laugh about you all the time. How you thought you were so smart when you were so damn stupid I could hardly believe it. You fell for everything, just like Alex said you would." She stretched her arms above her head, yawned loudly. "He knew just how to get you interested in doing my story." This time she laughed out loud. "He told me exactly what to write in that letter, how to flatter you in one sentence, tease you in the next. Then you went to see him and he told you that you weren't a good enough writer, that I deserved better, knowing it would make you all the more determined to do it. Just like he knew the best way to get inside your pants was to pretend he didn't want to. You fell for everything, didn't you, Charley?"

"Whose idea was it to murder those children?" Charley asked, once again trying to get the focus off her.

Jill began playing with her hair, twirling it around her fingers. "Alex's. I was complaining about having to baby-sit those brats every weekend, and he said we should just kill them. I thought he was kidding at first, but then he said how we could torture them first, like I told him I'd done with that kitten. His mother used to punish him by burning him with cigarettes when he was little," she added, almost cheerily. "Did you know that?"

Charley closed her eyes, refusing to feel sorry for him.

"Anyway, the idea just kind of took off from there."

"So, you knew all along what was going to happen to Tammy Barnet. You weren't sorry at all," Charley stated, remembering Jill's earlier disclaimers.

"Oh, no, don't get me wrong. I felt really bad about what happened to Tammy. She was a pretty neat little kid. I was really upset when she died. But, I mean, what choice did we have?"

"What choice did you have?" Charley repeated dully.

"Well, she could identify us. I mean, there was no way she was gonna keep quiet about what happened, and we couldn't take a chance of getting caught."

"And yet you did get caught."

"Yeah, but not right away. First we did the Starkey twins." There was an almost wistful look in Jill's eyes. "What'd you think of the video, by the way?"

Tears sprang to Charley's eyes. She stared at the table and said nothing.

"Aw. You were moved by it. That's so sweet."

"Shut up, Jill."

"I thought you wanted me to talk."

"I want you to die," Charley snapped, watching Jill's eyes open in alarm. "But we don't always get what we want, do we? At least not right away. Tell me, what was Alex's reaction when you were arrested?"

"Kind of like you just now. He almost lost it."

"Because he was afraid you'd cut a deal with the prosecution?"

"No!" Jill looked genuinely offended. "Alex knew I'd never betray him."

"And he was prepared to let you take the fall all by yourself."

"No point in both of us being locked up. Besides, he was always working ways to get me out of here. Whose idea do you think it was to do this book?"

"He thought the book would get you out of jail?"

"Off death row anyway. Once all that stuff came out about me being abused. . . ."

"Was any of it true?"

"Oh, it's all true. My father, my brother, Wayne. They all had their turn. Did you ever get ahold of Wayne, by the way?"

"No. He was killed in Iraq."

"Really? Can't say I'm too broken up about that." Jill twisted her lips from side to side. "Alex understood what I'd been through. Did you know he was molested by one of his mother's boyfriends when he was about eight?" She continued on before Charley could answer. "Anyway, we thought that even if nothing else came out of the book, at least we'd have a good time doing it. And it was a way of staying connected. Of keeping the dream alive, as it were. 'The family that plays together' kind of thing. And it helped pass the time. It can get awfully boring in here."

"And you picked me to write it because . . ."

"Because you were just so perfect. It was like you were made to order."

"Were my children always part of your plan?"

"Are you kidding? They were the driving force." Jill took a deep breath, allowed herself a small smile. "I mean, we had a good thing going. Why should we let a little thing like prison stop us from having fun? We wanted to do a book; we wanted to find some kids. Alex said we'd be killing two birds with one stone." She laughed. "Aw, come on, Charley. You have to admit that's kind of clever."

"You expect me to find something clever about killing my children?"

Jill shrugged. "Guess not."

"What about my brother?"

"The cherry on the whipped cream. I mean, well, he's not exactly Mr. Reliable, you have to admit. We knew we couldn't depend on him. But he sure came through in the end, didn't he? I mean, we always planned to implicate him in some way, if we could. But who could have ever predicted he'd show up that morning and make blueberry pancakes? We couldn't have written a better script. I mean, we were kind of flying by the seat of our pants, just waiting for the right opportunity. And then, bingo, Bram comes knocking. So Alex decided right there at your breakfast table to put those drugs in your juice. But if he hadn't done it then, he'd have done it later. You gotta know when to pick your moments. Like Alex telling me when to call his apartment and drop that bombshell about your brother. You were puking your guts out, so you weren't exactly thinking clearly. And it wasn't all that far-fetched. Bram had a history of substance abuse, he was irresponsible, **and** he knew my sister. All that was left was to give him another name."

"Jack," Charley acknowledged softly.

"Jack," Jill repeated with a smile. "But we had other options, too. Believe me, there were lots of potential suspects. That friend of yours, the one who gave you the dog? Glen? Alex made up that story about him maybe knowing my brother. And then, of course, all those threatening e-mails you kept getting, the ones targeting your children."

"You're saying Alex sent them?"

"He's so smart."

"Pretty stupid not to destroy the videotape," Charley reminded her.

"Yeah, that was unfortunate. Just when we thought everything was going so well. Guess we got cocky."

"Guess you did." Charley reached across the table and turned off the tape. She stood up, dropped the recorder in her purse.

"Wait. What are you doing? You're not going, are you?"

"I think I have everything I need."

"But you don't," Jill protested. "There's lots more stuff I haven't told you yet. We've hardly touched on what goes on in here, the guards, the sex. . . ."

Charley pushed her shoulders back, took a deep breath, and smiled from ear to ear. "Tell it to the judge."

37

WEBB SITE

Approximately nine months ago, something very interesting happened to me.
No, I didn't get pregnant. What I got
was a letter from a killer. The killer's
name was Jill Rohmer, whom I'd chris-
tened the Beastly Baby-Sitter in this
very space several years earlier, and she
had a proposition for me: agree to tell
her story, and she would agree to tell
me everything, including the identity
of her lover and accomplice, the devil
who made her do it. As we all know by
now, the devil's name is Alex Prescott,
and he turned out to be a triple threat,
being not only her lover and accom-

plice but her lawyer as well. He is currently recovering in a prison hospital from the near-fatal stab wounds he received at Raiford while awaiting trial. It couldn't have happened to a more deserving guy.

And I ought to know. You see, Alex Prescott was my lover, too.

"I think we have a lot in common," Jill wrote to me nine months ago. At the time, I thought this was a crock of you-know-what. Beyond certain superficial similarities, I couldn't see that we had anything in common. Yet as I got to know Jill, I came to believe we were more alike than I had initially realized. We were both the product of unhappy childhoods, our mothers having been either physically or emotionally absent, and our fathers physically or emotionally abusive. Our relationships with our siblings were strained and unsatisfying, while our relationships with men were mostly fleeting and ill-conceived. We both used sex as a means to getting what we wanted, which rarely worked because we rarely knew what that was.

Which brings me back to Alex Prescott.

Please bear in mind that when we met, I thought he was an upstanding member of the community, a dedicated attorney, and a sensitive and caring individual who drove an old convertible and played a mean guitar. Turns out he played me even better. Turns out he was the proverbial wolf in sheep's clothing. Turns out I can be fooled.

You see, in all the time I spent with Jill Rohmer, those hours spent talking to her, sizing her up, watching for the slightest narrowing of those big, chocolate-brown eyes, and listening for the slightest change of inflection in the misleading softness of her voice, I never really got to know Jill at all. What happened was that she got to know **me**.

Sociopaths are good at that. You give; they take. And they're experts at providing people with what they need to see. A good friend of mine once told me that. He also told me that being fooled doesn't make you a fool.

Liars and con artists prey on the good natures of others. And while no one has ever accused me of being especially good-natured, I've discovered some interesting truths about myself during these last nine months: I'm not nearly as cynical and hard-edged as I thought I was. Turns out that despite everything that's happened, or maybe because of it, I find I actually believe in the essential goodness of others. Turns out I believe people are capable of change. Turns out I'm even a bit of a romantic. I was, after all, named after Charlotte Brontë. (I was also named after a spider, which might account for my sometimes nasty bite.)

I've spent much of the months of my extended hiatus from the pages of this paper soul-searching, recovering my spark and equilibrium, and enjoying the two most fabulous children in the world. (Yes, I know. Your children are fabulous, too. Just not quite as fabulous. And must I remind you?—it's **my** column.) In the meantime, much has changed. My mother, for example, has straightened up, so to speak, recently marrying a man she met last year on a weekend cruise to the Bahamas. He's a lovely man, and they have a beautiful condominium on the ocean, where my children, my brother, my dog, and I are frequent guests. My two sisters, Emily and Anne, have recently contacted me about possibly coming to Florida in the not-too-distant future, maybe even bringing their children, for a long overdue family reunion. I even have two new stepsisters—Grace and Audrey, after Kelly and Hepburn—whom I'm having great fun getting to know. My brother just enrolled full-time at the College of Art and Design in Miami, and has been sober and drug-free for almost ten months. I'm very proud of him. There's also a new man in my life, the aforementioned good friend who is the very opposite of Alex Prescott—he is the **sheep** in **wolf's** clothing. I even have a new bathroom!

So maybe a seed was planted in my belly nine months ago after all. Only the baby I produced is thirty-one years old, stands five feet eight inches tall, and weighs one hundred and twenty-four pounds. I'm happy to report she has a full head of blond hair, an inquisitive mind, and an alarmingly big mouth.

I'm using it now to thank all the people who have supported me with their e-mails during my absence. Between bouts of navel-gazing, I was busy completing my book, **Down the Hill: The True Story of Jack and Jill**—which hits bookstores this week. To those of you who aren't so happy about my return to the **Palm Beach Post**, too bad. Remember, it's a free country, and nobody is forcing you to read my columns. But if you don't like them, please keep those nasty e-mails to yourself. As my mother used to say—well, maybe not **my** mother, but somebody's mother surely—if you don't have something nice to say, don't say anything. As for me, I'll continue to say whatever I please, as plainly and as clearly as I can. Because unlike Jill Rohmer and Alex Prescott, with me, there are no hidden agendas. And must I remind you again?—it's **my** column.

FROM: Happy Reader
TO: Charley@Charley'sWeb.com
SUBJECT: You
DATE: Mon. 8 Oct. 2007, 08:33:21–0400

Dear Charley, Welcome back!